James Greenwood

The Adventures of Reuben Davidger

Seventeen years and four months captive among the Dyaks of Borneo

James Greenwood

The Adventures of Reuben Davidger
Seventeen years and four months captive among the Dyaks of Borneo

ISBN/EAN: 9783337237585

Printed in Europe, USA, Canada, Australia, Japan

Cover: Foto ©Andreas Hilbeck / pixelio.de

More available books at **www.hansebooks.com**

THE

ADVENTURES

OF

REUBEN DAVIDGER.

W. DICKES.
LONDON.

THE

ADVENTURES

OF

REUBEN DAVIDGER;

SEVENTEEN YEARS AND FOUR MONTHS CAPTIVE

AMONG THE DYAKS OF BORNEO.

BY

JAMES GREENWOOD,

AUTHOR OF

"WILD SPORTS OF THE WORLD," "CURIOSITIES OF SAVAGE LIFE," ETC., ETC.

ILLUSTRATED WITH NUMEROUS ENGRAVINGS,

PRINCIPALLY FROM DESIGNS BY R. HULLULA, H. S. MELVILLE, AND E. LAW.

LONDON:

S. O. BEETON, 248, STRAND, W.C.

———

1865.

HARRILD, PRINTER, LONDON.

PREFACE.

NY time, I would sooner write the longest chapter of a story than the shortest preface. Doubtless it is all very well to affix an introduction to your book, if it is of so peculiar a sort as to make it desirable that the reader's patience, or forbearance, or charity shall be bespoke for it; but when the matter involved is of no greater moment than a yarn pitched by a grown-up boy for the amusement of his more youthful brethren, in my humble opinion, a preface—at least, of the sort known in Yankee land as the "high falutin" — may well be avoided. I like prefaces so little that, in ordinary, I never read them; but, being unfortunately pledged to this one, I have, in order to get in trim for the job, been looking through a dozen or so, and the result is that I like them less than ever. Generally speaking, they are horridly hypocritical, and as exceedingly polite and ceremonious as the bow of a dancing-master, and just as heartless and unmeaning.

We will have none of this sort of thing. The reader and I, I am proud to say, know each other tolerably well by this time, and thus I address myself to him: Here following are the adventures of Reuben Davidger, written for your amusement, and very heartily at your service. If spread through these pages you should light on crumbs of useful information—geographical, botanical, zoological, or other—I humbly hope that the dish, in its entirety, will not be deemed less palatable.

JAMES GREENWOOD.

CONTENTS.

CHAPTER I.

CHAPTER II.

CHAPTER III.

CHAPTER IV.

CHAPTER V.

CONTENTS.

CHAPTER VI.

LIST OF ILLUSTRATIONS.

THE

ADVENTURES OF REUBEN DAVIDGER,

SEVENTEEN YEARS AND FOUR MONTHS A CAPTIVE AMONG THE DYAKS OF BORNEO.

CHAPTER I.

My birthplace and parentage—Origin of my acquaintance with William Jupp—My first roving—I am tempted by thirst to commit a great sin—My struggle with the water-boy—The hut on Limehouse Fields—The friendly Malay woman—I get confirmed an adventurer.

WAS born on the 8th of July, 1798, in a little alley, in Goodman's Fields, in the parish of Whitechapel. My father was a tailor; and my mother, although she might have profitably employed the little leisure left from her domestic cares by helping in the meaner parts of tailoring, preferred working at her own trade, which was that of a pen-cutter. It is not on her authority, however, that I say that she preferred pen-cutting; indeed, if you might take her word for it, she would willingly have resigned the cutter for the needle, only that the ability to seam without puckering had been denied her; and that, though her life depended on it, she never could successfully accomplish a button-hole. My father, whose penetration was not remarkable, was content with this excuse, and, instead of regarding it as an obstacle to the extension of his business, was inclined to set it with the rest of my mother's valuable qualities, or at least, to regard it as a fact highly curious and interesting. Unless I am much mistaken, however, what stood chiefly in the way of the development of my mother's talent for making button-holes was her natural self-dependence, the offshoot of which was a desire to ascertain the exact value of her labour, and to have the same to display, though only for so short a time as it took my father to say, "You must have stuck well to the work this week, my lass. Ah! if you could only make a decent button-hole!" At the risk of convicting my mother of a small matter of deceit, I fervently trust that I do not misjudge her; it may seem a petty business in the eyes of those who will recognize chivalry only as assaulting a big-clawed dragon, and bravery but as picking the very teeth of Death; but for my part, when I think on her bony fingers and constant cheerfulness; when I recall the familiar picture of her bending over her board by candle-light, till her eyes, seen through her spectacles, were rimmed red, and all that folks might not know what a twopenny trade tailoring was, or, perhaps, even what a twopenny tailor her husband was, she becomes my foremost heroine and pearl of women, and I know not if I am most fond or proud of her.

My relations were not numerous. I had one brother and three sisters, all of whom were younger than myself. I had two uncles on my father's side, one of whom was of my father's trade, and the other a ladies' boot-maker; on my mother's side there was an aunt who was a spinster, and an uncle who was a stevedore, living close by Wapping Wall, and of whom the reader will presently learn some further particulars. As to my grandfathers, the one on my mother's side was a fellowship porter, and plied at Billingsgate; and my father's father (as I am informed, for he died before my time) was coachman and gardener to a retired sugar-baker.

From all that I can gather from the history of both my grandfathers, never in their lives did they travel farther from London than a coach would carry them; and it was their boast that they never once had laid down to sleep at night out of earshot of the watchman's call. My father must have been an even more insignificant traveller than they, for one of the recognized funny anecdotes of our family is to the effect that once upon a time he, my father, was over-persuaded to make one of a boating party to Blackwall Reach, but that, being overtaken by sickness, he was landed at Rotherhithe, and, having been put to bed, returned home by the road on the morrow. This was after his marriage. But, and despite his insinuations to the contrary, as a single blade he was not much given to roaming. He married my mother straight from the 'prentice board of his master in Eastcheap. It was the custom of this worthy to inscribe on the back of the indentures of his apprentices any serious act of ill behaviour of which they were guilty. I have my father's indenture in my possession, and its reverse side is unsullied, save for the following line:—"Out without leave till within seventeen minutes of midnight. August 13, 1795." To this is appended in my father's handwriting this explanation:—"Went to a tea-party with Miss Joyce (my mother's maiden name), and afterwards to the wax-work show in Holborn."

In case the reader should surmise, from my having made mention of so many of my relatives, that it is part of my plan to relate their adventures, as well as my own, it is only proper for me at once to disavow any such intention. To the best of my knowledge the most perilous passages of their lives was when colic attacked them, or a raging tooth sent them battering at the dentist's door; and as to adventures, the most momentous that dwell in my memory are, that once, when my grandfather Joyce was a lad, he was sent to Bridewell for three days, for letting off fireworks in Aldgate; and again, that my uncle, the ladies' bootmaker, was, in his younger days, stage-struck, and finally worked himself to such a frenzied condition as to essay the part of Macbeth on the stage at Sadler's Wells; his impersonation causing such emotion among the audience, that the manager was heard to declare that he would not risk a repetition of it for fifty pounds.

"Why, then," the reader may ask, "have you introduced these people? If they have nothing to do with your adventures, why have you been at the pains to make mention of them at all?"

To this my answer is, that it is just because that none of my relatives (with a slight exception in the case of my uncle the stevedore) have anything to do with my adventures, that they have been brought under the reader's notice. I don't know how others may think of it, but it seems to me somewhat curious that I—the son and grandson of folk bred and born to home pursuits, and following them as scrupulously as though trades were religious creeds, to infringe any of the articles of which would expose them to everlasting ruin; whose real knowledge of the earth extended to less than fifty square miles of it, the corner pillars being a work-bench, a pay-table, a porridge-pot, and a coffin; who, to a man, regarded the higher flights of science as atheistical bravado, and ballooning as flying in the face of Providence —I take it to be a marvel, albeit I am not quite sure that it is a mercy, that one so descended should be possessed of a mind so inquisitive as mine, with so restless a temper, and a disposition so urgently disposed to roving.

My very earliest reminiscence is one of roving. At the time I was about eight years old, I had made the acquaintance of a boy whose father kept a corn-chandler's shop in Crutched Friars. The sentiment that first drew me towards the lad (he was about a year older than myself) was one of envy, founded on his unlimited dominion over bins full and sacks full of peas; from which exhaustless stores I was wont to draw my humble ha'p'orth for parching. It was not uncommon for him to be allowed to serve such small customers as myself; but I never liked him to serve me, as, in his endeavours to appear an off-hand man of business, he would give many less peas for a ha'penny than his father did; consequently, many a time, when circumstances and inclination favoured a parched-pea banquet, I have, from prudential motives, endured the agony of waiting till such times in the day when I knew the greedy shopman was released from business. If ever I detested a human creature in my life, it was that boy at that period. Yet, after all, I discovered him to be a most excellent fellow.

The discovery began one sultry August afternoon. I had earned a halfpenny of my mother by taking some peas to Camomile Street, and, after mature deliberation, resolved to buy peas with it. The time of day was favourable for the transaction, as the corn-dealer boy would be at school. Confident of success, I entered the shop, and tapped the counter with my halfpenny. Nobody came. I tapped again; when, with an angry growl, the chandler's boy emerged from the shady bin where the pollard was kept, and fiercely confronted me.

" Well! what do you want?" said he

There was no retreating.

" A ha'p'orth of grey peas, please."

" Blest if you aint always wanting grey peas!" said he, plunging the measure savagely into the pea sack. " Come, be quick; hold up;" and he motioned towards my cap.

Aggravated as much almost at his rudeness as at the miserably few peas he was proffering, I felt it would be a cowardly thing not to rebuke him. I proceeded to do so, with a mildness for which he had to thank his superior size rather than my forbearance.

" If I kept a shop," I said, " and another boy came for a ha'p'orth of peas, I should give him a whacking fair ha'p'orth; and I shouldn't bite his nose off, if I happened to be asleep, as I had no business to be, when he came in."

"But suppose you *wasn't* asleep?" replied he, laughing and looking honestly ashamed of himself; "suppose you had got a half-holiday, and a fellow that you knew had lent you a jolly book about cannibals, and you had just laid down to it, and got to a stunning part—suppose a chap came in then? Why, you would have a jolly good mind to chuck a flour-scoop at him, wouldn't you?"

The young chandler had touched a subject concerning which there were no bounds to my sympathy. My wrath vanished, and I replied emphatically—

" I have no doubt I *should* throw a scoop at him. I know all about the book you mean, it is ' Robinson Crusoe.' "

" You know all about ' Robinson Crusoe!' " exclaimed he, regarding me with admiration. " You don't mean to say you have got the book of it?"

"My aunt Jane has," said I, with assumed carelessness, at the same time conscious that the boundary of peas that had hitherto stood between us was considerably diminished; and that, if I was not his equal, I was not far short of it. "I can go to my aunt Jane's when-ever I like, and read it. I could go this very moment, and sit in her easy chair in the garden, in the corner where the gooseberry bushes are, and read till it was dark—all about how he got the things off the wreck on to his raft; and how he stowed away his gunpowder; and how he met that old goat, don't you know? in the cave; and how he kept a reckoning of the days, by cutting notches in the pole; and how, don't you know? when the savages came, and he watched them from where he was hiding, and saw them dancing round the fire they had made to——"

As I progressed, Bill Jupp (that was his name) blinked his eyes more and more, and opened his mouth wider and wider; while the undelivered and forgotten peas in the measure dribbled to the ground in a stream. When I had proceeded so far, he suddenly plucked me by the shoulder, and pulled me towards the pollard bin.

" Here," said he, " come on, there's nobody at home; you aint in a hurry, I know. Let us get into the bin together, and then you can tell me all about it."

Luxuriously bedded on pollard with my late enemy, I commenced "Robinson Crusoe," and, to the best of my memory, proceeded with that truly wonderful narrative till late in the afternoon, when, all unperceived, his father entered the neglected shop, and, pouncing on Bill, laid into him with a meal-bag, while I scrambled out of the pollard and made my escape.

A friendship, however, of no ordinary character dated from the pollard bin. The very next morning he was lurking about our house, and, as it happened that about ten o'clock I was sent to the currier's for a penn'orth of French chalk, I encountered him.

"Come along," said he. "I began to think you were never coming. I have been waiting for you this hour and a half."

The determination and severity of his countenance was not that of a friend, and, as he seized my arm and hurried me up the street, I began to suspect that it was his intention to inflict on me what I had yesterday missed—my share of a drubbing.

"Have you got another holiday, Bill ?" inquired I, in a conciliatory tone.

" No," replied he, in a morose voice, and looking so ruffianly that I was quite afraid of him. " I have taken a holiday this morning, Reuben. You and I are going off together, and you are going to finish telling me all about Robinson Crusoe."

" But, Bill," said I, "I am going on an errand."

"No, you aint," replied he doggedly; " you are going with me. We are going together to Limehouse Fields. I've brought something to eat; look here."

He opened the mouth of one of his trouser pockets, and discovered it throttled with peas; the other pocket he did not open, nor was there any occasion, as the dog-biscuit with which it was crammed was projecting visibly.

" Only say you will come," said he persuasively, "and you shall have it all to eat, going along, or after we get there. Why, what are you afraid of ? You won't get a double lesson and a whacking at school, if we are found out."

This was true. As I had imparted to Master Jupp on the previous day, I had not yet been sent to school. That, however, was a fault— if fault it was—that, in justice to my father, I must confess did not attach to him, but to my mother. Eighteenpence a week was the

lowest sum for which a private school would have received me, and
that my father stoutly and justly maintained was an expenditure at
once extravagant and needless on the part of persons in our condition,
especially as there was an excellent parish school, that not only supplied education gratis, but also clothing and a gift of coals and meal at
Christmas time : but this was an argument little likely to prevail with
a woman of my mother's spirit; so, by way of compromise, she consulted her sister Jane, who, as I said before, was a spinster, and occupied the first floor of a baby-linen shop in Cable-street. Miss Jane
Joyce was a lady of superior education, and, what was better still, a
dear, good-natured creature. She at once agreed that a charity-school
was no place for me ; and, as regarded the alternative, advanced the
opinion that a man (she never liked my father) had no business to
marry if he did not see his way perfectly clear to paying eighteenpence
a week for his son's education. "However, Mary," continued she,
hastening to pour oil on the wound she had inflicted, " that is no fault
of yours, my dear, nor of his either, perhaps, as you say, but rather
his misfortune. One thing is certain—unless you wish the boy to
grow to be a scavenger, he must be taught something. Let him come
to me for an hour of afternoons, when I am resting from my stitching,
and I will do the best I can with him; that is," continued she, turning
her spectacles severely on me, " as long as he comes clean. I couldn't
have a boy with dirty boots trampling over my carpet, or one with
grimy fingers turning the leaves of my books. If such a boy were to
knock at my door, he would not be let in."

Finding that she scrupulously adhered to this resolution, I was
wicked enough, after the novelty of going to my aunt's to be taught
had somewhat subsided, to turn it to account by appearing before her,
whenever I wanted a holiday, with the boots of a mud-carter and hands
fresh from marbles and the gutter. After a short time, however, she
became alive to my design, and one Monday afternoon, instead of the
wished-for observation, " I can't have you here in that dirty condition,
Reuben ; go home, and come cleaner to-morrow," she considerably
astonished me by remarking, " Since you are so dirty, Reuben, you
may as well clean my candlesticks; after which, and when you have
blacked your boots and made yourself clean and respectable, you may
go home." At the time, I was disposed to regard this as one of those
side-blows of ill-luck to which the best-arranged schemes are always

liable; but finding, on the next occasion and the next, that my dirtiness was met by the candlesticks, which were tall copper ones, of a provokingly crinkled pattern, I began to see that I was out-generalled, and resigned myself to cleanliness. Thanks to my good aunt Jane, at the age of eight I was able to read most of the books contained in her little library, amongst which were "Robinson Crusoe," "Barnaby's Travels in North America," and "Parkinson's Voyage to the South Seas."

To return, however, to Bill Jupp, who all this time is waiting an answer to his daring proposition. How could I deny him? However wicked he might be—however iniquitous it was to play truant and to filch dog-biscuit—I was in no condition to condemn him, for I was implicated. Until he knew me, he had known the great solitary islander but by name. Out of my mouth had he tasted the palatable wonders that belonged to "Robinson Crusoe;" it was I who had roused his appetite, and I only who could satisfy it. Still, why he had selected so distant a spot as Limehouse Fields for the gratification of his craving was more than I could understand.

"Is Limehouse Fields a very fine place, Bill?" I asked him.

"I should rather think it was," replied he, enthusiastically. "There isn't a house for a mile round; none of your stupid grass, and green hedges, and flowers, but all barren and cut up in holes and rucks, with ditches and thick furze—a regular jolly wilderness; you might almost fancy yourself on Crusoe's desolate island. Oh! come on!"

Had the terms of Master Jupp's description been no more seductive than the description itself, I am inclined to think that I should have remained unacquainted with Limehouse Fields; in which case, as far as human discernment may be relied on, I might never have become a wanderer at all, and have missed the many rare adventures that have since befel me. But, there, it is idle to discuss what might have been. I might have been a dead man years and years ago; and when I am brought to consider the scores of narrow escapes it has pleased Providence to bring me past, I am warned to the observance of what is and what may be, unless I take care, and am content to let what might have been go.

I yielded to the linking of Bill Jupp's arm in mine, and sped off with him.

Limehouse Fields was a terribly long way off, or, at least, so it seemed to my small and conscience-burthened legs. Master Jupp knew the road very well, but he had never traversed it but in his father's cart, and just about noon was compelled to admit that he did not think the fields were so distant, and to beg back some of the dog-biscuit that, two hours before, he had pressed on me for my private consumption. Shortly after, as we fagged along the hot and dusty road, we met a boy carrying a pitcher of water.

Now, because of the husky dog-biscuit, we were both drooping as much from thirst as fatigue, and we civilly asked the boy to give us a drink; he, however, turned out to be a greedy fellow, and, instead of helping us at once to what we stood so much in need of, and which had cost him nothing, he set down the pitcher, and tantalisingly plashing its cold and sparkling contents, and sprinkling our hot faces with a few drops, refused us the smallest drink, unless we first gave him something. He was one of those heavy-jawed, bull-necked boys, ragged-headed, and with big, dirty fists; therefore there was no use in arguing the matter with him. Bill Jupp produced some slate-pencil and a piece of India-rubber, but at these the extortioner turned up his nose contemptuously, and an offering of peas met with like treatment.

"I don't want that sort of rubbish," said the water-boy; "I want money—I want a ha'penny a-piece of you, and then you may swig away as long as you like."

"I hav'n't got a farthing," said Bill Jupp; "have you, Reuben?"

"No; that is, it isn't mine. I hav'n't a penny of my own."

"Then you will have to go thirsty," replied the rascal. "Oh, jimminy! how thirsty you will be! You won't find a drop of water for more than a mile, and then it's a ditch with a dead cat in it; but you will be glad to take a pull at it by the time you get there, I'll be bound."

I think that of the two I was thirstier than Bill Jupp; my tongue felt harsh as a dried eel-skin. There was my father's penny! It was a shameful thought, and I looked hastily towards Bill to see if I was detected. Had he looked unconscious of the dreadful thing the Devil had put into my head, I should have been saved; but unluckily, as he returned my gaze, I saw at once that he, too, was thinking of my father's penny; his eyes were eloquent of it, and he looked very imploring indeed.

"I daren't do it, Bill," said I. "I'd rather go thirsty than be a thief."

"I'm jiggered if I would," said the wicked water-boy emphatically ; "leastways, I'd rather crib anything than go raving mad with thirst like the dogs do. Now, look here : you've got some money in you pocket at this very minute as doesn't belong to you. Aint I right?"

"I've got a penny of my father's," replied I, wondering how it was that he, a perfect stranger, should have known so much of my private affairs.

"I knowed you had," said the blackguardly water-boy. "Now, suppose I could make a jump from here to your house, and was to say to your father, ' D'ye hear, mister? here's your boy a-going mad with thirst, out Stepney way ; he has got another boy with him, and both their eyes are a-rolling dreadful. Shall I take that penny of yourn, what they've got, and let 'em have some of my water, which it will save 'em?' What do you think your father would say? What do you think his father would say, young un?" said he, turning to Bill Jupp.

"I know my father would give a jolly sight of pennies rather than I should go raving mad," replied Bill evasively, at the same time beginning to cry.

"Well, young un, if you die all along of your mate's hard-artiness," observed the little blackguard, still addressing Bill Jupp, "he'll be sent across the herring-pond for manslaughtering you. If you won't have any of my water, I'm off."

So saying, he swung the pitcher on to his shoulder, and slowly slouched away. The despairing look that poor Bill Jupp sent after him was more than I could bear. I plucked my father's penny from my pocket, and, running after the dreadful boy with the water, put it in his hand, and the next moment we had the deliciously cold brim of the pitcher at our lips, our thirst was appeased, and our friend walked off chanting a lively air. With the subsiding, however, of the first sensation of sweet relief the water afforded, my conscience began to quake more violently than before. My guilt stared me broadly in the face, and I cowered before it, and cried and wrung my hands. In my frantic despair, I attacked Bill Jupp with a ferocity that appalled him. I left him with his nose bleeding, and gave chase to the boy with the pitcher, who, by this time, was a long way down the road. I overtook him. I begged, I implored him to give me back my father's penny. I even went as far as threatening him, but he laughed alike at my prayers and my threats, and went on singing, as though he did not hear me. I made a rush at him from behind, kicking the calf of his leg, and causing the pitcher to tilt, and the water to slop down his back. This was too much for his equanimity. He growled some dreadful words, and, setting the pitcher down, turned about and showed me such an ugly, scowling face, at the same time whipping off his tattered jacket, that I sped away towards Bill Jupp, who immediately commenced howling, and took to his heels, making sure, as he afterwards informed me, that the water had come too late to save me, and that I had really gone mad. We parleyed at a distance, and on his generous promise to lay the whole case before his mother before I went home, and to obtain of her the precious penny, I was comforted, and we trudged on together to the fields, which we had now nearly approached.

They answered his description thoroughly, being just about as wild and desolate as could be well conceived. What little grass there was, was shabby, and stubbled, and brown, and the ground was all broken up into gullies and hillocks. At some time or another the place had been the scene of brick-making operations, and great, over-baked masses of brick-stuff and clinkers were lying about everywhere; and at one end of the field—the most marshy and miserable end—there was a ruined brick-making hut, and just outside of it an old clay-grinding machine, with its woodwork split and bleached from exposure, and its iron parts red with rust.

By this time Master Jupp had quite recovered his spirits; and with the weight of the penny lifted from my mind, although far from elate, I became soberly cheerful, and at once fell in with his proposition that we should adjourn to the ruined hut, and consummate the plan that had cost us so much peril to approach thus far. We squatted down in a shady corner.

" Where did I leave off, Bill ? "

" ' What was his surprise to see before him the print of a naked foot ? ' " replied he, promptly.

So at that point I took up the thread of the eventful narrative, and spun it out, doubtless with hitches and tangles innumerable, but still with sufficient precision to enthral my listener so completely, that, but for his laboured breathing at stirring parts and an emphatic sniff at a crisis, I might have been there alone, for all the sound there was, save that of my own voice. So intent were we both that we were unconscious of heavy clouds gathering and obscuring the sun, and had no suspicion of approaching rain, till it fell with sharp clicks and patters upon the crisp straw with which the hut was thatched.

"It rains, Bill," said I, for a moment interrupting the story.

"Oh! bother; can't I hear it? Go on," replied Master Jupp.

So I went on, but not however for more than another minute, for, at the expiration of about that time, the gloomy shed was lit up to its extremest corner, and there followed such a thunder-clap that the earth seemed to tremble. For a moment we looked at each other in speechless terror, and then said I—

"I won't stay any longer, Bill Jupp. It is so much like a judgment, I'm afraid."

No wonder, child as I was, that I was afraid; for the sullen clouds, just rent by the sharp lightning, had thickened, as though to resist its attack, and our hut was murky, so that you could barely see its extremity, and suffocatingly close; while the beetles and other creeping things, whose abode was the thatch, routed by the deluge, came swarming out and down the walls and about us with noises that, to unaccustomed ears, were weird and unaccountable.

"Come on, Reuben," said Master Jupp, rising and shaking the dust from him; "I'm afraid too. We will run all the way home."

"You had better stay awhile, my little gentlemen; there is a sharper flash, and a louder thunder-crash to come, and the rain has yet to fall its fastest."

If we were afraid before, what were we now? We clasped each other by the hand, and, pale as ghosts, were for flitting off, however the storm might rage; but barely had taken three steps, when there appeared before us, turning out from the shelter the eaves of the thatch afforded, a hideous old woman, sooty black, with a red hood over her head, and a stumpy pipe between her shrunken lips; that is, between her shrunken upper lip and an under one of wood, or so it seemed in the uncertain light by which we viewed her.

. "Don't be afraid of me, young masters," said she, in her thin, piping voice; "I'm only a poor old woman, weather-bound, like yourselves; let us go under cover, and have a little chat. What shall I talk to you about?"

"We don't want to be talked to about anything, thank you, ma'am," replied Master Jupp, giving me a nudge. "We don't think you could tell us anything we should like better than going home."

"Ah!" exclaimed the dreadful old hag, angrily, "you are afraid of me, that's what it is. You silly children, you are more afraid of the poor old Malay woman than of the lightning that could catch you, though you ran faster than the wind; yet why should you be? It

Master Jupp, the Malay Woman, and I.

makes me sad to see decent folks shun me. I don't mind frightening bad people, if I can frighten them into doing good. I don't mind scaring bad boys who cheat other boys out of their pence."

I could see her coal-black eyes peering keenly at me through a cloud of tobacco-smoke as she uttered these last words; and I could feel my face glowing with shame and humiliation at the hint conveyed in them. This seemed to tickle the old witch's fancy, as her keen eyes twinkled more and more, and her wooden lip wagged again. Then she seemed to fumble for a pocket among the folds of her tattered cloak, and, withdrawing something therefrom, beckoned me towards her. A thrill of joyful hope for a moment possessed me, conquering my fear and aversion, and I went over to where she sat.

It was the identical penny. I knew it from the circumstance of its being stamped with the letter C; and chalk being the article it was intended to purchase, struck me as rather an odd thing. She pressed it into my hand without a word, and shut my fingers over it.

So overwhelmed with thankfulness was I, that had it not been for her pipe and wooden lip, I verily believe her wizened black face would have been no obstacle to my hugging her round the neck and kissing her. I compromised the matter by shaking her bony hand very cordially indeed.

"Thank you very much, ma'am," said I; "I am sure I don't know what I should have done but for your kindness; though I can't help wondering how you could have found out——"

"Well, there was no magic about it, I can promise you," replied she. "I was at the other side of the palings, lighting my pipe, when you came after the boy with the water-pitcher, and I heard all that you said, and all that he said. When you ran away, I kept on the inside of the palings, and, walking faster than the boy, got out into the road ahead of him, and then turned back and walked towards him. He! he! he made no attempt to interfere with me, I can tell you; he struck into the road, leaving me all the path to myself; but, my little chicks, I wasn't going to allow the rascal to pass so easily. I walked straight up to him, and says I, 'Shall I tell you your fortune, my little dear?' And he answers me quite civilly, 'No, thank ye, old woman, I aint got a fortune as is worth telling.' 'Yes, you have,' said I: 'this is your fortune—you will come to the gallows, if you are not more careful how you get money than that penny you have in your pocket.' Ho! he! you should have seen how foolish he looked then, my dears. I think he would have run, but he couldn't for the pitcher. At last, says he—for I stood before him all the time—'Oh! well, if that's it, I don't want the penny.' 'Then,' said I, ' give it to me, and I will take it to the boy you took it from.' He was glad to get off so cheap;" and here the good-natured old soul began so to chuckle at the recollection of her exploit, that she swallowed some of her tobacco-smoke, and began to stare, and gasp, and look so hideous, that had we not, by that time, been fully convinced of her benevolent disposition, we should not have dared to have stayed with her another moment—not that the aspect of the weather encouraged us to be squeamish as to trifles. As the old woman had prognosticated, the fury of the storm was not yet spent, and, ever and anon, double and treble darts of lightning illumined our shelter, to be answered by the bellowing thunder. Finding the sort of old woman she was, indeed, we began to be thankful for her company; and at every demonstration of the angry heavens we edged closer to her.

"I never before saw such a storm as this," ventured Bill Jupp, when the black woman's coughing and gasping had subsided; "did you, ma'am?"

"Have I, chick?" replied the old woman. "Ah, that I have! I have seen storms beside which this would be but an April shower. I have seen great trees big round as the bodies of twenty men, wrung out of the ground, or broken short off as you could break a daisy. I have heard such thunder as has made the birds in the trees scream to hear, and the oxen to quake till their hides reeked with sweat. I have seen such rain as would strike down a strong man did he venture out in it."

"That must have been before I was born, ma'am," observed Master Jupp.

"Years and years before you were born, my dear—before your father was born, unless he is an old man. It is fifty years and more since my eyes last rested on beautiful Sooloo. Beautiful Sooloo, thousands on thousands of miles away, and fifty years ago and more, but fresh to the eyes of my mind as though 'twere only yesterday. See how good to preserve what is best of us love is, my little boys! Distance is nothing to it; time is nothing to it; else, my dears, the eyes of God in the skies, more miles away than the wisest man that ever yet lived dare consider, would never reach us to watch and take care of us."

The old black woman's latter remark was much more applicable than she could have known; it struck home, and brought remorseful tears to our eyes, though in the gloom she did not perceive them. She presently put an end to an embarrassing silence by commencing to speak again.

"But, my dears, although I should like to see beautiful Sooloo once more before I die, you must not think I wish myself there, living as I used to live. The Lord forbid! They don't know the Lord in Sooloo, my dears."

"Where is So—Sooloo, ma'am?" inquired Bill Jupp.

"Far away in Asia. As far as the shores of the China Seas," replied she, "where the tall cocoa-palm flourishes, and the woods cluster thick with beautiful fruit and flowers down to the very brink of the broad waters where the pearl-fishers work."

"That must be a nice place to live in," I observed—taking immediately to the cocoas. I never yet had had the good fortune to possess an entire cocoa-nut, but judging from the rare slices my means had permitted, together with some milk of the same I had once tasted, it was a food I would cheerfully have subsisted on till the end of my days, never asking for any other—"A much nicer place than England."

"Ay, ay!" said the Malay woman, shaking her head; "but, my little man, fruit and flowers are not the only things to be met with in the forests; there are great hideous apes, tall as men, and twenty times as strong, who lurk among the branches, and threaten you with their terrible teeth and their great hairy limbs; there the rhinoceros is to be met, and the wild boar, and the mighty elephant; as well as birds, big serpents nestle in the trees, and hang down their great, glittering lengths, plying their forked tongues in search of food; there, in these same forests, where cocoa-nuts and bananas grow, and where there are flowers of the colours of the rainbow, and some so large that a baby might lie in one and not be seen, and where great measures of wild honey are stored in the hollows of the trees—there lurk in the grass creeping things with stings as dangerous as poisoned arrows, and swarms of leeches that crawl about and cling to you and suck your blood. Would you call all that nicer than England, my dear?"

"But if one went to that country they would not be obliged to live where the rhinoceroses and the serpents lived, would they?" inquired Master Jupp. "Did you live among 'em, ma'am?"

"No," replied she; "I lived in a village where——"

But, even if it were my desire, I should find it impossible to relate in a narrative shape the wonderful things she told of that same village, and of many others forming one of the hundred islands that form the Malayan Archipelago—of the houses built of reeds and bamboo, and plastered with mud—of the trades of the inhabitants—how that some gathered india-rubber, and some were weavers of cloth of grass, and some went out hunting small birds for the market, their only weapon being a sort of gigantic pea-shooter, but with tiny arrows instead of peas—and some went fishing for pearls, diving to monstrous depths, and remaining below long enough to drown ordinary mortals, and that without the least assistance. She told us how the people lived, what their food was, how they dressed and decorated themselves (painfully illustrating this part of her story by removing the odious wooden plug from her bottom lip), with some of the curious ceremonies that attended their death and burial; she told us about the slaves—of how they were kidnapped, and who were the kidnappers, and how the Spaniards came in ships, and bought them and carried them away; of the wars and bloodshed that prevailed among the tribes, with some startling and incomprehensible information of one tribe going out on head-hunting excursions, the heads being human ones, and to be cut off and carried home in triumph, and kept for ever afterwards as precious trophies of valour. To this hour I am uncertain which most impressed me, this head-hunting business, or what she told us about the pirates— of whole nations being pirates to a man, ay, and to a woman and child; and if not every man, at least every family possessing a fighting-boat (prahus the old woman called them); and how that these prahus did not prey singly, but clubbed a hundred or more together, and put themselves under a chief, who chose his officers and led the marauders to fight and pillage. No petty cockboats were these war prahus, seemingly, but taut, capacious craft, carrying rowers and twenty armed men, besides each something in the shape of a cannon; so that a pirate fleet must have been a stirring sight, and a pirate battle a bloody one.

But I have not enumerated half—no, nor a quarter—of what the Malay woman told; though, without bringing her the least discredit, I might do so—all she related, as I afterwards had ample opportunity of proving, and as will be, by-and-by, made known to the reader, being strictly true.

She told us so much that it was waning towards evening, and the storm had disappeared, leaving the heavens bland and bright again before she concluded; and she bade us good-bye after accompanying us to the verge of the fields, going the contrary way.

I will not impose on the reader's patience by keeping him by the button till we reached home, that he may hear the wonderful conversation that transpired between Master Jupp and myself as we re-trod the weary road traversed by us in the morning. I trust this forbearance will not be regarded too lightly; for, were I to recount the comparing of notes, the agreements, the contradictions, the schemes for running away to sea that very night, the amendments that we should postpone it till next week—for a month—for six months—till we saved sufficient pocket-money to purchase an outfit; the cooling of our ardour as we neared home, the sneaking anxiety to shift the big share of the day's truancy each on to the other's shoulders, the final and tearful pause at the corner of Goodman's Fields, that the very best excuse might be adjusted—were the reader to be dragged through all this, he would, without doubt, appear at the Goodman's Fields end of it in a mood too unamiable to move another step.

This as regards the patient reader : as to the impatient one, I have grave doubts if I have not already incurred his lasting displeasure.

"Why 'home again' at all?" says he. "It was bad enough that you occupy a dozen pages in getting no farther towards Borneo from Whitechapel than Limehouse. Why back to so unromantic a place as Goodman's Fields? Why not take ship and be off at once?"

To which, with all respect, I reply to the impatient reader, that I know no more "why not" than he himself does. It was not so, that is all. It was not so till nearly six years afterwards.

"Then, Master Davidger, why did not you begin your story six years later? It was yours to choose the time to begin, and it is a little too hard to call us so long before we are wanted."

My dear, impatient reader, it is you who are a little too hard. True, I did not commence my more momentous adventures till I was nigh fourteen years old; but it was that little affair in Limehouse Fields that, finding my mind bent on roving, so hardened it, as hot iron is hardened by a souse in water. Far be it from me, however, to boast of this; alas! it was a sorry business for me, and, as I verily believe, launched me on that thorny road from which I was lucky enough, albeit so torn and battered, to escape with life.

CHAPTER II.

Y parents having arrived at the melancholy conclusion that I was either kidnapped or drowned, and that if ever they set eyes on me again it would be in a parish dead-house, or as brought to their threshold pallid, and extended on a shutter, were overwhelmed with emotion on my suddenly appearing before them.

This I was easily enabled to do by reason of the street-door of our house being fastened by a latch merely. There was mother at the window, her eyes red with weeping, my father before the neglected fire-grate, haggard, jaded, and with his hat on his head, as though he had but recently returned from a protracted and unsuccessful hunt after me ; and my aunt from Cable Street—who never visited our house except on extraordinary occasions—busily writing what I afterwards discovered to be a faithful description of my attire, height. and complexion, for circulation among constables and watermen. Hot, hungry, dusty, trembling with guilt and apprehension, I stood in the shadow of the open parlour-door beseechingly meeting the amazed glances of the three pairs of eyes that greeted me. This interesting picture, however, was composed and effaced in less than a tenth of the time it has here taken to describe.

" Thank God ! Oh, my dear Reuben, you cruel, cruel boy !" and in an instant my mother was cuddling me close to her, and kissing me so that my heart instantly changed its burden of fear for one of remorseful sorrow ; and as I piped my eye, and clasped my hands round her neck, I resolved that the most desolate island the world could afford should never tempt me to leave her. At this distance of time it will now and then occur to me, as food for mental speculation, whether, if my mother, at that time, had been allowed her way with me, my path in life might not have been entirely different. I know what she would have done if no one had interfered with her; she would have fed me and sent me to bed, and while I lay there, full of loving thoughts of her, and quite melted through her kind behaviour, she would have come in, all in the dark, and, sitting by the bedside with my hand in hers, talked to me, Heaven knows what about, but convincingly, and to the purpose, I am sure. What important results may have followed! My wayward inclination, put in train by Master Crusoe and the rest of the roaming crew, and clinched by the Malay woman, would have yielded to her persuasion, and, doubtless, I should have become a sober London journeyman, or, maybe, a rich and respected citizen. Well, if such would have been the case, and my parents and myself have been advantaged by it, the guilt of marring such a consummation lies at the door of my aunt Jane.

"Well, upon my word," exclaimed she to my tearful mother, "this is, indeed, a pretty way to reclaim him from vicious and vagabond habits! Mary, I am ashamed of you. Is he to play his pranks and befool you both in this way, John?"

Now, I must confess that at this period I was not overmuch attached to my aunt Jane; endowed as she was with many virtues, they were not discoverable by little boys (nor, indeed, by grown-up folk if they were strangers, and not particularly acute), by reason of the disguises she dressed them in. She always seemed as anxious to conceal her goodness as a miser to hide his gold; and as he secures his dear dross in unlikely rags and flinders, so she went about with her charity masked with stinginess, and her solicitude with disdain; nice enough to reflect on when you found her out, but until you did she was decidedly a loser, as you were liable to regard the good turns she did you as mistakes on her part, or diplomatic triumphs on your own. Undoubtedly she was actuated by the purest motives on this particular occasion; but, so far from appreciating them, I could not help regarding her interference as most unwarrantably vindictive and cruel; and observing my father, in obedience to her suggestion, casting about for some handy means of chastisement, I frantically exclaimed against her as a wicked old woman.

"You come with me, Mary," was her reply, marching across the room, and taking my mother's arm ; " and let his father deal with him."

Arming himself with a sleeveboard, my father proceeded to deal with me.

"Now, sir, tell me where you have been ?"

" To Limehouse Fields, father."

"To Limehouse Fields !   Pray what took you there ?"

" I went with a boy, father."

" Well ?"

" To tell him a story."

" Why, you audacious, false-speaking rascal !" replied my father as soon as he had recovered his astonishment that such a flimsy and ridiculous excuse should be attempted on him ; " d'ye think to come it over me in that way ?" Instantly I was subjected to such a series of spanks with the sleeveboard as, if they had not been deadened by my squealing, might have been heard on the other side of the street.

Was I the better for the flogging ? Alas ! bad, passionate boy that I was, I was the worse.   I went to bed, for the first time in my life, without saying my prayers, and cried myself to sleep with bitter and rebellious tears ; and, thanks to the wicked angels I had invoked, dreamt delicious dreams of commanding pirate prahus and diving for pearls, and riding magnificently-caparisoned elephants through palm groves, picking cocoa-nuts by the way.   This was bad for my unwholesome temper, and in no wise prepared me to partake, with humility and contrition, of the dry bread and sugarless beverage that composed my breakfast.

I became a changed boy ; it got into my silly head that my father, my aunt, my mother even, were against me, and strangely enough, I nourished the suspicion with a considerable degree of satisfaction. Regarded in this false light, my exploit of the previous day assumed proportions it had not before possessed—became a deed of daring that had convulsed my relations with terror, and brought on me heavy punishment.   To be sure, the nature of the punishment was not such as is inflicted on detected dare-devils ; and properly I should have been pilloried or placed in the stocks rather than have been spanked with a sleeveboard.

In this latter respect Master Jupp was luckier than myself, though in truth the poor fellow seemed not all alive to his advantage.   Knowing from personal observation, as well as from hints Bill had, in the midst of his tribulation, let fall, what a Turk the corndealer was, I was not a little anxious to ascertain how he had come off, and to that end made my way as soon as possible (which, by-the-bye, wasn't till late in the afternoon) to the shop, and sought, by hovering about, to attract his attention. My manœuvres, however, were unsuccessful. Spurred by my alarm, I approached close enough to see that he was not in the shop—nay, nor in the shop-parlour—although, as I well knew, it was long past his time for returning from school, and as I could see by peeping in at a corner pane, and availing myself of the chinks that existed between some meal jars, the family were preparing to sit down to tea.

What had become of Bill? Was he banished from his home? Had his inexorable father killed him? The nakedness of the upper windows, and the circumstance of there being no shutters before the shop-window, tended to negative this latter terrible supposition; still, Bill being a disobedient and reprobate boy, his parents might not have thought it worth while to avow their respect for his memory by any such demonstration; and even while his brothers and sisters were contentedly devouring bread-and-butter in the back parlour, the unhappy partner of my yesterday's atrocity might be lying stark—beaten to death—in the wash-house beyond. By-and-by, however, my horrified thoughts were turned into a fresh channel by observing the Jupp serving-maid emerge from the shop, bearing a jug that, by its smoking, evidently contained hot tea, and something wrapped in paper that might have been a hunch of bread, while depending from her forefinger was a great key attached to a ram's horn.

Bill was a prisoner! The bread and tea were his prison fare, and the great key was the key of his dungeon! My respect for so distinguished a boy increased prodigiously, and with eager, yet cautious, steps, I followed his gaoler. She traversed half the length of the street, and then turned down a narrow alley, which, from the cobblestones with which it was paved, and its general horsey aspect, I knew to be a mews. Into this unfrequented place I dare not follow her for fear of detection; but I watched her from behind a cart—saw her halt at a certain door, unlock it with the great key, disappear for a few moments, appear again, lock the door, and retrace her steps.

As soon as the coast was clear, I, too, was at the door, trying my

hardest to make out what was to be seen through the keyhole. There
was nothing to be seen through the gloom that enveloped the place
but the dim outline of a horse and a horse-stall; but there were to be
heard sounds of human mastication, blended with sighing and sobbing,
and ever and anon the clank of a chain.

I applied my lips to the keyhole.

"Are you in here, Bill?"

"Is that you, young Davidger?"

"Yes. What's the matter? What have they been doing to you,
Bill?"

"I'll let you know, you beggar! the first time I meet you outside;
it's all owing to you and your jolly lying old Crusoe that I'm chained
here!"

And the violence of his emotion caused the dry bread he was eating
to descend in an improper way, and he gasped and caught his breath till
his chain rattled in a manner terrible to hear. His mode of greeting
a companion in distress had been anything but courteous; still, I could
not bear to leave him till I had further acquainted myself with the
cause of his misery, and to that end climbed up the door-post, and,
drawing myself up by the grating over the door, looked in. There was
Master Jupp, hobbled by the leg with a chain horse-hobble, the block
end of which was passed through a ring by the manger; an upturned
stable-pail served him as a stool, by the side of which was a brown
stone pitcher, capable of holding about two gallons. Without doubt,
he must have heard me hauling myself up, and, with unaccountable
malice, made certain preparations on my behalf meanwhile, for no
sooner did my face appear to him behind the grating, than a blacking-
pot was hurled towards it. "Take that!" exclaimed he; and so I
should have taken it, to my great hurt, but that the bars were too close
together to admit of its passage. After this I felt no inclination to
pursue my inquiries, and, sliding down the door-post, left him to his
fate. That it was not extremely cruel I know from the fact of my
meeting him at Sunday-school only two days after; on this occasion,
as the last, he declined converse with me; this time, however, in mild,
though firm, language, and with a demeanour that convinced me that
he was a reformed boy.

Nor did I succeed in finding another agreeable companion to
accompany me in my rambles, for, as I have already hinted, I took to

rambling, and that in defiance of my aunt Jane's admonitions, stinted meals, the sleeveboard, and worse than all, of my mother's tears. Ratcliff Highway was my chief field of allurement, for in that neighbourhood in those days, and, for all I know, at the present, there existed many dingy little shops rich in the products of the most remote regions of the earth—of the Indies, of the Guinea coast, and of the ocean isles of the distant South—furnished by long-voyaging mariners who navigated spice ships and ships that traded in dye-woods and ivory, and, as I then firmly believed, guineas from the coast of that name, the medium of barter being beads, and brass buttons, and hanks of copper wire. Never yet was boy so bewildered, so completely enchanted, as was I at the marvels these dingy shops exhibited. There were birds dead and stuffed, with legs longer than mine but slender as a tobacco-pipe, with yellow bodies and green necks, and beaks the colour of blood ; others with staring goggle eyes, and with beaks long and sharp as skewers—some more gorgeous far than the peacock, but so small that at least six might have been stowed in one's jacket pocket ; one—he stood by himself in the middle—so tall that a hole was cut in the window-board, lowering him to the knees, and yet his head so pressed the ceiling that you were convinced, were he only to tiptoe, he would either break his neck or force his goose-like cranium through to the next floor—that is, if he had been alive. He was ticketed " Ostrich from South Africa," and between his legs, to the number of thirty or more, was piled a heap of freckled globes, each larger than a baby's head, and likewise ticketed " Ostrich Eggs." Then there were live birds, little as wrens and big as chickens, some savage and chained by the leg, others loose in giant cages, climbing and swinging and rocking and shrieking out in their foreign tongues such a Babel of sound that the mere reverberation of it lived in the ears an hour afterwards. All these birds had most outlandish beaks—some that turned up like scoops, some that turned down like hooks, and some with the upper part crossing the lower, like a pair of scissors ; moreover, they were of such various colours as are never seen out of the sky—indeed, it seemed doubtful whether the rainbow itself could match them, or whether a cloud of them would not furnish for the sun a more splendid setting than he often finds.

This is but an imperfect inventory of the curiosities furnished by one only of my Ratcliff shops ; but it dwells in my mind more distinctly than the others, because I always made it a practice to pause and have a look in as I went along, and as invariably gave it my attention as I returned, chiefly I believe, because the birds were merely a pleasantly wonderful collection; whereas the other marvellous shops—two of them in particular—were crammed with hideousness, including great man-apes, hairy-mouthed, with black lips and yellow fangs; and crocodiles labelled " Man-Eaters from the China Seas," or " From the Indian Archipelago," which seemed, indeed, a tremendously long way off; and live serpents, some no thicker than a sash-line, with " Poisonous" written on the jar in which they lived—one called " The Deadly Cobra," and another, who nestled in a tub and was partly hidden in the folds of a blanket, whose body was of the texture of floor-cloth, whose eyes were like precious stones, and who had a restless, quivering tongue like a miniature pitchfork, ticketed " Full-grown Boa Constrictor, sixty guineas."   Such trifles as " Carib Skull," " Ojibbeway Brain-Hatchet," " Tattooed Head of New Zealand Chief," " Cannibal Forks from the Sandwich Islands," etc., etc., made up the rest of the show, after feasting on which it was a real relief to hurry back to the bird-shop, and calmly contemplate the ostrich straining against the ceiling, and the sweet little birds of paradise, before I turned homeward.

There was another feature of interest attaching to Ratcliff, and which frequently turned the beam in favour of a visit there in preference to one to Holborn, to the coral and shell shop, and where tortoises were on sale, or to Drury Lane, where there lived an eccentric barber, formerly a man-of-war's-man, and who exhibited in his window an elaborate and highly-coloured model of an engagement between a single British frigate and two three-deckers of Spain ; the preponderating influence in question being the sailors of many nations who were constantly perambulating the Highway.   If there came along a squad of yellow-visaged men, long, lantern-jawed, and hungry-looking, shipstained, shock-headed, but still with an easy swagger, and bright-eyed, it was easy to make of them a party long becalmed at sea, and all exposed to the great, hot sun, till the water-casks were drained dry, and there was not a drop to drink, let alone to wash with—till the ship was hot as an oven, and favourable to the breeding of rats and weevil, and other creatures prone to batten on ships' stores.   Did I espy an African whose present pursuits were evidently maritime, despite the emphatic contradiction furnished by the unsailor-like wisp of red rag worn about his head in place of the honest tarpaulin, the rings in his broad ears, the sheathed knife slung round his neck instead of the clasped Sheffield blade dangling at his hip, the skimping pantaloons that revealed the scragginess of his shanks, when I furtively regarded his cat-like gait and his blubberous lips, I had no doubts as to his country or his proper occupation; he came from the land of cocoa-nuts and elephants, and his trade was hunting little birds with a blow-gun; it was pleasant to carry his image to the bird-shop, and then, by a bold imaginative effort, to convert Ratcliff Highway into a tropical forest, endow with life and let loose the golden humming-birds, the uncomfortable ostrich, and all the crew of dazzling, flaming, jabbering parrots and set at them my African, with his excellently-adapted lips, to blow tiny arrows at them and bring them down. True, the ostrich might defy the blow-gun, but then the legs of my African are little inferior as regards slimness to the bird's; and, having overtaken it, with one hand grasping its inviting throat, and the other the haft of his sheath-knife, the struggle would possibly be of short duration.

It must not be imagined, however, that, throughout the six
years that stood between my Limehouse Fields exploit and the time
when my real adventures began, my liberty was uncontrolled, leaving
me impunity to vagabondize as I chose. It was not so. After my
aunt Jane's signal act of meanness, it became impossible for me to continue my educational visits to her house either to her or to my satisfaction. With admirable courage she persisted for over a fortnight ; but,
at the end of that time, she happening to discover certain personal and
uncomplimentary allusions written on the title-page of her hymn-book,
we parted. Again there was a consultation of my relations, and it was
decided that, after all, a charity-school was quite good enough for the
sort of boy I was—at least, so my aunt Joyce expressed herself, and
with a view, I believe, to wound my feelings ; if so, she was unsuccessful. I had not the slightest objection to becoming a charity scholar,
only that it restricted my leisure in an alarming manner ; indeed it
was only on the afternoons of Wednesday and Saturday that I might,
with impunity, indulge my habit of roaming. How often I did so,
without impunity, and what came of it, it is unnecessary here to enlarge on.

I was just turned fourteen years old, and had grown to be so tall a
lad that the regulation small-clothes of the parish (made in sizes from
1 to 6, the latter being the largest size allowed), although eked out
with twine at the braces, and gored by my father at the knees, became
exceedingly uncomfortable, and the tail of my regulation jacket became
a mockery—jutting as it did in the abruptest manner at the beginning
of my back's smallness—when a sudden stop was put to my scholastic
career, and I was called on, without a moment's warning, to commence
the stern business of life. The call took place in front of the alligator-
shop (the full-grown boa was still unsold, although its price was reduced
more than a third), and the caller was my uncle, Sampson Joyce, the
stevedore.

Previous to this I had seen this uncle of mine but very seldom ;
indeed, to speak with certainty, not more than twice : once at Cable-
street, where he, by appointment, came while I was there to tea, and
when there was stout brown paper laid over the carpet, and the damask
curtains were taken down, and a spittoon borrowed from a neighbour-
ing tavern—he being a heavily-shod man, and an inveterate smoker ;
and once again in an inebriate condition, and on a Boxing Day, when

his sister Jane having been denied to him (a slight that, as he recounted
it to my father, compelled his tears and the utterance of dreadful language), he came to our house bringing some tobacco, strong and in the
leaf, and some ship rum in a stone bottle. He wasn't a tall man, but
he was tremendously broad, and had a purple face and bushy black
whiskers, and hands that looked as though his constant occupation
was the manufacture of cobbler's wax. He had plenty of money, and
was very generous, giving my mother a guinea as a Christmas-box, and
calling her "Polly," which seemed very strange to us children, and
appeared to be regarded by my father, who held singular notions concerning such matters, as an unwarrantable liberty.

It seemed to me, moreover, that our uncle Sampson was a man of
very uncertain temper; for when my father had taken a glass or so of
the ship rum, and began to speak his mind about Aunt Jane (decidedly, it is true, but in not nearly such violent terms as the stevedore
had used), the latter turned round on him in a jiffy, and bringing his
brown fist down on to the work-board with a bang that made the shears
and thimbles leap again, swore that the biggest man in London should
not speak ill of his sisters without first drubbing him past the power
to stand up for them. I must confess that the opinion my father
expressed of Uncle Sampson, as soon as he was gone, was also mine;
"that he was very likely a well-meaning, good-natured man, but a
great deal too bounceable."

It may have been about a year and a half from this last time of my
seeing Uncle Sampson, when I, being, as before stated, on a Saturday
afternoon, intent on admiring some recent addition to the marvels of
the crocodile-shop, was clapped on the shoulder from behind, and, looking round, discovered the well-remembered purple face and bushy
whiskers.

"Aint your name Davidger, young shaver?"

"That is my name," replied I; "how do you do, Uncle Sampson?"

"Oh, you know me, do you? Well, that's lucky. How am I?—
well, I'm only middlin';" and he shook his head lugubriously, and
sighed a sigh that at once conveyed to my senses an odour that had
not greeted them since Boxing Day twelvemonth. "What do you do
up this quarter? Have you found a job of work yet?"

This latter question—especially the look that accompanied it—
somewhat surprised me. I replied—

"I haven't begun to look for work yet, uncle; had you any reason for supposing I had?"

"Not at all—not at all," returned he, with a stern wag of the head; "on the contrary, I have precious good reason to suppose that you never do mean to look for it. Oh! it's not the least use you looking savage at me, I can tell you. I have heard all about it. Aint you ashamed of yourself? D'ye think it's becoming, now, for a great hulking chap like you to go dancing about dressed up like a farden doll" (here he lifted my coat-tail in the most contemptuous manner), " and living on your poor father and mother? Don't you think it would be more creditable to turn your hand to something towards earning your own living?"

I was so completely taken aback by his style of address, that for a moment it seemed to me that my proper course would be to bid him good day, and have no more to say to him; but then came the reflection that he was my mother's brother, and that it might happen (the Boxing Day effluvium certainly warranted the supposition) that he was a little tipsy; moreover, I felt not a little curious to ascertain what it all meant. Uncle Sampson seemed to read my thoughts, for he presently continued—

"Don't think it is your mother who has been complaining—not she; she would let you stay at home idling about and eating her head off before she would complain. Oh, no! it aint from that quarter I got my information; it's from this one."

He fumbled in an inner pocket of his jacket, and presently produced a letter addressed in the unmistakeable handwriting of Aunt Jane.

"Ses she," said he, opening the letter, and pretending to read, "'Dear Sampson—umph—'many thanks for your kindness'—umph. Ah! here's the part—that about you, young fellow—'he's a idle warmint as p'r'aps you might find a job for.'"

I could not help laughing at this base libel on my aunt's correct diction.

" You're a precious hardened rascal, I can see," continued he; " I aint had no time to answer your aunt's letter yet, but I mean to—to tell her that I can always find work for a lad as is early risin', and willin', and one as don't mind dirtying his hands, or care about being thought genteel."

It was not difficult to see that this latter observation was pointed at me, and might, indeed, be considered as an offer of employment.

Meanwhile, we had walked away from the curiosity-shop, and entered into a narrow lane that led to the river, I keeping my uncle's side, and puzzling my head to discover what sort of employment it was he could place me at, and on what terms. Presently we came to the end of the narrow lane, and in full sight of a sort of docks, in which a large number of merchant-ships, of all sorts and sizes, were discharging and taking in their cargoes amid such pulling, and hauling, and sweating, and swearing, and cuffing as I had never witnessed before.

My uncle was evidently well known among the shipping people, some of whom called him " Joyce," and "Sampson," and to whom he touched his hat, while others called him " Mr. Joyce," and touched their caps to him ; or, in cases where they wore no caps, hitched their slack trousers in a respectful manner. In a little while, one of the latter hurried towards him, and begged that he would step on board the " Shoreham Lass," as something had gone wrong with a crate of pottery. After cursing his informant in the heartiest terms, my uncle turned to me and observed—

" Now, look here, nevvey ; you've heard what I've had to say, and you see before you the sort of work you will be required to help at if we come together. Don't go to think that it's light work, or that it's pleasant work, because that's just what it aint. I shall be gone about ten minutes, and if so be you think you should like to have something to say to me, I shall find you here when I come back ; if so be you aint tired of skulking, and eating the bread of idleness, as soon as my back's turned you'll cut off, and I sha'n't see any more of you, which won't break my heart, I can tell you."

And, without more ado, he plunged his hands into the pockets of his monkey jacket, and, boarding a ship by means of a plank, made his way to the " Shoreham Lass," and was lost to view.

What should I do ? Next to going to sea downright (to do which I had long nurtured a hazy yearning), and sailing to far-distant lands, which were so wondrously fruitful, and where might be found in profusion the marvels of which my Ratcliff and Holborn treasuries furnished such interesting specimens, the next best thing must be to move among, and daily handle, and without doubt obtain frequent peeps into, the various quaint bales and packages such as, from where I stood, I could see being hauled from the depths of this ship and that —clumsy bales of savage packing wrapped about with the hides of beasts unknown in civilized lands, and secured with leathern thongs, hairy and untanned, and shapeless baskets of strange rush, which, when green, may have waved by the margin of remote African rivers, affording secure lurking for crocodiles and such other water monsters, whose nature it is to lie in wait for their prey.   Without doubt, I should like to have run home and consulted my mother before I engaged myself to Uncle Sampson, but it seemed only reasonable to assume that she and my aunt in Cable Street must have talked the matter over, and agreed to the writing of the letter, which I was very sure was of quite a different character as regarded myself from that my uncle's ignorance or malice made out, and, therefore, there was no need for me to be squeamish on that score.

Then, again, it occurred to me that, unless I embraced this or some such other opportunity, and that speedily, I should presently be called on by the parochial authorities to bind myself 'prentice to some trade for seven long years—perhaps it might be to a draper, or a shoemaker, or even, indeed, a tailor—a trade I disliked before all others ; in fact, there were serious grounds for dreading an apprenticeship to tailoring ; for my father, thinking it, perhaps, a pity that a stranger should get the benefit both of the parish premium and my services, had more than once hinted that he should not object himself to teach me his trade ; and though my mother was ever slow to encourage the hint, fifteen pounds was a nice bit of ready money, and if it should happen to offer itself at a slack time of the year, there was no knowing what might be the consequence.

All these considerations favoured my acceptance of my uncle's offer, as did one other, and that was my strong suspicion that my bearish relation made quite sure that I was too much of a milksop to buckle to such tough work as cargo stowing, and that, as soon as he was out of sight, I should take to my heels and run away—a circumstance he, doubtless, would have hastened to communicate, after his own peculiar fashion, to Cable Street.   I don't say that it was a desire to balk him of his expectations that decided me to take my chance with him, but when I had resolutely sat down on a handy barrel, it was very useful in keeping me there.

In a few minutes my uncle made his appearance.

" You hav'nt gone, then ?" said he, in what struck me as being a not particularly pleased voice.

"No; nor do I mean to go, uncle, if you please," replied I, as cheerfully as I could. "I want to go to work. Does it matter which of these ships of yours I step into to lend a hand?"

He seemed to think it a capital joke that I should have thought him such an extensive shipowner, and laughingly told me that, if I turned out as great a rogue as it was evident I was a fool, he was likely to have done a pretty thing through meddling with me; however, it was easy to perceive that his vanity had been pleasantly tickled, for, in quite an amiable tone, he presently continued—

"No, nevvey; I hav'nt arrived at having craft of my own just at present, though, maybe, I am as well off as many a one that has, and so may you be if you stay with me, and be a good lad. Let us see; this being Saturday, you begin work on Monday; so we may as well get you into a Christian rig at once, and then we will go to your mother's and settle the business with her."

So saying, he marched me straight to a slop clothier's, and in ten minutes I emerged, leaving my parish suit in a bundle, and equipped in a pair of substantial duck trousers, a checked shirt, a blue guernsey, and a glazed round hat.

"That's the ticket," observed Uncle Sampson, as we trudged down the street; "now you look something like."

He did not say what it was I looked like; but, in truth, if I looked as I felt—baggy where I was wont to be tight, and tight where I was wont to be baggy—I must have cut anything but a cheerful figure, or one that warranted the prideful glances with which from time to time he regarded me.

My suspicions that my mother knew of the application to Uncle Sampson were confirmed by the comparatively small amount of surprise we created. Of course, mother was somewhat taken aback that my transformation should have taken place in so unexpected a manner, as was my father, who, I verily believe, up to this moment had been kept in utter ignorance of the scheme; however, he was pretty much ruled by mother; and though, as I could see, he was inwardly furious that he had not been consulted, his meek nature succumbed before the will of his wife and the presence of her big, hairy brother, and he confined the expression of his displeasure to the hideous cut and scandalous workmanship of my new clothes, and offered no opposition to my uncle's suggestion that I should accompany him at once to his house at Wapping-wall, and that, in return for such services as it was in my power to render him, I should be lodged, boarded, and clothed, and receive, for the first year, an allowance of a shilling a week as pocket-money.

So that very night I left my father's house, and with a lighter heart than if I had known how very few times I should ever enter it again, or if I could have foreseen the hardship and misery in store for me almost from that very hour.

It was my misfortune to discover, and that within a very few days, that the man who was at once my relative and my master was no more nor less than a complete ruffian, and that, so far from his rough exterior covering a gentle nature, his outward semblance of manliness was his most tolerable part. His house at Wapping-wall was of good size, and well furnished. It seems he had been married, but that his wife had had the good fortune to die, leaving him a daughter, who had now grown to be a woman, and kept his house; but it would have been better for her—as she herself expressed it to me before I had known her very long —had she been dead and buried out of his way. At the best of times his foulest words were the fairest she got; and when he was drunk, which was every night, and sometimes in the day, he would cuff and shake her, sometimes aiming at her such blows as, had they been soberly directed, would have lain her senseless.

As for me, I had not a great deal to complain of. My uncle, himself a hearty feeder, honoured me with a seat at his board; my bed was soft enough, and as clean as Martha's hard-working hands could make it, and my shilling a week was paid with the greatest punctuality. Indeed, my name was entered in the labourer's book with the others, and I took my turn on Saturday night at the pay table. As to the quality of the labour expected of me, I at first found it tremendously hard; it blistered my hands and strained my joints, and my shins were black and blue through my awkward stumbling amongst the stowage. Indeed, for full a month after I entered my uncle's service, I should have much preferred, when the day's work was over, curling in a corner and there passing the night, to the labour and pain of walking home.

Hard as this was to bear, there was not much in it after all— nothing, in fact, to justify a word of grumbling on my part. I had freely undertaken the work, knowing its nature; it was work as I had only to look about me to be convinced capable of being performed by smaller lads than myself; and if my strength was unequal to it, it was my misfortune and nobody's fault. I didn't complain, but I don't deny that when, after a hard day's rope hauling, my hands were so raw that I could get no sleep for their smarting, I have lain and piped my eye at my hard fate, reflecting, in a spirit as bruised as my body, how much easier it would be to sit a tailoring. But as my skin hardened so did my courage, till, at the end of three months, with my palms as hard as a shoe sole, and of pretty much the same complexion, I wouldn't have changed my state for a seat in the best tailor's shop in Bond Street.

And so no doubt matters would have continued had I given my nature wholly to roughness and selfishness, till, by-and-by, I should have grown a great devil-may-care ruffian, such as abound in water-side alleys, working like a horse, and swilling beer like a hog, and so have continued all the days of my life. I am sure it is a wonder that it is otherwise; for my companions, from morning till night, were just of this class, and my uncle was no better, except that he had money, and swilled rum instead of beer. It was Martha who turned the scale.

Not, the reader will please to understand, that any such milksop sentiment as sweethearting came into the business; indeed, I have only to recall to the reader's mind that I was a mere youngster, and that she was a grown woman of four and twenty, or thereabouts; and further, to acquaint him that the poor creature was no beauty, being much scarred with small-pox, and wearing her hair, by her father's express command, in short rat-tail plaits, to convince him that anything of the sort is quite beyond the question. Had Martha been a giddy young woman, giving her mind to flirting and finery, all that she could have said would not have influenced me; but this she was not. She was a meek drudge, constantly at work (for her father insisted on her buying her own clothes, which she did with such earnings as she could get at sailors' slop-work), never complaining, and with such a motherly way. Thanks to her, I was about the only lad of all those who worked about the ships who could boast of a sound jacket and untattered trousers, or who wore stockings.

Martha told me all her troubles, and such as I had I confided to Martha. One of her troubles was, that for at least half the night in the week she was kept sitting up till twelve, and even one o'clock till her father came home from the tavern. She got no thanks for the office; indeed, he never failed to bully, and make an uproar about it, declaring that all he wanted was, that she should set up a candle and leave out some matches, and threatening all sorts of horrible things, if he ever again came home and found her sitting up wasting firing. Under such circumstances it would seem a pity that she did not give the ungrateful fellow his way, and so I think she would but for one reason. Uncle Sampson wore lace-up ancle-jacks, concerning the fastenings to which he was so very careful that the intricacies of bows, and loops, and knots, made by him in the morning, were altogether beyond his comprehension, when in a state of drunkenness, which the reader may depend was invariably more or less his state on his return from his evening carousals. Uncle Sampson, who, in his soberest moments, was an unceremonious man, in an inebriated state was infinitely worse; and so, since he couldn't take his boots off, he would go to bed in them. He had done so a score of times—muddy times, when the Wapping roads were ancle deep.

One night I offered to sit up in Martha's stead. She had been at work at the wash-tub all day long, and besides, had a bad headache; so that, come eleven o'clock, she sat dozing over the fire in a very pitiable condition. It was not the first time I had sat up for Uncle Joyce. Indeed on one or two occasions on the morning following a rumpus at sitting up, when he would growl out some sort of apology for having thrown things at her, he had wound up by saying, "If somebody must sit up for me, why not let that lazy lubber do it?" The lazy lubber was myself, and I saw no hardship in it either; I could sleep as well by the fire as in my bed, and he usually came home with such a thundering rap that there was no danger in indulging in a nap.

On the occasion in question Martha consented to go to bed, and I made myself comfortable in the arm-chair. Just as the clock struck one there came a peal at the knocker, and, hurrying down, I let Uncle Sampson in. He was in a much worse temper than usual, and very drunk—so drunk, that he took me for Martha.

"What did I tell you about sitting up, you brazen hussy?" he hiccupped as he floundered into a chair.

"It aint Martha, it's me, uncle," said I, dutifully kneeling down to unlace his boots.

"D——n ——n seize you," said my uncle, leaning forward and clutching my hair. "And who told *you* to wait up?"

"Nobody," I replied, trying in vain to wriggle my hair out of his grasp, and goaded to recklessness in the process. "I offered to sit up that she might go to bed; it's a shame to keep people up like this. You let my hair alone, will you?"

"What! you take it in turns, do you?" exclaimed Uncle Sampson, glaring with rage and shaking my head most painfully to and fro. "She and you take it in turns to watch and spy over me, eh! You're joined the conspiracy, have you, cuss you! I'll physic *you* anyhow!"

And so saying, still holding on by my hair, he unbuttoned his waistcoat and released one of his heavy buff braces, and with the buckle end of it laid into me until my resolution not to halloa gave way, and I howled my loudest with pain, so that the row roused Martha and brought her down in great fright with her nightcap on, and her shawl over her shoulders. As soon as she saw how matters stood, with noble courage she walked straight up to her brutal father and twisted the strap out of his heavy drunken hand, whereon with a big oath he let go my hair that he might pursue his daughter. I gladly enough slipped out of the room and hurried to bed.

For a long while I lay awake full of dismal apprehensions. This was the first time he had struck me. He had often threatened to do so; indeed it was part of his system of management to be always threatening to kick this man and knock down that. Had he kicked me I should not have thought so much of it, or given me a cuff and chastised me in any other fashion that was sudden and unpremeditated, but so deliberate a thrashing demanded more serious consideration. It seemed plain that the ice once broken I might expect a repetition of his ill favours. How was I to avoid them? Should I run away! go home; what should I do? I was still in a maze of bewilderment, when the handle of my room-door softly turned and a voice asked—

"Are you asleep, Reuben?"

It was my friend Martha. I slept at the very top of the house, and when my door was shut, could scarcely hear the loudest noise taking place below; therefore I was quite ignorant of how the poor young woman had fared since I last saw her. I had been so full of thought and trouble that I had neglected to put my candle out, and when I looked at her I saw that there was a great weal right across her face all puffed up and grazed, and that her eyes were swollen with grief.

"Yes, Martha, I am awake," I replied. "Good gracious, Martha, you don't mean to say that he has been beating *you?*"

"Never mind that," replied she; "are you hurt, my poor boy? He may have some right to beat me, but it is cruel of him to treat you so unmercifully. It was all through me, too," continued the tender-hearted creature, "all through me! Why did not I sit up for him?" And here her tears began to flow at a rate which made me feel very uncomfortable.

"Don't trouble on my account, Martha," said I, "I am not much hurt; not at all, indeed" (this was a fib, but I thought it might comfort her); "he won't beat me again, I dare say."

"Ah!" exclaimed she, "that is what I fear. Now he has once begun you will never be safe. I wish you were not bound to him, Reuben."

"Neither am I," replied I, "I only serve him for the sake of a spoken arrangement between him and my father. There's no other binding about the matter."

"Then," said she, very earnestly, "if I were you, I wouldn't stay here."

"Where would you go?" I asked.

"Hush," replied she, closing the door, "if he was to hear us talking together, he is in the humour to come up and murder us both. Where should you go, Reuben? why home. Go home, and tell your mother and father truly all that has happened. Leave it to your father to deal with his brother-in-law when he comes to make inquiries."

"I did not tell Martha so, but I had a distinct recollection of how my father was accustomed to deal with my uncle Joyce. It flashed to my mind how my father looked that time when my uncle Sampson dashed his fist on to the board, and swore that the man who presumed to do something or the other must first of all put him past boxing. Leave my father to deal with him! My father was a very worthy man, but I knew exactly how he would behave under such circumstances. He would talk spitefully and blusterously, and nothing to the purpose for a minute or so, edging his remarks with sneering allusions to the shortcomings of the entire Joyce family; and having thus extended the difficulty, he would make an excuse to go out for thread or a patch piece, leaving my mother to settle the whole business. Now my mother, I knew, thought no end of great things of her brother Sampson. He was such a bluff, big fellow in the first place, and knowing nothing at all of shipping matters, when he talked of *his* cargoes of silk, and spice, and rum, she firmly believed that they were *his*, if not entirely, at least in such degree as made him out a man with a good bit of money. He knew, moreover, that he started with nothing at all, but had worked his way up from the condition of a "lumper" (she didn't exactly know what a "lumper" was, but rightly imagined, that it was something very common), and shrewdly conjectured that the example of a man who had so successfully "made" himself, could not be but advantageous to her own son. Uncle Sampson bragged that he had made his way (knowing his sister's bent, he always made it out a broader and extensive "way" than it really was) by "roughing it" —by being cuffed and kicked from post to pillar. "It's that what made me. How should I get along with my gangs of rascals if I wasn't as tough as whalebone?" Therefore, if he brought this species of reasoning to bear on his argument with my mother, it is more than likely that she would incline to let me go back to Wapping Wall.

Altogether the notion of going home did not fit me in the least. Suppose it should transpire otherwise than as above suggested—suppose I should be kept at home! Would that mend matters? Would it suit me to sit at home threading needles or basting linings? Certainly not. But I didn't enter into all these particulars with Martha; I merely shook my head at her proposition.

"No," said I, "I can't go home, though I am quite of your opinion that I oughtn't to stay here. We must put home out of the question. Now, where would *you* go, Martha, if you ran away?"

"That's talking silly," said Martha; "where could *I* run to?"

"But," I urged, "suppose you were a boy?"

"Ah! then the case would be different," said she, shaking her head earnestly, "he should soon find *how* different. Where would I run away to? Why, I'd run away to sea! No fear!"

And Martha shook her head again with even more vehemence than before, and remained staring thoughtfully at the window for several seconds. "But where's the use of talking?" continued she, at last. "I am only a poor little woman, and so must be contented, and thank my lucky stars that it is no worse. I am at least thankful it is no worse with you; you squalled at such a rate I thought to be sure that some of your bones were broken. Good night. Think of my advice to you about going home out of this dangerous place. Good night."

I bade her good night, but so far from going to sleep, I was wider awake than ever, thinking of what she had said. Not of what she had said about my going home, that was not worth wasting a thought over, but about going to sea. *She* would go, she said, if she were a boy, and to hear her say it put aside the possibility that she was not in earnest. Why, then, should *I* not go to sea? As I have already stated, this was an old yearning of mine, but never before had it presented itself so forcibly to me. I was quite sure that it was a life that would well agree with me, and indeed if it did not, I should be none the worse for a voyage or so, and should then come back bigger, and stronger, and fitter to seek a living ashore. It should be done; I would go to sea.

Not only did I settle this momentous question before I went to sleep, but also another at least as important, viz. *how* I should go.

Now it happened at this time that my uncle had a job in hand at Deptford to stow the cargo of the " Margaret," an India-bound vessel, the said cargo consisting chiefly of Birmingham ware, with a little drysaltery, and some bales of printed cottons. I ought rather to have said that there were two of these Deptford jobs, for alongside the " Margaret " lay a Jamaica sugar ship, and as soon as the one vessel was out of hand our gang was to go to work on the other. I knew that, according to the terms of the contract, the " Margaret " would sail, as it were, to-morrow by the afternoon's tide; and my resolution was that I would to-morrow watch my chance, hide in the hold, and sail away with her, trusting to my luck to pull me through when I was compelled to reveal myself to the ship's company.

I do not pretend to any originality for my scheme. The fact is, not only had I heard of " stow-aways " since I had mixed with seafaring people, but I had met and conversed with more than one lad who, being bent on sea-going, and having neither friends nor money, had run the risk I meditated, and, as far as the attainment of their end was concerned, with success. In each case, however, there had been a penalty to pay; the mildest that came under my notice was a rope's-ending and the performance throughout the voyage of the most disagreeable offices for the crew and passengers. These penalties, however, had no terrors for me. I felt assured (alas for my ignorance!) that the end of any rope, howsoever vigorously applied, could afford no more exquisite or durable pain than the buff-leather braces with which my uncle had so recently chastised me; while as to drudgery, if they made me shift every article in the hold and re-pack it, it would be no harder work than I had been used to; and as for their swearing at me and calling me names, I was well salted to that, and would as lief they swore as whistled.

Thanks to my stow-away acquaintance, I knew that, however well my plan might succeed, there would be no chance of my discovering myself to the captain, that is, with any reasonable prospect of being allowed to remain on board, until the ship was well into the Channel, which could not transpire for at least three days after she weighed anchor. Therefore to provide myself with a sufficiency of food to keep me from starving during that period was an important consideration. As regarded means it might be easily accomplished, for I had so economised my shilling a week as to have something more than half-a-crown in hand—enough to buy food for three days—ay, or for a week either, at a pinch.

The difficulty was to hit on the proper things to buy. Under my belly's guidance I would have laid in a large loaf, or a half-crown cake; but it was essential, if I wished the first stage of my scheme to succeed, to be neither hampered nor rendered conspicuous by a hidden load of any considerable bulk. What sort of food, then, should I buy? After revolving in my mind as many sorts as would have stocked an extensive chandlery store, I finally fixed on cheese as being at once moist and nutritious, and an article of diet of which I was always exceedingly fond; and, having so far settled the business, I fell asleep.

The morning found me as fully, nay, even more fully, resolved to carry out my plan. The "Margaret" would sail in the afternoon, therefore there was no time to lose. To make my offence against my uncle as light as possible, I put on my oldest clothes. When I reached Deptford, and before I entered the docks, I purchased two pounds of the richest Cheshire cheese, which I had cut into four, and, stowing each quarter in a pocket of my trousers and jacket, presented no other than my ordinary appearance.

It was yet early, and as my uncle would not make his appearance much before noon, I had opportunity, while the finishing touches were being put to the stowage, to select a hiding-place; at last I discovered, towards aft of the hold, a considerable nook among some cases and barrels, and, marking the spot, returned to deck, and worked with a will till the dock bell rang the workman's dinner-time, then, in the bustle that ensued, I dropped my round hat over the side (it had my name written inside), and, slipping unperceived to my snuggery, lay still as a mouse.

Hour after hour I lay, expecting each moment to hear my uncle's gruff voice, calling my name, but nothing of the kind occurred, and presently I heard them putting on the hatches, and the hold, hitherto gloomy enough, became pitchy dark.

The darkness, however, had no terrors for me. I could shut my eyes any time, and make it just as dark; but any time I could not open them on what I hoped to by-and-by—the wide sea and the blue sky, and nothing beside. And after all, what was the penalty? What particular hardship was it to squat on the floor with one's back against a crate, with one's hands in one's pockets, at liberty to go to sleep or keep awake, with plenty of prog in one's pockets, and of the sort one was particularly fond of. Why, it was a joke. What a joke for my surly old uncle! How he would swear and stamp when he found that I did not return to dinner! How he would stare when my cap was fished up and taken to him! What would he do? Would he be glad or sorry? Would he write home about it? Of course he would; and when my reflections arrived so far, I began to think that, after all, it was not so good a joke as it at first seemed. He would write home, and my dear mother would be frantic with grief, and my sisters would be put in mourning.

This was melancholy enough to think on, and I began to blame myself very much for dropping my cap into the water. It would have been better to have disappeared without a clue of any sort; then there would have been room for my parents to hope that the worst had not happened. What would Martha think? Now a little hope came to me. After our conversation, it was not unlikely that she would have a suspicion of the truth, and would impart the same to my mother for her consolation. At this my spirits were so raised up, that I even began to regret lest she *should* have a suspicion of the truth, and should confer with her father on the matter, who would, without doubt, take a row-boat and follow the ship, even as far as Gravesend, and I might be thwarted after all. The ship seemed to move wretchedly slow; indeed, only that the cargo kept up such a creaking as it settled itself, I should not have known whether it was moving or no.

And having brought the reader to this point, I would so far crave his indulgence that he will spare me a recital of the horrors that speedily ensued. How that, within a very few hours, and all in the pitchy dark, I fell sick, so that I wished myself dead a hundred times, and willingly would, had I been able, have made myself heard, that I might have the company of a human being, though he were my executioner; how that, while still huddled helpless in my dismal corner, the rats found my trousers pockets, and devoured every scrap of my cheese, and my sickness only mended to expose me to a terrible prospect of lingering starvation; how that, in this wretched plight, I passed three days and nights and more, till my thirst made me mad, and I gave out such cries as woke the sailors sleeping in their hammocks—is all too melancholy for minute description. So we will skip it, and I will resume my narrative at the point where my life was renewed, when, suddenly, I was aware, as I lurked in my hole, of the flash of a lantern, and the sound of human voices, and when, within two minutes, I was hauled into the presence of one whose eyes flashed fiercer even than the sudden lantern.

My Introduction to Captain Jubal.

CHAPTER III.

I pass as a ghost—Am cruelly maltreated by Captain Jubal—Ill of brain fever, I am nursed by the crew of the " Margaret"—The " Margaret" overcome by a tempest—Our crazy captain—His wanton cruelty and miserable end—Three days and two nights on a raft—Our sufferings and ultimate rescue.

AS I have before observed, the aspect of the Captain of the " Margaret," when, in custody of the men who had discovered me, I encountered him on the deck, was terrible in the extreme. I had thought to be sure, that my uncle Sampson was the most ill-looking man alive; but I was in that, as, alas! in many another of my childish conclusions, much mistaken. I have alluded to Uncle Sampson as uncouth and bearish, and I will not retract the assertion, even though I apply no stronger term than bearish to the appearance of Captain Jubal. But there was this difference between the animals: one was the shaggy Indian bear, sly, cowardly, and more inclined to assault the honey-stores of little bees than to face and fight men; and the other was the great grisly bear of the Rocky Mountains, prodigiously strong, and loud-mouthed, and tyrannical. I had thought of the captain of a ship as a polite gentleman, neatly dressed, mild of speech, and never blusterous, except when the wind blew hard. This, certainly, was the sort of captain one met in books —nay, I am quite sure that the specimen or two I chanced to see about the docks, or in conversation with intending passengers, were amiable and gentlemanly persons. Very different was Captain Jubal; he was a coarse grampus of a fellow, heavily rigged in the roughest of pilot-cloth, and with his legs cased in tremendous sea-boots; he was far hairier than my uncle Sampson, and his face had grown red, and his voice deep and hoarse, through long contention with unruly winds: doubtless it was from the same cause, too, that his eyes had become so goggled, with their whites all webbed with red veins.

"What the Beelzebub does this mean?" asked Captain Jubal of the mate. "How long has that scarecrow been aboard, Mr. Jones?"

"No longer nor less than since we sailed from Deptford, captain," replied the mate. "We found him stowed away in the hold, squealing like a starved cat."

"Why, you don't mean to say that *this* is the ghost that has been haunting the ship these two nights?" asked Captain Jubal, glaring at me maliciously, and at the same time advancing and grasping the hair on the left side of my head, including my ear, with his iron fingers. "You don't mean to tell me that this rascal is the cause of the precious funk your fellows have been sweating under?"

"Seems so, captain."

"So you are Joe Manks's spirit, are you?" continued Captain Jubal, giving my ear a wrench fit to screw it off. "It's you I've got to thank for setting the old women who call themselves sailors, and who man my ship, quaking, and grumbling, and whispering about what they thought proper to call the ghost of almost as ugly a lubber as yourself who died last voyage? What the Beelzebub do you mean by it, sir?"

My long fasting, and dark loneliness and fright, had, as the reader will doubtless believe, mazed me to the extreme of my wits, and it needed not half the captain's brutality to put me clean past them. His ear-pulling I could have borne; indeed, if I valued my life at all at that moment, I had cause to be grateful to him, as the exquisite pain he inflicted on me certainly saved me from fainting and falling down; but when he began to address me as the spirit of a person whose name even I had never before heard, and to accuse me of haunting his ship, I began to doubt if there was truth in my discovery, and if this was not another added to the thousand myths that had visited me during my horrid bondage among the barrels and jagged crates below.

It was all, however, just as I have related, real enough; and, not to mystify the reader, I will here give him a bit of information that did not reach me for some days after, and which will fully explain what the captain meant by calling me Joe Manks's ghost, and why he showed such extraordinary ferocity towards such an ordinary being as a stow-away. Joe Manks had been a 'prentice aboard the "Margaret," and because that Captain Jubal often kicked him, and knocked him about the head, there was little love between them, and less still as the boy grew to be tall and strong, and to feel that it was a cowardly thing to allow any man, even his own captain, to kick him. It was during the "Margaret's" last homeward voyage (sugar-laden from Barbadoes) that the most serious disagreement had occurred between them. The captain, it seems, had fallen asleep one evening over the brandy-bottle, leaving it, as he imagined, about a quarter full, and when he awoke the bottle was empty, no one, meantime, having had access to his cabin but Joe Manks. Captain, with little ado, called Joe a thief, and sent him a full, swinging kick of his heavy boot; on which Joe, smarting with rage and pain, caught up the empty bottle, and shying it at Captain Jubal, missed his head by a very close shave. Joe came in for a furious thrashing on the spot, after which the captain ordered him to be tied up, and then he took a rope and laid into him again, and sentenced him to bread and water, and to sleep on deck for a fortnight. Now, whether it was the kicks, or the exposure to the rain and cold, or one as well as the other, none of the crew could positively say, but poor Joe Manks very shortly died, was stitched in his hammock, and hove overboard; his death being entered in the log as having been caused by "cold and fever."

It is a great chance if poor Joe Manks would ever have been

thought of afterwards (for you must know that, forty years ago, the British sailor, if he had the bull-dog's pluck, had also very many of that animal's worst qualities), but for the strange noises I was continually making while in the hold reaching their ears, and leading them to imagine that they proceeded from the unquiet ghost of the apprentice. I was likewise given to understand, for all his bluster and insinuations, that it was the crew who had been frightened and not he; that Captain Jubal's nerves had undergone a twisting such as they had never before experienced. From the position of his cabin he had a better chance of hearing my cries than any other man in the ship, and he had heard them,—heard them in the night, and made his appearance on deck shivering with fright, and much inclined for conversation with Mr. Jones, the mate, who was a man of serious mind, and less inclined to belief in the supernatural than the rest of the crew. But, after all, he found it easier to soothe his conscience out of the brandy bottle than out of the mouth of the pious mate. He would drink, and drink, and then come amongst the crew muttering, and cursing, and blustering, declaring that it was all a villanous conspiracy, and that he would cut the throat of the rascal who made the caterwauling; taking the men aside privately, and offering them heavy bribes to betray the delinquent, and cuffing and kicking them, when they solemnly declared their innocence. Then he would flout into his cabin and drink more brandy, drink it till he was mad, and then make his appearance, swelling with valour, and bidding defiance to the devil and all his angels. No wonder, then, that the sailors should exhibit such satisfaction that the cause of all this discomfort should be brought to light, or that the captain himself should be so full of spite against me who had caused him so much humiliation.

"D'ye hear?" repeated he, seconding his question by a cruel blow on the ear he was not holding; "what do you mean by feloniously boarding my ship?"

But I was too bewildered to answer him a word.

"Seems to me, captain, the lad's more than half dead," suggested the mate compassionately.

"Give him a souse overboard, then," said Captain Jubal; "p'r'aps it will revive him."

It needed but half a glance to perceive that the captain was in earnest, and there was no help but to carry out his orders. A stout line with a running noose was cast over my head and under my arms, and I was led aft and dropped over the side, sinking to the full length of the line, and then hauled up again—once, twice, thrice—Captain Jubal standing by to see it done. The little life previously in me seemed now quite drowned out, and at the final hauling I lay on the deck as limp, and as cold, and as dumb as any fish. Seeing it was so, the captain walked away, leaving me to the sailors.

When I came to life again, I was lying on an old sail in an out-of-the-way nook in the forecastle, with an old blanket wrapped round me. I felt no sort of pain of body, nor anxiety as to my condition; indeed, for so long as seemed a full half-hour, my reflections did not wander a foot from my bed. I only knew that I was lying down, and that it was nice to lie down. Somehow, I seemed to be awake, while my brain was still asleep. Gradually, however, my brain woke too, with, at first, a feeble pulse, that directed me to look about me; and as I obeyed and looked to the right and to the left, and saw the strange place I was in, with the hammocks, and a group of strange men sitting and lolling at the further end of the dimly-lighted chamber, my temples began to throb harder and harder, and all that I had undergone, from the time of my hiding aboard the "Margaret" till I was first soused in the sea, passed before me with swift and terrible vividness. It was plain where I was, but what was to become of me? I thought I would get up, and go and ask the men at the other end; and I accomplished the job well enough as far as getting on my knees, but, immediately after, my head became a humming-top, and I turned over on to the floor.

The noise of my fall roused the sailors. One of them, who had a bald head and thin, grey whiskers, came over to where I was lying, and, without a word, placed me back on the sail-cloth bed and covered me with the blanket, and was for walking off again, when I called after him—

"Will you let me get up, if you please?"

"Eh? why, you don't mean to say you've come back to your senses?" said he, turning square round and bending with his hands on his knees to get a closer view of me. "Why, dash my eyes! he means to weather it after all, I do believe! D'ye hear, my hearties? here's Joe's ghost alive and kicking, and talking as sensible as a ship's parson."

So the men gathered round—to the number of six or eight—and then I learnt that I had lain just where I now was for five days and nights, with no other than mad life in me, and that they had taken it spell and spell in my worst times to sit by me, feeding me with ship biscuit sopped in weak grog, and bleeding me on one occasion with a jack-knife. Captain Jubal, as I understood, had not inquired after me for two days after he had ordered my dipping, and when he did inquire it was to know "if that young devil's imp had not kicked the bucket yet;" but when he was gravely informed by the mate that my bucket of life, although not quite overturned, was fairly atilt, and might be expected to capsize within the hour, he suddenly altered his tone, and turned grumbling to his cabin, whence he presently emerged with a bottle of wine, which he handed to Mr. Jones.

"Let 'em give the rascal that," said he, "and tell 'em, if I come to know of his dying, they won't hear the last of it in a hurry."

The men dutifully received the wine with the message; but, sagaciously detecting the captain's design to poison me by "mixing my physic," broached the bottle and drinking it to the frustration of wickedness, continued to doctor me with weak grog. By this it was clear that the crew regarded his expressed solicitude for my restoration as a mere subterfuge to hide his real intent; but when I came to hear Joe Manks' story, and to set it against my own, it seemed pretty plain that the captain would rather I had live than die, for the sake of the pleasant government of his ship, if not for his conscience' sake. I explained these my views to Bill Ricketts, the bald-headed sailor beforementioned, and who, although our acquaintance was of brief duration, and ended with terrible abruptness, always treated me with great kindness, and, I have no doubt, was the means of saving my life when I lay in the forecastle, though he could never be brought to own to it. When, I say, I expressed my views to Bill as to Captain Jubal's intentions towards me, he shook his head, and said he—

"Well, my lad, wait till you get round a bit, and are took to the cap'n for further orders, and then we shall see how pleased he'll be to see you chirp and hearty."

To which I replied—

"I don't believe he will be glad to see me, Mr.—beg your pardon —Bill Ricketts (he wouldn't be called mister)—I only mean to say

THE NEGRO COOK KILLS CAPTAIN JUBAL.

he took it as a favour of me not to die; he'd as lief I had died, no doubt—liefer, perhaps, if it wasn't for my *being* dead. You understand me, Bill?"

"Can't say as I do," replied he.

But, although past danger of death from fever, I was a very long way from being well. I was woefully thin, and so shaky that it was full a week after my senses returned to me that I was enabled to creep as far as the mess-table and there sit down. Then, again, I could not at first take kindly to the ship's food, in spite of the frequent sips of rum, which my kind, blundering nurses insisted was appetising and good for my complaint. I think it was at this time that I thought more of my mother than at any other. I was qualmish, and dainty, and—well, I know of no word that will more aptly express my condition—"mother-sick." I wouldn't have let it out in the forecastle for the world; the fellows would have laughed at me; and, no doubt, to see a great, long-legged chap like me (I had grown at a tremendous rate lately) piping his eye for his mother, would have been a thing to have laughed at. But it was quite true, nevertheless. My pain and long suffering seemed to have stripped my heart of the husk that, springing from waywardness and obstinacy, and what I took for pluck and found foolhardiness, had been thickening round it for years, leaving it all tender and bare to ache at every remorseful reflection, and grievously flutter at every unkind breath. "Ah!" used I to think, "if I were but once more at home at that happy little house, and might lay my head on my soft white bed, with her to nurse me and make me well, that would indeed be happiness." Without doubt I was thoroughly mother-sick. I used, when I lay down at night, to bid my father and mother, and my sisters and brothers, good night, repeating, "Good night, mother; good night, father; good night, sister Polly; good night, Lizzie;" over and over again, till I carried one or the other of them sheer into the land of dreams, such being my intent at starting, with all the prayers I had ever been taught to say, that my most earnest desire might be gratified. Strangely enough, however, although in my dreams I frequently got home, it was never as the altered lad I had become, but as the lad of old—the obstinate and wrong-headed one! and I joined the family circle again but to put it out of joint—to quarrel with my sisters, to be cuffed by my father, and to provoke my mother to the utterance of that wish, the constant repetition of which had made it so familiar,

"Drat the boy; I wish he was a thousand miles away;" so that, after all, my dreams of home brought me but little consolation.

It will be recollected that I have spoken of the crew of the "Margaret" as kindhearted fellows who treated me with great good-nature, and never seemed to grudge the trouble I put them to. This is quite true, with one exception, and concerning this same exception there is something to be told that will, no doubt, appear to the reader just as wonderful as it did to me. When I had come out of my brain fever, and began to get about a bit and mix with the men, I was not long in discovering among them one who, had his example been followed by the rest, would have insured me treatment too scurvy to be borne. His ill looks I always had, and his ill word whenever a chance appeared, which was just as often as mess-time came round; for, as the reader may guess, no special ration was allowed me, and what I ate and drank came from the allowance of the crew. There was plenty and to spare, but that was a view of the question my enemy shut his eyes to. He protested and swore that he would have the meat he worked for to the utmost grain, and that he was not going to be mulcted to fatten such as me; moreover, he would not even sit to eat at the same board, declaring that the motion of my lean jaws, as I chewed my food, turned him sick; though, to judge from his outward appearance, he would never have been taken for a gentleman of delicate stomach, but rather as one whose knowledge of meat might have begun at the shambles and ended at the galley copper.

But what puzzled me most was, that from the very first I had been impressed with the idea that this was not our first acquaintance. Still it was in vain that I tried to recollect where, and under what circumstances, our previous meeting had taken place; nor, unless the said circumstances were very peculiar, was it likely that I should, for his was a commonplace, vulgar face enough, though, perhaps, somewhat distinguished from the herd by the extra ugliness conferred by its massy jaws and deep-set eyes. He was a young man, not more than eighteen, I should say; the youngest of the crew, in fact; which, to my thinking, made it all the more strange that he should be so set against me. At last the mystery was solved, and in this way.

For the men's amusement, I would recount to them the horrors of my imprisonment in the hold, and on one occasion Tom Cox, my persecutor, was present, though, unsociable as usual, he lay sprawling on his back on a bunk, smoking his pipe, and pretending not to be listening at all.

"The worst of it," said I, in the course of my narration, "was the thirst. Ah! that, indeed, was dreadful. I never, in my life, knew what thirst was till then."

"That's another lie," growled Tom Cox.

"And how should you know, Tom?" remarked my friend Bill Ricketts. "Granted you should be a good judge of a lie, if long practice may qualify a man; but how d'ye know that what he states is a lie, Tom Cox?"

I knows all about it," replied Master Cox sullenly. "I've met him afore to-day."

This direct confirmation of my suspicions amazed me not a little, and I looked over to where the young man was reclining, in rather an anxious way.

"Is that true, Joe's Ghost?" (for that was the name they pleased to call me) asked Mr. Ricketts.

"It may be true that he has seen me before," replied I; "but I don't recollect it."

"You don't recollect nothing wot aint conwenient," sneered Tom Cox. "P'r'aps you don't recollect ever prigging your father's money to pay for a drink of water? That makes you a thief as well as a liar, young mealy-mouth."

The mean rascal! I knew him now beyond a doubt, and only wondered that I should have been at fault so long. He was the water-boy that Bill Jupp and I had met out Stepney way, on the day made memorable by an interview with the Malay woman. But that he should attempt to vilify me about a business in which the most scandalous actor was himself was more than I could bear, so I up and told the men the true particulars of the whole business, including that portion of it of which he thought me ignorant, and which on the instant changed his aspect of wolfishness to one of sheepishness—the sequel to the story of the penny, where the old black woman met him on the road, and frightened him so that he was glad to disgorge it. This tickled him prodigiously, and brought on Tom Cox such a volley of jeering and forecastle sarcasm as drove him almost mad, and, without doubt, he would have taken summary vengeance on me, only that the chances of more than one better man than himself taking up my cause seemed tolerably certain. As for his abuse and threatening, I was too used to that to mind it a jot.

How it came about that Tom Cox so speedily recognized me after so long a lapse of time I never could comprehend until we became friends (for, unlikely as it seemed at the period of which I have just been speaking, we did become as fast friends as ever adversity brought together), when he told me that it was I who had disclosed the fact, or at least sufficient to give him a clue to it, while I was wandering in my mind, and it was his turn to take a spell of watching by my bed.

So passed full a month on board the "Margaret," during which time I had never once seen Captain Jubal, as it was unlikely I should so long as I was confined to the forecastle. By this time, however, I was quite recovered, had regained my strength, and could eat my allowance of beef and biscuit as well as the rest of them. From time to time I saw the mate, Mr. Jones, who, I was informed, had kindly exaggerated my illness to the captain, and still reported me weakly when I was well enough to work, in order that I might be well set up by rest and feeding, and as well as possible prepared for any sort of labour or punishment it might please Captain Jubal to sentence me to. At last, on a Sunday evening, my friend the mate came to me, and, after some kind and Christian discourse (for he was a God-serving man, and loved his Bible), informed me that the captain was growing impatient at my long idleness, and advised me to appear before him in the morning and endeavour to make my peace with him by humbly begging his pardon, and promising to work hard and cheerfully at whatever he might set me about.

"Possibly," said Mr. Jones, "he may order you a dozen with a rope's end, just for form's sake, but that, you must admit, is as little as you deserve, and had better take staunchly and without making a fuss, whereby he may take you to be a lad of mettle, and have the less hesitation in placing your name on the ship's books."

This advice I resolved to follow, and turned into my hammock steadily bent on showing the friendly mate that his confidence was not misplaced. But Providence had otherwise decreed. Hitherto we had pursued a steady course, with a fair wind and an easy sea, and no misadventure but mine own; but at sea one may never dare speak of to-morrow—nay, nor of this afternoon—though the sun rise in all its splendour, and the winds are as obedient as though rated on the ship's books and under penalties for rude behaviour. Surely no poor ship had more reason to bewail with astonishment the sea's uncertainty than now had ours. Fair as seemed the night when I retired to rest, I had scarcely got soundly to sleep when I was awakened by the banging of my hammock against the ship's side, and was, at the same moment aware of a most furious row overhead: scuffling, stamping, bawling, and, over all, a strange shrill shrieking, and a creaking, and flapping, and crashing, all blending to make such a hideous uproar that made me afraid to stir. Having had no experience of storms, my foremost thought was that the crew had engaged in a deadly quarrel, and that one half of them were bent on slaughtering the other. My difficulty was as to how they were divided. The captain would, without doubt, be at the head of one lot; but whom had he got on his side? To my knowledge, with the exception of the few who served before the mast, there was not a soul on board who did not hate Captain Jubal just as hard as they knew how. Perhaps the captain was fighting the entire crew single-handed; in which case he would possibly be presently over-powered, and the disturbance would cease.

But the disturbance did not cease, but each moment increased, as did the staggering of the ship; and presently she gave such a lurch as quite upset my determination not to stir, and bundled me neck and crop out on to the floor; and, as I crouched, shivering and holding on by a bunk (for to stand on so slanting a floor was impossible), there came down one of the crew in a mighty hurry, and with cheeks as white as a shroud, and, giving me nothing more civil than an oath in reply to my question what was the matter, possessed himself of a couple of axes, and scampered off again. Scarcely had he vanished when a great body of water came drenching down into the forecastle, com-pletely saturating the shirt on my back, as well as my trousers, into one leg of which I had just thrust a limb. This breaking in of the sea at once opened my eyes to the dreadful truth—the "Margaret" was sinking, and we should all be drowned!

Hastily forcing my legs into my wet trousers, and thrusting my arms into a stockinett or guernsey that happened to be lying handy, stumbled my way to the deck, where was to be seen such a sight as enchained me with horror. The night was pitchy dark—that is, the heavens were—but the great sea was white as snow, and built up into prodigious heaps, with yawning gulleys between—the hills becoming caverns, and the caverns hills, quicker almost than the eye could follow, and with a roar and turmoil as though compelled by the fierce wind, and most unwilling. As to our poor ship, had she been a reasoning thing and now gone crazy, she could not have behaved more strangely. At one time she would shriek, as it were, to the gale to help her, and the gale would, taking her on its wings and bearing her with its own speed through the heaps and holes of the frothy sea, that boiled with angry hunger that she would not sit still and be devoured; then, of a sudden, she would seem to mistrust the gale, and, shrinking from its urging, stand still shudderingly, and this despite the wind's mighty persuasion, its impatient shaking of her cordage as the reins of a horse are shaken, and its lashing of her naked spars with the sails, rent into a thousand whips. When she so stood still, it was the sea's turn to triumph, which it did, and with the maddest noises, roaring high above her deck, as though to take item of the luckless wretches with whom it hoped presently to make such close acquaintance, and ever and anon reaching its untiring arms over the poor ship's bulwarks to drag her down.

Meanwhile the crew of the " Margaret" was exerting itself might and main that such a dire calamity should not befall her. Where, even in calm weather, a cat could scarcely be expected to maintain a footing, were to be seen, looming through the darkness, sailors, barefooted and with their hair all to windward, furling sails or cutting away such as could not be furled, the wind following the knife and helping it till not more than a foot or so of the heavy canvas remained attached, and then, with an exulting whistle, tearing it away and bearing it high and afar, as though it were no more burdensome than a scrap of paper. It was so dark as to make it impossible to make out one form from another at half the length of the ship, and so noisy that to my unaccustomed ear it was hard to distinguish any man's voice save one, and that, belonging to Captain Jubal, was constantly engaged, and always to be heard, at every lull of the tempest issuing orders so thickly studded with oaths that it was a wonder how the men could get at his meaning; and cursing and swearing at the crew, and the ship, and the storm, as though the whole business had been planned for his special annoyance. Once, as he went to consult the compass, I caught sight of his face by the light of the binnacle lamp; and so vividly did it recall my first interview with him (I had not seen him since) that I involuntarily slunk from where I was standing, and, crawling on my hands and knees to a water-cask, crouched behind it, holding on to its lashings as tight as I could. Presently some one, in hurrying past, stumbled over my legs, and came with a smartish whack to the floor of the deck. It was Bill Ricketts.

"What the devil are you doing here?" asked he.

"No harm, Bill," replied I.

"Maybe," said he; "but why can't you try to be doing a little good? Every penn'orth of help is a Godsend to the ship just now. I reckon you wouldn't be content to lie skulking there if you knew the pretty strait we are in."

"What can I do, Bill?" I asked, impressed more than ever by his manner that something very terrible was impending. I'll do anything in the world so long as I may keep out of sight of the captain."

"Never fear the captain," replied the old sailor, bitterly; "he's too full of brandy to know you from me, or either of us from the stern-post. If it wasn't that we've got a decent sort of mate we should have all been at the bottom an hour ago, though, for that matter, last hour was as good for drowning in as next, for all I can see. Come on."

Not at all cheered by Mr. Ricketts' last ominous observation, I steadied myself by his arm, and in a moment or so we came on a gang of men stripped to their drawers, and labouring like very demons at the pump-handles.

"Bear a hand here," said Bill Ricketts, "and with a will, my lad, for I can tell you, if the pumps fail us, we shall all sup with Davy Jones as sure as we are here alive."

I had not been aboard a ship so short a time but that I knew who was meant by Davy Jones, and work with a will I did till my arms ached in their sockets, and till a voice, sudden and terribly near, made my heart leap to my throat—it was that of Captain Jubal.

"How now?" asked he, in his coarse, blustering way.

Thinking he had addressed me, I was about to fall on my knees and reply to him after the manner advised by the mate, but was checked by the voice of the last-mentioned worthy himself, who answered the captain—

"Very sadly, sir; the water in the hold gains every moment. At this rate she can't live another hour. Shall we make ready for launching the boats, Captain Jubal?"

"What the —— do you mean, sir?" returned Captain Jubal. "D'ye think I'll allow a set of cowardly whelps to desert my ship—*my* ship, sir, every plank and spar of her—because she happens to have shipped a bucketful of water? D'ye call that pumping, you lazy swabs? I'll show you how to pump."

So saying, he pushed away one of the tired crew, and for the space of about a minute laboured as only could a man of prodigious strength, and mad with liquor as well.

"That's how to pump," said he. "Talk of taking to the boats, indeed! Hanged if I wouldn't clear her as dry as a chip, and all by myself, in half-an-hour!"

And, after a few other senseless remarks, interlarded with more foul language than I may repeat, the drunken brute staggered to his cabin. At that very moment, however, and while the mate was evidently deliberating whether he should, or should not, disregard the captain's orders, the tempest seemed to reach its highest, and a tremendous sea broke over the starboard bow, sweeping from the deck the galley and the water-casks, and everything else it could lift, and, moreover, smashing the greater part of the larboard bulwarks. There was now no longer any hesitation on the part of the crew. Discipline was at an end; every man was his neighbour's equal, and neither richer nor poorer; each had one thing to preserve equally precious to Pompey the cook as to the captain—his life.

To this end the pumpers left the pumps, and the helmsman the helm, and gathered one and all about the long-boat, which lay on the deck. There was another boat besides this, but, as she needed some repairs, the carpenter had taken advantage of the prospect of a long spell of fair weather to begin his job, and was now about half way through with it; so that she could not have swum in smooth water, let alone the troubled sea that surrounded us.

The long-boat, then, was our only stay, and while some got together a few provisions, others busied themselves in rigging a rope and pulley to the mainyard, to lift her over the side. There was help in plenty, and in a short time the boat was being hauled up with a will, when Captain Jubal suddenly appeared amongst us.

Evidently he had spent the whole time since his last appearance in sucking at his brandy-bottle, for his gait was very uncertain, and his eyes were nearly as red as his face. He had, it seemed, rushed out of his cabin in a hurry, for his heavy jacket was all loose, showing his bare, hairy breast, and he was without the sou'-wester it was his custom to wear on deck.

"What the Beelzebub d'ye mean by this?" roared he, stamping his foot like a madman; "you infernal, mutinous dog, you, this is your work, is it?"

And so saying, he seized the mate, who was a spare man, and not very tall, and, after shaking him by the collar for a few moments as a terrier shakes a rat, flung him away so that he fell of a heap.

"Back to the pumps, I tell you—back to your duty, every man of you!" continued he, glaring about him like a wild beast. "I'll teach you who is your master, you villains!"

The mate had by this time risen from the ground, but was so bewildered by the shaking he had received, that we, who looked to him for the cue as to what we should do, looked in vain. It was plain the captain was mad with drink and excitement, and that it would go hard with the first man who opposed him. One man only of the crew was a match for Captain Jubal in bulk and strength, and that was the black cook, Pompey. Like all Africans, Pompey had very little courage, and this it was, although it, at first sight, seems paradoxical, that made him more daring than the rest; for, being so much more chicken-hearted than the Englishmen on board, he was the more alarmed at the prospect of drowning with the crippled ship, and was exceedingly loth to abandon the launch of the boat.

"What!" roared Captain Jubal; "am I to speak twice, you lubberly rascals?"

"Speak um bellyful, and be jiggered, you ole debil!" said the despair-valiant Pompey; "we wants no cap'n now, nor no drunken man. You go 'way; we gwine to launch de boat."

"Ay, ay," responded the men, "that's our intent, Cap'n Jubal." And, following Pompey's example, they took the hauling ropes in hand, and commenced pulling with a will. As, for fear of the captain, I had stood aside, I was well able to observe one party and the other, and I hope never again to see anything so dreadful as the expression of the captain's face when, finding himself so deliberately defied, he ground his teeth like a maniac, and, casting his bloodshot eyes about, spied an axe, which he caught up in a twinkling.

"That's your intent, is it?" said he, with a string of foul oaths; "then I'll show you mine. See! see! see!"

The boat, by this time, was suspended in the air at a convenient height, and with its bottom towards us. As Captain Jubal began to speak, he swung the axe round his head, and, as he hissed "See! see! see!" from behind his set teeth, at every word he dealt a smashing blow at the boat, making a ragged hole through which one might have put his head.

"Now," said he, flinging down the axe, "now launch her, and be —— to you all!"

For an instant every man was held dumb with rueful amazement. The tempest was still raging, and from time to time great waves swept the deck, so that, had the mate not had the foresight to secure the hatches, she certainly must have filled and sunk. Even as it was, we all knew the sea continued to climb in the hold, and would, within a few minutes, weigh us down for a surety. Therefore did this act of Captain Jubal's seem the more diabolical, since by it we seemed committed to death as certainly as though the axe had knocked holes in our heads instead of the boat. Little, however, did the poor drunken wretch dream of the swift and awful penalty he was to pay for his cruel act; nor, indeed, did I, or I should have taken care to have hidden my eyes.

Pompey was our avenger. With the shattering of the boat fled his last hope of escape from death, and there was roused within him his proper savage spirit. The deadliest passion bared his double row of white teeth, and, before five seconds had passed, he had caught up the axe the captain had flung down, and, springing forward, cried—

"Well, now me launch you—launch you to 'ternal fire! See! see!"

And at each "See!" the axe clove Captain Jubal's head, and down he fell, without a word or a groan even.

This was a critical moment with all of us, for the gigantic African, though struck with instant fright at the awful thing he had done, was none the less a desperate, furious savage, and still grasped the red axe in his great fist. I, for one, fully believe, if any one of the crew had resented the captain's murder either by word or deed, the axe would have been redder yet, and a few of us put past drowning. But, luckily, and in the very nick of time, Tom Cox spoke up—

"Well done, Pomp; serve him right; he deserved it."

"So he did, so he did," echoed the crew. "What say you, Mr. Jones?"

"Pompey had better finish his awful work," replied the mate, who had knelt down and examined the captain. "The Lord forgive him and us; he's dead enough. We can do nothing with him lying here."

Pompey instantly took the hint, and, brought to his sober senses by the forbearance of his shipmates, flung the axe over the side, and taking up the captain's body in his strong arms, tumbled it over too; and a charitable wave at the same moment breaking over the deck, we were rid of Captain Jubal to the last streak of his blood; his death and burial both occurring within the space of two minutes.

We now turned again to the boat, but found her even more shattered than was suspected; so that, without considerable repair, she could no more swim than a sieve. Of course there was no time to mend her; and now the mate and one or two others, after hastily inspecting the ship, pronounced that, at the very outside, half an hour was the extent of time she could live.

"There is one thing we might attempt," suggested the mate, "and that is, to make a raft."

The suggestion was at once admired and eagerly adopted. Planks were wrenched up with such other of the ship's timbers as could be detached by saw or crow, together with her heaviest spars, and lashed with cable and bolted as strongly as our scanty material and time would permit. The African did us good service by his extreme willingness and his great muscular strength, and when the raft was launched was the first to leap down on to it and assist in the lowering of some biscuits in a barrel, and about three gallons of water, which was tilted from a barrel into an empty brandy-anker found in the captain's cabin, as well as another anker with about a quart of brandy remaining in it. It was not our intention to put off with so little water, for there was plenty on board; but as, besides the empty anker, there were two empty kegs, the mate thought it would be prudent to take these three small vessels rather than one large one, the better to secure against accident; and, had his notion been fully carried out, no doubt it would have worked well enough; but, as ill luck would have it, although all three of the tubs were duly filled, one only was put on our raft, the other two in the hurry and scramble being overlooked. Besides the water and biscuit, the mate secured the compass, and somebody made a bundle of a tattered sail and pitched it over, and somebody else took a fancy to filling an iron pot with biscuit and lowering it down with a line through its handle. In hopes of being able by-and-by to enlarge our raft, some loose wood and a chest were likewise added, and that, I think, was about all. And just as the grey glimmer of morning broke through the leaden sky, the last man leaped from the miserable ship on to the crazy little platform that was secured at her stern, and then

The Wreck of the "Margaret."

we cast off and left her alone to her fate, though not without many yearning glances; for, though so glad to get away from her, yet when seen at a distance, and compared with the gimcrack thing to which we had preferred to trust our lives, she, despite her great ailing, still looked so staunch and homely that it seemed we had perpetrated a foolish act in abandoning her. I know that from the first this was my impression, and my first few minutes' experience of raft life tended very much to confirm it. But presently I had weighty reasons to alter my mind. We were about a mile apart from her, and riding on a wave, we looked, and there she was, seeming as sound a ship as ever floated; down we went in the trough, and then up again, and her fore and main masts had gone, and before we descended the mizen followed. Down we went again, and once more up, and there she was not, for the sea had swallowed her.

As the morning advanced the sea grew calmer, though still our weight bore so heavily on our frail raft that she was as often beneath as on the surface of the water, drenching us as we sat or crouched, and so benumbing our limbs that they could scarcely be felt. Worse than all, we presently discovered that the barrel that contained most of our bread was not water-tight, and that if we allowed it to remain it would speedily be utterly spoilt. As it was, before the discovery was made, a good three dozen of the biscuits were completely saturated, which was no trifling matter, when, including those in the iron pot, they numbered only two hundred and sixty, and there were fifteen of us to partake of them; so it was resolved at once to make a division of the dry biscuits in the barrel, each man taking his share and wrapping it in a shred of sail-cloth, its economy being left to his own discretion. As to the spoilt biscuits, it was agreed that they were unfit for food, and might be thrown away; but the mate, with commendable prudence, forbade this, sensibly observing that we might live to repent so rash an act; so the wet biscuits were spread on the head of the barrel, and covered over, to give them some chance of drying.

So passed the long and dreary day, our raft taking its own course through the wilderness of water, and no sign of succour appearing. Then the night fell, and, though our little raft held well together, and the sea was now quite calm, it was impossible to keep more than the upper portion of our garments dry, so that we were all shivering with cold. The quart of brandy the mate took possession of, and, having no more convenient measure, broke off the outer case of his silver watch (which was stopped, and of no use to note the time), which held about a table-spoonful, and, when it came midnight—as near as we could judge—he served round a second lot of it, the first having been served at noon on the previous day. There remained about half a pint, and that the mate resolved for the present to put by.

The little drop of brandy warmed us for a short time, but presently we one and all grew so famished with cold that our limbs shook as though with ague, and our teeth made a chattering distinctly to be heard.

"If we only had a fire!" spoke Bill Ricketts.

"Why not wish for a snug house ashore, with full pay and no work?" replied another derisively. "A fire out here indeed."

"A light's the thing," said the mate. "If we had the means of making a light, we'd have a fire in a jiffy."

Nobody thought it worth while to make any further observation on so hopeless a subject, but the mate, at least, was thinking it over, for presently he said—

"I wonder if we can muster a few scraps of dry rag among us? Feel about, lads; the breast part of our shirts, at least, should be dry."

In a minute a good handful of linen shreds was torn away from our shirts, and handed to the mate, all of us wondering what he was about to attempt.

"Now," said he, "turn the biscuits out of that pot, and wrap 'em carefully in a bit of sail-cloth; give the pot to me, and somebody lend me his knife."

Somebody lent him a jack-knife; and then, having put the shreds of rag in the pot, he commenced to strike his own blade and the other blade together, in hopes of raising a spark that would fire the rag; but, for a long time, his endeavours were fruitless. Knife after knife was handed to him, and at last he got hold of one that did, at distant intervals, strike a spark of fire; but the rags, though dry enough to our cold touch, rejected the sparks as though they had been sopping wet; and, indeed, there can be no doubt that they were very far from being dry as tinder. Even the tiny sparks, however, had warmed, at least, the hopes of the men, and set their ingenuity at work; Pompey kindly volunteering as much as might be required of his wool, which he assured us had been well greased only yesterday, and could not fail to take fire.

Suddenly I bethought me that my trouser-braces were of string, which had been substituted for my own proper ones, stolen by Tom Cox, who declared that braces were not allowed aboard ship. Without saying a word I slipped them off, and, to my great joy, found them quite dry, and in a minute or so I had unwove them, and stepping to the mate, who was still industriously peppering away at the damp rag, handed him the bunch of dry, loose hemp.

"The very thing, my lad," said he, snatching at it delightedly. "A good warming is your due, and you shall have it as soon as we are able to knock up a fire."

Happily, indeed, it proved the "very thing." With little further tinkering, the joyful words, "See, it has caught! Hurrah! it's all ablaze!" were uttered by all of us poor shivering wretches, while the mate, who, as I before said, was a pious man, covered his face with his hands for an instant, and gave thanks to God. Some of the loose wood had meantime been broken into handy bits, and with these and some bits of sail-cloth the iron pot was filled, and in a little time the flames were rising and crackling cheerfully. We were thankful for the fire for a double reason; not only did it warm us, it also served as a beacon should a ship chance to be passing within a few miles of us.

The second night on the raft.

But, alas! no ship passed, or, it so, failed to spy us, although the hope that one might do so tempted us to be extravagant with our fuel and even after the iron pot was nearly redhot, and diffused plenty of warmth, we continued to pile on the wood to make a high blaze. All in vain, however; and so broke the second morning.

Dismal, indeed, now was our prospect. Our store of biscuit was rapidly dwindling, and of fresh water we had remaining barely a mouthful apiece; so that we were fain to take it, as we had taken the brandy, in the hollow of the mate's watch-case, for fairness' sake. Still no sail appeared in sight, and the day wore on.

And now happened a circumstance by which I was much impressed as showing the awful and wonderful ways of Providence ; so, at least, it seemed to me, and I am much mistaken if the reader will not so regard it. As before observed, the biscuits that lay at the bottom of the barrel, and which were soaked with sea-water, were still covered over, and, as we thought, untouched. But in this we were mistaken. As well as the rest, Tom Cox had received his share of dry biscuit, but, being of a greedy disposition, he, instead of husbanding them as thriftily as did the rest, ate them all during the first day and night, and then, growing hungry again, had been tempted to filch the driest of the spoilt bread and to eat it. But the sin carried its own punishment. Previously adry, and lapping off his tiny dram of water with a discontented growl, within an hour or so of consuming the salt-soddened biscuit, his thirst became so raging that he could no longer contain himself, and begged and implored the mate to give him just a little drink, as his mouth and throat were parching. This seemed strange, as, though all were thirsty enough, no one else was so keenly distressed, and it set the mate, who was an acute man, considering what the cause might be. At last he hit on it.

"Tom Cox," said he, "I fear you have been doing a mean thing; you have been at the soaked bread."

"Yes, yes, I have, I confess it; but pray don't refuse me a drink, or I shall go mad," cried Tom Cox. And to see how he writhed, and how abjectly he implored, there really seemed reason to fear that his life, if not his reason, was in danger.

But the mate was a sternly just, no less than a God-fearing, man, and he replied to Tom's appeal—

"No more water can be dealt out till night; we have not got a drop to spare, for an honest man even, before that time, If you think you can't hold out as long—and, in truth, I much doubt if you can—you had better pray to God to forgive you while your sense remains."

At this Tom Cox fell despairingly at the mate's feet, and begged and implored harder than before for ever so small a drop, and, finding himself still refused, turned and appealed to the rest; but this he had better have let alone, for they one and all, bitterly incensed at his selfishness, were for pitching him into the sea off-hand, and I think would have done so, had not the mate persuaded them not to lay hands on him. In a little time, however, his thirst made him so reckless that he made a

PREPARATIONS FOR THE FIGHT ON BOARD THE "SULTAN."

dash at the anker in which the water was, and would have swigged it all off had they not thrown him down, and, for their security, bound him hand and foot.

Once more the night fell, and, with heavy hearts, the fire in the pot, which had been barely kept alive all day, was replenished, and the bright flames revealed even more vividly than the daylight our forlorn condition. The last of the water was served out, and, there being just half a watch-caseful after all were served, it was charitably poured into the mouth of the suffering Tom Cox, and that over and above his fair share; and then, weary and heart-sick, we lay about the fire to ponder on the awful fate that now seemed certain.

But He who rules the waters and the winds, and is as mindful of the sparrows' nestlings as of the sons of kings, at last pitied our woeful state and extended His merciful hand. Being in the midst of darkness, save for our pot of fire, the relief for which we had so long prayed came on us so suddenly that it seemed more likely that, like Tom Cox, our wits had left us than that it could be true. First came a plashing of oars. We all heard it, and looked at each other across the fire with eager faces, though without uttering a word. Then faintly, but unmistakeably, came the sound of a human voice—a sailor's voice—"Boat a—h—hoy!"

Much more startling must have been our response as it reached their ears, for we all cried it, nay, screamed, shrieked it, at once—"Ahoy! ahoy! Hurrah!"

"Hurrah!" was borne back to us by the wind, and we halloced, and cried, and laughed, and clapped our hands, and waved burning sticks plucked from our fire, till a boat, pulled by a dozen lusty arms, hove in sight through the gloom, and we were helped into it—Tom Cox, being lifted in and laid along the bottom—and gleefully shoved we from our trusty little raft, which pursued its solitary way with its pot of fire still leaping and glowing. That night we slept warm and snug on board the good ship "Sultan," bound from Liverpool to Shanghai, with merchandize.

And now, indeed, we had a glorious time of it. Only that I have so much to tell, and that the biggest book that ever binder bound has its limits, it would delight me to recount the many acts of humanity we received at the hands of the amiable captain of the "Sultan," as well as the crew and the few passengers she carried. Much as we overcrowded her, it was not we who experienced inconvenience, although we were all sick, and for a time turned the ship into an hospital. In a little time, however, we were restored to health, and then, with just enough work to keep us amused, and such living as amazed even Pompey (whose murderous act was confided to the captain alone, who resolved to take no step in the matter as far as punishment went, but to lay the whole matter before the British consul), and highly gratified the ever-hungry Master Cox (whose nature had become much softened by his recent adversity, and who now was seen in frequent converse with Mr. Jones), we were as mirthful as though there was no trouble in the whole world, nor ever had been. Since I may say so little of Captain Prescot and his crew, I would at least that that little were of a pleasant character; but, alas! stern truth denies me even this gratification. Adventurous as had been the past few months of my life, but a brief space was allotted between this and the time when new adventures beset me. Indeed, I fear the reader will begin to suspect me of romance; but of that I must take my chance, and not allow its consideration to balk the true course of my narrative. Still, in order that he who takes an interest in my narration may not accuse me of overwhelming him with shocking events, I warn him to take breath and compose his mind, as it now immediately becomes my duty to acquaint him with the dire particulars of how a still worse fate than that of the "Margaret" befell the "Sultan," inasmuch as the latter became the prey of savage pirates in the China seas.

Becalmed

CHAPTER IV.

I enjoy a short spell of happiness—Our ship becalmed—I overhear a mysterious conversation about pirates—Appearance of a pirate scout—Five piratical prahus bear down on us—The particulars of our bloody fight with them—I am wounded and taken prisoner.

THE "Sultan" was not a fast sailer; nevertheless, so propitious had been the winds—at least, since we found refuge in her—that, at the expiration of seven weeks and a half, we had approached the China seas, and were, according to the captain's calculations, not more than ten days from our destination.

Looking back from this distance of time, and remembering the sad mishaps and frequent troubles the sea has wrought me, does any one ask, "Were you permitted to begin your life anew, would you so readily yield to your inclination for ships, and foreign seas and shores?" I reply without a moment's hesitation, "Could so unlikely a thing happen as the renewal of my lease of life,

I should be most heartily glad to discover that a clause of the said lease provided against my sailing beyond Gravesend, or, at the very farthest, the Nore." But when I limit my retrospection of ocean experience to that through which I was carried by the good ship "Sultan" during that same seven weeks and a half, then I say, if this is the sort of life a sailor leads, why, place on the one side the most exalted post the land can boast of—even the lord mayor's chair itself— and on the other the "Sultan," with Mr. Prescot for my captain, and leave me to take my choice—especially if you make the time of choosing evening, and I can hear Bill Ricketts playing on the fiddle, or Jack Wilkins singing "Homeward Bound" or "Gosport Hard"— my mind is made up before you can reckon two and two, and I turn my back on the lord mayor's chair to applaud Bill Ricketts, or join Jack Wilkins' chorus.

There was never a more comfortable ship than the "Sultan," nor a stronger contrast between any two captains than between Captain Prescot and the unfortunate wretch who had commanded the "Margaret." What the latter was like the reader already knows, whereas the former was a sleek and fat little man, with mild grey eyes and a shining bald head, with a kind word or a pleasant nod for everybody about him. He was a sober man: not a drop of grog or wine did he ever touch till after dinner, and then only enough to promote harmony between himself and the passengers who were his guests. It must not, however, be imagined that he was a slatternly captain. No officer in the king's fleet had a severer eye for shipboard proprieties, or was prompter at setting right things that were awry; but, withal, he had such a happy knack of ship management that the heaviest work seemed light, and a grumbler would have been regarded by his shipmates as an ungrateful fellow who did not know when he was well off.

As for me, I was as happy as ever I have been or hope to be. My recent adversities had quite weaned me of my boyishness, and I began to consider, with proper seriousness, my present condition and future prospects. I found them to be not at all satisfactory; for, though I had shared with the crew of the "Margaret" their dangers and privations, I was not entered on any ship's books, and had no title to call myself a sailor, or to expect from the British consul, whom we should find when we reached Shanghai, and to whom the case of the

"Margaret's" crew would be submitted, any of that relief and assistance he was bound to render to the others; indeed, unless he kindly stretched his authority, or helped me from his private purse, I could not be provided with a passage back to England, but should be left behind in a strange land to get along in the best way I was able.

All this was melancholy enough, and, doubtless, would have weighed very heavily on my mind but for the great kindness I experienced on all sides. Clearly enough my mainstay was the compassion my condition might excite in those about me; therefore, I thought it no harm to make my story—dating from my service with my uncle Sampson—fully known to every one who inquired into it; and, by great good luck, this curiosity presently extended to the passengers, who were glad to beguile a tedious hour by calling me in to hear all about it. There were five passengers—four gentlemen and a lady—one of the former being a tea-merchant, one of the heads of a European agency in Shanghai, whither he was returning.

"And what are you going to do, boy, when we get to Shanghai?" asked this gentleman, when he had heard my story.

"That is more than I can say, sir," replied I; "it doesn't matter to me; by sea or by land I mean to do the very best I can by any master who will be kind enough to take me;" which reply was double-shotted, and aimed as well at Captain Prescot, who was present, as at the tea-merchant. To my disappointment, however, the captain did not take my hint, but turned to talk with the lady; but the merchant, first asking me if I could write, and then, testing my arithmetic, dismissed me with the intimation that, if I behaved myself, something might be done for me. This, of course, was a great relief to me, and I was only fearful that, having so few opportunities of seeing the merchant, I should presently slip from his memory, and his half promise come to nothing after all. In this, again, however, fortune favoured me, for the captain's boy having the misfortune to run a rusty nail into his heel, laming him so that he could not walk, I was installed in his place till his health mended; and now, indeed, such a jolly time did I have of it—good words, the best of food, and many a sixpence from the passengers, for whom I found ample leisure to perform little services—that if the captain's boy had had a mind to regard my interest, he certainly would have remained lame during the remainder of the voyage.

Such, then, was my condition at that time—that is to say, when I had been aboard the "Sultan" seven weeks and a half. Little, however, did I dream that the end of our voyaging was so near at hand, or that in a little time it would not matter a single straw who the "Sultan's" captain was, or who her cabin-boy; least of all could I imagine what would be the manner of our voyage's ending, as well as that of the good ship herself; how, this being Thursday, she was doomed to-day to die, but not, as is the case with other ships whose ending is out at sea, at once to disappear, and so an end to the tragedy, but to linger inanimate on the face of the ocean for full two days and nights, and then to go down to her fathomless grave, with her poor carcase all maimed and crippled, with flame and smoke for her shroud.

I speak of the "Sultan's" dying on the Thursday; and so she did die, if a dead thing is one from whom the breath of life is withdrawn; for in the morning part of the day in question, the breeze, which for some hours past had blown so faintly as scarce to help the ship at all, suddenly expired, and what were before the vessel's great and little sails (but now had no more claim to be so called than has a corpse to be called a man), hung from their separate pole mere dead and idle rags, and our ship stood silent and still.

And so we lay throughout that day, moving, if at all, but at a snail's pace, veering sometimes a little to the right, and then again to the left (as we could judge from the position of the sun), like a ship at single anchor. To my ignorant and selfish mind, however, there was nothing very alarming in all this; on the contrary, the present condition of things had the charm of novelty, and possessed at least this advantage, that it enabled me to set out the captain's table in a proper manner, and without that slopping and clatter which, thanks to the vessel's motion and my inexperience, invariably distinguished my performances as a waiter. Nevertheless, to have seen our captain's anxious face, you would have thought that he was in momentary expectation of some great calamity, while the elder men of his crew—men who had served with him a dozen years and more—went about the ship with gloomy faces, and, instead of joining in the ordinary fun of the forecastle, kept together and wagged their heads and whispered ominously. As to the passengers, four out of the five moved about with but small abatement of their ordinary content; but the fifth—the tea-merchant—was much flurried in his manner, and at least half-a-dozen times in the course of that first day came knocking at the door of the captain's cabin, and, on being admitted, engaged the captain in very earnest conversation. The last time the two conferred together the captain called to me—

"Boy, ask Mr. Patching to step here for a minute."

Now, Mr. Patching was the first mate; and the circumstance of his being sent for in such a hurried and unusual way filled me with such curiosity that I was tempted to the meanness of listening, that I might learn something of the purport of the mysterious conference. It was easy enough to find a job that kept me very close to the cabin-door, but the door was so thick that, unless I laid my ear close to it, I could not hear a single word. The passengers were about; so that, for fear of detection, I could only give a sharp look round, then listen for a few seconds, and look out again. This was the result of my listening:—

Captain: " —— be left to you, Mr. Patching, to inform the crew of the danger of our position. Do so without exciting unnecessary alarm, taking care to provide each man with weapons——"

Here a footstep alarmed me, and I went on with my pretended job for awhile, and then placed my ear to the door again. The mate was talking.

" —— cutlasses being things easy enough to handle, though a man had never seen one before—especially against the naked bodies of these villains."

The merchant: "True, my dear sir, but cutlasses are of no account unless it came to boarding. You may depend that our best security are the two six-pounders. I should advise that they may be seen to at once. Is the other man as good a gunner as yourself, Mr. Patching?"

The mate: "He should be a better, sir. He's one of the picked-up crew, and served four years in the war-sloop 'Turtle'—or so I understand —before he took to the merchant service. How many small arms can we muster, sir?"

Captain Prescot: "Eleven muskets and seven pistols. Besides these there are two fowling-pieces belonging to this gentleman, and ——"

Again I was obliged to take my ear from the door, and this time for full a minute, that being the time occupied by two of the gentlemen passengers, who at that moment came in view, in exchanging pinches of snuff. Even when they had turned their backs, and I was free to listen again, they commenced such a trumpeting with their pocket-handkerchiefs that all I could make out of the conversation going on within, and which now had become so painfully interesting, was something about "a good look-out," "as well to tell them, if such a thing should happen, that they may expect no quarter," and "it may please God, after all, to send us a wind, and so put us out of danger of these blood-thirsty robbers." This last observation being made by the merchant, and to it the captain replied, as the three came out of the cabin together.

"Well, if the worst should come, we are lucky in having with us the crew of the 'Margaret' as well as our own; they owe us a good turn, and will pay us, without doubt."

As the reader may imagine, these disjointed scraps of conversation not a little bewildered me. It was impossible to arrive at but one conclusion—that "a good look-out" was to be kept for certain "blood-thirsty robbers" who gave no quarter; that "if a wind sprang up" it might keep them off, but that if they approached they were to be met with the contents of our "two six-pounders," and, "if it came to boarding," with cutlasses, and the guns, and pistols, and fowling-pieces. That was the best I could make of the puzzle, though who the "robbers" were, and from what quarter they were expected, was as great a mystery to me as ever. Under these circumstances, the look-out man at the mast-head, spying this way and that through his glass, became to me an object of extraordinary interest.

Having half-an-hour to spare in the evening, I went aft, and there found the men—my own shipmates, as well as the crew of the "Sultan" —busy as bees at polishing and sharpening cutlasses, and cleaning and oiling muskets and pistols. They smoked their pipes over the job, and seemed to enjoy it as a good bit of fun. There was Jack Wilkins singing like a nightingale while he rubbed away at a musket, while Pompey was grinding a boarding-pike, his eyes glistening with delight to find how sharp he was making it; while my old friends Billy Ricketts and Mr. Jones were solemnly repairing the edge of two cutlasses. I went up to Pompey.

"What's the row, Pomp?" said I, affecting much more surprise than I felt; "what's all this for?"

"Dunno, Mas'r Rue," returned he with a grin; "jes to keep fellahs' j'ints from rustin', I s'pose."

"No, that can't be it," replied I, anxious to learn how much of the plans made in the captain's cabin had been confided to the men.

"What is the matter, Bill Ricketts? Are we going to have a sham battle?"

"We aint going to have a battle of no sort that I knows on," answered Mr. Ricketts. "You may take Pomp's answer for mine, as I can't find you a better."

At the same moment, however, Bill exchanged a look with Mr. Jones that convinced me that they were in the secret, which it seemed was confided only to a few discreet hands; while by this, the mate's judicious management, the important end, that of preparing and placing the arms at hand, was as well attained as though the alarm had been sounded in the most public manner.

But the sun went down and the moon rose, and throughout the night a mast-head watch was kept, and all in vain; the "blood-thirsty robbers," the thoughts of whom kept me awake from the time of my lying down till my rising, never troubled us, and the sun rose as gaily as though there were none but good people to give light to, and we had nothing to fear. But, alas! besides ourselves the sun was the only thing that appeared alive; the air remained dead, and our hot sails hung stiff and still as though held in bond by unyielding frost. By noon of this, our second idle day, our two six-pounders being put in working order, and our small arms brought to proper condition, it was by no means likely to excite the suspicions either of our lady and three gentlemen passengers, or of such of the crew as were kept in the dark as to why such preparations were made, that the captain should suggest, as a pastime, that the men should try their skill as marksmen; and to this end a tub was carried out in the ship's boat to a distance of forty yards or so, and then, with a bit of a flag stuck in it, set afloat by way of a butt. And, to be sure, the hearty praise that each fair shot called forth—especially from a certain few, including the captain and the tea-merchant—was such as to encourage the gunners to do their very best. So the game continued as long as ammunition could be spared, and again the sun went down, leaving us aboard the dead ship in sole possession of as much of the great flat sea as could be swept by the glass of the look-out, who still kept rigorous watch at our mast-head.

Another night passed peacefully, but towards the dawning of morning there was a sudden bustle aboard; the captain was roused by the merchant, who, by-the-bye, during the last two nights had not retired to rest at all, but passed the time in pacing the deck, smoking cigars, and chatting with the watch.

"The vultures have spied us at last, I am afraid, captain," said he, as Captain Prescot joined him, and they proceeded on deck together.

"What is it, Dick Rood?"

"Well, I can't rightly make it out through the haze, sir," replied the look-out; "it aint a sail nor it aint a ship's boat; it is a mite of a thing that I should have let pass as a bit of drift timber, only it happens that the sea is too dead for drifting as much as a bung just at present; and this thing, whatever it is, is cutting its way at a spanking rate—towards us, too."

By this time the haze had cleared a bit, and half-a-dozen spy-glasses (for our passengers had roused to see what the matter was) were brought to bear on the distant black speck moving on the water.

"It is a fish, I believe," observed one of the passengers; "I can clearly distinguish the movement of its fins. I have no doubt that it is one of those grampuses that one hears about, and when it comes closer we can have some prime sport with it with our big guns—eh, captain?"

"If it is the sort of fish I take it to be, no doubt we very shortly shall have some sport, or something worse, with our guns, and our cutlasses as well," replied the captain. "What is your opinion, Mr. Aitchison?"

"A sampan belonging to a pirate prahu," replied the merchant coolly. "I know a little of the ways of these sea-devils, you see, gentlemen," continued he, turning to his fellow-passengers. "This villain approaching in his boat is a scout; should he find us a man-of-war, it is a chance if an attack would be ventured; but when he discovers nothing more terrible than a becalmed merchant-man, he will carry back the glad news, and they will be down on us like buzzards."

In a very few moments the nature of our peril was made known through the ship, and the whole number of hands on board of her, thirty-eight, including the passengers, crowded on deck to watch the approach of the little canoe that was now so close that, with the naked eye, it was easy to make out her shape, and that the man who worked her paddle so deftly was naked to the waist. On came the sampan till no more than a quarter of a mile stood between it and the stedfast ship, and then he paused, and, laying aside his paddle, shaded his eyes with his hands, and gazed intently towards us.

"Give him a shot, Mr. Patching," said the captain. "He may as well take back to his friends a hint of the sort of reception they are likely to meet with if they venture too close."

In less than a minute one of our six-pounders was pointed towards the inquisitive sampan, and, with a tremendous bomb, a shot was sent flying fair and true towards her. The boatman's behaviour, however, was highly significant; his quick eye had caught the flash the instant the match was applied, and as the ball left the mouth of the piece, so did the rower leave his boat, shooting into the sea as though, too, impelled by the power of gunpowder. As soon, however, as he found that his sampan was untouched (and to strike so small and flat a thing from a ship's gun was almost impossible) he just bobbed his head and shoulders out of the sea, and, clutching the edge of the sampan with one hand, swam with the other till he was fairly out of gun range; and then, climbing into the little cockle-shell of a thing, he waved his paddle, and, uttering a defiant yell, shot off as quickly as he came.

No longer was any mystery observed on board the "Sultan." All hands (with the exception of the husband of our poor lady passenger, who had been in horrible hysterics ever since the news of a probable attack by pirates had first reached her ears) were mustered, and Captain Prescot, who, as a fighting captain, was as admirable as he had shown himself as a captain of cargo, delivered to them a short and spirited speech, telling them what they might expect, and what he expected of them. He explained to them that, should the pirate prahus bear down on and attack them (as, being propelled by rowers and independent of the wind, they easily might), every man would have to fight for his life, for that the Dyak pirates were the most blood-thirsty on the sea, consigning their prisoners to instant death, or to what was worse, to everlasting slavery; on hearing which, the men, one and all (although not one in any ten had smelt more powder than was burnt in a Guy Fawkes' squib, or handled a more prodigious cutting weapon than a dinner knife), gave a most hearty shout, and declared that they would most prettily cut the buzzards' wings should they make up their minds for a swoop; and laughed and jested amongst themselves, and exhibited nothing like the serious concern of men about to engage in deadly strife. Perhaps they were not at all sure that they were, and that the captain's alarms were not groundless.

If so, they were vastly mistaken, for, before the excitement consequent on the captain's address had nearly subsided, the look-out spied a sail, and immediately after, another and another, till he had told five.

"What d'ye make 'em out to be?" inquired the captain.

"I never saw the like of 'em before, sir," replied Dick Rood. "They might be Thames barges for all that their hulls show above the water, and they mount no colours at all. Swarming with fellows like him who came to have a squint at us just now! Pulled along by oarsmen! There's at least fifty of 'em in the foremost one, judging from the double row of blades!"

These scraps of information, which Dick Rood jerked out eagerly and at intervals, as, according to the rapid approach of the strange craft, he made his successive discoveries, were received by those on deck with breathless interest; but, as I was delighted, and, as a Briton, proud to see, nothing like fear was visible on any one face—only a grim and sturdy determination to sell their precious lives at such a price as should, at least, make the purchasers repent their bargain.

In a little while the shape of the foremost of the piratical prahus could easily be made out from our deck (for the rowers worked with such will and precision that the vessels seemed to fly through the water), and at the same time we were aware of a shining thing at her bows, plainly revealed by the sun, that blazed full upon it. What the shining thing could be was a mystery to most of us; but we were quickly relieved of any doubts and guessings, for a spurt of something brighter than the glistening thing leapt from it, followed by such a bellowing as never could have found utterance in any but a cannon's mouth. At the same moment the other prahus, as though acting on the signal, fired each a gun (though we were, as yet, far out of range of their shot), and then the crews, uniting their voices, sent forth a yell shrill and appalling, and compared with which their cannonading was a mere whisper.

Such a thrilling, high-pitched shriek was it that the savages gave vent to, that it seemed impossible that any human throat could sustain it for more than the space of a single breath; but, to our surprise and dismay, the horrid yell proved but the first note of a war-song, the

performance of which was accompanied by the rumbling of drums, and
such music as is made by the clashing of gongs and cymbals. I say
that these sounds filled us with dismay as well as surprise, and so the
reader would have said had he been there to hear. I believe that if
they had made no other demonstrations than from the mouths of their
cannon, though it had been fifty times more formidable than that
already displayed, our fellows would only have been nerved by the
sound, and spurred to the very bent of their mettle; but to know of
this horde of black and naked barbarians approaching our helpless ship
with such hellish harmony and rejoicing, and as though a feast, and not
a fight, was their aim, was not a little disconcerting to men with
Christian lives to lose, and so small a prospect of saving them. It was
hard to believe that any enemy would approach with music and singing,
and there seemed a chance that our captain was mistaken, and that
the approaching fleet was a friendly one. There were those among the
crew, however, who had sailed these seas before, and knew better; as
did Captain Prescot and his friend the Shanghai merchant; indeed, it was
this gentleman who, at this moment, set at rest the doubts of all as to
the quality of the strangers, whose music and yelling became, each
moment, louder and more discordant.

"Men," said he, "one short hour from this time will see the settlement of the pretty bit of business we have before us. I won't waste
words in urging you to meet these cowardly rascals with courage;
as my fellow countrymen—as Englishmen, hailing from English homes,
and with the honour of the old country in your hands, you will, of
course, fight pluckily, and, let us hope, win, and with no great amount
of credit to us either, although our naked, caterwauling friends yonder
outnumber us six to one. You can't expect, however, to win without a
few scratches, and therefore the prospect of a trifle of shin-plaster may
be worth your consideration and acceptance. In the captain's cabin I
have a certain strong box; and as sure as ever we manage to beat off
these sea-robbers, I'll give every man in the ship a shoeful of silver
pieces, full measure."

This timely promise, which was hailed with a shout the leading
pirates must have heard, furnished the key to the secret of the extraordinary anxiety and alarm the good merchant had displayed since
first the fatal calm fell on the sea and stopped our ship.

By this time the pirates had approached to within a quarter of a mile of us, never for a moment ceasing their infernal din, to which, as we could now make out, half-a-dozen fellows, who wore monstrous rings in their ears, and heavy armlets of copper, executed what we supposed was a dance, while they yelled like furies and brandished naked swords. This was in the fore-part of the vessel; and besides these dancing warriors there were none others to be seen, owing to the strange construction of the vessel, which, immediately behind the bows, was partitioned with rough planks to the height of a man; and through this partition protruded the brass gun we had seen in the distance. This partition prevented us seeing the rowers, of which, to judge from the number of sweeps the blades of which might be seen, there must have been at least forty. The man at our mast-head informed us that, besides the rowers, there were, at least, thirty armed men; but concerning the nature of their arms he could give no very satisfactory account. Some few, he said, had crooked swords, like the dancers, and the rest sticks and slings; a bit of information that was, as I noticed, highly relished by our fellows, but not so much by either the captain or the tea-merchant, from whose manner I gathered that the look-out did not know what he was talking about; as, indeed, was presently made clear enough. Arrived within the above-mentioned distance, the large prahu halted, to enable the other four, which we found were considerably smaller, to come up; and then, stem on, and with their five guns pointed at us, on they came, yelling and thrashing their tom-toms and gongs harder than ever.

Meanwhile, our six-pounder on the side of the ship the pirates were approaching was being carefully tended by the gunner of the "Turtle"— Mr. Patching lending a hand for the present. And here it was, as it afterwards appeared, that the captain's humanity was displayed to our disadvantage; for either from lack of confidence in their guns, or from their peculiar mode of warfare, the prahus approached amazingly close, but, as yet, had not fired a single shot; still the captain gave no order for our gunner to fire, although he had trained his gun to play full on the big prahu; and, his experience telling him what a chance it was, he stood, match in hand, impatiently waiting for liberty to let fly.

"I think we had better fire, sir; we shall catch it else," at last suggested the mate.

"I had rather they open the ball, Mr. Patching, while there is a shadow of doubt as to their——"

If "intentions" was the word with which Captain Prescot was about to conclude his humane observation, the pirate guns spoke it for him with singular aptness. With a thundering report the contents of the three out of the five brass guns were directed towards us, and, had they been well aimed, considering their closeness, it would have gone hard indeed with the "Sultan" and all aboard of her; but thank our lucky stars, they were but bungling gunners, and in two cases fired over our heads, making great havoc amongst our rigging, but that was about all; the third pirate gun, however, was more effective, for its shot came smashing through the bulwarks, carrying to their long account three of our poor fellows, and wounding two others in so shocking a manner that they were at once carried below.

The chief of the leading prahu—the large one—judging, I suppose, by the crippled appearance of our rigging, and the quantity of splinters he had raised, encouraged the savage crew to give forth an appalling yell of triumph, and to pull straight to us that they might board us, and complete their devilish work. But there were two to this bargain, the other one being our stedfast gunner out of the king's ship "Turtle," who was so intent on his business as to be deaf and blind to all that was passing around him; presently, however, and when the big prahu was not more than thirty yards away, our gun, responsive to the swift descent of the match, discharged its iron messenger, which striking full and low at the partition in the big prahu's bows, rent a great ragged hole therein, and then ploughed its way through the double hedge of rowers and fighting men, raising a shrieking of a very different quality from that to which the gongs and tom-toms had beaten the measure.

If I am not mistaken, I found occasion to impress on the good reader how that my callous nature had become changed by adversity. And this was true. I could think placidly of all my ill doings, and was free to the bottom of my heart to admit that so far from receiving my deserts, I had been mildly punished, and would indeed be an ungrateful wretch if ever I harboured any other thoughts except those of meekness and humility again. But this was not exactly the case, and indeed furnished no bad illustration of how utterly incapable of perfect sincerity the human mind is. I was grateful and satisfied with my lot, simply because it was one that left nothing more to be desired; and my resolution to walk in proper paths for the future, simply meant that so long as my present good luck lasted, I would take particular care to put myself in the way of enjoying its results to the full.

My heart was quite changed I thought, but what a blunder! There was still a great deal of the devil in it, for when their shot struck our rigging, and caused the splinters to fly about our ears—when I heard our poor fellows cry, and saw them carried past me mere huddled bundles of rags, all covered with blood—when I saw this, I could do no other than clench my fists, and cry out aloud against the cause of the carnage in language which I thought myself no longer capable of uttering; and when I saw our shot strike *their* ship, when I heard that horrible shriek, and saw through the smoke the water about the stricken prahu all stained red, and in the midst of it a score of human beings beating the red water into foam with their torn limbs, when I saw all this, was I sorry? No, I was wild with delight. I could have kissed and hugged our valiant gunners, and laughed and shouted "ha! ha! that's good! that's glorious! hurrah!" and would have clapped my hands, only that by this time one of them was encumbered by the cook's big cleaver, of which, as the handiest weapon about, I had possessed myself. I was grievously disappointed to find that the prahu did not at once sink and drown every soul aboard of her, or that, finding the vessel so crippled, they did not either sheer off or yield. Had I known as much of the nature of those sea-devils as it was my fate by-and-by to do, I might have spared myself the idle speculation.

What happened was this. So far from being daunted by the calamity that had overtaken his ship, the chief, who, unluckily, was not hurt, only flourished his kris savagely in our direction, and proceeded to such swift arrangements for the mending of his damage that, before our gun could be again served and brought to bear on him, his men were brought to rowing order, and had shifted the prahu out of danger, leaving their sampan, or ship's boat, to pick up the wounded.

During this time, not more than two or three minutes, the four smaller prahus were not idle, and, having discovered the position of our guns, made preparations for attacking us, so that we might make little or no return. True, there were our muskets and pistols; but, owing to the strange way in which each prahu was partitioned, it was impossible to get a successful shot, except when, in their manoeuvring, het rowers were for a moment exposed; and, although this frequently

happened, and never without, at least, one fatal result, their numbers
were so great that, do all we could in this way, our prospects seemed
not at all mended, but, on the contrary, grew every moment more and
more desperate, especially when the two prahus that at present had taken
no part in the firing took up their position at our stem and stern, and
commenced to ply their guns.   As for the others, including the one the
number of whose crew we had so considerably thinned, they kept continually edging in closer and closer, and were evidently bent on boarding us
as soon as we were driven to panic by the shattering of our ship.   And

The Pirates boarding the "Sultan."

indeed, to lie still and helpless, while the murderous pirates were
mauling us so dreadfully, seemed so preposterous a thing, that, so far
from dreading their assault by boarding, we wished for it that we
might have something to do.

We had not long to wait.   The prahu at our bows had delivered
into our wretched ship not more than half-a-dozen shots (which, by-
the-bye, owing to the weakness of their gunpowder, or some other
cause, did very little more than penetrate the outer timbers of our
hull), when the damaged vessel, which, though its gun was rendered

ineffective, still assumed the leadership, made its appearance at our
stern, and, signaling the other to cease her firing, made a great dash
at us to board us, and, as fortune would have it, with such hot eagerness that they served us a good turn; for, coming head on and with
all their rowers' strength, they met our bows with such a thump as to
cause our becalmed ship to veer half round, and in such a way that
one of the prahus lay directly before our larboard gun, to the huge
delight of our gunner, who, since his first shot, had been fuming with
the most savage impatience for a second.   Now was his chance;
instantly his eager match kissed the touch-hole, and simultaneously,
with a thundering roar, came a greater wailing than had as yet been
heard; for the well-aimed shot, plunging down and striking her amid-
ships, played such havoc with her bottom planking that the prahu
sank like a stone, leaving her savage crew, who swam like eels, to
swarm up the sides of the other vessels, and even up the sides of our
own, by means of the hooked poles many of them bore, and which, as
I afterwards discovered, are weapons peculiar to the Dyak pirate, and
used for the purpose of dragging off the men of an opposing vessel.

Of these stragglers, however, not many reached our deck, and
those who did made their exit from it at a much quicker rate, being
pitched into the sea in a condition past swimming; for our men, who
were by this time furious, and eager to shed blood, shot, and slashed
and clubbed without mercy.   But it was for no more than a minute
that the boarders were confined to the survivors from the wreck.   First
the big prahu, and then two of the smaller ones, came close along, and
the Dyaks commenced swarming up the sides, climbing with both
hands—for their krisses, and spears, and other weapons were borne in
their mouths—and, in an instant, were about us, thick as flies.

And now ensued a spectacle than which a more terrible, one even
bred to battle and making it their trade never yet saw.   Our brave
fellows, reduced by this time to less than thirty in number, knew—
it was plainly to be read in the eyes of each—that all hope was fled—
all chance of saving life *under any circumstances*.   All that remained
was to live as long as their arms were able to defend them—to expend
their little remnant of life in taking revenge on the ruffians who for
their profit had attacked them in such cowardly fashion.

It is marvellous what miracles of valour men will achieve, when the
chances of war have put them beyond hope; when, by a dozen murderous

tokens flashing before their eyes, and heard behind them, and round about them on every side, they are made fully aware that their account of life is at an end, and there remains nothing to expect, but the closing of the ledger; none but such as have witnessed such mortal fights can judge *how* men fight when reduced to such extremities, or imagine how, on a certain instant, the arm just now fagging, stretches itself out anew; how the head is lifted up; how the eyes, dulling with loss of blood, and faintness, leap alight again and become glareful of strength and power. It is such spectacles as this that turns the tide of many a battle, but only when the odds are slight; but, what could one poor thirty do against three hundred at the very least, or so few clumsily-handled weapons against their terrible krisses, sharp as razors, and handled with that easy dexterity that can only be acquired by life-long practice, against spears of iron and wood, and the stone-headed clubs, all of which these sea-robbers used with deadly effect?

Nor were the krisses, and spears, and clubs the only hand weapons the pirates brought against us; otherwise, excepting for their big guns, we should have been able to have reckoned the full number of our assailants among the black horde who besieged our ship as thick as ants. Those in the prahus alongside, and who could by no means manage to board us, were armed with a weapon simple-looking as a cane for walking, but in its use more to be avoided than the stone club or the jagged spear. The innocent-looking instrument, as I afterwards learnt, is called a sumpitan, and is no more nor less than a hollow reed, and through it are blown insignificant-looking barbed darts no longer than the hand, and seeming fitter for the boyish pastime of killing sparrows than for the handling of men-of-war; but God help the sparrow, or indeed any other living creature up to the size of a Patagonian giant, whose body gives lodgment to one of these tiny darts. The venomous poison with which each of them is tipped, at once conveys such tormenting heat to the blood, that nothing but the cold hand of death can allay, and which in all cases it does with charitable promptitude.

I have spoken of the hooked poles, somewhat resembling sheep-crooks, used by the savage crews that lay alongside us for dragging an enemy overboard. Many of our poor fellows were ruined by these preposterous engines, and that at a moment when they least expected it. Tom Cox was one of these unlucky ones. While our deck was slippery with blood, and encumbered by the many carcases that had made it so, among which might be counted our captain, the merchant, the lady passenger, and Bill Ricketts, poor fellow! whose head was gone, and whose body I only knew because of the lion and unicorn tattooed on his naked arm—when, seeing poor Pompey standing like a black lion at bay, wielding his terrible pike, while around him was a savage host hacking and thrusting at him, Tom Cox ran to his assistance, and was on the point of spitting Pompey's foremost assailant, when he was grappled in the rear and lugged over into a prahu. As for me, being but a lad, it was not to be expected that I should fight at all, or that my life should be aimed at.   As regards the latter, I only know that I found myself speared through the thick part of my left arm, and with a gash over my right knee.   How I came by the wounds, or whether I paid my assailant in his own coin, I cannot recollect.   One's memory is very apt to fail him on such occasions. True, my cook's cleaver was red to the very handle; but then, might I not have dropped it on the sloppy deck?   Of one thing I am quite sure; whatever mischief I might have done with my cleaver was before Tom Cox was kidnapped, for almost the next instant I was stunned by a blow of a stone club, and on recovering, was a bound prisoner at the bottom of a prahu, whose crew was still yelling and hauling with their hooked poles, and blowing poisoned darts through their reed sumpitans.

CHAPTER V

I am shocked to my senses by the sight of a red foot—I discover, to my great joy, that Tom Cox is a fellow-captive—The "Sultan" plundered and burnt—We are carried to the pirate island of Magindano—We find that the whole of the inhabitants reside under one roof—Our treatment by the doctor—We go to bathe, and are fetched in a hurry.

WHEN I say that I recovered from the senseless condition into which the blow of the stone club had cast me, I beg that a not too literal construction may be applied to the expression; my recovery, indeed, was very gradual, and would, I have no doubt, have been even more protracted but for the excruciating pain in my left arm, through which, as before mentioned, some ruffian had thrust his rusty spear. My feet were bound together, and my hands, drawn behind my head, were served the same, and it unluckily happened that I was lying on my damaged side, and with the weight of my heavy head on my arm. The pain that this position occasioned at length brought such life back to me that I languidly opened my eyes.

The first spectacle which they encountered was the naked legs of the rowers, who did not fight, but kept their seats at their paddles ready to manœuvre the vessel into such convenient points as the captain might direct. In the sight in question there was, however, nothing very alarming, for my head was in such a whirligig state, that, beyond the fact that they were legs, and black, and that there were a goodish number of them, they served in no wise to aid me in the realization of my condition; nay, at present, so limited was my power of comprehension, and so benumbed my senses, that the double row of black legs became objects of trivial speculation and amusement. I noted how broad was the heel of this foot, how the toes of this curled under, and how that one big toe amongst the number had altogether lost its nail, and I puzzled the little brains that were in working condition to find the reason why. Had the unlucky toe been trodden on? Had the owner sacrificed the nail to ill-fitting boots? Had it been chipped off by a spear? This last suggestion came, no doubt, rather from my own speared arm than from the head which rested on it.

Presently, however, as my but half-conscious eyes wandered among the black and naked feet and toes, they rested on something that instantly restored them to perfect wakefulness, and, indeed, loosed all my senses, as though previously bound with a thong, and the said thong had now burst. I could smell the intolerable closeness that pervaded the prahu, and to which the bilge-water and the grease with which the bodies of the savage men were anointed largely contributed. I could hear the yelling, and jabbering, and shouting on every side, and which, although uttered in an outlandish tongue, were unmistakeably the notes of victory and triumph. Now and then—very rarely, alas!—I could hear an English voice swearing a big English oath, or crying out in despair that last and universal prayer, " Lord, have mercy upon me !" I could hear the clash of steel against steel, the sharp crash of the pirates' brass artillery, and the rending and splintering of tough wood, and could feel the ship at whose bottom I lay shiver and complain as the cannon at its bows was discharged. In an instant, I repeat, the true state of the case; the attack, the unequal fight, with its terrible details ; my wounds ; even up to the very instant when that merciless stone club came " blob " on to the crown of my head ; all was restored to me, the key being a great patch of blood spreading over one of the before-mentioned black feet.

I raised my throbbing head a little, and discovered that the red foot derived its colour from a small pool close by it, and in which a man's hair was dabbling ; it was hair of a peculiar colour, and I recognized it immediately ; it belonged to Tom Cox, and Tom Cox's head it was that was the fountain-head of the crimson stream.

Was poor Tom alive or dead? This became with me a very serious consideration, involving more hopes and fears than ever I thought to find the greedy Stepney water-boy the subject of. Bearing in mind Captain Prescot's speech to the crew of the " Sultan," that the captive of the Dyak pirate preserved from death was invariably doomed to slavery, it was evident that there existed no immediate intention of killing me ; therefore I might regard perpetual bondage as my certain doom, and how much easier might this melancholy state be borne with one of one's own countrymen for a companion! As far as might be judged, however, by the stillness of his head, Tom Cox was beyond further persecution; but if so, unless these wretches wanted him to eat, it seemed unlikely that they would allow their already crowded ship to be lumbered by his carcase; besides—and I am ashamed to confess the reflection caused me at the time considerable satisfaction—Tom Cox was a very cunning fellow. True, he had mended considerably since the good mate of the "Margaret" had taken him in hand; but I felt convinced that he had enough of his old nature remaining to sham death or anything else likely to serve his aims. It chanced, however, that I was not to be kept very long in suspense as to Master Cox's condition, for the captain of our prahu presently gave an order that concerned the boatmen, and the one with the red foot, finding that his actions were likely to be impeded by the young man's prostrate form, grasped him by the hair, and so swung his body round that his head was brought to within a foot of mine own, and at the same instant my ears were delighted to make out Tom Cox's voice consigning the ruffian who had served him so to eternal punishment.

"Not that it's any use talking to such ignorant heathens, who don't even understand as much English as to know when you swear at 'em. I wish they'd throw me over the side; I'd better be dead and among my dead mates than alive and alone among this precious cannibal crew."

"Cheer up, Tom," I said in an under tone. "Not quite alone, shipmate; you never liked me over much, I know; but since we are both in the same strait, it seems to me we had better shake hands and be friends."

He turned his head as I addressed him, and showed me a face pale as a shroud, and all encircled with red, very frightful to look on, but still with so much delighted amazement and gratitude in it that I thought I had never seen it so pleasant.

"What! you, Reuben?" said he. "Well, now the Lord really *is* kinder to a fellow than he deserves. I've found it so a dozen times since that precious good sort of fellow, Mr. Jones, first put me up to it, but it never came down on me so strong as this. Friends we are, Reu; but as for shaking hands, these—but I won't swear any more, that I've made up my mind to—these thundering rascals have treated you better

than me if they've left you power to shake a hand, or a foot either. I'm
bound fore and aft, Reu."

"So am I, Tom," I replied, "although I forgot it when I made the
offer.   They needn't have been so particular, though, as they've served
one of my arms in such a way that, if I might write my own discharge
out of their devilish hands with it, the thing couldn't be done."

"That's precious hard on a youngster who didn't do them any
harm," said Tom.

It was quite certain that he had not seen me with the cook's
cleaver, and I was very glad that he had not, otherwise he might have
been able to confirm a suspicion of mine that I *had* hurt more than one
naked Dyak, and that to a considerable extent.   I'm sure I hope it was
not so.   I only know that the villain's back was towards me, and that
in another moment poor Mr. Patching would have been cleft from his
shoulder to his chest with that terrible kris, had I not——but there, let
it pass; as I have before observed, on such occasions one's memory is
not to be relied on.

" Is the hurt to your arm the only one you've got, Reu ?" asked
Tom Cox.

" Well, there's something the matter with my right knee, but I
don't exactly know what," replied I.   " You seem in bad case, too,
Tom."

" There you're mistaken, my lad," said he.   " It aint a thing to
brag about, but I shot one fellow over the ship's side, and scattered
the brains of another with the butt of my piece; and as you may
see, I've come off with as mere a scratch on the side of the head as
one might get in a forksal row."

As the reader may imagine, I was considerably astonished to hear
him talk so, as, from the very beginning of our whispered conversation,
I had been aware that one of his ears was shaved off as neatly as though
an hospital surgeon had performed the job.

" I suppose you can see the scratch ?" said he, seeing that I was
gazing very hardly at his head.   " Is it a deep 'un ?"

" There's one thing, Tom," replied I, "that will never need scratch-
ing again as long as you live, and that's your right ear; it's sliced
off as clean as a carrot top."

This bit of information coming so suddenly on the poor fellow seemed
for a moment quite to overcome him.   His white face flushed red with

rage and indignation, and quite forgetful of his good resolution not to swear any more, he turned towards the oarsmen and abused them in so hearty a manner, that, had they been able to understand but half of what he said, it might have gone hard with him. As it was, they seemed to attribute the sudden outburst to the pain of his wound, and one of the oarsmen compassionately took from his own head a strip of greasy rag and bound it round Master Cox's, thereby nothing improving either his personal appearance or his temper. Indeed, so ludicrous a figure did Tom cut when the savage had adjusted the bandage to his fancy, that I could not forbear congratulating him on possessing the handsomest figure-head in the ship. I never paid so severely for a joke in all my life.

"I begin to think, young fellow, that you haven't yet seen all the figure-heads aboard this vessel," said Tom seriously. "P'r'aps you are not aware of the awful pile of heads without figures—heads of old acquaintances and friends, they've got aboard this floating slaughter-house?"

I began to fear that the loss of his ear had set Tom's head wandering.

"I don't exactly understand you, Tom," I replied. "What heads are you speaking of?"

"Look if you can, towards the midship's partition and down in the right-hand corner," whispered he. "I can tell you well enough where to find 'em, for I had my face that way when the first two were chucked down, and counted 'em one by one as the rest were brought in, till I was glad to close my eyes and keep 'em shut."

Raising my head cautiously, I looked in the direction indicated by Tom Cox, and could scarcely repress a cry at the dreadful sight that met my eyes. There, in the corner, was indeed a heap of human heads, seven in number, the faces of four of which were towards me, and instantly recognized, despite the marks of violent death by which each was distorted. Topmost of the buried pile was the head of our lady passenger, and so it was well placed, as its beautiful long brown curls (which many a time, as I waited at the captain's table, had caused my heart to flutter with admiration) hung down and over the other ghastly heads, partly concealing the features. Attached to the brown ringlets by a long copper hair-pin was a tag of red cloth, placed there, as I suppose, by the ruffian whose spoil the lady's head was, that he might know his own.

I have said that the brown curls hung about the other heads, partly concealing them; only partly, however. It was easy enough to make out the round face of Captain Prescot, with his mouth still ajar, as though his decapitation had taken place at the very moment of his giving some important order. There was the long, sallow face of my friend the tea-merchant, and the big black woolly head of Pompey the cook. No face of the whole number looked so awful as the African's, and this not so much because it was black, or that it betrayed in a shocking way the manner of its death; on the contrary, it looked like a live face, and this it was that made it so terrible among the others that were so very dead: the eyes were open, and a grin parted his lips, showing his double row of closely-set white teeth, and in his wool the owner of the head had stuck a white feather, giving it quite a holiday air.

Knowing nothing of the manners and customs of these savages, or their peculiar and invariable mode of treating the heads of such as fell by their hand in battle, I thought to be sure that they must be cannibals, and that our reservation from death was a mere matter of larder convenience; still, on the other hand, it seemed strange that, in the case of the slain of our ships, the head, the most inconsiderable part of the carcass in the eyes of the ordinary butcher, should be preserved, and the remainder wasted. To my horror, I found that Tom Cox, when questioned on the subject, quite agreed with me that our doom was the spit or pot; and when I asked him, did he not think it rather strange that the bodies and not the heads of our friends should be saved, he gave me no comfort by replying that he saw nothing strange about the business, as no doubt the bodies of the unfortunate crew were somewhere safely stowed away for the use of the captain and his officers. the heads being the perquisites of the commoner sort.

Meanwhile, and during this whispered conversation between Tom Cox and myself, the pirates had not been idle. It could not have been very long since I had left our ship, for at that time the slaughter was at its briskest, and there remained at a rough guess, not more than eighteen men on our side who were doomed to certain destruction in less than as many minutes. According to this, my swoon must have been of very short duration; indeed, it would seem that, deprived of sense by the stone club, my resuscitation must have commenced with my unceremonious bundling into the prahu.   The fight was still progressing, indeed, it was under cover of the din that Tom and myself had ventured to converse.

By this time, however, it became evident that the end was rapidly approaching.   True, the savage yelling was as loud as ever, nay, much louder for that matter; but the firing of the brass guns each moment diminished, as did, alas! every sound betokening that an English ship was lying so near.   Presently there arose a frightful yelling, more prolonged and universal than any that had before been heard, and the gongs were banged, and the whistles blown, and the tom-tom drummed, all telling as plainly as spoken language, that at length the last "white devil" was overcome, and the victory won.

Then began the work of plunder.   Like vultures round a dead camel the prahus now swarmed about our poor ship, leaving only the rowers and the prisoners behind.   From our position, we were spared the sight of the barbarians pillaging the worthy vessel which had been to us an ark of refuge in our direst extremity, but by the tremendous uproar that prevailed, by the sudden exclamations of surprise and wonder, by the loud tones of authority and the occasional painful cry of some pilfering wretch whose shoulders the staff of authority had visited, by the devilish gabble and the incessant joking and laughter, it was certain that the work of plunder was proceeding with full activity; indeed, if we had entertained any doubts on the subject they would have been but of short duration; for presently, bales and bundles and boxes of the "Sultan" cargo came tumbling into the prahu in which we lay, and which the slaves proceeded to pack with such an infernal din, that Tom Cox gravely declared that, if it was to continue, they were welcome to his other ear, and that as soon as they pleased to lop it off.

Presently, however, there was a panic among the robbers.   The Babel of sound ceased, giving place to one single word, which was uttered in every variety of tone, as well by rowers as fighters, the former waving their arms and pointing at something with gestures of the greatest alarm.   "*Api*" was the word as far as we could make it out; but who or what "api" was, was a sore puzzler.   Certainly it carried with it a most potent meaning, for, crying "Api! api!" the fighting men of our prahu came tumbling back into her as though Satan himself was at their heels, while all around were sounds of heavy splashing in the water, occasioned either by living bodies or the bales and boxes abandoned while but half-free of the ship from which they were being taken.

What could "api" mean? Could it be the lingo of these savages for ship? Was there a ship in sight? An English man-of-war, perhaps, arrived just in the nick of time to rescue us from our peril "Api! api!" was still the cry, while every face about us was aghast with apprehension, and the rowers clutched their paddles and looked to that part of the vessel were the captain was, as though eager for the order to pull away for their lives. I was filled with delight at the thought, and nudged Tom, whispering that he might depend that deliverance was at hand.

"Why do you think so?" asked he incredulously.

"Don't you hear their shouting?" replied I. "Don't you hear how everyone is crying 'Api! api!' and preparing to make off? Api means ship, Tom, I believe; an English ship, Tom, bearing down on these wretches to avenge the murder of our countrymen and deliver us out of their hands!"

But Tom answered my remarks only by a grunt of contempt. "What dy'e mean?" said he. "How could a man-of-war or any other craft, except of this cursed sort that is pulled by oars, make way in such a calm as this! If it's a ship at all they are making such a yelping about, it must be the 'Flying Dutchman.' And good luck if it is, I say; since we're bound for Davy Jones, the sooner it's all over the better."

Still, I could not help clinging to the hope that, despite Tom Cox's glooming predictions, "api" meant deliverance of some sort, and with much eagerness watched the movements of our captors. Without doubt, the work of plunder had ceased, and presently the rowers bent to their oars and pulled with a will. But alas! at the same moment my senses were greeted by sensations which provided a dismal solution to the mystery. A smell, as of burning wood assailed my nose, and a sound that is like no other smote my ears. Crack! crackle! crackle! It was clear enough now the "Sultan" was in flames, and as columns of black smoke rolled sluggishly above her, the prahus cleared off.

Now, as the vigorously-plied paddles bore us rapidly from the burning ship, did we begin to realize to the fullest our woeful plight.

Although it may be true enough that our prospects were not a bit more melancholy at this moment than a half-hour before, it had not till now seemed so completely all over with us. Hopeless as had been the struggling going on between our people and their people, still it *was a* struggle, and, by a miracle, the weaker might be victorious, and we released from our perilous position. Now, however, even this feeble glimmer of hope was extinguished; the bloody wreck of the good ship was abandoned to the flames which had seized her, and we were being borne away hopelessly as sparrows in the talons of a kite! So overwhelmed was I as I so reflected, that my tears, which had been pent up since the time I was recovering from my illness on board the "Margaret," began to flow abundantly. As for my companion, he was one of those whose natures seem rather to parch than to soften under the influence of sorrow; but still, if one might judge by his closely-shut eyes, and the groans and husky noises he was continually making, his dismal apprehensions were of a piece with mine own.

On sped our prahu (the others, as we could hear, keeping her close company) for fully three hours, during which time Tom and I exchanged but few words. No doubt we were intimidated by the comparative quiet that now prevailed, though for that matter our heads lay so close together that we might have conversed in whispers, and they not have overheard, even had they understood our language.

Although, however, they could not converse with us, they understood signs readily enough, as Tom Cox unluckily found to his cost. It happened that he was more exposed to the sun than I was, and, what with the heat and the worry of his wound, grew very thirsty; and presently, finding one of the rowers regarding him, Tom opened his mouth, and humbly expressed his great want of a drink of water. The only reply, however, to his desire was a squirt of saliva, accurately aimed by the disgusting fellow at poor Tom's cheek, and which exploit elicited the laughter of such of the sooty villains as chanced to witness the filthy trick. I perceived, by the sudden lowering of Tom's brows, that his will was good to give the fellow the full benefit of all the Billingsgate at his command; but, in a hasty whisper, I enjoined him to keep his temper, fearing that, if we showed ourselves fit objects for the amusement of such a crew, we should, in all probability, have a bad time of it. So Tom contented himself by concentrating his wrath within the compass of a few brief and powerful expressions, which he directed at the chief aggressor, on whom, however, from his ignorance of the English tongue, they were happily lost.

In the course of the afternoon we neared what I afterwards discovered to be the Island of Magindano, one of a hundred piratical strongholds situated in these regions. And here, for the reader's edification, I may as well impart a few particulars of these bloodthirsty sea-rovers. It must not be imagined that they are skulking hang-dog fellows, keeping their calling a secret, and never venturing to pursue it except when far from home, and secure from the observation of the authorities governing the country where they dwell. There is no occasion for secresy; the authorities are pirates to a man, and the governor is the pirate in chief. The inhabitants, man, woman and child, subsist on the produce of sea-robbery—that is as we call it —but they give it no such hard name, nor do they regard their avocation as a matter to be ashamed of. It is their sole means of existence, and they think no more of skimming the sea for its treasures than do honest men when they cast their nets therein for a haul of fish. They are born to the business; their fathers followed it, and the young men will exhibit the kris worn by their grandfather, and all notched and rusted, with as much pride as we feel when we contemplate the dented swords and battered head-pieces of our warlike ancestors.

Neither must it be imagined that, in their piratical undertakings, a system of private enterprise is observed. Every such stronghold as Magindano owns a fleet comprising sometimes as many as fifty vessels and a crew numbering a couple of thousand men and more. As with civilized fleets, there is a chief officer corresponding, as regards his authority, with our Lord High Admiral, with a captain and his senior officers to every ship. As to the rowers, they are chiefly slaves —Papua, and the three easternmost islands, contributing the chief supply. Indeed, although when they can in safety attack a merchant ship, they never miss the opportunity, the getting of slaves forming the chief feature of their trade, and the Malays being their best customers. They have their laws and regulations, which are scrupulously observed —the chief of them being that the captains and the rest of the head men claim all slaves, guns, and money, and the finest sorts of silks and cloths; the rest being divided among the free crew and the slaves, who by this means are sometimes enabled to purchase their liberty.

To return, however, to the prahu, in which Tom Cox and myself were lying, bound and helpless, prisoners. By the gestures of the crew I saw that we were approaching land, and signified the same to my companion, who lay with his eyes shut, utterly indifferent to all that was passing around him.

"I think we are near land, Tom," I whispered, eagerly.

"Are we?" answered he, with miserable indifference, and without opening his eyes.

"Come, Tom," said I, "rouse yourself, man; let us show these savages that we can meet our fate, whatever it is, without flinching. Hark! don't you hear the people on the shore shouting?"

"Pshaw! where's the good of rousing?" said Tom, despondingly. "They can as well knock us on the head as we lay here; besides, if they could more conveniently do it, if we roused, as you call it, I don't feel in the humour to oblige 'em. Lay still, Reu; what does it matter? we shall be roasted and eaten before the morning!"

"I am not so sure of that, Tom."

"Well, then, boiled—baked, if you like it better," said he, with ghastly merriment.

I was much younger than Tom, nor did I possess half his brute strength; but somehow I could not bring myself to regard our position as so utterly hopeless. It is true that the best of our chances were no better than to become slaves, and that it may be said is a condition not a bit preferable to death. But this opinion, as I have observed, is chiefly held by people who have no reason to apprehend either one calamity or the other. But put these to the test. Stand them before two individuals—the one with a sharp axe in his hand, and the other with a leg chain and a slave whip; give him his choice at whose hands he will be dealt with. Nay, give him the merest hint that by begging and imploring, his head may be allowed to remain on his shoulders, on condition that his leg submits to the shackle! Will he accept the terms, or will he connive at his own murder, valuing his sense of pride, love of worldly conceits and calculations, before his precious life with which God entrusted him?

"Tom," said I, "if it is indeed our forlorn case either to be eaten or to become slaves, very much will depend upon ourselves as to which fate will befall us. If we show ourselves crippled and near to death's door, it may appear more convenient to these rascals to push us fairly in than to trouble themselves about our cure, or the chance of our living bodies fetching a price that shall remunerate them. Now, I'm more damaged than you, Tom; and though, as I assure you, my arm shoots and burns as though it were in an oven, and my wounded leg is not the most comfortable, I shall put a light face on the matter, and make as though I thought nothing of such trifles. And unless you have come to have so poor an opinion of yourself as that you are only fit to become a roast or broil, I should advise you to adopt the same course. Besides, has it slipped your consideration, Tom, that in the other prahus there may be shipmates of ours whom we may be very glad to see?"

This last view of the matter seemed to afford him more comfort than any other, and he became from that moment much more contented and cheerful.

By this time we were fairly into port, and the rowers and crew proceeded to land the plunder amid the rejoicing acclamations of the inhabitants of the island, who were assembled on the shore. The seven human heads were not forgotten; indeed, they were evidently regarded as no inconsiderable portion of the booty, and were the property, not of the common sailors or the rowers, but of the leaders and chief men in command. As the proprietors of the ghastly trophies assembled round the pile and selected each his own, he behaved towards it with none of that coarse brutality that might have been expected, especially when their conduct towards the living owners of the craniums was taken into consideration. I expected to see each head seized by its hair and so carried off, but the pirates observed much ceremony. They endeavoured to smooth the tangled locks, and with great care attached a string to them, and tied them to the belt at their waist. The owner of the head with the brown ringlets I expected to see especially careful of his prize; but the savage in question was no admirer of silken tresses, and finding that, drooping down to the floor, he was in danger of being tripped up by them, he caught them up, and whipping out his knife sawed them off, and flung them over the side. We now had an opportunity of inspecting the three of the seven faces we had not yet seen, but death had so completely disguised them, that we could not for certain make out to whom they had belonged. By so much of the white whiskers that remained unstained on one of them we guessed that this was another of our passengers, but we couldn't have sworn to it.

The plunder and the heads carried off, came our turn, and two of the fellows coming up cut the lashings that bound our legs and arms, and with an insolent kick intimated that we were to rise. This Tom Cox found it not very difficult to do, but with me it was sadly different. My leg had swollen very much, and had grown so stiff and heavy that, had it been a leaden leg, it could not have been more useless; and the best I could accomplish after receiving a second kick was to scramble into a position which was half-sitting, half-crouching, upon which one of the villains roughly hauled me up, and endeavoured to stand me on my legs. But I was down again quicker than he had lifted me, and hurt so very much that I uttered a loud shriek; while at the same time the violence done to my wounds caused them to stream out afresh. Tom rushed to me and lifted me up, which the two pirates perceiving they became somewhat more humane, and took me between them to assist me, while they drove Tom Cox on before.

In this plight did I first set my foot in a country which fate had ordained should become so familiar to me—a country which was to reveal to me so much that was admirable as well as horrible, and was to be an abiding place for so many years, every month seeming a year almost, and every year a lifetime.

As the reader may imagine, my landing was not auspicious. After my vain boasting to Tom Cox that I would put a light face on the matter, and make believe that my wounds, ugly as they appeared, were of such small account as not in the least to interfere either with my activity or cheerfulness (especially the latter, as it seemed to me that of all possessions that of a cheerful disposition must be most desirable in one doomed to pass his life in unrequited labour), it came about that, so far from being a pattern of hopefulness to my companion, I could see from the pitiful glances he was continually casting behind him, that my sorry plight was breaking him down; indeed, as he afterwards informed me, as he gazed on me leaning my trembling weight on the arms of the two pirates, he thought it was all over with me, and fully expected to see me presently sink down and die there and then.

We found the greater part of the plunder from the "Sultan" piled on the shore, and surrounded by a guard formidably armed, while three or four fellows who bore no arms, but who appeared a sort of custom-house officers, were busily engaged daubing each bale and package with certain marks with a stick dipped in a bowl of white-wash, doubtless by way of distinguishing them as the property of the king.

Besides the guards and the mob of women and children, there was a vast number of the sailors belonging to the fleet. One especially there was, who had served in the prahu in which we had been conveyed. We knew him at once by a large grey scar, which extended from under his right eye to his chin. But it was not his scar which now made him particularly noticeable. It was because of a certain horrid waist-ornament which he wore, and which was nothing else than a human head, a white one, suspended in a sort of potato net made of string or fibre, and tied to his belt. Who the head had belonged to, it was impossible to recognize, nor indeed at the moment did we take particular kind of notice, our attention being entirely taken up by observing the manner in which the ruffian comported himself with his hideous trophy. He strutted with it with his arms folded proudly, and his nose in the air as though its possession entitled him to the respect and admiration of all beholders. Nor if such were his sentiments, did he seem to be in error. He was very much admired, and this more especially by the women who came up to him with smiles of welcome, and with eyes beaming as they gazed on—nay, touched and caressed the gory head in the potato net with much the same sort of expression as one of my own countrywomen would assume, were she shown a handsome gown-piece or a shawl. Even the young boys made much of it, and pointed at it longingly, and would have handled it had they dared. Ugly as was the spectacle it was one from which, as it seemed to me, some consolation might be drawn; since if white heads were held in such high esteem—dead heads without sense and animation,—it was only natural to infer that living heads of the same description, properly and naturally mounted on a pair of useful shoulders, need not fear much damage.

But there was one sight we saw not, eagerly as we looked about for it, and that was the sight of a living white prisoner. Faces there were in plenty, but, alas! they were all of the black or copper-coloured sort, and it seemed certain that, of the "Sultan's" bold thirty-eight, we were the miserable remnant. True, there remained a faint hope that one or more of our fellow-countrymen might be still aboard some of the prahus; but this was not very likely, as the sailors had ceased to go to and fro, and the work of unlading seemed at an end.

We were kept for some time on the beach, surrounded by the nearly-naked mob, which crowded about us in a manner that, owing to the abominable grease rubbed over their bodies, was anything but agreeable; but though they jabbered and pointed, and lifted up the children that they might not lose the show, no one did us any violence. This was better than we expected; indeed, it had seemed likely enough that, as soon as the islanders were informed of the damage we had inflicted on the lives and property of their friends and relatives, they would turn on us and take summary vengeance. On the contrary, they exhibited considerable friendship, and, in one instance, a degree of good nature that could not have been excelled in the most civilized country in the world; for we had not stood there many minutes when a woman, observing the blood trickling down my leg, came forward, and, enlarging the rent in my trousers caused by the slash of the kris, examined the wound just above my knee, and then proceeded to chew some green leaves to a mash, which she applied to my limb as tenderly as though I had been her son. The salve made me smart terribly at first, but in a few moments the pain subsided, and, what was of much more importance, the bleeding entirely ceased.

So touched was I at this kindness of the woman's, that, forgetting that she did not understand a jot of what I said, I thanked her in the heartiest way, as did Tom Cox, who, moreover, and as proving that he had profited by the good teaching of the mate of the " Margaret," added that she might depend that God would reward her for her goodness. The woman, however, seemed inclined for some more immediate reward, and, handling the clasp-knife which still hung at my waist, plainly enough intimated the wish that I would give it to her. Only too glad to convince her of my gratitude, without a moment's hesitation I slipped the lashing of the knife and offered it; but at this one of our jailers took mighty offence, and, raising his bamboo sum-pitan, dealt me a blow over the knuckles that made them tingle again, at the same time reproving me in such a bullying tone as to recall me at once to the miserable truth that now I was a slave whose very life, let alone his worldly gear, was the property of his masters.

Presently the mob began to cry out and look in a particular direction, as did we, and saw coming towards us an individual, who, by hi superior dress and the extra massiveness of the silver rings whic adorned his arms and ankles, we saw was a person of some conse quence; indeed, when he approached closer, we at once recognized him as the commander of the pirate fleet, and whose vessel was the first to be mauled by the "Sultan's" six-pounder. He was accompanied by several who appeared to be petty officers, and when he came within a dozen yards or so of where we stood, the fellows who had us in custody made signs for us to fall on our knees and kiss the earth. Now, although both Tom and I had mutually agreed to endeavour to conciliate our captors by a show of ready and cheerful obedience, we were not a little astonished at this monstrous request. It seemed like nothing else than voluntarily subscribing to the bond that consigned us slaves till death to these ignorant barbarians—a setting of our lips to the dust as a seal is set to the wax, and resigning irrevocably all that was Christian or manly in us.

"What does this mean, Reuben?" asked Tom, as the crowd continued to gesticulate to point to the ground, and make signs of kissing.

"It means that we are to fall down and salute the earth before the mighty fellow now approaching," returned I, in the same hurried whisper.

"I'll see them all ——"

Where or what it was that Tom intended to express that he would see them all before he would so demean himself, I can't say, for it happened that he had got no further in his rebellious answer when our custodians made short work of his objections by tripping up poor Tom's heels, so that he fell flat on his face; and, fearing a similar fate, I, too, flung myself down, and, by way of compensating myself for the indignity, instead of kissing the earth, I joined Tom Cox, as we both lay on our faces, in cursing the villain in the great silver bangles, and all the rest of the savage crew, in the heartiest manner.

Presently, however, we received orders to rise, Tom assisting me in the tenderest way, and then politely pulling his forelock to him who, for the present, I will call the captain, at the same time pointing to my leg in explanation. The captain, who was an old man with a shrivelled visage and scarcely a tooth in his head, as soon as he saw how matters stood, ordered one of those who clustered about him to examine us. Tom's turn came first, but they made light of his injury, grinning and nudging each other when the rag was raised, and the place where his ear had been exposed. Tom grinned too, but if they imagined his was a mirthful grin they were much mistaken. After pulling at his legs and arms, and punching him about the chest, the doctor pushed him aside with a grunt of satisfaction, and then took me in hand.

As I expected, my case was not so easily disposed of. The rough

The Dyak Doctor.

usage I had lately been subjected to had set me trembling and fainting almost, and the bitter thought that I was looking ten times worse than I was in reality, no doubt greatly aggravated the lugubrious expression of my countenance. Even the villain who proceeded to strip me, the better to judge of my condition, gave a grin and shrugged his shoulders. It was not a grin of pity, however, for he hauled off my jacket without ceremony, and as though it was not worth while to waste time over so worthless an article as myself. My shirt sleeve was saturated with blood, and had clung to my wound, but taking the sleeve by the wristband the rascal gave it a pull, which tore it away from the shoulder, causing the gash in my arm to stream afresh, and inflicting on me such exquisite pain that I cried out.

My arm ready for inspection an old fellow, of rather more decent appearance than the rest, and who wore a pouch at his belt containing healing herbs and such other things as pertained to his business, which was that of a doctor, stepped forward and examined the injured limb with much concern, and then turned to report his opinion to the chief, who, finding little interest in the examination of a damaged slave, was by this time busy with the plundered merchandise. While the two were talking, however, the brute who had torn off my shirt sleeve perceived the bloody condition of my trousers' leg, and inserting his finger in the hole the weapon had made, ripped the cloth, and brought to view the wound. The doctor was recalled, and after a moment's inspection shook his head in a way that was not to be misunderstood, and once more went away to talk with my owner, the great pirate captain.

Ignorant as I was of the language of the people about me, it was easy enough to perceive that the present was a very ticklish time for me; but *how* ticklish it was I never knew till long afterwards, when I had learned to speak the Dyak tongue, and could converse with individuals who were present during my surgical examination.

" Well," asked the chief, " may he be cured ?"

" Great care and skill may save his life," replied the doctor, dubiously.

" And make of him a sound slave ?" said the chief, interrogatively.

" Nay, I said not so," replied the doctor. " He may be made sound to eat and to drink, but sound and able to labour he will never be. He will go lame as long as he lives."

" Bah !" replied the old savage, contemptuously, " we war for our profit, and not to fill the country with cripples; since you cannot cure him, the sooner you take off his head the better." So saying he turned away, while a great villain, armed with a tremendous sword of the sabre pattern, and who as it turned out was the chief executioner and the constant attendant on the great captain, stepped forward and clapped his hand on my shoulders.

As before observed I could not understand a word of the conversation that had taken place between the old doctor and the captain, but their gestures were significant enough; and when, as a climax, the hideous swordsman took me in hand, I could no longer doubt what my fate was, and now completely overcome I cried good-bye to Tom, and drooped my head that the barbarians might not see my tears.

And truly my case did seem utterly hopeless. My case had been fully considered, I had been condemned to death, and the executioner had hold of me. Nay, he had turned me about, and we had advanced a few paces in the direction as I suppose of the spot where my murder was to be done, when suddenly there occurred some stir among the group we had just left, and a name was uttered aloud, whereon the giant, who still held me by the shoulder halted, and after listening to a few words which some one in authority addressed to him he gave a growl of impatience, and walked me back to where the old doctor and the captain stood, conversing with a youngish man, whom I had observed narrowly watching the doctor as he was examining my wounds.

As I approached the group this young fellow (who certainly possessed a countenance far more intelligent than any other I could see about me), addressed himself to a close scrutiny of my injured limbs, turning from time to time to report to the captain, and in such terms as made the old doctor, who stood by, protest, and grunt, and distort his ugly face in such a variety of ways by way of giving additional force to his expressions of contempt for the young man's opinions, that the captain grinned till he displayed the whole of his toothless gums, and evidently was much tickled at the joke involved in the contest of medical opinion. As for me I saw nothing to laugh at, though to be sure nobody had a greater interest in the matter than I had. I was so low-spirited and plunged in wretchedness, that had I been able to understand the talk of the doctors I should have had no heart to have listened, as who would on whom sentence of death was already passed, and at whose side stood the executioner fidgeting to carry me away and complete his job? Had I thought, however, how momentous that conversation which seemed so funny to the captain was to me, I should indeed have opened my ears to their full, albeit I should have benefited nothing from the outlandish babble which would have been poured into them.

Being quite without hope, the stroke of good luck fell on me all the more astonishingly. All of a sudden, and to my great amazement, the captain spoke a single word to the executioner, whose hand at once fell from my shoulder, and then the young man with a kindly gesture led me over to where Tom was, and stood me by his side. For full a minute I could scarcely believe my senses, and judging from his appearance Tom was in pretty much the same condition.

"Well," whispered he at last, "if ever you hear me denying that there is such a thing as a 'sweet little cherub that sits up aloft,' just you call this miracle to my mind, Reu. I set you down as dead and gone a minute ago, and here you are with a free pardon, as one may say."

"Perhaps it's only a respite, Tom," I replied, feeling at present quite afraid to believe in my good fortune. "Perhaps it isn't quite suitable to kill me just now; they have seasons for killing, may be, and laws to abide by."

"That I don't believe," said Tom, bluntly. "Unless I'm much mistaken, any season is killing season with these villains, and their laws are fitted to their pockets. Did ever you dream of such a horrible crew, Reu?"

"Nay, Tom," said I, "you cannot expect me to speak hardly of men who have but just now spared my life."

"And pray are you such a fool as to imagine that it is saved for your own using? D'ye think if curing your wounds would cost a ha'porth more ointment than you will be worth when you are made sound, that you would have had a head to your shoulders by this time? Nonsense, my lad. I can argue from eyesight as well as any man; and you may take my word, that the reason of this bobbery and shilly-shallying this way and that is to settle whether you will pay for plastering. They think that you will. Very good; and on that account, and as far as you're concerned, I say good luck to 'em."

And here I may inform the reader that Tom was, at least, partly right in his conjecture as to the motives of our captors; but he was not entirely right, nor could he possibly have been so without knowing something of the character and condition of the rival M.D.'s, who had in turn inspected me. The young man, it seems, Anakraja by name, had, by dint of cunning, and, as I verily believe, of superior intelligence as well, pushed his way from a position of insignificance to one of con- siderable importance in the old chief's service; indeed, excepting the

old doctor (who, by the by, had taught the young one all he knew of the
healing art) no one was more respected; and though the chief himself
was still inclined to favour the old man before the young one, the latter
had a fast friend in no less an important personage than the chief's
mother, and who, in consequence of her great age and increasing infir-

Reuben Davidger and Tom Cox approach the Pirate Village.

mities, kept the young man pretty constantly engaged at the palace, thus
affording him opportunities of currying favour which his rival was
debarred from.   On this account great jealousy existed between the two.
The chief, despite his ripe years, was still most submissive to his mother's
will, and obeyed her in all things; therefore it was not politic in the
old doctor to express all the disgust he felt for the thriving Anakraja,

lest that young man should carry his plaint to the old woman, who
might advise her son to pack him—the old doctor—about his business.
Nevertheless, he lost no opportunity where he might, with apparent
fairness, dispute Anakraja's skill; and as precisely the same feeling
animated both men, thus it was that my life was saved. As the old
doctor was turning away to leave me to certain death, the young one
went up to the chief, and begged that he might be allowed to look at
my wounds, at the same time hinting that white slaves were of the
very best sort, full of all kinds of cunning and contrivance, and that
if there was a possibility of saving me it would be much to the chief's
advantage. The old doctor replied sarcastically to this, but, nevertheless, the chief intimated that the young fellow might examine me.
This he did, and, for the furtherance of his own ends, affected to
regard my hurts as the merest trifles, and pledged his word to the
captain to set me up as strong and able as ever I was in all my life,
and that in the space of six weeks. The captain laughed at this, and
told the young doctor that since he promised so confidently he would
be expected to keep his word, as otherwise it might be the worse for
him. This business concluded, he passed on with his officers to inspect
his fleet, and see what injury it had sustained, while Tom Cox and
myself—I leaning on Tom's shoulder—were shortly afterwards
marched into the village. I call it a village because I have no other
term for it, but, regarded in an English sense, it was no village at all,
but rather one gigantic homestead enclosed by a slight stockade.

It was by this time quite dusk, and, seen in the uncertain light,
the spectacle presented by this single and vast abode of the pirates
was very amazing. I have said it was more a homestead than a
village; but, if the reader pictures it as an English homestead, he will
be again mistaken. It was like this: Atop of a long row of piles,
consisting of the green trunks of trees, with the branches but roughly
lopped, that the projections might serve as the spars of a ladder, was
a wide and long platform of split bamboo. This platform was as wide
as Cheapside, and, I should say, as long; maybe, if you included the
Poultry, it would not exceed the length of the platform; for, afterwards having a fair opportunity of measuring it, I found it could not
be paced from end to end under four hundred and seventy steps,
which I take to be equal to four hundred yards. This terrace, the
proper use of which seemed to be as a promenade, served as the resort

of pigs, and dogs, and chickens, besides several monkeys, large and small, which climbed the posts, and chattered and grinned at the uncommon sight of a man with a white skin. At the back of the terrace the dwelling-place was constructed, extending from one end of it to the other, and built chiefly of bamboo, and grass, and mud, with doorways screened by mats, and no windows. Only a few very old folks and some young children were at these mat-hung doors, so that we presumed that the entire population, or, at least, as much of it as was capable, had turned out to escort us. Over this vast shed was another shallow story, which, to judge from the odds and ends that were visible through the apertures, must have been used as a store-place for tools and such articles as were only required at particular seasons.

However, as the reader may imagine, we were in no case to examine very critically; besides, if we had been at liberty to do so, it was, as I have before observed, growing quite dark, and we could not distinguish anything about us very plainly. What we were chiefly concerned about was as to what sort of treatment we should receive, where should we be lodged, and what should we get to eat; for it will be remembered that very many hours had passed since we had either drunk or eaten.

At last we arrived at the end of the perched-up platform, and came upon two or three little huts, not vastly bigger than pigsties, and looking as though they were capable of affording about the same amount of satisfaction to a human tenant. One of these, however, was selected for our lodging, and, though there was evidently a debate whether we should be housed together or separately, we were rejoiced to find that we were not to be parted, and were presently thrust into one of the huts, the entrance to which was overhung by a mat, which descended from the roof to the ground.

Having thus provided us with lodging, the men who had escorted us turned out of the place, and left us to ourselves. There was plenty that we wanted to talk about; but having no doubt that our jailers were on guard outside the door, and not knowing but that one or other of them might have some knowledge of the English tongue, for a considerable time we refrained from opening our mouths, except once, when Tom asked me if I had such a thing as a quid of tobacco about me, and with which I luckily—for curiously enough we had not been searched—was able to supply him. At last Tom whispered—

"The fellows outside are mighty quiet, Reu."

"Perhaps they are listening. That may be the reason why they have put us together," I replied in the same guarded whisper.

"Well, they won't hear any good of themselves if they listen for a week," said Tom, making himself comfortable in a corner.

But although we both endeavoured to make believe that it was a matter of indifference whether or no the sentries were listening, we could not rest easy under the suspicion, and presently Tom crawled stealthily along the floor, and applied first his remaining ear and then his eye to a crevice in the mat door. The moon by this time had got up, so that he had a fine view.

"Why, I don't believe there is any one on sentry at all," said he; and then, to make sure, he thrust out his head, and looked far and wide.

"Well, this is a rum go!" he exclaimed. "Hang me, Reu, if they haven't gone away, and left us free to cut and run!" And having relieved himself of this speech, Tom gave way to a succession of grins, that made him a more cheerful object to look on than I had seen for many an hour.

"But perhaps they're only gone to fetch us some supper, Tom," I observed.

"Well, perhaps so," replied he; "let us hope that they will look no sharper after us then, than now; eh, my hearty?" said Master Cox. "We won't put 'em to the expense of providing us with breakfast; will we, Reu?"

"They'll be put to the trouble of eating the supper they are cooking for us if they are not quick with it," said I.

"Did you ever hear tell of such ignorant beggars?" chuckled Tom.

"They'll stare to find the empty cage and the birds flown," said I; and, despite our aches and ailments, we quite enjoyed a laugh at the expense of our foolish captors.

"As soon as they settle down for the night, and the coast is clear, we will slip off, and——"

"And what, Tom? Where shall we slip off to?"

The hopeful clasp with which each held the hand of the other relaxed dismally as this important feature of the running away question occurred to us. We were on an island, and whichever way we ran we were certain in the end to be stopped by the sea, if even, in our ignorance of the geography of the place and the customs of the inhabitants, we did not betray our intention before we had journeyed a mile. To " slip off," therefore, would but be to get from the gridiron into the fire ; and all in the dark, and very much chopfallen, we were compelled to admit that our friends the Dyaks were not nearly so foolish as they at first appeared.

Besides, in what condition was I to run away ? My unlucky leg had been not at all improved by our walk from the landing-place to the hut, and so weighed me down, that to recline on the rushes or grass, or whatever it was, with which the floor of the hut was strewn, seemed the most desirable thing in the world, and I was not at all sorry when, in despair, Tom flung himself down too, and disturbed me by no more propositions in the carrying out of which my lame leg would be bound to assist.

We may have lain there rather more than an hour when we heard approaching footsteps, and saw, through the chinks of the walls, three men coming our way. They turned out to be the young doctor who was pledged to cure me, a man with a great bundle of soft rushes, and another who carried two wooden vessels, one of which we found contained about half a gallon of water, and the other a mess of rice and fish seemingly stewed together. These things they set on the ground ; and while, by the light of the torch of wood-splints, one fellow spread the rushes, and the other assisted the doctor in making ready his salve, we set to work on the contents of the two tubs. We first gave our attention to the one containing the water, and by a long and grateful swig each, entirely emptied it. In this, however, we were wrong ; the water being intended for washing our wounds, and not for drinking ; and one of the villains, discovering Tom Cox in the act of draining the biggin, caught him a sounding spank with his open hand, and made as though he would take away the other tub which contained our supper. At this, however, the doctor interfered, and sent the fellow off to re-fill the water-vessel.

But now there appeared another difficulty. Truly we were much in need of victuals, and there it stood, smoking and savoury enough ; but how were we to get at it ? I should have mentioned that when we were first left to ourselves our jack-knives had been taken from us, and they had evidently forgotten to bring us either knife, fork, or spoon ; at least, being in ignorance of their hoggish ways, we thought they had forgotten these things, and I thought I might venture to remind one of our attendants of the oversight. So I nudged him, and, showing him my empty hands, and pointing to the stirabout, shook my head. The fellow, like all the rest with whom we had any correspondence, was quick enough of comprehension, and at once proceeded to show that he understood my signs by plunging his dirty fist into the mess, and, helping himself to a great mouthful of the rice, grinned and nodded his head, as much as to say, " There ! that's the way to do it." What our feelings for the moment were may be easily imagined, but we were in no condition to affect squeamishness ; so, first cleansing our hands as well as we were able on the rushes, we took the tub between us, and, with many a rueful grin, scooped up the mess to the last scrap.

Then the physician, whose salves were ready, did his very best to make me comfortable; so tenderly and carefully did he set about his business, that I wish I could lay it all to his good nature ; but I could not help reflecting that he was curing me for his own sake, and not my own, and that if I should happen to die in spite of him, he would be much more ready to curse me for marring his plans than to mourn me. That this really was the state of the case he presently furnished ample proof; for, having finished with me, Tom stepped forward and presented his raw stump for surgical treatment, but the doctor turned about scornfully, and gave one of the fellows with him orders to furnish Tom with a little ointment. Again he showed how small was his concern in my companion's welfare. I found that the fresh rushes the man had brought in were spread in one corner, and just of sufficient width for one to lie on ; but seeing which way our jailers were bent, and that to thwart them would very likely make matters worse, I winked at Tom to take no notice, but laid down on the soft heap, while he pretended to compose himself on a few old rushes which he raked together in an opposite corner; but as soon as we were left to ourselves we altered this arrangement, and, quite worn out, were presently asleep.

We were awakened next morning by a sound so familiar and English, that, ushering us out of our dreams of home, it saved us from the momentary shock that might have ensued on our opening our eyes to the walls and barbarous garniture of our bed-chamber. It was the sound of crowing of cocks, and neither Tom nor I having heard a cock crow out of England, could but associate the sound with civilization; indeed, after we had become sufficiently awake to discover the true state of affairs, and to review the proceedings of the previous night, the cocks still continuing to crow brought us no inconsiderable amount of comfort.

"How do you feel this morning, old boy?" asked Tom kindly.

"Why, ten pounds better at least, thank ye, Tom," I replied, and truly, if the degrees of so precious a thing as health may be measured by such dross as money. "D'ye hear the cocks, Tom?"

"I do, Reuben," replied he cheerily, "and I hear the pigs squealing. Now, in my opinion, where there's pigs and cocks, and that sort of thing—things in the farming way, you know, Reuben—the people can't be such cannibal wretches as we at first supposed 'em. One can't fancy a man-eater making hay or digging potatoes, you know."

"Well, Tom, let us get outside, and have a peep at the sort of place fortune has tossed us on."

So we went outside—my leg being so far improved that, though I was obliged to limp, I was put to very little pain—and first of all were for rambling towards the great terrace we had passed the night before; but we could see in the distance that, though the poultry and the various animals that lodged there were awake and on the move, there was no sign of a human being, which could scarcely be wondered at, considering that it was as yet barely broad daylight.

"Perhaps it will be better for us not to make too bold, Tom," said I; "if one may judge from their stowing us so far from where they live, they would rather have our room than our company; and no doubt they will come after us quite as soon as they want us. Suppose, therefore, we venture on a bit of a bathe in the sea?"

To this Tom was quite agreeable; and so we made our way towards the back of the village, which was so near to the ocean that there wa only room for a few sheds (likewise built on piles driven into the shore, and beneath which several small prahus and countless sampans were sheltered) between it and high-tide mark.

For my part, the hurt to my arm prevented my swimming; so I could do no more, when stripped, than paddle in waist-high, holding my bandaged limb high and dry, and laving myself with the other. But as for Tom, he could swim like a duck; and when I had had enough, and was dressed again, he was still frolicking about fifty yards from the shore, and enjoying himself as little like a one-eared slave as can be imagined. Presently, however, and before Tom seemed to have had nearly enough of it, casting my eyes about, I saw a troop of people coming from our deserted hut; and no sooner did they spy me all alone on the beach than they set up a terrible whooping, and came rushing up at the top of their speed.

As almost all the savages were armed, and seeing that they seized me in a very threatening manner, Tom hesitated whether he should come ashore; but, on reflecting that drowning was the only alternative, he altered his mind and came, and was seized too, such being their hurry to march us somewhere that Tom was only allowed time to slip on his drawers, and walked along with his jacket and trousers slung over his shoulders.

Taking into consideration the evident eagerness of the messengers, together with their vehement gesticulation and excitement, it was impossible to avoid the suspicion that something had occurred sudden and unexpected, and which nearly concerned us. Whatever it was, certainly it was not of a secret character, for the fellows about us talked loudly one to the other, and made signs with their fingers, and addressed observations to us, all bearing, as it was easy enough to understand, on the business in hand, but of which neither Tom nor I could make either head or tail; so we could do no more than shut our ears to their unintelligible jargon, and discuss together where we were probably going, and what our fate would be.

Tom's chief concern was his trousers. " I wish they would allow me just to slip my slacks on," said he; " 'pearances are everything, my boy, all over the world; and s'pose we are now on our road to the mayor or the magistrate, or something in the savage way that answers for one or the other, a pretty figure I shall cut!"

But our conductors seemed in no way inclined to slacken their pace for a quarter so long a time as it would have taken my companion to adjust his habiliments decently; a strong hand was on each of our shoulders, and there were men in front to show the pace, and men behind to hustle us along. This, however, only lasted just so long as we remained in view of the village, from the houses of which,

especially from the middle and tallest house, we could see a great
number of people beckoning with their hands, and waving scraps of
cloth, as though to urge us to greater haste; but presently, when we
came to a bend in the road from whence the village was shut out, to
our great dismay the whole party halted as though by common consent, everybody uttering a hurried ejaculation which might very well
have been, " Now's the time !" and beckoning one to the other, and
looking eagerly up and down the road as though they had business in
hand which had best be executed before no more witnesses than such
as were then present. They clustered round us in a ring and elbowed
each other, every one seeming anxious to lay hands on us.

"It's all over now, Reu, my boy !" ejaculated Tom Cox dolefully.
" Didn't I tell you that it wasn't for our sakes that ———"

But before he could finish the sentence a dozen great hands were
extended towards his throat, one indeed stuffed into his mouth, as
though to stifle his cries. Presently Tom was down on his knees,
but whether he was forced to that devout posture, or voluntarily
assumed it as proper to one in his last extremity, I had no time to
judge, for in an instant I was seized in a similar fashion, my throat
being squeezed in the most cruel manner, while as many dirty fingers
as could find room were poked at my lips, some endeavouring to
force my mouth asunder. I could not see Tom, but I could hear him
gurgling and spluttering in a way that made my blood run cold to
hear, especially when it suddenly flashed to my mind that among the
punishments inflicted on their slaves by Eastern barbarians was that of
plucking out the tongue ! To save myself from such horrible torture
I set my jaws close, determined never to open them while I had the
strength to resist. This was not long, however, for, observing my
obstinacy, extra pressure was applied to my throat; presently my
senses began to fail and my jaws to fall helplessly ajar, and I was
conscious of a great finger and thumb being thrust into my mouth.

The finger and thumb bungled about my mouth, but to my surprise they seemed to have no business with my tongue, only with my
teeth. Molars and incisors they grasped them every one, and endeavoured to shake them; while the mob craned their necks, and
leant over a-tiptoe with eyes full of wonder and expectation. This
was all; in a few moments the finger and thumb were withdrawn, and
my tongue was at least for the present safe and sound.

I had been forced to the ground in the struggle, and as they assisted me to rise, Tom was rising also; and as our eyes met there was so much of sheepish consciousness in each that for once we had halloed before we were hurt, that we simultaneously burst out laughing, an act which our custodians regarded with evident suspicion, and regarded each other as though they thought that what they sought in our mouths was there after all, and that they had been baffled by our cunning. However, it seemed that there was no time for a second inspection, and so forming in the same order as before they set forward at a brisker rate even than before, as though to make amends for the delay.

What could this mysterious proceeding mean? Tom Cox suggested that perhaps these barbarians judge of the age of animals as English horse-dealers judge of their steeds, by an inspection of their teeth, and that they were anxious to try the same means to ascertain how old we were. Let this be how it might, two things were certain: firstly, that the inspection of our mouths had not been satisfactory, for since that performance they had done nothing but whisper ominously ogether, and shake their heads in a disappointed way; and, secondly, it was equally clear that they had no right to examine our jaws at all, for, on presently discovering that their rough handling had made my mouth to bleed, they all instantly stopped, evidently in great consternation, and ran about here and there, hunting along the wayside for certain leaves to eradicate the tell-tale. This was accomplished with great alacrity; but the stoppage was evidently suspected by the impatient ones at the village, for, before we could emerge from the bend, a gun was fired as a hint that a little more haste was desirable.

At length we came to the commencement of the high-perched row of huts, and, pointing to one of the notched logs before mentioned, and which were substitutes for ladders, we were motioned to ascend. This to Tom, although still incommoded by his misplaced trousers, was an easy matter, and he was aloft while I was painfully endeavouring to make with my lame leg good toe-hold for a second step; but the fellows behind, and who since the firing of the gun had been in a mightier hurry than ever, commenced pushing me in the rear, and hustling me in a manner that would speedily have undone all the good the young doctor had effected, had it not happened that that identical worthy came hurrying up in a great rage, and, unlucky for my assaulters, with a thickish bamboo in his hand. With this he laid over the heads and shoulders of the fellows, abusing them at the same time in terms so hearty and indignant, that one might have suspected that I had been his nearest and dearest blood relation rather than a poor slave whom he had undertaken to cure for charity's sake; then, having laid about him till he was tired, he beckoned to a sturdy savage, and bade him take me on his back, and carry me up the notched log, which he did, and with as much freedom as though he had been a monkey and I his kitten.

Escorted by the entire population, from the oldest to the little naked toddler of three or four years, we traversed half the length of the terrace, which was not pleasant to walk on, being composed of bamboo lashed together in parcels of about a foot in width, and laid down with a space of about five inches between. I may as well here mention that, at the time, we imagined that these openings in the flooring were for sanitary purposes merely, and, considering the large number of birds and animals herding on and about it, the inference was not unreasonable; but we afterwards found the real use of these openings was to afford a means of attacking any body of besiegers who might fall on the village. The most favourite mode of assault by an enemy was, under cover of their shields, to rush under the flooring of the elevated village, and then to make several great bonfires, first hacking away the ladders that the miserable inhabitants might not escape. By means, however, of the slits in the floor, the attackers could be thrust at with spears, and shot at with poisoned arrows from bows and sumpitans, or deluged with measures of scalding water.

In a little while we arrived at the centre hut of the row, which, as already mentioned, was somewhat taller than the rest, and further distinguished by a length of yellow stuff hung out from a hole near the roof, bannerwise. The doorway of this, the chief hut, was concealed by a great heavy mat of plaited grass, and before this stood two herculean fellows, naked but for several broad rings of metal worn about their elbows and ankles, and a short petticoat, made of some sort of tree-bark, about their waists. Each of these guards bore in his hand a curved sword, and with the handle and the flat of it did not scruple to push off such of the mob as pressed too hardly on them.

As we and our conductors approached, the people fell back, and the sentries drew aside the mat screen, and in another instant we were introduced to a scene never to be forgotten, though I may live to be a hundred years old. The floor of the place was of the same material as that of the outer terrace, but plentifully strewn with green rushes, which were deliciously cool to the feet. The building itself was about thirty feet long, twenty broad, and fifteen high, and the walls on every side were plentifully decorated with curious shields, and bows, and arrows, and sumpitans, and krisses, and ranjows, and many other weapons of Dyak warfare, concerning which the reader will, by and by, hear further particulars. Neither were the samples of weapons of war confined to those of native manufacture; there were, besides, many English weapons—cutlasses, and muskets, and boarding-pikes, polished bright as mirrors, and looking very familiar and homely with the English letters—the king's brand, G. R.—plainly to be seen. As well as decorating the walls, some of these war tools hung suspended from the beams overhead. Nor were these the only symbols of battle and bloodshed that hung there; and what else there was was of so repulsive a nature, that only my full determination to omit no fact of interest from this history should compel me to describe it. Full in view of all who entered at the door were hung by hooks nineteen human heads, in a double row. At first glance I fully expected to find among them the heads of our crew and passengers, but was much relieved to find that they were all even blacker than the living native heads about us, and were, moreover, as mummified as that of the New Zealander I used to see in the shop at Bloomsbury. Some of the hideous relics had the teeth dyed red, others wore them quite white and glistening, while others, again, were jetty black as ebony, showing distinctly behind the dusky narrow lips that clung to their bases. Had these heads, however, been those of their dearest friends, they could not have been better preserved; they were brushed and polished, and, lacking eyes, were furnished each with a couple of shining white beans, painted in the centre, and making an imitation horribly true. No brush of fox or antlers of stag that ever graced the hall of a huntsman, could have been more carefully kept than were these ghastly trophies.

But, at the risk of offending my reader by making a very abrupt digression from the level passage of my story, I will give a few particulars of this head business; and this both for my credit's sake—for doubtless, the reader, ignorant of the true state of the case, must begin to suspect me to be a person with a morbid inclination to linger about horrible matters—and for the sake of the character of my masters, the Dyaks.   Really, there is nothing villanous in this one of their most singular customs, repulsive as it must appear to a Christian people.   Head-getting is with them a very ancient and respectable institution, and its observance as honourably regarded as the capture

The Dyak Head Dance.

of ordinary war trophies among ourselves.   Nay, it has this advantage, that it has a religious as well as a social consequence.   The Bornean implicitly believes that the head is the seat of man's spirit, and that, even after death, this fleshy tenancy is maintained until the habitation decays and perishes.   Great, however, as is this barbarian's respect for " spirits," he has much more for his own cunning, and, in time of war, he sets this latter ruling quality of his against ghostly power, and seeks through it to make his advantage.   For example, when a

Dyak warrior brings in from the battle-field the head of an enemy, he takes it first of all to his family, and then the women-folk paint and otherwise decorate it, and the whole family proceed rejoicingly with the trophy to the council-house, where it is hung up, and addressed by the soldier whose property it is something to the following effect :— " Oh, good spirit, do not be angry with us for removing you in your house"—the head—" to this our village; it was to your good that we did it. Had you been lain with your decaying body in a narrow hole in the earth, there you would have remained lonely and without a single companion; now you may look around, and see peeping from the windows of their houses the spirits of many of your countrymen, and, should you desire the society of an acquaintance—of a brother, or your father even—you have only to beguile him into our path, and we will surely bring his head here to you, and hang it so close that you can converse together and be comfortable."

Nor is a state of war necessary to the furnishing the house of council with heads. Should a man lose his son, or his daughter, or his wife, he will leave his house, and never return till he has avenged the death by slaying one of his nation's enemies, whose head he brings home as indisputable evidence that he has conformed to the custom proper to be observed in such cases. Again, no young Dyak may take a wife until he has proved himself a worthy man and a warrior by robbing a fellow-creature of his head. He sets out on his errand with the blessings of his parents and the good wishes of his friends, and is regarded by all who know him much in the same light as the virtuous young Suffolk labourer who shoulders his bundle and sets out for London, that he may make his fortune, and return and marry the ambitious grazier's daughter. The chances of both young men are about equal; for whereas he of Suffolk may haply miss the road to fortune, and, instead of picking up gold and silver, be brought to picking an uncertain crust from the city's byway, so may the young Dyak, lying down on the road to sleep away his fatigue, and dream that he is already in possession of the gory key to a life of happiness, be overtaken by the enemy, haply likewise in search of matrimonial credentials; then the business is settled in the flash of a kris, and the hand of the maid of Magindano remains unclaimed.

To return, however, to the point of digression. At the farther end of the council-chamber into which Tom and I were ushered, and squatted on a pile of mattresses, which, without doubt, had seen service in the cabins of some honest European ship, was the old chief of the pirate fleet, and beside him an ugly old woman, withered with age, and bearing about her lean brown body a donkey-load almost of gold and precious stones. Her legs, from the ankles to the knees, were covered with bands of the precious metal, as were her arms, both below and above the elbow; while the lobes of her ears were dragged far down towards her shoulders by the weight of the clumsy rings they afforded hanging to. These latter were set with brilliant stones, as was a strange-looking circlet of gold about her forehead, her white hair sticking out in every direction from between its inner rim and a crimson velvet smoking-cap, with a golden tassel, that was perched jauntily on the summit of her cranium.

Her most conspicuous feature, however, has yet to be mentioned— it was her mouth. What made it conspicuous was a monstrous set of teeth—not monstrous from their crookedness or ill colour, but from their great size. Her mouth was filled to overflowing with them; they projected even beyond her lips, and their shape was visible through her thin cheeks. Both she and the old chief were most obsequiously attended by those in waiting; and while one of them was oiling the old woman's shoulders and arms, another was fanning off the flies attracted by the odoriferous process.

As soon as these two grandees observed us, they at once beckoned us forward, and forward we came, the crowd of courtiers falling into line on either side to make way; and seeing that it was expected that we should do homage in the customary manner, it occurred to us that this was no time to be fastidious, so down we floundered, and for a moment cooled our noses among the green rushes. So eager, how- ever, were the chief and his mother—for such we afterwards dis- covered her to be—to proceed with the business in hand, that we were speedily lifted to our feet, and made to kneel before the mattresses.

Still reclining, the chief addressed to us a few words in a quick and haughty tone, and which, no doubt, conveyed some command, of the nature of which we were, of course, no more aware than if he had not opened his mouth. Not to give more offence than necessary, we signified by dumb motions our ignorance of his language, and our great sorrow that such should be the case, whereon the chief turned with a gesture of impatience to a man on his right hand, and doubtless, bade him make known his commands to us. This minister was evidently a shrewd fellow, and discerning at once that it was no use addressing us in terms of speech, at once proceeded to a very lively correspondence in pantomime. He clapped both his hands to his jaws, made the motion of eating, put his fingers into his mouth, and made pretence to pull out all his teeth, and then commenced to nod his head very knowingly, and to point at our mouths, as though it was impossible that we could for another moment fail to comprehend his meaning.

As the reader may easily imagine, however, our former confusion was, by his antics, only worse confounded, especially when it flashed to our recollection that the messengers who had fetched us in such a hurry from the beach had manifested much the same sort of curiosity respecting our mouths.

"What on earth can they mean, Tom?" said I, turning in bewilderment to my companion.

But Tom, whose head was fairly in a maze, clung despairingly to his original notion that their inquisitiveness about our teeth all arose from a desire to ascertain our respective ages, and at once proceeded in the most energetic way to convince our interrogators that he quite understood them by holding up his fingers till he had exhibited a number corresponding with his age last birthday; at the same time earnestly advising me to lose no time in following his example, as it was evident that the old chief was growing each moment more angry. But, to my companion's infinite distress, this display of his digits seemed not at all to mollify the old gentleman; on the contrary, with a frown and a growl, he unsheathed his jewel-hilted kris, and made as though he would whip off Tom's head on the spot; but his mother, laying her hand on his arm, gently restrained him, and at the same moment put up her other hand to her mouth, and drawing therefrom an entire double row of grinders, held them before our eyes, regarding us with a grin which, now that her jaws were allowed to close naturally together, was rather startling to contemplate. Indeed, it would have been difficult to decide which of the two was the most repulsive, the face of the old chief's mother or that of one of the unlucky passengers, whose head had hitherto been concealed in the folds of a cloth lying on the mattresses, and which the old woman now held up before our eyes, pointing, as she did so, at the mouth of it, that we might see

its emptiness, and at once understand the source from which the
artificial teeth were derived.

Tom, whose apprehension at best was not of a rapid character, at
this terrible sight was plunged deeper than ever into the slough of
perplexity, and could do nothing else but gaze bewilderedly about him,
and wag his head in wonder. The true state of the case, however, at

Our Jaws are Inspected in Search of Movable Teeth.

once flashed to my mind. It had been discovered that one of the
heads captured from the "Sultan" was furnished with movable teeth,
set cleverly in the gums, and provided with bands and springs of fine
gold, and making altogether a remarkably neat specimen of English
mechanism. It seemed, however, that it was not in this light that the
prize was regarded. Although the Dyak chief's intercourse with

Europeans had been of the most limited character, rumours of their wondrous attributes had, doubtless, reached him; and, therefore, he might be excused if his discovery had led him to jump to the conclusion that detachable teeth were a natural advantage pertaining to the favoured race. That it *was* an advantage he could not but believe, for had he not seen the beautifully sound and white teeth taken from a grey head, whilst he, with hair not nearly so venerable, had scarcely a stump left in his gums? True, the other heads had been most carefully examined, and the teeth in them found to be too firmly bedded for removal, except individually; but then it was possible that their setting might be affected by the rigidity of death, as was the rest of the body. This, as I was afterwards informed, was the line of argument adopted by the chief, and, combined with his vain old mother's unscrupulous appropriation of the splendid teeth, led to our hasty summons to attend before him.

Our position was a critical one. What was to be done? The chief had evidently fixed his mind on a new set of teeth, and seemed not at all inclined tamely to brook disappointment. There was nothing left but to put a bold face on the matter; so, affecting great meekness, I took the artificial teeth from the old woman's hand, and, approaching the chief, endeavoured to make him understand that they were but a substitute for real teeth, the handiwork of man, and a contrivance never resorted to except in cases of premature decay of the masticators originally supplied by nature; and, as a proof that I was telling him the truth, I opened my mouth to its widest, and invited him to inspect it, and to see that neither springs nor metal had a place in its conformation. He at once accepted the invitation, and, with his councillors, minutely inspected my open jaws; while Tom Cox, with his mouth stretched to its fullest capacity, formed a centre of attraction for another group.

The inspection seemed to mollify the chief somewhat; and when they had stared their fill, and satisfied themselves by all sorts of practical and painful experiments that the portable grinders differed in every particular from my own, I was allowed to shut my mouth while the chief and the fellows about him consulted together. Chief among his councillors was my friend the young doctor, and, after Tom and I had been kept in anxious suspense for several minutes, that worthy came over to where we stood, bringing the old woman's artificial teeth in his hand. He moved me a few paces apart from Tom, as though our business was of a nature of which he understood nothing, and then began to handle the teeth in a very significant way, pointing at the springs and the gold plates in which they were set, and then regarding me with an expression that said as plain as speech, "You see how all this is done; you must make an article exactly similar."

It was of no use affecting to misunderstand him; to do so would be but to irritate the old chief, who all the time kept his eyes on us anxiously, even condescending now and then to assist his minister in his explanations by bawling out a few words, and making all manner of hideous contortions with his sparsely-fanged jaws. To tell the truth, I most heartily wished that the job had been one which I could have confidently undertaken, as such a chance of making a friend of the chief of our captors might never occur again; and, besides this, my friend the young doctor had evidently set his heart—and pledged his word, for aught I knew to the contrary—on the proper execution of the work, and, after all he had done for me, I felt no way disinclined to oblige him; but so astonishing a demand, as the reader may very readily understand, took me not a little aback, for I had never worked at any trade—with the exception of now and then basting a straight seam for my father—than stowing a ship's cargo. Still, had it been any rough work that had been asked of me—a job at carpentry, or to build a wall, or even to cobble a pair of shoes—I should have gone at it readily enough, trusting to luck and industry to carry me through; but to be called on, without a moment's warning, to perform the work of a practised mechanical dentist, which would involve measuring and taking a cast of that dreadful old griffin's mouth, and, may be, the extraction of a few obstinate tooth-stumps! I had better be beheaded immediately than prolong my miserable life by attempting it.

I shook my head vehemently, in token that I knew nothing at all about such work, on which my friend smiled and put on a knowing air, as much as to say that that excuse would not avail me. I pointed at my wounded arm; he shrugged his shoulders impatiently. In despair I held out my empty hands, and intimated, as plainly as it was possible by dumb show, that to make a set of artificial teeth, without a single item of the necessary material, was simply impossible; but at this he frowned, and gave a little stamp of impatience. What did I mean? there were teeth to be had in plenty. He pointed

at a dozen gaping mouths, and finished by pointing at mine, and this
with an air of threatening, as though to convey the pleasant hint that
it was not to be expected that the chief should be at a loss for a
grinder while I, or any other fellow in the town, had one left in his
head. In my extremity I took the false teeth, and showing their
smooth under part, and then pointing at the spiky condition of the
chief's mouth, made him understand how impossible it would be to
make a decent job of it. This seemed rather to stagger him in his
confidence; he looked perplexed, and presently went over to the old
chief, and held a longish consultation with him on the subject. To
my great satisfaction the conversation was marked by several dissatisfied grunts on the part of the great man, and most fervently I hoped
that the prospect of having his grinders extracted would induce him
to abandon the entire project. But, alas! the old fellow's vanity was
superior to his dread of the pincers, and in a few minutes my friend
the doctor came back to me radiant with satisfaction, and intimated
that even this last difficulty was overcome; and then, observing that
my distress had not abated, he laughed, and, laying his hand first on
his own breast and then on mine, seemed to convey the intimation
that he would see after minor details, and that between us we should,
no doubt, make an excellent job of it. A little while after the doctor
beckoned me to follow him; but, on Tom Cox attempting to accompany me, he was ordered to stay where he was; and so, to our
mutual distress, he was obliged to remain while I went with the
doctor.

The hut in which the doctor lived was at the extreme end of the
terrace, and consisted of but a single apartment, the interior of which
was perfectly clean; while several large and white mats hung against
the walls, one specially large partly covered the floor. At one end of
the place was a little platform on four legs, somewhat resembling the
humble English stump bedstead, only that the hinder legs, which were
about eighteen inches high, were nearly double the height of those in
front, causing the structure to slant considerably. Moreover, its
upper part was of no softer material than rough planking. Nevertheless, it could be mistaken for nothing else than a bedstead, and such I
afterwards found it to be. Besides this piece of furniture, the hut
contained a sort of low square bench, on which was an iron pot, and
before the pot squatted a woman, pounding away with a sort of minia-

ture paviour's rammer at something the pot contained in the most vigorous way, leaving off only to stir or replenish a wood fire that burned in the middle of the room, the smoke finding its way out at a hole in the roof. The walls of the place were decorated with three or four copper and iron pans, a string of little bells, a shield, the ordinary Dyak weapons of war, and a couple of human skulls slung together and hanging from one string.

As soon as we entered, the doctor motioned me to be seated, and ordered his wife to give me something to eat. She complied by going to a corner before which hung a mat, and bringing out a wooden trencher containing things which from their shape were eggs, but which from their colour might have been black plums, and from their smell anything but human food. I could not forbear a gesture of disgust as the dish was presented to me, when my host, to reassure me, took up one and whipped it into his mouth, smacking his lips as though it was very delicious. However, I was not to be persuaded, and, peeping into the iron pot, and discovering it was rice the woman had been pounding, I expressed my preference for a little of that in a cooked state, if I might be served. In an instant it was yielded by the corner cupboard, cold certainly, but not to be despised by a hungry man, especially when there came after it a hearty draught of a mild, sweet sort of wine, which possessed the flavour of the cocoa-nut. After this breakfast he attended to my wounds, and having dressed them with cool ointments, and bound them up as tenderly as on the preceding night, he showed me to the plank bedstead, and handed me a mat on which to recline. I did as he desired, and shortly after the doctor went out, leaving me to reflect on the sudden and favourable turn my prospects had taken, and to gaze at the outlandish things about me, including my fellow-tenant of the hut, who had returned to her pot, and was again pounding away with a monotonous and muffled clangour.

But for my anxious thoughts respecting Tom Cox—where he was and what he was doing—there was nothing in my situation—that is, for the time—that a reasonable man would have grumbled at. Truly, I was lucky in securing the patronage of a person of so exalted a position as the doctor evidently was; for I could but observe, as we passed through the village, that the people made haste to draw their children out of his path, and one man, whose pig obstinately refused

to turn aside till he had consumed a rotten pumpkin he was engaged
on, went on his knees almost to apologize to the doctor for the unlucky
accident. And not only did this grandee condescend to honour me
with his countenance; he seemed, even more from his manner than
his actions, to be very anxious that I should understand his intention
to be my friend. Did this arise from generosity and common
humanity, or did he have a notion that I was a wonderfully clever
fellow, and one whom it might be worth while to comfortably stall
and tether, while he used me as a stepping-stone to the chief's favour?
When this view of the matter occurred to me, it seemed that I had
best make the most of my snug quarters while they lasted, as, without
doubt, a day or two would serve to convince the doctor what a
thorough ignoramus I was, and that it would be a saving to send me
about my business.

I had no means of noting the passage of time, but the doctor must
have been away four hours, at the very least, and I began to grow
anxious to know what was going on outside. Was Tom Cox still in
the village? The place was not a large one, and I had no doubt that
my voice might be heard from one end of it to the other. Should I
bawl out his name, and see if he answered me? But then I reflected,
where would be the use? If he was safe and sound, well and good;
and if he was in trouble, I might only add to it by interfering where
I could give no aid. But, strangely enough, no sooner had I resolved
not to call out for Tom Cox than I was startled to hear my poor companion calling out for me.

"Oh!—oh-h-h!—oh! Leave me alone, I tell you! Reuben!
Reuben!—Oh-h-h!"

In an instant I started up from the bedstead, and, having no
weapon of my own, darted to the wall, and, seizing a broad war-knife
that hung against it, bounded to the door, despite my lame leg, and
fairly leaped over the doctor's wife, who had dozed to sleep by the side
of her pounded rice, and now rose to stop me. However, I got no
farther than the door, for, dashing away the mat that hung before it,
I was about to run, when I tripped over something, and came down
heavily; the "something" turned out to be "somebody"—a man, in
fact—who, I suspect, had been placed guard at the door, and, lying
down, as the easiest way of performing his task, had fallen asleep.
The kick in the ribs I had administered, however, effectually roused

him, and before I could regain my legs he had pinned me with a grip like that of a vice, and, first twisting the knife out of my hand, hauled me back into the hut, and laying me along with my face to the ground, sat himself on my back—a method of securing a prisoner for the efficacy of which I can vouch.

Although I listened most intently, I could not hear anything more of my unfortunate shipmate, and had little doubt in my own mind that I should never see him again—that he had been barbarously murdered, and that the cries I had heard were the last it was in his power to utter. This reflection so completely unnerved me, that, had it been an easy matter to shake off the fellow on my back, I should not have attempted it. My companion was dead, and, rather than exist among such bloodthirsty villains, I would pefer to die too! In the midst of my tribulation in came the doctor.

In a few words my guard explained how matters had arrived at their present condition; but the fellow, instead of receiving thanks, at least, for his vigilance, was fairly cuffed out of the hut by the doctor, who assisted me to rise, and, imagining that my grief had no deeper source than the violence of the man he had left sentry over me, endeavoured to comfort me.

But I was deaf to his soothings, and replied to all he did or said nothing but "Tom Cox." I wanted Tom Cox, and could listen to nothing until I was acquainted with that poor young fellow's fate. To my great surprise, when I had uttered Tom's name, the doctor repeated it, and in a way that convinced me that he knew perfectly well what the words signified—a circumstance I can only account for by supposing that he must have overheard me address my companion by name.

"Tomcox! Tomcox!—bisi! bisi!"

Being at the time perfectly ignorant of a single word of the Dyak tongue, I did not, of course, know that "bisi" was Sea Dyak for the simple word " yes;" and taking the word at its English signification, I understood the doctor to intimate that Tom was "busy," and couldn't come. But, fearing that my poor friend had been put past all business, I was not to be put off so easily, and covering my face with my hands, uttered Tom's name over and over again.

In hopes, as I suppose, to divert my thoughts, the doctor produced from a little pouch he wore at his side several little packets, which he

placed on the low table. These packets, which were secured in shreds
of cloth, he undid one by one, and looking through my fingers, I spied
the following articles:—A model of a human mouth in beeswax; a
small coil of fine wire; a small ball of something the nature of which
I could not make out; about a couple of dozen of human teeth,
molars, and incisors. Most of the teeth appeared to have been lately
pulled, and filled me so full of wonder as to whence they were derived
—nay, with such woeful foreboding—that I could not refrain from
calling on poor Tom more lamentably than before.

In vain the doctor led me to the table, and by all sorts of eloquent
gestures made me understand that here were all the requisite materials
for a perfect set of artificial teeth for the chief, and that I had better
set about their adjustment at once. "Tom Cox! Tom Cox!" was the
only answer he obtained from me. He coaxed, he stamped, and
presently, losing all patience, he snatched up the broad, razor-like
knife, and threatened; but, finding that I was not to be moved from
my resolution to see my companion before I consented to stir in his—
the doctor's—business, he uttered an exclamation of rage, and hurried
out of the hut—an example I was about to follow, but found the way
barred by the same individual who had before hindered me, and who,
moreover, was now armed with a formidable naked kris. Turning
back, I flung myself on to the wooden bedstead in a very miserable
mood, but was almost immediately roused by approaching footsteps.
In another instant the mat was lifted, and beside the doctor, Tom
Cox, alive and hearty, stood before me —that is, hearty in comparison
with how, if alive at all, I expected to see him. In reality, however,
he looked very savage and rueful, and carried his hand over his mouth
as though afflicted with a bad toothache; indeed, from the thickness of
his utterance while returning my congratulations on his safety, I came
to the conclusion that such was his unlucky case.

"There don't seem much amiss with you, Tom," said I. "What
was it that made you pipe so loud a while ago?"

For a moment he did not reply, but his eyes, rolling with morose
curiosity round the chamber, presently lighted on the pile of teeth
yet lying on the bench. Hurriedly approaching them, he selected
from the pile two sturdy molars, and held them up for my inspection,
at the same time shaking his fist at the doctor in the most daring
way.

"Ask him, the gallows rascal!" said he, "ask him what I piped about. I reckon *you'd* pipe, my hearty, if a couple of right and tight grinders were screwed out of your jaws."

And the poor fellow, with the wisp of coloured rag slouched over his sore ear, his lugubrious countenance, and the wistful way in which he gazed on his extracted teeth, combined to make such a ludicrous picture, that I could not forbear laughing, neither could the doctor, who stood looking on. Seeing, however, that Tom took my mirth amiss, I hastened to condole with him, though the best comfort I could give him was that it might have been worse.

As indeed it might, and very easily, as the reader will agree when he is made acquainted with the particulars of the case. It seems that, in his search for teeth—*where* he searched is too easy to guess—wherewith to fulfil the chief's order, he had come upon a set perfect but for two molars, and that, among all his dead stock, he failed to find a couple that would match either in size, shape, or quality; in this strait he had recollected that Tom's teeth were of the very sort he wanted. Nothing remained but to send one messenger for Tom and another for a pair of pincers, and then followed the yelling I had heard, and which I supposed to be Tom's death-cries. So, you see, it might have been much worse; had three, or five, or a round half-dozen teeth been wanted to make up the proper number, the supply would, without doubt, have been drawn from Tom's mouth; nay, if, on inspection, his entire mouthful had seemed but a shade preferable to those in hand, I have not the least doubt that out they would have come.

Having gratified my desire for a sight of Tom, the doctor was evidently anxious to hurry him off again, so that I had little opportunity for conversation. I, however, learned from him that he was lodged at the farther end of the village, and that, an hour or so before his teeth were drawn, he had been taken to a shed and shown several sorts of tools, with a view, as he supposed, to his taking up a trade to which he had been used; and that, seeing some hammers, and some other such tools as might be used in a smithy, he intimated that he knew something of their use, as indeed he should, having been bound 'prentice to a blacksmith at Deptford, whom he served for two years, and then ran away to sea.

"But," added Tom, "they'll get no smith's work out of me unless they treat me better. I don't know how you have been getting on, Reuben, but I've had nothing to eat since that rice and fish last night. A pretty way to treat a fellow—pull out his teeth instead of giving him his breakfast!"

Knowing Tom's obstinate nature, especially in matters of eating, and fearing the consequences if he gave way to it just at present, I earnestly persuaded him to have patience, and by and by we should find ourselves comfortable enough; but in the midst of my exhortation, and thinking, no doubt, that we had whispered together long enough, the doctor called in his man, who conducted Tom out of the hut.

Once more alone, my master—for so I suppose I must call him—called my attention to the business in hand, and invited me to inspect the material on the bench. He had provided himself with the properly-made artificial set of teeth belonging to the chief's mother, and showed me that he had provided all the requisites—the wire, the teeth, and the grey resinous ball already mentioned, and which he designed to be used in making gums to set the teeth in. Now, ever since this precious job of dentistry had been proposed to me, I had resolved within myself to have nothing to do with it, and for the best of all reasons, I knew no more about it than of flying; but finding my gentleman so determined on believing that I knew all about it, it seemed my best course to let him have his way.

First of all, and with the most business-like air I could assume, I took up the model of our patient's mouth, and at once discovered that several projecting stumps had been allowed to retain their places, and at once pointed out to my patron that before anything could be done these obstacles to a correct fit must be removed; but at this suggestion my patron vigorously shook his head, and, to my great relief, proceeded to make me understand that the teeth were not required so much for use as for show, and that, no doubt, the chief would follow his mother's example, and take them out whenever he took his meals. This bit of information quite cheered me, and encouraged me to set about the business with much less timidity.

But I will not tire the reader with a circumstantial account of my first attempts as a mechanical dentist. I should rather have said *our* attempts, for my master busied himself fully as much about the matter as did I, and, after helping me all he could while daylight remained, took on himself the office of torch-holder, and kept me pottering at the distasteful job till late in the evening, encouraging me by the promise of a good supper. From my experience in the matter of the stale eggs, I felt little disposed to trust his judgment of what *was* good, but presently observed his wife bring in a couple of plump and ready-plucked chickens and pop them into the pot, and was comfortably reassured. Come bedtime, I slung the heaviest mat I could find over a rafter, and so parted off a snug corner from the rest of the apartment, and, rolling myself in another mat, with my jacket for a pillow, slept like a top.

By dint of rising at cockcrow, and sticking to our job, by about noon it was accomplished, and nothing remained but to colour the gums, for which purpose the doctor crushed some scarlet berries, and produced a dye which answered the purpose admirably. So delighted was he at the success of our undertaking that he embraced me very cordially, and then, beaming with pride, wrapped the teeth in a leaf, and strutted off to present them to the expectant chief, and thereby secure at once his lasting favour and a signal triumph over his rival, the old doctor.

To confess the truth, I, too, was not without sensations of self-gratulation. It was evident that I was much cleverer than I had ever supposed. Who but a born genius could have taken in hand a job so strange and ticklish, and successfully accomplished it? What might not be the result? I know from story-books how generous savage potentates could be towards the gratifiers of their vanity. What if the pirate chief should take it into his head to honour me—to give me the command of a prahu, perhaps, or load me with gold and jewels, and make me his chief councillor?

With such idle castle-building did I consume half an hour. The pastime was interrupted by the sound of hastily-approaching footsteps. "Doubtless," thought I, "this is my friend the doctor hurrying to tell me my good fortune."

Never was I so miserably mistaken. The reader who has seen a full-blown soap-bubble radiant and lovely one moment, and the next forming nothing but an insignificant smirch on the dust, may realize my case. It was indeed the doctor, but no longer my "friend." His eyes, so lately flashing with pride, now burnt with fury, and as he entered he dashed to the ground the wreck of our joint handiwork.

The false teeth had miscarried! The chief's delight at their appearance had been unbounded; they had fitted his mouth to a miracle; but on opening his jaws to laugh at the chagrin betrayed by the old doctor, the brittle gums were shivered to fragments, filling his potent mouth with dust and bitterness. This I learnt afterwards, as well as the fact that the chief was so enraged that my patron was lucky to have escaped with his head, which presented a fair chance for lopping as he stooped to gather up the rubbish the chief spat out of his mouth. As it was, he had suffered what to the Dyak is detestable next to death—derision : he had left the council-chamber amid the gibes and jeers of all there assembled.

Had I known all this I should have been inclined to make some allowance for the furious passion he exhibited. What had I to do with the failure of the gums ? He himself had introduced the material, and well knew its properties, while I was ignorant of them. Nevertheless, he seemed resolved that I should share the indignity to which he had been subjected. Calling in his man, he bade him strip me of my jacket and shirt, and then, while the strong ruffian held my hands in front, the doctor gave me a most cruel flogging with a slim cane of bamboo, and which I believe was the more severe because my pride would not allow me to cry out and tell him how he was making me suffer.

Nor did his spite end with the flogging, for the condition of my back at last satisfying his bloodthirsty mind, he bade me take off my shoes, and, without allowing me even the covering of my shirt for my wealed shoulders, led me out, naked but for my trousers. When we had descended from the terrace and walked towards the woods, we met a gang of slaves, marshalled by an overseer, who carried a whip of raw hide. The slaves were each heavily laden with rough planks, and were hurrying towards the beach, so that I imagined the wood was for use in ship-building. Bidding me stand where I was, the doctor threw himself under a tree, and there lay in the shade—no doubt chewing the bitter cud of reflection—while I stood scorching in the sun. After some time the slave-gang came trotting back again, and when they came up to us the doctor called the overseer, and gave him certain directions ; whereon I was ordered to fall in with the rest, and marched into the woods to work.

As may be easily imagined, this sudden alteration of my prospects cast me down not a little, and it was with a heavy heart that I tailed on to the string of slaves, and shambled along as fast as I could to keep pace with them, and save my already smarting shoulders a visit from the ugly whip which the driver was so handily smacking and whisking just behind me.

From dentistry to tree-felling! True, I knew as much of the latter business as of the former, and from its character it should be easier to perform. But I had but to cast my eyes about me to discover what promised to be a very formidable difficulty in the way of my success as a woodman—the sort of tools the men had to work with! The man trotting on before me had the implements of his craft over his shoulder, and when I looked on them—on the axe, scarcely fit to chop billets for a kitchen fire—on the adze (for so I suppose the thing was called), with its blade no wider than a broad chisel—when I looked on these toy-like things, and then on the mighty trees which surrounded us, I could not help reflecting that my chances of a taste of the overseer's whip were considerably greater than that I should give satisfaction by my tree-felling.

My fears, however, only lasted just so long as it took us to jog from the entrance to the wood to the place where the men were working. Working, I have said; but certainly my impression, on first catching a glimpse of them, was that they were idling, for every man was sitting down. I thought to myself, " My lads, you don't know how close the man with the whip is; you'll be made to jump up presently in double-quick time." But, although we continued to approach them, they still remained squatting, and then I found, to my amazement, that, although in that position, they really were at work. There was a great company of them—a hundred or more; some perched on great boughs, peck, peck, pecking at them with their little choppers; others—generally in gangs of four—were squatting at the stems of the lightest of the trees, chipping at them from opposite sides; while several more were sitting down with logs before them, wielding their tiny adzes, and working away, evidently with the hope of ultimately reducing the rough, heavy tree-trunks to the dimensions of a plank.

Ludicrous, however, as was this method of felling and preparing timber, it luckily was nicely adapted to my lame condition ; and when one of the drivers came and put an axe in my hand, and motioned me that my business was to cut down a certain tree (about eighteen inches through), I was very glad to squat down like the rest; and even then, although I took care not to punish my tree a bit more than the others were doing, the jarring of the axe against the hard wood gave me such pains in my wounded arm, that it made me grind my teeth at every stroke. By and by, however, a good-tempered-looking little black man, with a woolly head and monstrously thick lips (evidences that he was no more a native-born Dyak than I was), having finished his long task of lopping off a bough about as thick as the calf of my leg, took his seat opposite to me, and likewise commenced chopping at it. I at once saw that his method of holding and swinging his axe was very different from mine, and he, making the discovery as soon as myself, politely showed me the way, grinning round the trunk at me, and setting me right over and over again, till I chopped to his satisfaction and to my own, for I now could hack away without jarring my idle arm in the least.

So I continued to work till it began to grow dark, when the banging of a gong was heard, and the wood-choppers ceased their work and hurried in a body deeper into the wood, and my companion (who by this time had, I believe, confided to me his entire history, had I only been able to understand him) took me by the hand and beckoned me to come too. After a little while we came on about a dozen huts of the very roughest sort, and in front of them was a man with a sack of rice, which he was measuring out to the wood-cutters at the rate of about a pint to each man. When my turn came, I had nothing to hold my ration, and should, doubtless, have been passed over, had not the little Papuan (for such I afterwards discovered my friendly fellow-slave to be) kindly allowed me to mingle my allowance with his in the same pot.

Although I had not eaten since noon, and then not over-plentifully, the fussing and eagerness manifested by my fellow-slaves to light fires and fetch water wherewith to cook their dole of rice failed to inspire me with emulation; and, since my Papuan friend had obliged me by affording room in his iron pot for my supper as well as his own, I was content to leave the matter in his hands entirely, and, retiring to some distance from the noise and clatter, sat under a bush to indulge in the melancholy pastime of reflection.

And truly, if my mind's appetite for misery had been as voracious as that of the parched ground for rain, there was food enough for it

and to spare. What was I ? A slave of the lowest sort, "a hewer of
wood," kept alive for the profit of my heathen masters, as a packhorse
is kept alive or a mill in motion.   Had fortune, indeed, done with me ?
Was this the finish to my romantic dreaming—this death of heart and
hope? Had I for any space of time been acquainted with ill luck and
good, alternately swimming and sinking in the stream I had ventured
in, I might have regarded my present ignominy as but a transient
thing—a mere stranding that would, in natural course, be remedied
when the tide turned ; but, after knowing but one short day's tolerable
comfort, to be so suddenly reduced to the very lees of misery—plunged
and fast stuck in it beyond hope of escape! All these thoughts
brought me to so wretched a state that I wept more plentifully than
I should have cared the savages about me to have witnessed, and
uttered aloud my regret that I had not perished on the raft, or that
my arm had saved my heart from the thrust of the pirate's spear.

In the midst of my lamenting, the little Papuan came forward with
the mess of rice smoking on a dish made of a great green leaf. It was
evident from his expressive features that he interpreted my distress as
arising from doubt of his honesty, and he very generously set down the
dish before me and stepped away a little that I might eat what I pleased,
and leave him the rest. But, even had I been in cue for eating, I
could not have touched the smoking mess, for the Papuan had dressed
it to please his own palate, and had so saturated it with oil and pepper,
that was rancid and stinking, that the very smell of it caused me to
shudder with disgust. This involuntary expression of my feelings did
not escape the Papuan, who, poor fellow, never having in the course of
his life experienced a trouble that fat and rice could not assuage, was
at once impressed with the notion that I must indeed be ill, and,
hurrying off, found the taskmaster, with whom he was in favour, and
who gave him permission to show me to the hut where I was to sleep.

I have before remarked on the appearance these paltry hovels presented, but I was agreeably surprised to find them—at least, the one
I was shown to—much more commodious than I imagined. True,
there was nothing in the shape of bed-clothes or of bedding either,
except from a horse's view ; but with the former it is easy to dispense
in such a climate as Borneo, and as to the latter my recent experiences
had taught me not to be over-nice ; so down I flung myself, hoping to
escape my misery in sleep.

And, despite the humming and clicking of the great beetles in the thatch, and the tormenting stings of the mosquitoes, I was on the point of succeeding, when, to my astonishment, the hut I lay in was boisterously entered by at least a dozen fellows, so that there was not more than fair standing room for them, and who deliberately began to squat and huddle down on the rushes, pillowing their heads on each other's haunches, and evidently bent on staying all night. Luckily, I had previously edged close to the wall by the doorway for coolness' sake, and was not in a convenient position for pillowing. Evidently it was a common thing for the slaves to sleep in this way; indeed, had I taken the trouble to compare the number of huts with the number of wood-choppers, I might easily have avoided my erroneous conclusion that the hut was for my separate accommodation.

But, although I saw the necessity for resignation, sleep was quite out of the question. In a little while the heat and evil odour became intolerable, while the beetles seemed to regard the snoring of my companions as a challenge, and commenced to ·lick, and chirp, and buzz at a harder rate than ever, while the mosquitoes warmed to their work, and set to with a vengeance. I can hardly believe that the rest were bitten as cruelly as I was, for, beyond an occasional tossing of arms or a more emphatic snort than ordinary, not one of the sleepers betrayed the slightest inconvenience. Perhaps the tiny demons thought it their duty to pay me, as a stranger, special attention.

At last I became so frightfully stung that I resolved to stay in the hut no longer, and, crawling out at the doorway as stealthily as I could, gained the outside without disturbing any one of my bedfellows. I should have liked a walk to the beach, and a good look at the sea, but I neither knew the way nor what might be the penalty if I were discovered attempting it, so I did the next best thing—I climbed a high tree, and, the night being clear and bright, my eyes were speedily refreshed by a sight of the wide-spreading ocean, which, though it had served me so unkindly, I was still faithful to—nay, yearned to it more than ever, I think, and not without reason, for, when it had first attracted me, it was but as a speculative path, leading, perhaps, to riches and things curious and desirable, and perhaps to peril and hazardous adventure. It was, doubtless, this very uncertainty that constituted the chief charm; now, however, there was the charm without the uncertainty—I *knew* what the sea parted me from,

and I knew to the utmost grain the value of the treasures on the far-
away other side—treasures which I had deliberately abandoned.
Should I ever get back to reclaim them?   Should I find the custodian
of the choicest casket—my mother, with her heart so full of love for

Reuben Davidger in the Tree.

me?—should I find her alive, or dead and buried, perhaps without a
message or ever so trifling a token left behind that she died thinking
of me?

And here I would tender my advice alike to young boys and

elderly lads not to regard sneeringly or with impatience what I have just said or may have to say concerning this milksopishness of mine. Don't be too hard on it unless your determination or some insurmountable obstacle precludes the possibility of your running away to sea. Sure as ever you do so run away—and remember it is old, grey-haired Reuben Davidger, and not the harum-scarum young fellow who climbed into the tree at Borneo who writes this—thoughts of "mother" will cause you more choking sensations than anything else you are likely to meet with. In my opinion, that peculiar little bump in the throat known as "Eve's apple" was not so called because of the original apple of sin Adam was beguiled into swallowing, but because it is symbolic of the bitter fruit of remorse which rises to rebuke us when we inflict on those dear Eves, our mothers, wanton grief and anxiety. So it happened that, as I nestled among the green boughs, and gazed over the great sea, homeward, I thought——

But there—out of my thoughts, and vows, and good resolutions nothing came, so I will not repeat them. Something, however, came of my climbing into the tree. While I was still astride the bough, resting my melancholy head against the tree-trunk, my quick ears detected a sound as of some living creature moving among the thick brushwood at a short distance away. Ignorant of the fact that rapacious animals of any great size are unknown on the Borneo coast, my instant thought was that it was some prowling lion or tiger. But the thought caused me no great alarm. The tree I occupied was a tall one, and above my head there were boughs to a considerable height and of such dimensions that while they would afford me safe refuge no great animal would venture his weight on them. Besides, it was growing towards morning, and even should the forest prowler scent me out and try my nerves by endeavouring to get at me, my anxiety would not be of very long duration. My mind, however, was not so easy on the subject but that I kept my eyes pretty constantly fixed on the lurking object which continued to move stealthily from place to place, its attention seeming to be attracted by the huts in which the slaves slept, as though its object was to find a convenient opening through which it could creep and drag off some poor wretch lying handy.

This behaviour on the part of the mysterious beast perplexed me even more than if it had nosed me in my retreat and made endeavours to secure me for his breakfast. What should I do? If I ventured to get down and awake the inmates of the huts it would be at the risk of being carried off myself for my pains; and at the very least I should probably incur the driver's displeasure by showing that I had crept out of the hut in which it was expected that I should peacefully abide till the gong sounded in the morning. Yet it seemed cruelly selfish and unchristian to sit perched in a tree while it was in my power to assist a fellow-creature, especially after the many recent instances of divine interposition I had myself experienced. Perhaps I might be able to scare the animal away without descending.

For this purpose I cast about me, and presently spied, hanging just above my head, a stoutish, time-withered bough which might be easily broken off. Noiselessly I climbed a bit higher, and having secured the rotten piece broke it to a convenient size, and taking aim hurled it as hard as I was able at the bush behind which I could dimly make out the rapacious brute to be crouching. The missile hit the bush, but judge of my astonishment, when, instead of seeing a lion or, at least, a leopard emerge, the animal reared up and discovered itself to be a *man*—a white man with a wisp of rag tied round his head! It was Tom Cox.

So astonished was I at the apparition, that for some time I could only stare in wonder, while Tom was busy peering through the gloom this way and that, to discover who it was that had thrown at him. At last he seemed to have made up his mind it would be no longer safe to play the part of a lurker, and set off at a half run down the path that led to the village. In a moment I slipped down the tree and made after him, which at first only made him run the faster, till I called him by name, when he stopped with an exclamation of satisfaction, and turned to greet me.

"I'm precious glad it's you, Reu," said he, shaking me by the hand in a very earnest manner; "I thought to be sure he who was coming after me was the same fellow who cast his spear at me as I was skulking behind the bush."

"It did not wound you very badly, Tom, did it?" I asked laughing.

"No, but it might," replied he solemnly; "it passed within a foot of my head, and buried itself in the scrub. But how is it, Reu," continued he, "that I find you in so easy a humour? Has your luck taken another turn? Have they released you from slavery, and made you captain of a gang?"

Tom said this with so much bitterness that it grieved me not a little.

"Look at me, Tom," said I reproachfully; "do I look like a captain? do I look aught else than a wretched disgraced slave?"

"Such it was I expected to find you," replied he in a kinder voice; "it was because that I knew how miserable you must be, that I stole out of the village to find you."

"Then it was to seek me that you came here?"

"For no other purpose I assure you," replied Tom; "if I could have made my mind easy as to your condition, had I not known that with the spite of that villain upon you, you would be ready to dare and do anything, I should have gone without you."

"Gone! gone where, Tom?"

"Anywhere!" replied Tom fiercely; "to the devil if to no better. I'll have no more of this, Reu. It's knocking every bit of good out of me that poor old Jones set me up with, and it's better for me to bolt now, than to wait till I'm exasperated to knock somebody on the head, and then bolt."

It was plain that since we had last met, something had happened to Tom, to put him in such ill-humour, and by a very little questioning I discovered what it was. It seemed that Anakrajah, the young doctor, in the fury of his spite, and with all the meanness of his brutal nature, was not satisfied with the punishment he had inflicted on me As soon as he returned from consigning me to the tender mercies of the slave driver, he had gone straight to Tom's quarters, accompanied by the executioner, whose office it was, as it is with our Jack Ketch, to inflict whipping on offenders sentenced to that punishment. The charge against Tom was just as flimsy as it was possible to be. The doctor declared that he was in league with me to befool the chief in the matter of the artificial teeth; that on the very day on which the job was begun, I had insisted on seeing my friend (the villain forgot to state *why* it was that I had been so anxious to see him) and that when he had come, we fell to whispering together, and the result was that the materials used in putting together the sham grinders, were bewitched, and so adapted as to fall to pieces when the chief put them into his mouth.

Such serious charges as befooling the chief, and indulging in the hateful work of witchcraft, were more than enough to have cost Tom Cox his head, and so they doubtless would, had the chief seriously entertained them; but as the young doctor had on one occasion served me, so now the old doctor served Tom. His rival disgraced, he was now of course in high favour, and charitably hinted to his august master, that a man like Anakrajah, who was fool enough to undertake to make a set of teeth, was doubtless rogue enough to cast the cause of his failure on some one else. The chief taking the same view, commanded that Tom Cox's life should be spared, but that as probably he was a little in fault, he might be whipped.

And to a surety the poor fellow *had* been whipped. Anakrajah had superintended the operation, indeed, as Tom indignantly informed me, had assisted in his degradation to the utmost; for while tied to a post the executioner laid on him with the cow-skin lash, Anakrajah stood before him, mocking him, and spitting at him, and buffeting his face with the flat of his hand. Poor Tom stripped off his jacket, and showed me his back, which was indeed wealed and bruised in a very shocking manner.

"So I'm off, Reu," said he determinedly. "It *must* come to bolting, and I'd rather not do a murder first if I may be spared. I couldn't help it. If I were to stay another day I should let fly at that mean whelp, as sure as I met him."

"Well, Tom, I too am sick of the accursed place," said I, as in truth I was, and none the less at my present prospect than at what had gone before. "I'll go with you. Where? that's the question."

"Through the forest," replied Tom, with a promptness which showed that he had considered the matter. "We can't find a worse set than we are now among."

"But how do you know we shall find a set of any sort?" I inquired. "Suppose, when we have penetrated through the forest, which is goodness knows how vast, suppose, then, we find ourselves in a wilderness uninhabited except by savage beasts?"

But Tom explained that he knew there was another tribe of men somewhere upon the island, and how he came to know it. It seemed that a day or two previously, while tinkering at his smithy, a fellow had marched up to the door of the hut, with one of their hideous war trophies hanging at his belt, and which he was proud to show to the strange white man. It was the head a Dyak by the features, but distinguished from those of Magindano by having a circle of crimson dots round each eye. Tom, whose sense of delicacy was not unfathomable, and had since his arrival seen enough of such horrible things to somewhat familiarize him with them, felt some curiosity about the crimson eye circles, and made signs to the native to know where the men lived who wore such ornaments, and the fellow had pointed directly across the forest.

"And it cannot be a very long journey either," said Tom, "for, as far as I could judge, he couldn't have been in possession of his prize many hours."

There was no time for deliberation; in less than an hour the morning would break, and very shortly after that one or other of us would certainly be missed, and pursuit commence. Of course there was such a mischance as jumping out of the frying-pan into the fire, but the pan in which we both were had lately grown so very hot, that even if it came to the worst a jump on to coals could not find us seriously worsted. At once we resolved to attempt our escape, and there and then turned back, and ran towards the thick of the forest as fast as was consistent with prudence.

Very earnestly did I hope that Tom's conjecture as to the shortness of the distance that parted us from the abode of the men with the crimson dots might be correct, for never did two poor fellows set out on an adventure in a more wretched plight. We were unarmed, half-naked, sore-backed, and empty-bellied; added to which, I was still so lame as to halt as I walked or ran. It happened, however, that the most serious impediment to the success of our venture—hunger— was of all that most easy to surmount. Once fairly into the wood, we found that the cocoa-nuts hung on the trees in vast profusion, while the bushes were festooned with clusters of berries richer looking even than cherries or Hamburgh grapes; though, as to their perfect wholesomeness, I cannot say, nor, I think, should I waste time in inquiring, were I very hungry and they before me. However, as we were quite sure of the cocoa-nuts, it was not worth while being foolhardy; and so, when we had pushed on for fully two hours, and thought we might venture to halt, we shook down a few nuts, and made a hearty breakfast off them. Then we set off again.

Our progress, however, was not nearly so rapid as at first. The deeper we penetrated into the forest the more dense it became, and so gloomy, on account of the massive overhanging branches shutting out the sun, that, but for the singing of the birds and the chattering of the monkeys, it might have been evening. It was very hot and oppressive too, and though, in the cool of the morning, I had been inclined to envy Tom his jacket, I now pitied him sweltering under it. Still he was better off than I was in one respect, he had a pair of shoes, for want of which my feet were sadly pierced and torn by the thorns which lay concealed in the rank grass.

I have spoken of the monkeys as doing us some service by chattering and gambolling, and thus convincing us that it was day time, and bright and pleasant, when we had the good luck to make our way out of our present tangle. But these were the little monkeys. There were others, monstrous fellows, with bodies big almost as our own, and great hairy limbs, and hands with fingers and thumbs. I don't say that creatures so hideous had never been seen; probably there were such to be met with in London at the wild-beast shows. But I had never seen them, and, even if I had, I question if the sight would have gone far towards preparing me for the horrid spectacle that awaited me that morning. I have since seen orang-outangs, but they were no more like that grim monster I first saw in the depths of the Bornean forest, than the purring puss of our domestic hearth is like that fierce and bloody grimalkin, with her bare crooked teeth and gleaming eyes, now and then found in the woods of northern Europe.

We both heard this great man monkey together shaking the boughs and chattering in our rear, and thought to be sure it was our Magindano friends in hot pursuit. The fright came so sudden, that, tired as we were—from the glimpse we now and then got of the sun it must have been long past noon—we set off running faster than we had since breakfast time, taking no heed of small impediments, but dashing through the network of creeping plants that laced the trees together, and leaping over bushes as high as English hedges. But our haste seemed only to stimulate our pursuers to greater exertion; the rustling of branches and the impatient grunting grew each moment more distinct, till it seemed as though hands must be presently laid on us.

"I can't run any farther, Tom," said I, as plainly as my exhausted state would let me; "I think I would rather use the little breath I have left in fighting, since it seems that we must fight. Let us make a stand, Tom."

"A stand it is, then," replied Tom, suddenly coming to a halt, and both of us wheeling round.

But only that we were held to the ground with terror, we should at once have turned again and ran, though our lives had paid for it. Our sudden halt had taken our pursuer by surprise. He was coming headlong on, swinging himself along by the hanging branches. He had no time to check himself, and plump he came cheek and jowl with me, with his hideous green eyes and his leathern lips, knocking me over and making such a hideous mouth at Tom that he slunk down too; and then the hideous man-monkey, as though he thought it an excellent joke, swung himself into a tree and was off and away, chattering and barking with all his might. When, as we sat panting and resting our tired limbs, we considered his awful aspect—his double row of snow-white teeth and tremendous limbs, we could not but think that our escape was a perfect marvel of good fortune. But, as we afterwards discovered, we were in more peril from fright than from the ferocity of the orang-outang. Indeed, according to our experience, he would sooner run than fight, and has nothing of the hobgoblin nature ascribed to him in the picture-books. True, there were two of us, and except in one instance, when we espied a great ape squatting on a forked bough, suckling her baby, we never met them but singly. How it would have been had the odds been reversed I am quite content to leave to conjecture.

We were so knocked up through our flight from the man-monkey, that, although there still remained many hours of daylight, we made but little further progress when the gloom increased and we knew that night was coming. And now we were forced to halt, for even though we had been fresh and fit for journeying, now that the sun was gone we were as helpless as blind men, and were as likely as not to grope our way back to the hated spot where the slave huts were. While our guide, the sun, reposed so must we; so while there was yet sufficient light we gathered some nuts, and then making ourselves as comfortable as we could on the convenient fork of a tree, we talked till we were sleepy and then took watch and watch, as they do aboard ship, till the morning.

As soon as the sun rose, so did we, or more correctly speaking, we

REUBEN DAVIDGER AND TOM COX'S UNEXPECTED ANTAGONIST

descended. But alas! our luminous guide was in much better trim
for beginning his day's journey than were we. It is not at all comfortable sleeping up a tree, as anyone who has tried it will vouch.
You are obliged to hold on even in your sleep, and you dare not turn
about in the least for the easement of your cramped limbs. It would
have been better had we squatted on the ground, and so we should
but that Tom was equally ignorant with myself that the larger sort
of carniverous animals are unknown in Borneo, and there seemed a
chance that however vigilantly one watched while the other slept, one
or the other of us might be snapped off.

So with our tattered garments saturated with dew, with our feet
blistered from the violent exercise and the thorns of yesterday, and
with our legs aching from thigh to heel, we drearily noted the position
of the sun, and shaped our course for what we supposed was the abode
of the savages with crimson spots round their eyes. Neither of us
said a word about breakfast, and as we presently found, for a very good
reason. The only eatable we could safely indulge in were the cocoa
nuts, and one day's feeding off them had given us both such a sickening that to go without was preferable to renewing the repast. So
instead of breakfasting on cocoa-nuts, I entertained Tom, as we limped
along, by narrating what my sensations were when the old Malay
woman (we had come to talking about the old woman in a friendly
way enough by this time) told me about a country in which you could
gather cocoas as you walked—how that with my passionate fondness for the milky nuts, I had dreamt of what she had told me
many and many a night, and felt as though I could have given
my head, if I could have spared it, to have lived in such a glorious
country.

But our endeavour to beguile the time by such conversation was not
long successful. Still we limped on, still the hours flew by, but the
forest was as dense as ever, and we relapsed into moody silence, each
engaged with the same dismal reflection—either that there *was* no way
to the country of the speckled-cheeked men, or that if there was, we
had lost it. A dozen times in the course of that morning we came on
places which I could have declared we noticed yesterday, and though
for the present I kept such disheartening convictions to myself, I had
but to look at Tom to perceive that suspicions of much the same
character were haunting him. But in this matter we may both have

been mistaken, the great green and flowery forest being throughout alike as the waters of a river.

To add to our other misfortunes, come the middle of the afternoon Tom fell sick. He had not been able to withstand the sight of some purple fruit, blackberry shape, and looking wonderfully cool and luscious, as they hung in the heat. He tasted them, and pronouncing them more delicious than any fruit he had ever tasted, went in for a largish quantity. No doubt I should have done the same, but I had no appetite; whether it really was the large quantity of cocoa-nuts I had eaten on the previous day that made me feel so poorly I cannot say, I only know that I did feel out of sorts, and cared for nothing but to drink, which I did whenever we came to a pool or rivulet.

With his usual obstinacy Tom would make out that the purple berries had nothing to do with his illness; it was the cocoa-nuts he said, but I judge it was otherwise, on account of the difference in our symptoms. As for me I was merely qualmish and afflicted with a sort of stomachache, but Tom was violently sick and trembled very much, though the air was suffocatingly close, and presently he began to swell in a very alarming manner. He couldn't walk, and his only craving was to go to sleep, and so even earlier than on the previous day we made a halt, and Tom flung himself down on to the moist earth, and in a very little while fell into a profound slumber, so profound indeed that I began to be very much afraid that he would never wake any more. I did not so much mind while the daylight lasted, but when the shadows of night began to gather, and presently it grew quite dark, and still Tom lay like a dead-drunken man, responding to my shaking and pinching and shouting only by groans and broken ejaculations as though he were dreaming, I grew much frightened, and bitterly regretted that I had listened to his advice, and ran away.

My constant fear was of wild beasts. I thought that if I could only rouse him sufficiently to get him up a tree the danger would not be so great; but there he lay like a log. I endeavoured to lift him and did manage to hoist him on to his feet, but there he hung like a dead man, with his head all on one side and his knees bent, so there was nothing for it but to lay him down again, and, sitting by his side, keep the best watch I was able.

I sat with my back against a tree, and with Tom's head resting on my lap. For a very long while, or so it seemed, I kept my eyes open as well as my ears, but the odd sounds which at first startled me gradually grew familiar, and without my even suspecting its approach, sleep stole over me. How long I slept I don't know, but it must have been some considerable time, for during my unconsciousness it had changed from the blackest gloom to bright moonlight, which I dare say served to increase my amazement as I was startled into wakefulness.

It was Tom's voice that woke me. He was shaking me by the arm.

"Hist! Reu! wake, lad, wake," said he. He spoke quite clearly and in his own natural voice. As well as I could see, too, the swelling of his face had subsided, and he seemed to have quite recovered; but still he was strangely agitated.

"What is it, Tom?" I inquired; "you have had a decent spell of sleep yourself, my hearty, and I am glad to see that you are all the better for it. Now let me have a turn while you watch."

"It seems to me that it will fare ill with either of us if we sleep another minute in this horrible place," said Tom, seriously; "though which way to turn with the cut-throats all about us is more than I know."

"Cut-throats all about us! why you are dreaming, Tom," said I; "you've been dreaming since yesterday afternoon, you foolish fellow."

"Maybe," replied he; "but I was not dreaming when I saw what I did see—it was you that was dreaming, my lad, or you would have seen it too."

"Seen *it!* what do you mean, Tom?" I began to fear that poor Tom's malady had taken the form of insanity.

"One of the speckled cheeks!" whispered he softly. "What it was that woke me I don't know, Reu; but I did wake softly as a baby might, with my head on your lap, and looking up there in the boughs above us—along that crooked bough with the gnarls in it—saw peeping down on us just such a head as that fellow brought to show me at the smithy, only that it was alive, and attached to a body and legs. The villain had a spear in his hand, Reu, ready for casting, but as soon as he saw that I was awake he somehow vanished."

Earnestly, however, as Tom related the particulars of the singular sight he had witnessed, I was still sceptical. The moon shone brightly so that it was not difficult to look about, and as it happened the spot where we halted on the previous evening was singularly destitute of great trees ; indeed, with the exception of that against which we rested, there was no other near in a circuit of twenty yards at least. All about were low, scrubby bushes, insufficient to afford shelter to any animal as bulky as a man ; but though I peered earnestly in every direction no trace of a speckled-faced savage was visible.

"You are sure, Tom, it was a *human* face ?" I asked. "There may be stranger-looking man-apes in this quarter than those we have yet seen."

But at this suggestion Tom shook his head. "There may be some strange monkeys hereabouts," said he, "but monkeys don't carry spears, neither do they wear earrings."

"Well, what do you propose, Tom ?" I asked. "You say the savage you saw was one of the ring-eyed sort; how d'ye like the looks of him ? D'ye think we had better push on, or——"

"Or what ?" said Tom, as I hesitated, not knowing how he might take the remainder of my observation.

"Or turn back, Tom ?"

"Turn back I never will," exclaimed Tom, decidedly. "You may be so inclined, Reu, and not without some reason, for since you have been in this country you have tasted of its sweets as well as of its sours, and are able to set this against that in a manner of speaking; but my lot has been all sours, and it is because nothing can be sourer, that I mean to push on. As for these speckled-faced rascals, if——"

But at this very instant occurred an incident as though specially planned to convince Master Cox that there were sours which he had not yet tasted. He had been half-starved, suffered the lopping of an ear, the extraction of a couple of sound double teeth, he had been abused and whipped, but inasmuch as all these punishments fell short in their severity of that of death, he had been not unlucky ; but even as he spoke he was in danger of tasting the bitterest sour of all, for a flutter like that of a bird's wing was momentarily heard, the next instant a spear gleamed between Tom's side and the arm he had raised to add emphasis to his declaration that he never would go back to Magindano, and penetrating into the trunk of the tree, there stuck quivering.

For a moment we were both too astonished to do anything but to gaze blankly at each other. It was evident that the apparition Tom had seen was a veritable man and no monkey, and that in the tree was a sample of the weapons with which he was armed.

"Quick, Tom," said I, "let us get to the other side of the tree ; he can't aim at us there without shifting his ground."

"*He!*" exclaimed Tom ; "Lord send there may be only one of the speckled wood-devils ; more likely to be a dozen, my lad. This is our last hour, I'm afraid, Reu."

"We thought so before, Tom," I replied, trying to speak cheerily ; "even if there are several of these savages lurking in the forest they may mean us no harm ; they may merely wish to question us."

Tom pointed grimly at the spear in the tree.

"Had not skulking somewhat spoiled the villain's aim," said he, "one of us at least had been put past questioning by this time. However it shan't be wasted ; it is an outlandish thing, but better than no weapon at all."

So saying Tom began to wrench at the handle of the spear to pull it out of the tree, while I stood by his side very anxious to see the operation completed, that we might then adopt my suggestion and hide at the side of the tree which must conceal us at least from the savage who had thrown the spear. But I was destined not to see the extraction of the spear. Sudden as a flash of light I felt a tremendous sting between my shoulders, and down I fell flat on my face without the sense to put out my hands to break my fall.

My awakening sensations were of an extraordinary sort. I could feel that my face was wet, as was my breast, and I could indistinctly make out the bustle of some one in close attendance on me. I felt no pain, but as my consciousness gradually returned the latest events of which I had recollection flashed to my mind, and I was afraid to open my eyes. What was it that my face and breast was wet with ? Who was it that was pottering about me ? Was it one of the speckled-eyed men, and thinking me dead was I being subjected to some savage ceremony peculiar to the tribe ? If this were the case it were better, at least for the present, that I continued to sham dead.

And so I believe I should had not the supposed savage presently growled out with an unmistakably English voice an equally unmistakably English oath.

"Devil take him, the villain," it said. "Thinking you was only stunned, my poor chum, I began to repent cracking his skull ; but now that I find you are really dead, I'm precious glad I hit him as hard as I did !"

"Not quite dead yet, Tom," said I, opening my eyes, whereon I was very much affected to see the poor fellow bending over me, with big tears rolling down his cheeks. I was lying beside a stream, where he must have carried me, and my wetting was occasioned by his laving me with the water in hopes of restoring me. His delight at seeing me come to life again was unbounded; he sprang to his feet, and skipped about and laughed like a madman; he hugged me in his arms and kissed me, the last-mentioned act more than another showing his grateful joy, for, as the reader may judge from as much as has been told of Tom's character, he was of any but the kissing sort. But I may here remark on the singular fact of which Tom Cox's behaviour in this instance furnished an apt instance, that kissing among men is disgusting less according to nature than the usages of civilization. Among savage people the practice is quite common, and this not only with the more brutish, but also with the most decent and modest, of which the Touga islanders furnish an example. Here, as I have often witnessed, when a brother goes on a voyage, he kisses his father and his brothers as well as his mother and his sisters, though I must confess I never liked a man's kiss, and would much sooner he shook hands. But we need not go to Tonga to find male kissers; Irish hodmen do it habitually, as soon as they have imbibed sufficient whisky to melt the artificial nature they have acquired during a residence among cold-blooded Saxons.

To return, however, to the Bornean rivulet and to Tom Cox. As soon as his extravagant delight had somewhat subsided, I begged him to give me an account of what had happened since I was last awake, and what he told me was, in brief, as follows:—The stinging blow at my back, which had so effectually felled me, and knocked the breath out of my body, was inflicted by one of those club-like instruments already described, and which are fashioned simply by inserting the end of a short length of bamboo into a hole drilled into a great round stone, the said instrument being alike efficacious when used as a club or a projectile. At the very moment of my fall, Tom had succeeded in wrenching the spear out of its setting, and instantly turning about, he spied just above the top of a distant bush the same face which had, a short time before, looked down on him from the tree under which we were reposing. Tom's courage was marvellously like that of the bull-dog; a groan in the dark would make him quake, a mysterious sound of any sort make him feel currish; but *show* him his game, let him be aggrieved and the aggressor visible, and then he had the heart of a lion. So it came about that as soon as he caught sight of the painted savage behind the bush, he caught up the stone club, and with that in one hand and the spear in the other, he gave the savage chase.

"He would have got off too," said Tom, "had he been satisfied to run away, for while I had to dodge round bushes, he leapt them like a Whitechapel hurdle-jumper, but the silly fellow must needs stop and poise another spear, to take a parting shy at me; but as he had already had a couple of throws, I thought it was my turn, and I let fly with the mallet as neat as ever I flung a stick at a Greenwich-fair cock-shy, and bowled him over like a nine-pin, Reu. After that, as you may depend, I thought it no harm to help myself to the villain's weapons, and a few other handy trifles he had about him. See here, Reu."

And as Tom spoke he pointed to quite a heap of oddments lying just by.

"But, Tom," said I, "did that single crack on the head so completely knock the pluck out of him, that he allowed you to plunder him without farther struggle?"

"Without farther struggle!" echoed Tom, turning away his head, and looking, as I thought, as though he would rather the subject of conversation were changed.

"Well, at all events he has spoilt the purpose of our journey," said I; "we may rely on his hurrying home, and telling his friends of the treatment he has received. There can be no doubt as to their being able to recognize us from his description, Tom."

"There is a matter we may rely on much better," replied Tom, "and that is, that he has done us all the harm he ever will do."

"What!" said I, laughing, and never suspecting the truth, "did you make him promise he would not split on us, Tom?"

"Nothing at all was said about splitting after the mallet had cracked his ugly head," replied Tom, trying to put a bold face on the matter; "he's dead!"

"Dead!" I repeated with horror.

"Dead enough," replied Tom, brazen now that the cat was out; "not deader, though, than we should have been had he had his way.

Why! what's the matter? He's served better than he deserves if it comes to that, for I did leave him with his head on his shoulders, and that's more than he would have done for me."

"That's only a guess, Tom," said I, feeling strangely melancholy that my companion had taken a human life. I say strangely melancholy, and so it was, considering how that I had helped at the slashing and slaying when the pirates fought the ship "Sultan," and never lay awake a single hour being sorry for it.

"And not a bad guess either, though no credit is due to me, considering that I was helped to it by this pretty thing."

And Tom, walking up to his plunder heap, picked up a little net made of bark fibre, and in appearance exactly matching with those we had seen the pirates wearing, and in which they carried their horrid head trophies. So far, however, from feeling shocked at the sight of this one, I experienced considerable relief, for it went far in favour of Tom's suggestion that it was only in defence of our lives that we had taken that of the savage. I further tried to comfort myself with the reflection that the Bornean's death had ensued on a chance blow, but Tom's replies to one or two questions I asked him on this matter were so evasive, that I thought it prudent not to pursue it. No doubt it was just as Tom had related as far as knocking the fellow down went, but I have grave suspicions that when Tom came up to him he had life left for scuffling, and that Tom's blood being up he was rather unmerciful.

"This is no time for going into particulars," said Tom; "he got what he deserved, and there is an end of the business."

"An end of *that* business let us hope, Tom," said I; "but what about our own affairs? What are we to do next?"

"Have some supper," replied he coolly, and resorting once more to his heap of plunder, he produced five stout stumps of what looked like bamboo, about a foot long. Had they been placed in my hands, I should no more have thought of making a supper off them than of any handful of rushes that grew by the water where we were sitting; but Tom, while at Magindano, had had better chances than myself of roaming about the place, and noticing the various occupations of the inhabitants; and on one occasion he had observed an old fellow busily engaged in boiling rice till it was as sticky as honey, and mixing it with what looked like treacle. The old man from time to time tasted the stuff, so that Tom knew that it was good to eat. When it had grown cool, he brought out a bundle of just such reed stumps as those that Tom now held in his hand, and stuffed each one of them with the sweetened rice. We afterwards discovered that this method was

the one adopted not only in Magindano, but also throughout Borneo, for the convenient carrying of food by travellers, the bamboo possessing certain qualities tending to keep the rice sweet; otherwise, in a climate as hot as this is, very few hours would serve to convert it to a state too nasty to be eaten.

Sitting in the bright moonlight by the edge of the quiet stream, Tom and I each grasping a bamboo rice-holder as though it were a marrow-bone, scraped out the contents with a bit of stick, and though perhaps if the same mess were put before me now I should turn sickening from it, I assure the reader that never in my life did I sup with greater relish, or (although in the five holders there was much more rice than might be supposed), with a more intense longing that

Dyak Weapons.

there had been more to eat. As was easy to see Tom was in exactly the same humour, and so complete was our own enjoyment that for the time all else was forgotten. With our last mouthful, however, our respite was at an end, and the question of "what was next to be done?" presented itself with such urgency as was not be resisted. It

was, however, a question much more easily asked than answered.   By
killing the Dyak Tom had quite spoilt the purpose of our journey.
True, we might reach the country to which the dead man had belonged, and we might be well received; but, knowing the way we had
come, as soon as the body was discovered, we should undoubtedly be
suspected of the murder, and be punished according.   On the other
hand, we had now been away from our masters over two days and a
night, and if we returned might reasonably expect no more tender
treatment than was usually accorded to runaway slaves.   So that
between the two fires it seemed pretty clear that we were in for a
roasting.   There seemed no possible way out of the mess, and this was
the only conclusion we could arrive at after full a half-hour's deliberation.   At last, when we had both been silent for several minutes,
Tom seemed suddenly to be inspired by a brilliant idea.

"Look here, Reu!" said he, "according to your way of thinking,
leaving the dead Dyak out of the business, our chances are much about
the same if we turn back or go forward.   I know you think so, though
you don't like to say as much!"

"If that is not what I think, it is pretty much like it," I replied.

"Very good, now comes in the dead Dyak.   If we go forward he
does us harm; if we turn back——"

"He does us neither harm nor good," I interrupted.

"But suppose we can so contrive matters that he is made to do us
good? that he is made to secure us a welcome from our Magindano
friends instead of a whipping or worse?"

"Why, then," said I, laughing, "if we could manage so neat a
trick I think we might justly call ourselves clever fellows.   But is it
to be managed, Tom?"

"Suppose we cut off his head and carry it in!   It is of no further
use to him, and since heads appear of such high value in these parts
it seems a sin to see one lying idle when it might be made of use.   If
you had only seen how proud that fellow I told you of was of his
speckled-cheeked prize, and how the people came round him and
praised him and caressed him, you would catch at my proposition a
little more eagerly than you do."

Tom was right when he said that I did not seem to take his suggestion eagerly.   To cut the Dyak's head off now that he was lying
dead seemed a crime little less than that of killing him, nor was that

the worst part; the horrid trophy would have to be carried by one of us—by both of us if we expected to share in the benefit which would arise from its possession.   It would have to be carried the live-long day—the ghastly thing must be guarded in the night while we lay down to rest all in the stilly darkness.

"I can have nothing to do with such a shocking business, Tom," said I, "nor will you, I am sure, when you think further on it."

"But I don't mean to think further about it," returned Tom, obstinately.   "Since you won't have anything to do with it, I will take it all on myself, as is quite proper since it was I who killed him. Since we are to turn back we may as well set off at once; we have supped and we are rested, and it is almost as light as day.   Here, Reu, take these things—I would put the goat-skin cloak on if I were you—and go on; I will overtake you."

The things Tom alluded to were such as he had stripped off the Dyak, and consisted of a skin-cloak and a cloth to be worn about the loins, a sort of skull cap of monkey skin, two spears and a water-bottle; so that Tom must have stripped the body entirely. One item of the dead man's goods I have omitted to mention, and that was his kris, a very handsome weapon with a handle of what might very well have been gold from its appearance.   Tom took possession of the kris, while I slipped on the skin cloak and took up the other things; then he pointed out the road I should go, and saying he would presently overtake me he turned into the thick of the wood.

I walked on as he desired, feeling for the first time since we had been travelling together, not all afraid of being alone, but rather inclined to take to my heels and run that Tom might not overtake me; indeed, when after a lapse of a few minutes I heard his well-known whistle I could not forbear a shudder, as I thought of the horrid thing he would bring swinging in his hand.

He had, however, exercised more delicacy over the ugly business than I should have thought him capable of.   As he came up facing me I saw that he carried nothing in his hands but the kris, which was bright and untarnished as when he left me a few minutes before, and a thrill of delight possessed me as I thought that he had altered his mind.   But in this I was mistaken.   As he came closer and half turned to avoid a low, hanging bough, I saw that he carried a bundle at his back, a round bundle done up first in green-leaves and then deposited in the net before mentioned. It however fitted the net so exactly that it was impossible to doubt what it was. Not a word was said respecting it, however, and though as we trudged along hour after hour and discussed what sort of reception we were likely to receive when we got "home," and speculated how long a time was likely to elapse before we reached it, the bulk that, slung round Tom's neck, hung between his shoulders might have been a natural hump, for all the conversation it provoked; nevertheless, it was present to both our minds every minute of the time, as was certain from the fact that whereas before Tom had taken the lead he now insisted on my going first, so that I never once caught sight of the net.

So we journeyed till the sun was blazing hot, and then having picked the Dyak's monkey skin cap full of berries we halted beside a stream to rest and refresh ourselves, intending after spending an hour or so in this manner to push on again till the evening, hoping by this means to reach that part of Magindano whither we were bound some time next morning.

Judge, then, our surprise as involved in deep thought we both lay in silence on the rugged grassy banks, we both became aware of a sound which could have proceeded from none but a human animal, for it was neither a sound of wings, nor of bird-music, nor such as could be made by any beast of the forest, but a regular "click! click!" as of a chopper against a tree trunk. We simultaneously raised our heads and regarded each other with amazement.

"Surely, it cannot be, Tom!" I exclaimed, "we can't have arrived there in this little time!"

"Arrived where?" asked Tom, looking much scared.

"At one end of Magindano."

"I am afraid not," replied my companion, ruefully, "the fact is we have missed the road, Reu, and—and come unawares on the country of the speckled-cheeks!"

And as Tom said this he hastily broke the cord to which *his* specimen of a speckled-cheek was attached, and was for pitching it into the stream.

"We had better get rid of that fellow's goods as soon as we can, Reu," exclaimed he, hurriedly, "our heads are not very secure on our shoulders as it is; but to be caught with these things about us would be nothing short of asking them to cut our throats off-hand.

Take off that jacket, my lad, quick! let us make a bundle of the lot and sink it in the water with a stone." And in his hurry he began helping to disrobe me with no gentle hand.

"Stay a bit, Tom," said I, "it may be as well to make sure, or, at least, as sure as you are able; it would be a pity after all your pains in carrying that disgusting trophy about with you, if you should throw it away and presently wish in vain for it back again. There is a chance that, after all, we may be nigher to Magindano than we think. Suppose we climb a tall tree and take a survey. If the choppers we hear are those of Magindano, the village should not be very far off.

Close at hand was a rare tall tree of the palm tribe, and assisted by Tom I swarmed up its smooth lower part till I was able to reach the branches, when to mount to the very top was an easy matter. A single glance showed me the true state of the case. We were indeed approaching Magindano; it was yet far distant, some three or four miles perhaps; but in the clear bright morning it was easy enough to make out its general shape and arrangement in a manner that left no room to question its identity.

Tom was so full of dismal apprehension that looking down from my perch I saw that he had already found a stone, and was trying the depth of the stream with a stick to find a deep place in which the terrible parcel might presently be sunk; but when I called down to him that it was all right, and by telling him of the signs by which I knew that it was so, convinced him of the impossibility of there being any mistake, his spirits revived, and by the time I reached the ground he had resumed his net-load and was ready to start.

It was evident from Tom's demeanour that he expected to gain something beyond simple forgiveness by the possession of the head of an enemy of the people who owned us, and stepped along in a way I had never hoped to see, at least on that road. I must own, however, that I was not over sanguine. I had no wish to dishearten Tom, but I could not help reflecting, that after all he might be mistaken in supposing that the speckled-cheeked race were the enemies of our pirate friends. It is true, Tom had seen just such a head as he had in his net in the possession of one of them, and the ghastly thing was highly prized; but Tom was quite ignorant of the language as well as of the manners of the inhabitants, and for all he knew to the contrary the speckle-faces instead of enemies of the Magindanos, might be their dearest friends, and the man who had the head to exhibit might have been actuated by love and respect and not by savage triumph and malignity. If this were the case Tom Cox was about to put his foot in it, as the saying is, in a rather alarming manner.

We agreed that if we could manage it, it would be better for us to slip out of the forest and march straight into the town lest we should meet a party sent in quest of us, and whose orders might possibly be to kill us as soon as we were caught. But in this plan we were baulked; the only path we could find led straight to that part of the wood were the choppers were at work, and that we were now pretty close upon them we knew by the increasing noise. Indeed, after a little further walking we came in sight of the slaves' huts and could hear the harsh screaming voice of the driver, and now and then the cracks of his whip.

Not knowing what might be in store for us we paused irresolute; but presently Tom exclaimed, "Come on, Reu, it's no use to shilly-shally, we've got to face, so here goes."

So saying he strode bravely towards the spot where the wood-choppers were at work, I keeping close to his side. Presently we stepped from the cover of the bushes into an open the men had cleared and stood fairly in their sight.

Instantly there was such an uproar and consternation as I will not attempt to describe. Every woodman started to his feet, uttering every conceivable sound of astonishment, and ran towards us in a body still bearing their axes in their hands and flourishing them with gestures which seemed so threatening, that it really appeared that the order to kill us wherever we were found had been given. At first the slave driver did not perceive us, but when he did, he set up a whooping and yelling and came bounding towards us as though the very moment he laid hands on us his fortune was made.

Without doubt his intention was to seize us, but when he came nearly close enough for the purpose, he suddenly looked, as I thought, full in my face, and, coming to a dead halt, clapped his hand over his mouth—the customary method among these savages of expressing extreme astonishment. With hurried ejaculations he kept pointing at my head, as did the others gathered in a large ring about us, but had we been afflicted by the plague they could not have kept at a more respectful distance.

"What on earth are they staring at, Tom ?" I asked him ; "there's nothing more than common about my face, is there ?"

"It is not your face but the cap that they are making all this fuss about, I believe," replied Tom ; "try the effect of taking it off, my lad."

I did as Tom suggested, holding it out towards the driver. I expected that he would come to take it, but as it was held towards him he gave a cry and fell back further than ever, as did all the rest of them, and that with such evident demonstrations of awe as made the whole business perfectly unaccountable. Tom, however, was not at all perplexed.

"I told you how it would be, my lad," he softly whispered ; "since they find so much to admire and respect in the cap, what will they say when they see the head that fits it ?"

"It is not so much what these fellows say, Tom," I remarked, at present only half convinced that he had done a wise thing in bringing away the Dyak's head ; "it is for the opinion of the great guns of the town we have most to care ; suppose we try and make them understand that we wish to be taken to the chief ?"

This was not at all difficult. We had only to point towards the town, when the driver replied with a vigorous shake of the head, and began hurrying in that direction, beckoning us to follow. The slave gang would have come too, but the driver, with furious gestures, forbade them ; so, still keeping a considerable distance between himself and us, he trotted on, we following.

As we neared the town, however, and encountered the inhabitants in the pursuit of their various employments, our escort rapidly increased : indeed the magic of the monkey-skin cap was as effective with everyone we met as on the slaves in the forest. Certainly it was now a more conspicuous object than ever, for it having occurred to me that a thing so tremendous for good or evil was no fit ornament for a head in jeopardy, I did not replace it when I took it off, but handed it to Tom, who, glorying in the sensation it was creating, stuck it on the hilt of the kris and carried it aloft ; and a very curious figure he must have cut, with his tangled hair and ragged jacket, and the net seemingly stuffed with green leaves slung behind him.

By the time we came within sound of the clatter of the monkeys perched about the platform, we were surrounded by at least a hundred of the inhabitants, all yelling and hooting and eagerly pointing, but none so bold as to approach us closely; nor were we to approach the house of the chief unannounced, for swift runners had gone before to tell the news, and looking ahead we saw the head men of the place coming to meet us, and among them, to our alarm, were our enemies Anakraja and the old doctor, and heading the procession the terrible old chief whose mouth had, through my instrumentality, been defiled. There was, however, nothing in his appearance to denote that he entertained vengeful feeling on that score; he looked amazed and expectant, and that was all. One thing, however, struck us as being not a little singular; the cap the old chief wore resembled exactly, in shape and material, the one Tom carried on the hilt of the kris, while no such thing was to be seen on the heads of any of the head men and captains who attended him.

And, to keep the reader no longer in suspense, this was the key to the whole mystery. Like certain badges of royalty in civilized nations, the black monkey-skin cap was, among these Dyaks, a covering sacred to the heads of chiefs and their sons; indeed the article represented royalty as does the queen's sceptre, and may no more be approached unceremoniously than her majesty's august person. How then could have happened a thing so marvellous that we two runaways should become possessed of the precious emblem?

As we approached, the chief and his party came to a standstill, and we both falling on our knees, Tom presented to the old chief at once the cap and the kris. He heeded not the kris, however, but taking the cap eagerly in his hands, examined it curiously, and then proceeded to ask us a string of questions, not one of which we could understand. Under the circumstances, however, the natural inference was that he wanted to know how we had come by the cap. In a hurried whisper we both agreed that this was the case, and that the sooner his curiosity was satisfied the better, so Tom at once unslung his net, and disrobing the loathsome thing within of its leafy covering, displayed it to the chief and his counsellors.

The effect was tremendous. From the peculiarity of the tatooing or some other reason, the pallid face was instantly recognized, and chief and counsellors at once set up a chorus of delightful surprise that was highly gratifying to us to hear. The ghastly relic was taken in hand and passed about and admired, everyone having a question to ask Tom, who by this time was looking as proud as a general who had achieved his first victory. Tom was perfectly right in his surmise that the Dyak's head might prove something more even than a peace-offering. Everyone, including even Anakraja (though it evidently cost him a twist to accomplish the deceit), looked kindly on him; especially after when, in dumb show, they had made him understand the question, "Did he perform the feat single-handed and without my assistance," and Tom had very heartily jerked his head betokening "Yes."

This, however, was a sad question for me. "Honour to whom honour is due," would seem to be a maxim adhered to with extreme exactness among these barbarians. Tom had served his master by cutting off the head of the chief of their most inveterate enemies and to Tom, and Tom alone, must honour be given. Beckoning my companion to follow him, the chief, himself carrying the head, turned towards his house, but when I attempted to go too, I was rudely thrust back by one of the chief officers, who, at the same time, snatched the spear from my hand and the goat-skin cloak from my back, and called to the driver of the wood-chopping slaves, who still stood by, to take charge of me. Looking back Tom witnessed the outrage and made a stop, and as I could see by his manner, commenced a vehement harangue in my favour. I was too far off to hear what he said, but that it was ineffectual was too plain; the crowd moved on again, and the driver, giving me a push with his whip-stock, directed me the contrary way. At that I felt particularly lonely and wretched, and but for the shame of the thing, would have wept outright. Tom, however, even at the risk of giving offence to his new friends, could not let me go without a word of comfort, so bawled out loud enough for me to hear—

"Keep a good heart, Reu. I'll soon have you with me again."

"The sooner the better, Tom," I hallooed in return. How Tom fared for his daring I durst not turn my head to see, but I caught a crack of the whip, and so with smarting shoulders I was led back to slavery.

The axe I had abandoned was once more placed in my hand, and I recommenced the monotonous labour of chipping trees down, broken only, for the space of about an hour, at midday, when we were allowed to eat our handful of rice and lay down and rest, or smoke tobacco if we were lucky enough to possess any.

So passed day after day till nearly a week had slipped by, but still I had neither seen nor heard anything of Tom, and I was fast arriving at one of two conclusions—the one scarcely a whit more dismal than the other—either that he had been made so much of that he had no time to think of his **poor companion**, or that he was after all mistaken in the nature of the wages he had earned for cutting off the Dyak's head, and was by this time dead and buried, or languishing in some prison. I grew weary of ever watching the road to the village looking for the coming of Tom Cox or some friendly messenger of his; I grew sick of my employment, of my food, of my companions—of my very self. At times ugly thoughts would so thickly beset me, that I had a mind to settle my score of wrongs with the bully driver with the blade of my adze, and make an end of the business altogether. At other times, as I lay awake at night in the hot and suffocating hut, I would picture Tom luxuriously housed and clothed and fed, and reflect whether it would not be possible for me to run away again and hunt for a Dyak with speckled cheeks and slay him, and make a good **market of his** head as Tom had done. Had I possessed any sort of weapon I really believe I should have attempted this wicked and absurd venture, but as soon as work was over in the evening, the driver very carefully collected the axes and secured them in the hut in which he himself slept till the morning.

I think it must have been on a Sunday morning (not that any difference in the behaviour of my companions warranted the conclusion, for Sunday and Saturday, and indeed every other day, except once or twice in the year, when they perform their heathen ceremonies, are all working days among these barbarians), and about the eighth day of my renewed slavery, when **my despondency** was greater than ever before. This perhaps arose from the fact that I was left to myself and had not the jabber of my fellow slaves to distract my thoughts; and why I was alone happened in this way. To save time the rice for our dinners was all boiled in one pot, and in turn each of the slaves had to be cook to the rest. It happened on this day that the office fell on me, and all the morning I was engaged in tending the fire and keeping the pot boiling. Melancholy as ever human being yet was, as I sat I pulled a forked stick **towards** me, and thinking of anything but what I was doing, began raking the hot embers with it, and using it, in fact, as a poker is used.

Who can tell when his luck may change, or, indeed, what is good luck and what bad? The threshold to the Temple of Fame is not always of a piece with the inner splendour, but ofttimes is so unpromising that we unconsciously pass the door that would open readily by a push. But there, one can do no more than avail himself of fair opportunities as far as he may see them; if they extend beyond his range of vision—as he afterwards discovers—let him console himself with the reflection that a blind man would have been thankful to have seen only half as far as he, the short-sighted one, saw himself.

I, sitting on the trunk of a tree, and cowering over a smoky fire, with a bare back and an empty belly, was as nigh the threshold of fame and of vast wealth as any man who ever lived. As I sat stirring the red embers, I held in my hand a wand more potent than ever yet was wielded by enchanter. The said wand was the forked bough.

As I poked at the fire there oozed from the jagged end of the stick a gummy whity-brown substance, which, as I indolently watched it, trickled on to the embers, and, there melting, died away; when, however, I held up my stick, the gum seemed to harden as it cooled, and hung from the stick as birdlime would. I idly gathered a pendent string of the stuff in my hand and rolled it into a ball, and speedily it became as hard as leather and as tough, for I could not indent it with my finger-nail. I stuck the ball on the crook of the stick, and toasted it till it fell flat and soft, and then I moulded it round my wrist bracelet fashion, kneading the ends together. Then for the first time I began to think with some degree of seriousness of what I was doing, for the stuff had become a hard, tight ring round my wrist, and try as I might I could not break it away. I had no knife to cut it, so I took to biting it, and, hurting my teeth, was reminded of my late disastrous failure, and no sooner were the two subjects—the gum ring round my wrist and the dentistry business—brought together in my mind than they seemed to fit each other so exactly that it seemed a pity to disturb them, so I let them alone and quietly brooded over them; and this was what was hatched from my brooding. Here was a vegetable substance hard as wood, light as cork, tough as whalebone, and, under the influence of heat, ductile as dough. What an excellent material wherewith to make artificial gums!

To regain the favour of my masters—to escape from my present mean condition—was my chief desire, and, since this new and curious substance promised to help me to this, it was all I hoped of it. Knowing what I now know—what all the world knows—how ridiculously modest my ambition seems! What might I not have demanded of the good genius who had placed round my wrist that magic bracelet! The reader will be able himself to make the calculation when I inform him that the dingy bracelet was gutta-percha!

Full of hopes and fears, I distilled a few more drops from the end of my magic stick, and tested the new material in all sorts of ways. I stuck chips of wood into it, and allowing it to cool tried to pull them out again, but they resisted all my efforts until I held the substance to the fire, and then their release was easy enough; it was as smooth as silk to the touch, and, though pulled out to quite a thin string, was not to be broken, pull how I might. Never doubting for a moment but that the substance must already be well known to the natives, I puzzled my brain for a reason why Anakraja had not used it; but after all, and as the manufactures of my own country furnished abundant testimony, one very often seeks far afield for the very thing that lies unheeded at his door.

Of one thing I was determined, I would seek Anakraja at the very earliest opportunity, and submit to him my discovery. How to get at him was the difficulty. To ask permission to visit him would, I knew, be useless, and it might be weeks, or even months, ere he visited the forest where I was at work. Now, more than ever, I yearned to see Tom.

I am afraid that my preparation of that mess of rice did not go far towards gaining me a fair reputation as a cook. Indeed, I forgot all about the fire as well as the pot, so that the latter emitted a smell of scorching, and the former died out almost to the last ember. However, they for whom I was caterer were blessed with appetites not easily offended; so sousing some more water among the rice, and fanning up the fire beneath, I had a steaming boil ready for them by the time the gong sounded, and the meal passed over without a complaint.

Although I ate no dinner, the fault lay with my head rather than with my stomach. Instead of squatting down with the rest, I sauntered off a little way to give my mind to thinking on how the stuff which composed the ring about my wrist might be made to serve me in the shortest possible time. Then it suddenly occurred to me, that if I wished to keep my secret for the present *quite* to myself, I must remove my brown bracelet, which looked conspicuous enough on my right wrist, and would probably excite the curiosity of my fellow-choppers, when I presently sat down to work with them; but, though

Davidger at work in the South Pacific.

I tried very hard, I found it impossible to remove it. I could not pull it over my hand; I could not bite it through; I tried to cut it by rubbing it against the edge of an adze, but the weapon was too blunt for the purpose; and to squeeze my hand through it I found to be impossible; and, unfortunately—as it seemed to me at the time, though as the reader will presently see, it was the luckiest thing that could have happened—in the midst of my endeavours to remove my bracelet, the gong sounded for work, and I was compelled to desist from my efforts, and join the gang.

But it was no longer as a hopeless, miserable wretch that I returned to the labour of tree-felling; the bracelet seemed to have quite a talismanic effect on my spirits, and as my arm and leg were by this time nearly well, I seemed in better humour for work than I had felt since my arrival on the island. Never before did the Dyak method of tree-felling seem so ridiculous as that afternoon, when, tailorwise, I took my adze in hand like the rest of the workmen. Suddenly it came into my head that I would show them the English method of felling a tree, and how superior it was to their tinkerish mode. The axe, to be sure, was but a sorry substitute for the axe of the English woodman, as well as I was a sorry substitute for the woodman himself; but when I had selected a not over-large tree, and, swinging the axe over my shoulder, commenced making the splinters fly, the rest of the choppers, who were, as usual, squatted on their hams, desisted from work and stared aghast, especially when they presently saw the tree fall. Attracted by their wondering ejaculations, up came the taskmaster, and he, seeing how matters stood, to my astonishment began to look angry, and to regard me with glances which were anything but friendly; but when I came to understand that he had risen to the position of driver solely on his merits as a skilful woodman, my surprise ceased. It was not to his interest that one of his fellows should chop timber faster than he himself could.

In a moment, however, he masked his anger by a forced laugh of contempt, and, looking about him, selected two trees, and, taking an axe from a slave, motioned me to one tree (the largest by some inches), squatted at the foot of the other, and invited me to test my skill against his. Had I been allowed time for consideration, I should have foreseen the danger of beating my master, and taken pains to have lost the match; but, luckily, pride of country stepped before the meaner sentiment, and I straightened my back and went to work with a will—England against Borneo.

Borneo didn't have a chance after the first half-a-dozen strokes. Considering his tailor-like position, he chopped with marvellous dexterity; but his blows were weak, and took but slow effect; while I exerted myself to the very top of my strength, so much so that, about midway in the job, the axe was broken in the middle of the handle, and I had to provide myself with another, and the result was that my tree was brought with its crown to the earth while the marrow of his had not yet felt the axe. The taskmaster was signally defeated on his own challenge, and the slaves, who bore him about as much good-will as might be expected, clapped their hands to see it.

The taskmaster's copper-coloured face turned ash-colour with rage, and, starting to his feet with his axe still in his hand, he rushed towards me. Whether it had been his intention to cut me down with it I can't exactly tell; I only know that he raised the weapon very suspiciously, and I, too, raised mine. In an instant a curious change came over him. Like a man seized with sudden fright, he stepped back a pace or two, and his axe dropped from his shaking hand, and there he stood with his great mouth ajar, and his eyes staring in a way that would, under ordinary circumstances, have been very ludicrous to behold. For a few seconds I was much puzzled to know what act of mine had brought about this extraordinary change in the driver, but happening presently to raise my arm—the one with the ring on—I noticed that his staring eyes were raised too, and then the truth was apparent enough; it was my bracelet that had caused his dismay, that it was on which his eyes were fixed, at which his finger pointed. Seeing the taskmaster so strangely affected, the slaves had desisted from their work, and though they did not dare approach close enough to see the reason, they knew it must be something unaccountable, and, as I have invariably found with every savage people among whom it has been my lot to be cast, to be un-accountable is to be dreadful; and so they remained looking from one to the other in a strange, uneasy manner, and evidently uncertain whether they should stay and hear an explanation, or run off at once out of harm's way.

It seemed to me at the time, that the driver's surprise and terror, were assumed to suit his own ends; but now I come calmly to consider the matter, I am of a different opinion. Although he was invested with some sort of authority, he was in no way superior in intelligence to the brutish crew he governed, and in all probability shared with them in their ignorant superstition. Anyhow, if his horror was assumed, it was a most excellent piece of acting, and when presently he found his speech, and cried out, "Antu! antu!" had it been the apparition of the devil himself that called forth the exclamation, it could not have been given, uttered with greater heartiness.

But, for that matter, it *was* the father of evil at whom the driver had taken fright. "Antu" in the Dyak tongue means "spirit," and "spirit," means a minister of Satan. My bracelet was the antu the task-master alluded to, and as soon as he had uttered the dread word, every slave in the gang leapt to his feet with a cry of terror, and skipping behind the trees to be as much as possible out of my reach, peeped out on me with faces full of fear and quaking. The driver however kept his ground, or if he had at all shifted it was not more than a few steps. Had my silly notion of escaping into the woods again still possessed me, I could now have put it in execution easily enough; armed with my adze I might have walked off, and no one would have dared to follow me; and indeed it did seem as though to run away was as good a course as any to pursue, for there was a great deal of rage as well as of terror in the faces that surrounded, and I could not be sure one moment from another that they would not fall on me and murder me off-hand. But somehow the bracelet seemed to inspire me with perfect confidence, and I felt not the least afraid; on the contrary, I think I felt a little proud at having produced such a decided sensation.

"Why, what does this mean?" I asked, forgetting in the excitement of the moment that they did not understand a word I was saying; "what is there to frighten anybody in this simple thing? Here, examine it for yourselves and see."

And as I spoke I flung aside my adze, and walked open-handed towards the driver. If, however, they did not comprehend my spoken language, they had wit enough to know that the devil himself without an axe, is less dangerous than with one, and seeing that the driver did not scruple to seize me by the wrist, in an instant they were all upon me, holding me powerless, though I had possessed the strength of an ox. But though they grasped at every other part of my body, including even the hair of my head; they studiously avoided the arm on which the bracelet was, and when in my struggles I happened to touch any one of them with it, the fellow would shrink away as though it was red hot, and had burnt him.

The conversation which then transpired was, as I afterwards made out, pretty much as follows :—

"See how we have been deceived!" said the driver; "this is not a man, but a spirit—a spirit of the devil! See, his arm is

Davidger's Match at Woodcraft with the Driver.

strengthened by a charm, the like of which was never before seen. Come here, Lunak Sada, and you, Kara Tiku, and tell us whether from your old memories, you have a knowledge of this strange thing."

So Lunak Sada (the "fat fish") and Kara Tiku ("monkey tail") stepped forward, and, handling my fingers as fearfully as though they had been the tails of venomous serpents, examined the ring long and curiously.

"It is neither iron, nor brass, nor any sort of metal," pronounced Lunak Sada gravely.

"Nor wood, nor stone, nor anything that grows on the face of the earth," was the equally emphatic decision of Kara Tiku.

"Iain antu! bunoh iya! bunoh iya!" shouted the slaves in one voice; and though their vengeful emphasis alone made the foreign words very terrible, they would have been even more so had I known their import, which was, "A bad spirit! Kill him! kill him!"

But the driver, while he evidently regarded my death as a consummation by no means undesirable, was withheld, as it would seem, by certain directions he had received from the young doctor when the latter had given me over to the task-master's custody.

"Nay," said he, "it would be of no use for such as us to try and kill him; his body, destroyed by us, would only spring up in another shape—in shape of a son or a daughter of ours, perhaps, for these white devils are very malicious. The way of putting him altogether out of the world is known only to our priests. Let us take him to Anakraja, that he may deal with him."

I must once more remind the reader that, at the time, this was to me not intelligible talk, but mere gibberish, accompanied by all sorts of violent and threatening gestures. Nevertheless, I found myself listening as attentively when one and the other spoke as though able to understand every word; and, at the end of the discourse, as the savages unanimously repeated, "Anakraja!" and, after binding my arms, began, in a body to move, taking me with them, I had little difficulty in arriving at the conclusion that to "Anakraja" I was about to be taken.

As the reader is already aware, Anakraja was the young doctor, but at the time in question I was quite unacquainted with his name, and what the word signified I could not even give a guess. "Anyhow," thought I, finding that to Anakraja I was to be taken, "if it is anything bad"—and I could not suppose they were putting themselves to so much trouble for the purpose of conferring a favour on me—"it may happen that I shall find a friend at court," thereby meaning master Cox, of whom I had heard no tidings since the day I left him in such illustrious company. If Tom was alive, no doubt he was in high favour, and it was not likely he would see his old comrade come to grief, if it were in his power to save him.

They led me out of the forest, and towards the village, shouting and clapping their hands as they went, while I was busily revolving in my mind how I should make my case clear, and how, supposing I should be able to see Tom Cox, and not be able to approach him on account of his dignity, I might in as few words as possible make him understand how matters stood. Judge then of my surprise, when, on our arriving very nearly to the outer palisading, I beheld Tom Cox, tattered as ever, and grimy as a sweep, squatting before an anvil, and banging away at a bit of red-hot iron, while his assistant was blowing the forge fire out of an instrument looking rather more like a highlander's bagpipes than a smith's bellows.

I lost no time in shouting Tom's name, which, on hearing, he answered by shouting my name in return, and scrambling to his feet in such a hurry as to capsize his bellows-blower, bagpipes, and all. In his rough way he pushed aside the fellows who would have hindered him, and shook me by the hand in the heartiest manner.

"Why, what's up now, shipmate?" inquired he with astonishment ; "what new devilry are they brewing for you? But I'm glad to see you alive, Reu," continued he, giving my hand another squeeze ; " I began to give up all hope of ever seeing you again."

"The same thoughts have been troubling me concerning yourself, I assure you, Tom ; but one thing I made quite sure of, and that was that if I found you alive it would be as a sort of nabob—a lord chancellor, maybe, or something of that kind. How comes it, Tom, that you are still a blacksmith? What did all their fussing and caressing mean if nothing better than this was to come of it?"

But by this time the mob who surrounded us began to grow impatient of the delay, and urged me forward in a way there was no resisting, so Tom walked by my side towards the council house."

"Well you see, Reu," replied he to my question, "there is a longish story attached to that business, and this is no time to begin a long story. Tell me where they are taking you and what for?"

But as the reader already knows all about that part of the business, I need not recapitulate. It occupied a certain time, however, and that it may not be lost to the reader I may as well here relate how that in consequence of being ignorant of the customs of the country, Tom lost a good chance of being made a great man.

Going back to that day when, with the Dyak's head slung in the net behind his back, and the Dyak's monkey-skin cap on the point of the kris, Tom encountered the mob of grandees who came out to meet him, I may state that the cordiality and respect with which they greeted my companion was perfectly genuine. As luck would have it the head Tom had brought in was, of all heads, the one most desired by old Ribut Bungat (for such was the name of the chief of Magindano) and his friends; for not only was the owner of the head with the speckled cheeks the only son of the chief of the tribe, but scarcely three months before, while Ribut Bungat and his chief officers were out hunting in the forest, a famous young captain, who was one of the party, and whose father was one of Ribut Bungat's chief counsellors, happening to lag somewhat behind, was attacked by the Speckled Cheek, who lay in ambush, and slain, the assassin bearing away the head of his victim, but in his haste leaving behind his short, broad-bladed knife, by which they knew him.

Now, according to ancient Dyak law, should a man fall by the hand of the enemy, and another pursue and take the assassin's life, the last-mentioned individual finds great favour with the friends of the first. If the chief representative of the slain one's family is an elderly man, and the avenger is an elderly man, that the two swear eternal brotherhood, and for the remainder of their lives treat each other as though come of one mother; if the avenger is a young man and the slain one's relation an old man, the relation of father and son exists ever afterwards between them.

Nor is the ceremony which makes men, strangers yesterday, to-day the dearest friends, one of words only. Certain rites have to be performed, and of a character that should obtain no mention from me for fear I brought on myself the suspicion of dealing in romance—only that scores of Bornean travellers since my time have observed and recorded the same. This is the ceremony:—As many friends as maybe are invited and on a certain day they take their places seated on the ground in a circle, in the midst of which are the men about to enter the holy bonds of brotherhood. Besides these two men in the middle there is a pig. The witnesses keeping an intent eye on the actors the performance then begins. One of the would-be brothers draws his knife and cuts a line between the pig's shoulders, and the other one immediately draws his knife and crosses the first line by a second on

the back of the unlucky porker. Then some one cuts the pig's throat
—he must be a man of importance among the tribe—and bedabbles the
blade of his kris in the blood of it. The brothers then take off their
jackets and exchange them one with the other; and while their
shoulders are naked the man with the bloody sword touches them
with it in the same fashion as the queen touches a man to make him
a knight, leaving a crimson stain which must remain till it wears off.

If this were the beginning and the end of the ceremony it would
be one in which the most fastidious might engage at a pinch, and that
without burdening his mind with much horror; but the most repulsive
part of the rite has yet to come, and consists of the newly-made
brothers imbibing each other's blood. There are two methods of doing
this, but the preliminaries are the same. These consist of each man
baring his breast just over the heart, while the man who marked their
shoulders with the sanguinary sword, brings a little cup. Each man
then makes a slight incision in his breast and catches the blood in the
cup, so that it mingles. Sometimes water is then added to the contents of the cup, and thus diluted the brothers drink each a share, at
the same time calling on the invisible spirits to witness the action, and
to deal with them according to their sincerity. The other way of dis-
posing of the blood is to spread it on a leaf of the tobacco plant, and
rolling it up cigar fashion, it is lit and puffed at alternately by the
brothers until it is entirely consumed. The former method, however,
is the one most generally adopted, and is considered much more sacred
and binding than the latter. Had it been otherwise Tom might have
fared better.

It happened at the time when the head of the speckled-cheeked
Dyak was brought in, that the old counsellor, the father of the young
captain whom he had slain, was lying ill abed, and knowing that
nothing would so gladden his heart as the news that his son's death
was avenged, Ribut Bungat, instead of conducting Tom to his treasury
there to reward him for his prowess, took him to the hut of the
sick counsellor, who shed many joyous tears and kissed Tom over and
over again, as he himself informed me, till he was nearly sick. Queerly
enough, as Tom thought, he displayed an equal amount of affection
for the hideous relic of his son's murderer, and with affecting earnestness begged of Tom to give it to him. Of course Tom had no use
for the nasty thing, and had he been left to his own devices would

gladly have thrown it into the first hole he met, but finding such high value set on it, he very prudently affected an inclination not to part with it, until even Ribut Bungat himself joined his supplications to those of his servant's, and then Tom gave it up.

The old Magindanoe was overwhelmed with joy and gratitude, and on the spot declared his intention of making Tom his son and sharing with him his worldly possessions—an announcement which everyone present highly applauded, and congratulated Tom, although he couldn't understand a word of what was said, on his good fortune. All Tom could make out was that everyone seemed mighty civil towards him; and when the company presently took its departure, and the old counsellor sent his servants to fetch a rich pelisse of costly skins and placed it himself over Tom's shoulders, and presented him besides with a magnificent pair of earrings and a set of golden bangles to be worn round his wrists, and set before him a rich repast with abundance of palm wine, he was much delighted, and laid down to sleep that night fully impressed with the comfortable conviction that now his fortune was made—that he might cease to trouble himself about the future.

True to his word that he would make Tom his son in the course of the following morning, the old fellow caused preparations to be made for the performance of the ceremony already described. It was customary that it should take place in the open air, at a spot specially set apart for the purpose; but being confined to his bed and being too eager to wait until he grew well, it was arranged that it should take place within the hut, which was a spacious one. Ignorant of how deeply the preparations concerned him, Tom witnessed the arrival of the guests and the sacrificial pig with no more than amused curiosity and it was only when the circle had been formed and he was invited to take his place within it beside the pig that he became aware that the assemblage was on his account, and began to feel a little anxious as well as curious. Presently the sick man was lifted from his mattress and placed in a sitting position beside Tom and the pig, and the ceremony commenced. A knife was placed in Tom's hand, and when the old counsellor with his knife made a gash in the pig's back, Tom, obeying the signs of those present, followed suit, much wondering what it all meant. Then came the ceremony of the exchange of jackets and the shoulder marking with the bloody sword. In the next act, the drawing of blood from the **breast**, the old man led off, and Tom, though **not much fancying it, submitted to** a like operation with the best grace **at his command, feeling, as he said, how neces-** sary it was to affect **good fellowship. But even the** great interest he had at stake **was not sufficient to outweigh his 'natural and** English horror at **what was** immediately to follow. Clasping Tom's hand and with **eyes beaming with** affection, **the old cannibal drank** from the cup and then courteously handed it to honest Tom, invit- ing him, by unmistakable signs, to drink it up. "What! drink that!" exclaimed my shipmate, "I'll see you all jammed first!" and flinging the cup to the ground he rose and made his way out of the circle.

Never since Magindano had been an inhabited island had such an outrage been perpetrated. In an instant a dozen krisses were drawn, and it was only Tom's half-father's earnest intercession that saved him from being cut down on the spot. His disgrace, however, was com- plete, and after being kept a bound prisoner for several days he was set again at the blacksmith's work at which I found him.

And now to return to my own affairs. By the time I had ex- plained the chief events which had happened to me since we had last met, we were very nearly arrived at our destination and I hinted to Tom that perhaps he had better not come any further.

"Well," replied he, "perhaps it will be as well for both our sakes that I turn back, though I shall have a hard time of it, wondering what is happening to you, Reu. How d'ye feel about it, my lad?"

"Livelier than I should, perhaps," I replied. "There's one thing I may tell you, Tom, if *Anakraja*, or some such outlandish word, means death, I think you may shake hands with me for good and all."

"Anakraja!" repeated Tom; "why, that's the scoundrel who pulled out my grinders! I've heard his name a dozen times."

"Well, if that is it, Tom," replied I, "my case is not so bad as I thought, for, if there is a man who can save my life, the one you speak of is he. Just you get back to your work quietly; I shall see you again before long, you may depend."

So off Tom went after shaking hands with me, and leaving me much relieved. And, sure enough, he was right in his information; for when we came to that part of the village where the doctor lived we halted, and, accompanied by the driver and two other fellows, mounted to the terrace and approached Anakraja's hut.

Luckily, he was at home and gave us audience. What the terms of the accusation were I did not understand, but I could see that the doctor listened with much more curiosity than indignation, eyeing me from time to time with a puzzled expression, to which I believe my confident demeanour contributed not a little. When they came to speak of the bracelet—as I knew by their motions—he came up and examined it eagerly, and then, cutting short the slave-driver's harangue, ordered him and his companions out of the place, and Anakraja and I were left alone.

His first act was to endeavour to remove the ring from my wrist, but, finding that he could not, he cut the withe that bound my hands and signed for me to take it off; but this I could do no better than himself, as far as pulling it over my hand went. Finding this, he handed me his knife, but the blade, like all I ever saw there, was of poor stuff, and the edge of it turned back from the tough ring as soon as it touched it. At this, Anakraja's face began to assume an expression something of a character with that I had seen on the faces of the slaves in the forest, when the driver first announced to them his discovery of my true nature. Anakraja couldn't make out how the little ring could have been drawn over the broad hand; neither, as it was easy to see, could he divine of what material the ring was composed; and, as he firmly believed himself less cunning only than the devil himself, he began to smell brimstone about the business, as the saying is. How to remove the bracelet was at first a puzzle to me, till I recollected how fire would soften it, when—the doctor all the time looking on in amazement—I thrust the point of the knife into the fire, and then applying the hot edge to the gutta-percha, divided it easily enough, creating, however during the process a fume and a smell that evidently went far to confirm the doctor's brimstone suspicions. After a little hesitation, however, he took the severed ring in his hands and examined it minutely, but he could make nothing of it. I begged it back, and, holding it on the point of the knife till it was quite soft, drew it out to a longish string, and, waiting a moment till it cooled and hardened, twisted it into a sort of fancy knot and placed it in his hands. Again he took it to the light and tried its strength, and smelt at it, but all his manœuvres failed to make the thing less inexplicable. I took it again, and, once more softening it, picked a chip of wood from the ground and stuck it into the putty-like mass, and when it had cooled the chip was fast fixed, so that, in trying to release it, the doctor broke it short off. Instantly a light seemed to dawn on him. He uttered a cry of joy, and, clapping his hand to his mouth, intimated at once his appreciation of the happy discovery and his desire that it should be kept a profound secret from every one else.

Going to the door, he dismissed the driver and his attendants in terms, as was evident from his tone, of banter and ridicule at the mare's-nest they had discovered. Then he pulled the mat close over the entrance, and, sitting down, invited me with great cordiality to seat myself at his side. Producing the little cake of gutta-percha, which he had thrust in his girdle, he again examined it, and began to ask me a long string of questions respecting it, to all of which, for the best of all possible reasons, I could only shake my head. I might have made him understand easily enough how and where I had discovered the singular substance, but it occurred to me that to do so would be to throw away the better part of the lucky chance that presented itself; should the newly-discovered material prove valuable, my importance, while I held the secret of its source, was secured. Little, however, did I suspect the manner in which the doctor accounted for my possession of it; despite his pretended ridicule of the tale brought him by the slave-driver, Anakraja was not so wise but that he, too, regarded the bracelet as a "witch thing," a gift to myself from the Prince of Darkness, whom I had exhorted to help me out of my difficulties; indeed, Anakraja afterwards told me so himself, and when I expostulated with him on the rashness of meddling with goods he had believed came direct from Satan, he laughingly replied that that was no concern of his—that the white man's "Great Spirit of Bad" was not the black man's, and that any reckoning I had incurred by the transaction it would be my business to settle.

Certainly, any scruples he may have entertained as to the source of the "liem-besi," or *iron-wax*, as he chose to term it, did not stand in the way of his setting about applying it to his pet project—the fixing of the chief's artificial teeth—with the most cheerful alacrity. It happened, too, that, since the failure of our first experiment, it had occurred to me that if the tops of the teeth could be drilled, and securely threaded with fine gold wire, they could be formed into a sort of chain, and admit of much more secure setting than if fixed individually. The doctor caught at the suggestion very readily, and undertook to get the job done. The drilling of the teeth and weaving them together occupied nine days, and, though I saw nothing of them meanwhile, I was convinced that the work was progressing satisfactorily, because day after day my patron's kindness increased so, that the end of a week found me quite set up by good feeding, and with my shoes returned to me, which was a great convenience, as in those regions the ants that swarm about the ground are very apt to attack the feet, depositing their eggs under the toe-nails, and causing them to swell and ulcerate in a very painful manner. As for my jacket, the doctor, with many apologies, declared his inability to return it, as he had given the buttons belonging to it to his wife's sister to make a necklace, and the garment itself to another female relative, who had converted the body of it into a sort of petticoat, and the sleeves into a head-dress; however, in compensation, he procured the skins of two goats, and out of these his wife contrived as comfortable a cloak as I would wish to wear. While aboard ship I had learned to smoke, and I had but to express the desire, to find a pipe and a handful of native-grown tobacco at my disposal. Indeed, it seemed that nothing was denied me but liberty; on this point the doctor was very particular, and whenever he himself went out gave me the strictest injunctions to remain within the house.

At length the teeth came home, and a most excellent job was made of them; so good a job indeed, that I could scarcely believe it was native work, not knowing at the time that, as a worker in wire, the Dyak is second only to the Chinese, of whom he probably learnt the art. Prepared as they were, to fit the teeth into the plastic "liein-besi" was an easy task enough; and by the morning of the eleventh day of my release from wood-chopping my master again set out on his dentistry mission, on the success of which depended what he held most dear in life, while in my case liberty, and perhaps life itself, was at stake.

On this occasion, however, fortune was less unkind. Scarcely more than half an hour could have elapsed from the time of his setting out when he returned, and at a single glance I saw that it was all right. His face was radiant with joy; he wept, he laughed, and, throwing his arms about my neck, kissed me on both cheeks. He called me his "dear brother," his "heart's pulse," and several other extravagant things; and at the termination of his tiresome endearments bade me put on my cloak (for, the morning being hot, I had been lying on a mat smoking my pipe without it) and come with him.

We approached the centre hut, where the two sentries, with their bark petticoats and drawn krisses, kept guard, and were speedily ushered into the presence of the chief, who, as on the occasion of my first introduction to him, was seated at the upper end surrounded by his counsellors, among whom I observed the old doctor, whose lips were compressed, and his eyes flashing with ill-concealed fury. As for the chief, he wore his new teeth, and, without doubt, his appearance was much improved by them; a fact he himself, with the vanity of a girl of seventeen, was verifying as we entered, by the aid of a small mirror. As soon as the chief saw us he kindly beckoned us forward.

Of Anakraja's conduct on this occasion I have no reason to complain; indeed, whenever I reflect on the deep villany he afterwards practised towards me, this generosity of his the more amazes me. One thing, however, should not be forgotten; he had promised to cure my ailments in the space of a month, and here I was (thanks to my luck rather than to his kindness) hale and hearty in little over a fortnight. Moreover, he had, more, I believe, by way of inducing the chief to entrust me to his care than that such was his actual belief, expatiated on the cunning and ingenuity of white men, which made them so much more valuable as slaves than any other sort. Here, then, was an opportunity of convincing the chief at once of his skill as a physician, of his wisdom as a counsellor, and of his profound knowledge of mankind.

"Here is this wondrous white man whom I have cured after my elder brother (the old doctor) had pronounced him incurable, and here is a specimen of the cunning work I bespoke him capable of performing."

This, as nearly as I could make out—for, as I should before have stated, during the eleven days I had been confined to Anakraja's house I had mastered a goodish many words of the Dyak tongue— was the address of Anakraja to the chief, who was thus made to understand, what really was not the fact, that the work which had so pleased him was solely mine; and that all he (Anakraja) claimed w the merit of skill in curing me, and of shrewdness in foreseeing what a clever fellow I was. This address was graciously received, and Ribut Bangat (or, "the hurricane,") gave us his hands to kiss, an act which so infuriated the old doctor, that, forgetful of the etiquette of the council-house, he stamped his foot and rushed out of the place, without the least respectful salutation to his chief. This, according to Sea Dyak law, is an unpardonable offence, and may be visited by death.

Ribut Bangat, however, whatever were his thoughts on his late physician's strange behaviour, only smiled scornfully, and motioned Anakraja to the place vacated. As for myself, I was fairly bewildered when the old fellow turned to me, and bade me name the reward I desired. On account of his new teeth he spoke the words very indistinctly, but "reward" happened to be one of the very words for which I had been at pains to learn the Dyak equivalent.

Now, like all ardent and inexperienced young fellows, my mind was susceptible of the most insignificant influences, and the turn of a straw, as one may say, would plunge me to the depths of despair, or raise me to the topmost pinnacle of expectation. Therefore it came about that, while in the latter mood, I had asked myself this very question: "Suppose you should find such favour with the chief that he would promise to grant any request you chose to make?" To this my immediate reply was, "I would ask for my liberty." But it instantly occurred to me that, if the chief valued my services, this would be the very last favour he would be inclined to grant, and that, indeed by asking it I might give him such offence as to forfeit his good-will altogether. It would be better to observe a little patience—to further please him, and advance another step towards my ultimate aim by an affectation of modesty. It was as well that I had thought the matter over, for when it now became my good fortune "to name the reward I desired," I, with much promptitude, intimated, by signs and words, that I desired nothing better than to be placed in a position to be of such use to the chief as my ability might permit and his wisdom suggest, only stipulating for the company of my companion, Tom Cox. Now, at this time I was quite unaware of the manner in which Tom had put his foot in it, and was therefore much surprised when the latter part of my request was made known to the chief, to see him frown ominously, and shake his head in a very determined manner

while the sages and counsellors about him grunted and wagged their
heads too.   All except one old fellow, who, approaching Ribut Bangat,
addressed him in a beseeching tone till the frown was gradually dispersed from the august countenance of the "hurricane," and consequently from the countenances of his courtiers.   It was not hard to
guess that the conversation concerned Tom—as indeed it did, and, to
his credit be it said, the only man who had a word to say in his
favour, who indeed begged for his forgiveness, was the young captain's
aged father, he whom Tom had so grossly outraged—so, by way of
giving my friend a lift, I beckoned to Anakraja, and intimated to
him, as plainly as I was able, my desire that, if, as I supposed, Tom
Cox had given offence, and his crime was of such a nature as might
be compensated by a gift of goods, any present the chief might have
it in his heart to make me might be applied to that purpose.   My
suggestion, which was interpreted to the chief by Anakraja, so pleased
him that he at once despatched an officer to the treasure-house, and
presently that functionary returned, accompanied by two slaves, who
were loaded with fine mats and native-made cloth, while the officer
himself bore half a dozen rings, as large as those used for curtains,
and as thick as my thumb.   From their weight and general appearance it was plain that they were of solid gold, and Ribut Bangat,
taking them in his hand, slipped three on to each of my wrists, at the
same time uttering certain words which, though they certainly did
not seem so at the time, were much more valuable than the six gold
rings, inasmuch as they conferred on me the rank of an officer of his
household, with certain pay and privileges.   I believe that, in his fit
of excessive generosity, he was about to grant my application for Tom
Cox's company, but, seeing him about to do so, one or two of his
grey-headed counsellors commenced whispering with him, and I was
finally given to understand that Ribut Bangat, although a liberal
chief, and ever anxious to reward merit, could not confer favour on
any one who did not in some way distinguish himself, and that, until
Tom Cox did "distinguish" himself, we could not be allowed to
meet even.

This decision, arbitrary and unaccountable as it seemed at the
time, was, by and by, rendered intelligible enough.   It seems that the
counsellors had advised Ribut Bangat that, though the wisdom and
cunning of white people was unbounded, they were very jealous of

their knowledge, and could never be brought to impart it to strangers unless compelled, at the same time broadly hinting that the chief had already been too ready to reward me for the trifling service I had performed, and that, if he had held back and treated my handiwork lightly, I might have been induced to make a much more extensive and useful display of my ingenuity; and I regretted to see that, although Anakraja did his best for my cause in a long and energetic speech, Ribut Bungat's avarice nearly overtopped his good nature, and he shook his head dubiously, and was evidently inwardly resolved not to let my unlucky fellow-countryman escape so easily.

Finding how the case stood, and being very anxious that Tom should, at least, be made acquainted with my safety and fair prospects, I begged permission to write to him; but, though I made the most graphic signs—forming words on the palm of my hand with my fore-finger, and reading them off audibly—I could obtain no other answer than a look of bewilderment from every one present, including even the learned Anakraja, to whom the chief naturally turned for an explanation.

"Look about you," said Anakraja to me, as the readiest way out of the difficulty, "look about you, and touch the thing you want, that we may understand."

Provided I could have seen in any part of the council-house a pen, a pencil, or even a scrap of paper, Anakraja's hint would have been the exact thing to have acted on; but nothing in the way of writing material was visible, which was no great wonder, considering that the art of writing was utterly unknown in Magindano. Of this, however, I was unaware at the time, and, marvelling in my mind at their thick-headedness, I begged a slip of bark from the petticoat of a gentleman standing by, and a knife from another, and on the smooth side of the bark scratched in big letters—

"DEAR TOM,—I am safe and sound. They have given me presents, and made an officer of me. The same honours await you. Make them something new and novel in blacksmithery, and your fortune is made. Try and accomplish this, for they won't let me see you even till you do.—REUBEN."

When I had finished I gave it to Anakraja, at the same time begging him to send it to "Tomcox," as he was here called; but Ribut Bungat snatched it from his hand, and for the space of a minute examined the scrawl with the greatest wonder, turning it sideways and upside-down, but could make nothing of it, so he returned it to Anakraja, directing him to question me about it. He commenced by asking "Why?" meaning why did I wish the slip of bark to be carried to Tom. I replied, "To tell him I was well and kindly treated." This reply Anakraja interpreted to the chief, whom the notion of the bit of bark being able to "tell" anything seemed to tickle amazingly. He laughed outright, as, of course, did the entire assembly, and said it was impossible, adding that mine must indeed be a marvellous country if speech was given to the very trees; but I maintained my seriousness, and did my best to make them understand that the words on the bark, and not the bark itself, were what would acquaint Tom with my condition; but my attempts at explanation were anything but successful, and seemed but to lead Ribut Bungat to the conclusion that with the point of the knife I had cut the "tongue" of the bark, and so let free its powers of speech, in some such sort of way as the ignorant among English folk cut the tongues of their starlings. The end of the business, however, was that a messenger was despatched with the bark letter, with instructions to bring Tom Cox back with him.

In a little while the messenger returned, bringing Tom fresh from his smithy, with his shirt-sleeves rolled above his elbows, and his face and hands within a shade of the colour of those about him. This it seems was the first time he had been brought face to face with the chief and the head men since he had given them such great offence, and therefore it was no wonder that he should look rather sheepish. At first he did not perceive me, and when he did, what with the goatskin cloak and the golden rings on my arms, he stared as though he could scarcely trust his eyes. No sooner, however, was he quite convinced that it was me, than, with no regard for court etiquette, he elbowed his way towards me. Before he could approach me, however, he was stopped by command of Ribut Bungat, and led to the farther end of the hall. There was no objection to our holding a conversation, the chief said, but it must be through the "talking bark," as he was particularly anxious to witness the process. At the same time we were both furnished with slips of bark and knives.

By way of easing Tom's bewilderment (for, of course, he knew not a word of the writing controversy), I first of all sent him a few lines of an explanatory character, to which he replied in such an uncomplimentary strain as regarded the chief and his counsellors, that it was a mercy that " bark talk " was a secret known only to ourselves.

CHAPTER VIII.

OR all the knowledge, however, the chief and his people were
likely to derive as to the art of writing by simply watching
the passage of our correspondence, they might as well have
stared at a sound egg in hopes of penetrating the mysteries
of the growth of the chick within; it happened, therefore,
that, by the time the exchange of bark notes had continued for ten
minutes or so, the chief began to yawn and exhibit signs of impatience, pushing away the last note which was submitted to him with
a gesture which plainly implied his growing suspicion that we were
fooling him.

To allow his suspicion to continue was to let his favour cool, yet
how to reassure him seemed to me the most difficult thing in the
world. Suddenly, however, my good genius put into my head an idea
on which I resolved to act instantly. First warning Tom as to what I
was about to do, I took from my arm one of the six gold rings, and
placing it in the hands of Anakraja, made him understand that he was
to conceal it where he chose, I meanwhile turning away so that I
might not see, but Tom looking on, and assisting me to discover the
whereabouts of the hidden ring by means of a few words written on a
piece of bark. In fact, it was nothing but the old English game of
"hot boiled beans" simplified by the hunter being informed where the
game lay.

Ridiculous as it was, however, it captivated their ignorant minds
at once; and no sooner had Anakraja explained to the chief the
miracle I was about to attempt than the old fellow brightened up

wonderfully, as of course did his court, with the exception of Anakraja, who was evidently very anxious, and fearful that this new experiment of his *protégé's* would fail. He, however, took the ring, while I turned my head and covered it entirely with the goat-skin cloak; but, to make quite sure, by the chief's direction my head was further enveloped in a cloth, so that I had difficulty in breathing. After about a minute the cloth was removed (though I was not allowed to look round towards my confederate), and a slip of bark placed before me. On it was scrawled, " Look under the right foot of the little man with a scar on his cheek." Of course I walked straight to the individual indicated, and, touching his right leg, discovered the ring, amidst the wondering ejaculations of all present, except Tom, who could not forbear laughing outright, and who audibly expressed his conviction that the chief and his party were a set of nincompoops ; and, indeed, it was ludicrous, though at the same time pitiful, to witness their amazement at the performance of a feat easy to a baby who only knew its A B C. For a moment it seemed a shameful thing to practise on their ignorance, but there instantly ensued the reflection that the art of discoursing without the assistance of those prime organs of understanding, the tongue and the ears, was indeed a marvellous business, and one that might very naturally excite surprise among a people becoming acquainted with it for the first time.

Taking the tell-tale bark, the chief scanned it with great earnestness, and then calling the little man with the scar forward, took to glancing from his figure to the figures written, evidently supposing that he should find some resemblance ; but he presently shook his perplexed head, ejaculating—

" It isn't a bit like him ! Where are his hands ? where are his legs ? Even though he were chopped into the smallest pieces he would be more like a man than this is !"

After a little reflection, however, he seemed resolved to put the magic art to a severer test. Taking the ring, he went out, accompanied by his counsellors and Tom Cox, and leaving me in the house in the custody of Anakraja and some others. After awhile the party returned without Tom, but bearing from him a written intimation that the ring was concealed in a bag of rice under a mat at the foot of the great post at the end of the village. Thither I immediately turned, followed by them all, and, arriving at the post, turned back the mat, plunged my hand into the rice-bag, and, with-drawing the ring, handed it to the astonished chief. He turned the ring over and over with a serious countenance, and it was evident that the matter had got fast hold on his mind, and was not likely to fade from it with the subsidence of his astonishment. His followers had, no doubt, expected an afternoon's entertainment with the " talking bark," and looked not a little astonished when, with the exception of Anakraja, they were all dismissed, and while Tom and I were com-fortably installed in the house of the chief doctor, the latter and the chief retired to consult together.

A feast of fowls and goat's flesh, with palm wine and tamarinds, was speedily placed before us, and ere the repast was over there arrived from the " palace" a present for Tom of cloth and gold rings, with the additional present of a handsome kris for myself. A very satisfactory evening was that for Tom and me, though, to speak the truth, we regarded our situation from very different points of view, Tom's prac-tical mind ignoring the romantic, and finding nothing enjoyable in reclining in an outlandish hut surrounded by the presents of an out-landish potentate, who, while to the rest of the Christian world he was nothing but a pirate and a barbarous cut-throat, to us was favour-ably inclined. Nevertheless, while Tom insisted that the chief was a rascal whom he should like of all things to knock on the head, and that, rather than lay puffing villanously strong tobacco on a Bornean mat, he would be smoking Virginian and drinking beer in an honest Stepney tap-room, he could not but admit that the gold arm-rings were worthy of some consideration, being worth, as he computed, at least ten guineas each. In the midst of our discussion, however, a messenger made his appearance and conducted me to the council-house, where the chief and Anakraja awaited me.

Our conference was very long, and, on account of our mutual ignorance each of the other's language, very tedious. This, however, was the gist of it. The chief, who was a shrewd and sensible man, had at once been struck with the importance of the art I had intro-duced, and was very anxious to be informed whether it was in my power to confer it on him, on Anakraja, and on a few others, in whose hands the government of Magindano was, " so that," said he, " my words may live after I have uttered them, and be no longer at the mercy of ears which are wilfully deaf or inclined to treachery."

Now here was a proposition! I, the Whitechapel charity lad, who, on the very last occasion of attending school, was whipped for spelling "worshipful" with two l's, was suddenly called on to induct the rulers of a nation into the arts of reading and writing! However, there was no help for it; had I declared myself incapable, I should not have been believed; besides, I could not but be alive to the fact that in my attempts to teach them I should myself be gaining knowledge, and, if successful, it was impossible to say what amount of advantage I should get out of the business. So I boldly replied that it was very possible to impart to persons who were patient enough the arts which had so astonished them, but that, in the first place, it would be necessary for me to acquire a knowledge of the Dyak tongue. To this the chief at once agreed, and on the spot gave Anakraja instructions to afford me and my companion every facility for learning the rudiments of the Dyak language; in fact, intimated that, for the present, he was to devote himself entirely to our instruction.

Matters having arrived at this pass, I thought it a good time to push them a little further, both for the success of the hare-brained scheme I had embarked on, and for the comfort of Tom and myself while it was progressing. I therefore informed the chief that quiet would be chiefly essential, and that it was impossible to obtain in or near his village; whereupon he graciously replied that I might select any spot I chose for a house, and that his slaves should set about building it at once. I also inquired if he had any paper or pencils in his possession, thinking that, amongst the plunder of ships which, from time to time, had fallen into his hands, it was not unlikely that such things might be included. But neither he nor Anakraja understood what I meant, till at last a bright idea seemed to strike the doctor, and he hurried off, to return presently, bearing in his hand a sort of short-handled birch-broom, covered with what seemed to be fresh whitewash, and placed it in my hands with a confidence which betokened his conviction that he had hit on the very thing. This implement, however (which I afterwards discovered to be a Dyak paint-brush, and used for decorating prahus), I was compelled to return to my obliging friend, at the same time intimating that the article I required was of a somewhat smaller and more delicate character, whereon the chief beckoned me to follow him to his store-house, which, as before mentioned, was at the rear of the audience-hall.

This place, which was of considerable dimensions, appeared to be treasure-house, and armoury, and granary all in one; for, besides a great quantity of European cases, and boxes, and shipping gear, there was a stock of loose rice rising as high as the rafters, besides heaps of such vegetables and fruits as might be dried and stored, and which included yams and pumpkins, and onions and garlic, as well as lemons and pomegranates, and the nauka, or "jack," and the pomplemose; all these fruits and vegetables, and very many others, flourishing in this delicious climate most luxuriantly. About the walls were hung all sorts of arms, and piled against several pieces of brass ordnance were shot and gunpowder in bags and barrels, the latter branded "Dartford," telling, undoubtedly, of its source. I will not here, however, stay to enumerate the contents of the store-house, which the chief invited me to inspect with a view to my finding what I wanted. For some time the search seemed hopeless; but presently I spied, lying in an out-of-the-way corner, a ship's ledger, with the clasps (which had doubtless formed the inducement to bring it ashore) wrenched off. This, however, was of small moment to me. I was only too thankful to find its pages not more than a quarter covered with writing, leaving me a good two hundred leaves, clean and fairly ruled. "I will make shift for a pencil after this stroke of fortune," thought I; but, at that very moment, my eyes lighted on a cabin-desk, forced and empty, and upside down; but, as there happened to be just such a one in Captain Prescot's cabin, I knew that it had secret drawers between the real bottom and the false, and thought it likely that these same receptacles might have remained undiscovered. I gave the bottom of the desk a tap with my fist, and, 'sure enough, my surmise was correct; there were two secret drawers, and neither had been opened.

Seeing that the desk itself had been much knocked about, had lost its hinges and its lock, and was otherwise spoiled, I made no scruple of giving the bottom a vigorous kick, when, to the chief's wonder and delight, a litter of curious things were immediately brought to light and strewn over the floor. It must have been a Spanish merchant-man that had yielded this article of plunder, for among the things that tumbled out were five rolls of Spanish gold pieces, which, being scattered from their rotten papers by the fall, the chief hastily scrambled together and thrust into the folds of his robe. Besides these there was a goodly roll of foreign bank-notes; and as the chief, after glancing at them, threw them away contemptuously, while he gave his entire and delighted attention to a stick of red sealing-wax, I thought it no sin to clap the notes within the leaves of my ledger, thinking that one day they might be of considerable use to me. There was, in a shagreen case, a pair of gold-rimmed spectacles, which, for Ribut Bungat's amusement, I set astride my nose, and caused him to laugh very heartily; then he must needs try them on his nose, and they happening to be well adapted to his failing sight, his delight, as he looked about him and saw things plainer than he had seen them for years, was extreme; and, indeed, they really were valuable to him, and would, no doubt, have afforded him many an hour's comfort had he been allowed to keep them; but no sooner did his greedy old mother see them, than, although she might as well have worn them on the back as the front of her head, for all the assistance they lent to her purblind eyes, she insisted on having them, and to the day of her death they were added to the skull-cap, the false teeth, and her other adornments, and made of her such a figure as is never seen in England except on the fifth of November.

However, to return to the contents of the desk. Besides the gold and the notes, and the other things already enumerated, there were many papers and documents, the nature of which I did not understand, and a set of ivory tablets, and, better than all, a bundle of quill pens. Ink, as might have been expected, there was none; but that I knew was an article for which a substitute might easily enough be made in any place where berries grew. So with my ledger and my other treasures I walked off contentedly enough, leaving the old chief busily kicking at the bottoms of European sea-chests and packing-cases, in hopes of finding them false and the depositories of further wealth.

Our first business was to fix on a convenient site for a house, and then to set about building it. The first was a matter easily decided, for about a hundred yards from the beach there was a gently rising hill of considerable elevation, and delightfully covered with verdure. This spot, both Tom and I agreed, was all that could be desired as the site of our abode, affording as it did both retirement and a fair look-out over that vast and trackless road by which alone we could ever hope to escape; for, after all, to escape was our foremost desire, and could we have spied a ship of any sort within swimming distance, we would cheerfully have turned our backs on Magindano and the fair prospect it offered, and, leaving our rings, and our necklaces, and our raiment of costly fur, and every other present we had received on the shore, swum naked away.

Not that we were for the present at all depressed because no ship came to relieve us. We had suddenly grown to be individuals of importance, honoured by the chief, and with the services of his slaves at our command. We resolved that our house should be after the English pattern—that is, as far as our ingenuity would serve. On the summit of the hill we planned the building, and round about it, stretching about forty yards either way, we had the ground cleared, and fenced, and an outhouse built for our poultry, and an enclosure for our goats and bullocks, and a sty for our hogs; for Ribut Bungat was kind enough to give us permission to select such poultry and animals as we might desire from his own stock, which, by the bye, in reality meant the entire produce of the island. We should have liked to have added a horse, or at least an ass or a mule, to our establishment, but such animals are unknown in this region, as is likewise the dog. This latter fact rather alarmed us when first we were informed of it, as, from the little we had seen of the gloomy woods, we imagined that they must be inhabited by lions and bears, and that, without the warning voice of a dog, we should some night be attacked by a troop of ferocious animals, who at the least would devastate our goat-pens and pigsties, even if they failed to penetrate to our house and devour us also; but to our satisfaction we were, with truth, informed that neither the lion nor the tiger, nor, indeed, any of the larger breed of the feline species, were known at Magindano. Neither could we hear that a wolf, or a bear, or a fox had ever been seen on the island. In the forests are found the rhinoceros, or "bodok," as these people call him, and the stag and the buffalo, also such "small deer" as the rabbit and the mouse, and the rat. Nor must I forget to mention the ourang-outang, the "wild man of the woods;" indeed, it would be unciril not to make mention of a beast who, on our first attempts at settlement treated us with marked attention, rooting up our fences, and devastating our sprouting crops of beans, and cucumbers, and strangling our fowls, seemingly for the mere pleasure of the performance. Nor should I forget the host of little monkeys, some of them no bigger

than a squirrel, who, from the very commencement, paid not the least
respect to the fences and our other devices for privacy, but came in
and took up their abodes above our very doorway; indeed, it was not
till we had trained a biggish ring-tailed fellow to the duties of watchman, and taught him how to handle a stick, that we could keep them
out of the parlour.

Our House on the Hill.

During the progress of our house scarcely a day passed but we
were honoured by a visit from the chief and Anakraja, as well as
others of the chief's counsellors; and on no occasion, from driving

REUBEN DAVIDGER SEARCHING FOR WRITING MATERIALS IN
RIBUT-BUNGAT'S STOREHOUSE.

the foundation-piles to the elevation of the chimney-pot, did they go away without being much edified and astonished. And not without good reason; as, for instance, never before had they seen such a necessary ingredient in the construction of a house as sawn planks, nor was it likely that they should, considering that they were ignorant of such a tool as a saw. Here occurred Tom's chance to astonish them; and, though I much doubt if his talent as a saw-cutter would have gained him credit in Sheffield, the specimens of that implement—both cross-cut and single-handled—were here regarded as miracles of perfection. It was with these sawn boards that the walls of our house were composed, being overlapped and pegged (we had no nails) to the corner-posts. As for the roof, as we could obtain no substitute for tiles, we were obliged to call in the native thatcher, who, to do him justice, did his work in a style that in its way was very superior to ours. We had a door hung with hinges (another wrinkle for the Bornean architect), and secured with a latch, and in the door was a sliding shutter to admit or shut out the light just as we pleased, while round the walls were bored holes, which, together with the chimney-space, afforded us ventilation. Then recollecting the prahu-painting implement Anakraja had previously shown me, I made inquiries for it as well as for some paint.

They know but two colours of paint in this country, red and white, or, as they say, "hot" and "cold;" and I may as well here state that these colours are not used promiscuously or according to fancy, as colours are among us. Red with the Dyak is symbolic of war and bloodshed, and white of peace. Their war-prahus are "hot"—red hot, in fact, for they are painted entirely of the fiery colour; and should war threaten, the council-hall in which the warriors meet to discuss the imminent business would be daubed red from floor to ceiling; and should peace be restored it is no hard task to obliterate the sanguinary symbol, as the colours, white as well as red, are prepared in water— the former being made of sea-shells manufactured into lime, and the latter by crushing the seed-pods of a certain plant.

Ours, however, was to be a house of peace, and so the whitewash was brought and applied plentifully within and without, giving the whole place a beautifully cool and cleanly appearance. Our house-furniture was neither elegant nor elaborate, but it suited our purpose; we had a large table and a couple of three-legged stools, and two long forms for the use of company, should they prefer sitting in Christian fashion instead of squatting down on a mat. Up-stairs were our two bedrooms, and, having no fancy for bedsteads, we slung to the cross-beams, by means of ropes of twisted bark, hammocks of stout native cloth; and two wide bags of the same, stuffed full with soft grass, made us decent beds.

When our house was quite finished the chief brought his mother to see it, and the novelty of the whole concern so enraptured the old woman that, as I was afraid would be the case, she wanted to take up her abode in it, and, knowing her son's disposition to oblige her in everything, I thought he would consent. One would have thought that he would have been glad to have got rid of the mercenary old creature, but filial affection is very remarkable among these barbarians; I have known a married man of forty or more reduced by his grief for his mother's death to a bed of long sickness. In the present case this peculiar Dyak characteristic luckily suited us, for Ribut Bungat, while he bemoaned his pain at disobeying his parent, implored her not to think of living apart from him, and compromised the matter by engaging to escort her to the coveted abode just as often as she chose to visit it. With this she was forced to be content, and at last was got away with no more serious loss to us than both our three-legged stools, to which she took a fancy, and had conveyed to her abode in the village.

And now commenced the happiest time it was ever my lot to experience. My wounds were so completely healed that I had forgotten all about them, as would have been the case with Tom only that he was afflicted with deafness on the side from which his ear was missing. We were as well clothed as any grandees in the land, and as well fed, and, according to our way of thinking, better housed. Every morning we were waited on by two slaves from the village, who brought us a plentiful supply of fresh water, and took our orders for anything else we might require. We rose generally a little after sunrise, and, strolling down to the beach, took a bathe, or, loosening a couple of sampans from their moorings under the prahu shed, went a paddling race for half a mile or so; and though we at first got more exercise for our lungs than for our muscles out of the amusement, by reason of our laughter each at the other's bungling attempts to handle the paddles, after a few lessons we could manage them deftly enough. After our row or swim we would return to our little house on the hill and set about getting breakfast—adapting its ingredients to our appetites. One morning we would bake a sago cake, grill a couple of young chickens, and draw a quart or so of rich milk from our sleek little cow; or we would clap a joint of a fine young porker into our oven (Tom contrived a capital oven), and that, with a custard of rice and cream and eggs, and a bowl of palm-wine, furnished just such a meal as a couple of hungry and hearty young fellows could do justice to. Then, and before the sun grew too hot, we would attend to our gardening and farming operations—Tom taking to the latter, and I to the former. Our garden was of the useful rather than of the ornamental sort, and, while it contained no flowers, yielded us a very plentiful supply of cucumbers, and pumpkins, and onions, as well as a very sweet but coarse sort of greens resembling sea-kale. Not, be it understood, that there is a dearth of flowers at Magindano; on the contrary, wherever you walk the woods are all aglow with them, from the little vivid crimson flowers no bigger than the English forget-me-not to the gigantic and gorgeous pitcher-plant, which I shall presently have an opportunity of describing. It is on account, I suppose, of so many magnificent flowers growing in a wild condition that the Dyaks of these parts never think of cultivating them; indeed, the island is nothing but a vast garden from one end to the other.

Our gardening and farming completed, it was time for Anakraja to make his appearance, when we would hold " school " for two or three hours; that is, Anakraja and I would hold school while Tom laid on his back and smoked his pipe, till, wearied with what he disrespectfully called the doctor's gibberish, he turned over on his mat and went to sleep. Indeed, all poor Tom ever learnt of the Dyak tongue was not much, and that at second hand from me. For my part, however, I gave the subject my best attention, so that within three months of the commencement I could hold easy conversations with my tutor, while he, being even more assiduous than myself, had learnt to spell and write such easy sentences as, " Come and eat with me to-day," and " At time of high sun I will come to the house up hill." Very proud of the achievement he was, too, and a very severe time his man had of it, bringing " notes " from the village to " the house up hill " from morning till night. Indeed, at such a furious rate did he take to letter-writing, and such a great sprawling hand did he write, that, had I allowed him to draw freely on my limited stock of writing-paper, he would have consumed it in less than a fortnight, so after the first few days I suggested that he should make do with bark instead, using a quill pen and some of the white lime-wash as ink.

It was not, however, till I began to teach Ribut Bungat that the business began to be really lucrative. The old chief was not apt at learning, and the task of teaching him involved twice the patience, and at least three times the writing-paper, compared with that expended over Anakraja; but when he had mastered only as much of the art of writing as enabled him to play the game of "hot boiled beans," as introduced by me, his delight was unbounded; and I never went to his house but I came away with a present either of cloth or gold rings; and on one occasion he gave me a great yellow diamond from the island of Landa, of the value of which I had no idea till, many a year afterwards, it was submitted to a diamond-merchant in Bishopsgate.

Ribut Bungat was now never contented unless I was with him, except when he accompanied his fleet on piratical excursions, when we were invariably "advised" to keep within doors, or, at all events, not to stroll away from the foot of the hill atop of which our house was built. Nor were we at all likely to forget the said "advice," for if ever we attempted, while the chief was absent, to set out on a longish walk, or to take a boat for a row, we were sure to encounter some "head man" or other who would politely intimate the propriety of our turning back—if from the woods, because of a vicious rhinoceros, or because of head-hunters of a distant tribe who were known to be prowling there; if from sea, because of an approaching storm, because of sharks—any excuse, in fact, to induce us to refrain from a journey. Thus we were never so unhappy as when the chief was away, because it was at those times that the fact of our being prisoners was made so manifest. The saddening reflection was not, however, without its consolation; since the chief was so careful of us, and so alert that we did not escape, it was certain that there existed a means of escaping if we could only find it out! It was I who urged this argument, and sorry indeed was I afterwards that I should have been so indiscreet. Notwithstanding his repugnance for the inhabitants and their manners and customs generally, since our residence in the little house on the hill, Tom had become much more contented with his fate, as indeed was not surprising, since he was so well provided for, and his only em-

ployment was pleasure. It is true that he did not often see Ribut
Bungat (the old fellow never seemed entirely to forget the insult
towards the sacred ceremony of brother-making of which Tom had
been guilty), and consequently did not come in for so many presents,
but he was only half as poor as he might have been on that account, for
we made it a rule to divide everything equally. On the whole then he
was quite reconciled to his lot, and if ever he talked about the old
country it was with a placidity that betokened no vast amount of
anxiety. Indeed I think it was chiefly because he seemed so apathetic
on the subject that I took pains to rouse him, and pointed out to him
that it would be a shameful thing for two Englishmen to exist till the
end of their lives as we were existing; that after all, and however
much our wealth might serve to gild over and conceal the fact, we
were nothing but slaves, and dare not lay our hands on anything—not
even the jacket on our back—and say " this is mine."

" Why," replied Tom, " you talk as though it was a mere matter
of ' go if you choose,' and that I rather preferred staying. Where's the
use of crying for the moon ? Here we are and here we are likely to
stay. That being the case I will make myself as comfortable as possible, if you have no objection."

" I can't make myself comfortable, Tom," I replied, " while I am
haunted by the thought that there *is* a way of escape if we could only
find it."

" And why do you think so ?" asked Tom, becoming so interested
as to let his pipe go out. " The only way of getting out of this, as it
seems to me, is to take a journey across the forest to the country of the
speckled-cheeked fellows, who, for all we know to the contrary, are
greater savages than these."

But I told Tom that to try our luck with the speckled-cheeks was
the very last of my thoughts ; it was across the sea that our road lay
if anywhere ; and called to his mind how anxiously we were watched,
and debarred even from our amusement of paddling in a cockle-shell
of a sampan whenever the chief was away. Finally my efforts were
rewarded beyond my foolish desires, for not only was Tom roused to
such a sense of his present degradation as prepared him to avail
himself with alertness of any opportunity that might by and by
present itself; he immediately became full of discontent, and instead
of happily smoking his pipe in the sun, or whistling while he pottered

among the garden plants, took to brooding and hatching, and when I returned from a visit to my pupils in the village, I invariably found him ready with a plot for our escape, and which, if attempted to be carried out, would certainly have cost us our heads. And when I laughed at him and endeavoured to joke him out of his melancholy, he would reply that it was very fine for me to be light-hearted who did not lack companions and friends, but for him who, three days out of the week, was left from morning till evening without a chance of exchanging a word with any one, it was a very different matter.

Nor was Tom the only individual to whom my constant visits to Ribut Bungat failed to give satisfaction. The old fellow had grown so attached to me that nothing would have pleased him better than to have had me with him constantly; and, flattering to my vanity as this marked inclination for my society on his part may have been, it not altogether tended to my comfort. For hours I was closeted with the chief privately; I ate and smoked with him, and was present at his councils. Of course there really was nothing in all this. True, I had been able to serve Ribut Bungat in various petty matters, but all of them strictly applying to domestic economy, and none to political; indeed, it was impossible for me to make a single suggestion concerning the government of his territory, being ignorant of the commonest matter pertaining thereto. But the wiseacres about the chief chose to think differently; in their ignorance and superstition they attributed all the chief's vagaries to the influence of my "talking paper;" and, though I believe that Ribut Bungat was now not a bit more wilful or obstinate than ever, they thought that he was, and argued against and combated his simplest decisions in a way that made him furious as well as obstinate, and brought against them in reality what they before only suspected they laboured under—the chief's mistrust. And the more uneasy the old fellow was made the more he resorted to my company —purely for the sake of pastime, without doubt. That, however, was not their way of construing the matter; the unwelcome change was entirely laid at my door, and, though they affected to treat me with extreme civility, their envy and jealousy were too apparent to be mistaken. Nay, from what afterwards came to my knowledge, I suspect that we should, about this time, have been kidnapped and drowned, or secretly put to death in some other way, were it not for fear of the wonderful "talking paper," which might tell tales and make known the assassin.

So things continued for something more than a year, at the end of which time I stood higher than ever in the chief's esteem, as did Tom, who, though his discontent had not at all abated, had contrived, by the introduction of a few common English appliances in iron in boat-building, to win for himself the distinguished post of head ship-builder. I question, however, if he would so well have succeeded had it not been for our old friend Anakraja, who of late had displayed towards Tom as well as myself the most unbounded friendship, which was the more remarkable as Tom's bluntness of speech and manner rather increased than softened with his prosperity, and never on any occasion did I know him even to assume an ordinary friendliness towards Anakraja, let alone to court his patronage. Nevertheless, for the past few weeks he had given to Tom more of his company than to me, and it was no uncommon thing for me, on my return from a visit to our house on the hill, to find Tom and Anakraja in very close con-fabulation.

"What have you been talking about, Tom?" I would ask.

"Oh, the prahus and that sort of thing," he would answer; but there was an end to his report, and he seemed much relieved when I pursued my inquiries no further.

One evening, however, as he and I sat in our garden, refreshing ourselves after the labours of the day with a pipe and a calabash of wine, Tom, after a deal of fidgeting and uneasiness, broke out at last with the following astounding question:—

"Reu, my lad! how would you relish being Governor of Magindano?"

"Nay," replied I, laughing, "if we are to pass an hour in castle-building, let it be of the right sort. I would rather be King of England a hundred times. Ah, Tom! if I was King of England, and you——"

"Nonsense," interrupted Tom Cox impatiently; "you are so full of your romantic notions that there isn't a serious matter-of-fact idea in you, I believe."

"Why, it was you who started the castle-building, Tom; did you not ask me how I should like to be Chief of Magindano?"

"That I did," replied he, laying down his pipe and sinking his voice to a whisper; "and what's more, Reuben, I meant what I said."

"Very well, then," said I, "here's my answer, as sober and

serious as a monk, since it is your humour:—I should like it very much indeed."

"Or," continued he, "would you rather sail away to England with enough of gold and diamonds to make you a rich man for the rest of your life?"

He continued to talk in such an anxious and serious tone that I began to suspect that he had been working in the sun without his palm-leaf cap. Anyhow I thought it best to humour him, so I answered—

"Well, I think that, of the two offers, Tom, I should accept the chieftainship. This is a wonderfully rich island. Any fellow with English wits who held the reins here might make a very pretty thing of it."

"One prize or the other would be worth running a considerable risk for, eh? don't you think so, Reuben?"

"Any risk almost," replied I; "that is, any risk that endangered only a fellow's life. There are things, you know, Tom, that neither you nor I would venture for the greatest kingdom in the world."

"I'd like to know what they are!" observed Tom grimly.

"Well, there's a longish string of them, Tom; here's one, anyhow—murder!"

I saw that Tom winced at this; and, inasmuch as it showed that he was in his senses, I grew more alarmed, especially as he maintained his earnest demeanour and his low, whispering tone. Singularly enough, too—though why I can't say—while I could not but think that something was amiss, it likewise flashed to my mind, "Anakraja is at the bottom of this business!"

"Why, yes," observed Tom Cox, after a moment's uncomfortable hesitation, "murder is a thing I should be as loth to dabble in as yourself, my lad. I don't think I could be brought to kill a fellow-creature—a fellow Christian creature, you understand, Reu—for all the jewels in the Tower. But killing ain't always murder. It ain't murder to knock a dog on the head—no, nor a bloodthirsty piratical old Dyak either. There, now you've got my opinion flat."

But I could plainly see it was not only Tom's opinion that I had been put into possession of, but also of the clue to the secret that he was harbouring—that he was ashamed of, I am glad to add, for as he spoke he got up, and, walking away, stood leaning over the fence that

encircled our little estate. I followed him quietly, and presently was
by his side, leaning over the fence too.

"Go on, Tom," said I; "it's plain enough you've got a cat in
your bag, and maybe, from the small bit you've shown of her, I don't
much like her colour. But let her out, Tom; perhaps I shall like her
better when I see her fairly on her legs."

"Well, it's no cat of mine, Reu, I assure you," returned he, half
laughing. "You ought to take kindly to it, as it belongs to a friend
of yours."

"To Anakraja?" said I.

"A good guess," replied Tom. "And now just listen to me
patiently for a few moments."

Then, still maintaining his cautious whisper, he revealed to me the
particulars of about as diabolical a plot as could well be conceived,
even by an unscrupulous savage such as Anakraja was, for, as I suspected, this latter worthy it was who had concocted it. With praise-
worthy delicacy, Tom Cox approached the main of the plot with some
reluctance, justifying and excusing himself in a rigmarolish way.
This, however, was the gist of the business:—In three days Ribut
Bungat would set out with a fleet of war-prahus, in search of such
game as fortune might send him. As usual, he would take with him
his best fighting men, his most faithful adherents, as well as the
greater part of his rowing slaves, who, it was known, were much
attached to him, and would fight for him to death. Tom, as inspector
of ships, was to be prime mover in the devilish tragedy that was to
ensue within ten hours of the fleet leaving port. A plank in the
undermost side of each prahu was to be partly removed, and the hole
to be neatly plastered over with a glue-like substance which Anakraja
knew of, and which, though soluble, was very tenacious, and would
resist the action of the water for a considerable time. The chief and
his adherents thus disposed of, Tom and I were to be placed in his
stead at the head of affairs, with Anakraja for our chief counsellor
and guide, and with such other men to fill the higher offices of the
State as Anakraja might please to nominate; or, if Tom and I preferred it, Anakraja would take the reins, and, rewarding us with a
shipload of wealth from the chief's treasure-house, lend us a vessel
and crew to carry us to Shanghai, whence we could proceed to England at our convenience.

"There you are, my lad," said Tom, as he completed his precious revelation; "now the cat is out entirely. What do you think of her?"

For a few minutes I could not reply to Tom's question. I was so completely astonished, and bitterly regretted that I should, however unwittingly, have been the means of provoking the discontent out of which had grown so prodigious a mischief.

"What is the present condition of the plot, Tom?" I asked him; "is it ripe for hatching, or near ripe?"

"Well, the truth is, Reu, it is a little over ripe," replied my companion with a laugh in which there was no mirth. Five of the prahus are already prepared, and there remains but the largest in which Ribut sails—and which is of course the most important of any—and two others. The obstinate old savage can't be persuaded that his ship wants patching, and unless he is, the ship can't be brought close in shore, so that I may serve her as the rest are served. It must be managed somehow, though, for we've gone too far to back out."

"But is there no way——" I began.

"Why, there *is* a way," interrupted Tom, quite misunderstanding the purport of the observation I was about to make; "but though it won't do to be over squeamish in such matters, it is a way that doesn't exactly hit my mind. It is Anakraja's idea. He says that if Ribut Bungat is still obstinate come the morning, that he may be brought to his senses, if the cement with which one of the ships is already patched is loosened a bit so as to send her to the bottom, as a hint of what comes of not letting the master shipwright do as he thinks best."

"Good Lord, Tom!" I exclaimed, "you surely will never lend a hand in such a horrible business?"

"I don't think I shall," replied Tom; "at least I'll hang back as long as possible; as you say, Reu, it *is* a bloody business, and since it's got to be done I'd rather see it done at a stroke than piece-meal. I wish it was over."

"And are you so mad as to think that it *will* be 'all over' when the prahus go down, and the water closes over the heads of that host of unsuspecting wretches?" I asked him.

"No, my lad," replied he, briskly; "I am *not* so mad as to suppose that there and then will be an end of the business. If it were so, you wouldn't catch me stirring a peg to bring it about. No, Reu,

after the cut-throats have been put away, then comes the best part—
the reward! The gold and the diamonds, Reu!"

"And the remorse and the agony of mind," said I, "the mistrust
even of the wind's breath, the terror of darkness, the life-long torment
of a murderer's conscience, Tom. Oh, Tom! why did you not tell me
of this infernal business before?"

"It's too late now," he replied, gloomily, "at least for me. I
hardly know for which to be most sorry, that I did not tell you before,
or that I have told you at all, for it don't seem that you are inclined
to stand by me."

"I should be no friend, Tom, if I did stand by and see you plunge
into such a gulf without lending a hand to save you," I replied;
"but answer me this question, does Anakraja suppose that I have been
all along acquainted with this horrible conspiracy? Did he tell you
to inform me all about it?"

"That indeed he did not," replied Tom, in a confused sort of
way; "he made me promise not to mention it to a soul until it was
all over."

"But, tell me now, did he not expressly mention me as one who
was to know nothing of the conspiracy?"

"Well, since you push me into so close a corner I must confess
that he did," replied Tom: "'Don't mention a word concerning what
we are doing to Orang Reu,' (so I was called) said he; 'not but that
he's staunch enough, and would go through fire itself to gain his
liberty, as he himself has told me a hundred times, [the lying villain!]
but he has grown so foolishly attached to Ribut Bungat that he
would be sure to warn him——'"

"As I most certainly would," said I.

"But I knew different," continued Tom, not heeding the interruption. "I said to myself, 'Reuben may not like the plan, nay, he may
so much dislike it as to decline to have a finger in it; but of this I
am sure he will never be such a dastard as to 'peach on his old chum
after all we have gone through together;' and so, finding the secret
growing too heavy for me to carry, I up and told you."

As Tom concluded, he fixed his eyes on me to know what would be
my decision after his appeal. Not, I believe and hope, that he for a
moment suspected that I would betray him, but with a lingering hope
that I would after all fall in with the scheme and take an active part

in it. Against this, however, my heart was completely set; not all the
wealth in the world should have tempted me. Besides, it was plain
enough to me that, even were both disposed to be actors in the horrible tragedy with the outline of which Tom had acquainted me, we
should not be a penny the richer thereby. That Anakraja hated me
because of the favour I found in his master's eyes was certain; indeed,
despite all his savage cunning, he found it so difficult to conceal that
Ribut Bungat had observed it, and warned me against intimate dealings with him. Without doubt the scheme had but one aim and point,
and that was Anakraja's aggrandizement; and a splendid stroke it
would have been to have deposed the chief, set himself up in his place,
and destroyed his two clever white enemies at a single sweep; and the
latter part of the business he could easily have accomplished, and at
the same time have secured the admiration of the people to himself by
denouncing Tom and myself, who had contrived the massacre of the
chief and his fleet. These were the thoughts that with the speed of
lightning came into my mind as Tom paused for an answer; but just
as I was about to explain my views of the case to him, I happened to
cast my eyes down the hill and to my great surprise saw the very individual in whose diabolical brain the conspiracy had been born hurrying towards our house with such speed that his toga and ornamental
streamers fluttered in his rear.

"Is not this Anakraja, Tom?" I asked.

"What scudding along up hill at that pace? No, he's too much
of a gentleman ever to be in a hurry; more likely—— by jingo! it
is Anakraja!" exclaimed Tom. "Why, what can be the matter?"

And as he spoke, poor Tom's face became white as paper, and he
looked the picture of detected guilt.

"Perhaps," said I, "he has come on business with which I have
no concern. Suppose I walk down to the beach, Tom, and have a
pipe while you have your palaver?"

"No, no, stay here," said Tom, nervously; "there is only *one* business that could put him in such a mighty hurry."

"I hope nothing has gone wrong, Tom; could your plot have
been——"

"Discovered?" interrupted Tom, anxiously. "Good Lord! I hope
not. If so, I shall be glad of your counsel; so don't go away, my lad.
You are safe, you know, for you have neither said nor done anything.

You are supposed not even to suspect the existence of the conspiracy.
Whether or no, you won't breathe a word of what I have revealed to
you?   You'll promise that, won't you, Reu?"

"I will say nothing that will make a bad business worse for you,
Tom.   I need not be called on to promise, I should hope.   But let
what will come, let me implore you to take this bit of advice, don't
trust Anakraja.   He would make catspaws of us, Tom; he would
use us to rake the chestnuts out of the fire for him, and then pitch us

Tom Cox and Reuben wait to hear what the Doctor has to say.

in neck and crop with the nutshells, that we may have an extra
scorching."

"Say no more, he is coming in at the gate," said Tom in a
whisper.

But we need not have troubled ourselves to discuss the merits of Anakraja's scheme, and its probable chances of success or failure, or to argue the policy of my joining the confederacy; our dismal forebodings were realized, the secret was blown. Ribut Bungat himself, as will presently be seen, made the discovery, the details of which were at this very moment horrifying such of the chief's counsellors as he had chosen to take into his confidence. This was the cause of Anakraja's hot haste, and, as he burst through our little garden wicket, his demeanour was that of a man well-nigh crazed with fear and apprehension.

"It is all discovered!" cried he, as we entered the house together. "Alas! that a scheme so wise and perfect should miscarry! Ah, Orang Reu! ah, Tomcox! from my heart I pity you—I tremble for you. But Anakraja will not desert his dear friends in their trouble. Fly, my brothers! Take the smallest and most precious of your goods, and flee into the depths of the woods. To-night I will take care that a sampan shall be ready for you on the shore, and by that means you may escape to another island, and avoid those who at this moment are thirsting for your blood."

All this he uttered in the most rapid and earnest way, laying his hands first on one and then the other intreatingly, and even catching up such portables as he knew we valued, and attempting to force them into our possession. As for Tom, weakened as he was by conscious guilt, the doctor's panic had immediate effect on him; he turned deadly pale, and was for accepting Anakraja's advice, and acting on it on the instant. That I was not similarly affected seemed much to astonish him, and he remonstrated with me in an angry manner for what he mistook for my helpless terror.

"Rouse yourself, Reuben," said he. "Why do you stand there freezing with fright? Pluck up your manliness, and let us be off while there is yet time. Are you deaf? don't you hear what the doctor says? The plot is discovered!"

All this time I had stood with my arms folded, regarding Anakraja steadily, and becoming each moment more convinced that solicitude for our safety was not the real purport of his visit. Besides, what did I know of "plots"? Tom's very latest words to me, when we were discussing the matter, were that I should not acknowledge to the secret, and I had distinctly told him that I would have no finger in the precious pasty in course of concoction; therefore, when Tom urged me to run off because the "plot" was discovered, I turned to the doctor, and said—

"What madness is this that seems to have afflicted my friend as well as yourself, Anakraja? Who has been plotting, and to what purpose?"

"Hear him!" exclaimed the hypocrite with well-feigned astonishment. "Hear him, Tomcox! he asks *who* has been plotting!"

"And I ask it again," said I, "who has been plotting? Not I; I defy you to show me a plot I am engaged in. Take me to my accusers."

"You talk a little too fast," said Tom, in confirmation of my declaration of innocence, "he knows nothing of this damnable business, and that nobody is better aware of than yourself."

"I know nothing," replied Anakraja, shaking his head in a manner that betokened the length he was prepared to go in support of the lie. "How should I know how to meddle with such matters? I am too ignorant. It is only you wise men who can make paper talk, and who hold the spirits of the air and of the sea at your command, who would attempt such a tremendous conspiracy as this. But why should we waste time, precious time, in idle talk? You two understand each other; you *know* that you do. Fly at once, let me beg of you. You know not how terrible my people are in their vengeance; you know not the horrible torture and certain death that is even now hungering for you; you would never dally here if you knew how close at hand danger is."

"Since it is so close," said I, perceiving plainly enough that, however much truth there might be in what the villain told us, his aim was to save his own skin at the expense of ours, "since it is so close there is no use in running away from it, I would rather have danger before my face than at my heels."

"But think of me!" whined the base wretch, "think of the many acts of friendship I have performed for you. They will be here in a very little while, and surely you will not peril your friend's life by letting him be discovered here in friendly converse with you."

"No, that would not be right," said Tom, who seemed by this time to have a glimmering of the true state of the case; "but still, as Orang Reu says, he is innocent, and has nothing to fear, let him stay, and you and I will run off together; eh, doctor?"

But this proposition was just the very last likely to suit the rascal's views.

"It is only the guilty who run," said he, doggedly.

"The guilty!" exclaimed Tom, now completely roused. "Why, hang you, what d'ye mean? Arn't you as deep in the mud as I am in the mire? Deeper—ten times deeper. Which are you, my lad, a rogue or a fool? What d'ye think will become of you if we go, and leave you here to bear all the blame?"

"But they don't suspect me," Anakraja replied, with an ugly grin. "I am the chief's faithful friend and prime counsellor; it is my zeal for his safety that brings me to arrest you two for your treason; but if, on arriving at your house, I find that you have already taken alarm, and made your escape, it is no fault of mine. Surely I speak plainly enough," continued he meaningly.

"You speak like your true self, as I have ever known you, and that is as a designing villain," said I, for plainly enough I now saw through this double traitor, and that his design was to entice us to furnish undoubted proof of our guilt by running away; that accomplished, nothing would be easier than for Anakraja to heap all the blame on to our shoulders. "This time, however, you are a little mistaken in the fellows you have to deal with. We want neither you nor your advice, but you are quite welcome to a bit from us; be off, else you may find yourself helped down the hill at even a quicker rate than you ascended it."

"Nay," said he determinedly, "it is for you to go; here I stay; if you are so unwise as to stay too, it will be my duty to hold you prisoners till the chief sends me some assistance. But you will not be such fools as to hold out your necks to the kris; for that, or worse, will surely be your doom. You will run off. You may rely on me, the sampan shall be ready an hour before the moon rises, and——"

Here he suddenly paused and caught in his breath, while his face became blanched with terror, for there suddenly reached the top of the hill the shout of a mob, and, looking towards the village, there, through the twilight, we saw approaching a great number of persons, all very eager, and with the blades of their naked swords flashing in the fading rays of the sun. It was only for a moment, however, that Anakraja was silent; after but a single glance at the vengeful mob his rage broke through his dumb despair, and his mask of friendliness slipped

TRIAL OF REUBEN, TOM COX, AND THE CONSPIRATORS.

off with an ease that showed how paltry a thread had hitherto upheld it. He happened, as was very unusual with him, to have come to us unarmed, as, indeed, so were we, having no fear that we should need our weapons. There was, however, lying on a bench close by, a contrivance of stone with a wooden handle with which we used to pound our grain, and, catching up this pounder, Anakraja made full aim with it at Tom's head.

"You crocodile spawn! you breeders of mischief!" shouted he, "if I may not save my life through you, you shall not live to see my disgrace. Die!"

Tom put up his hand so as to ward off the first blow, but before he could prevent it the pounder was swung the other way, catching him such a blow on the forehead that poor Tom came down like an ox before the pole-axe. Doubtless the same fate would also have been mine had I not been pretty nimble, but, in the nick of time, I seized and cross-buttocked the villain, after a fashion imparted to me by my unlucky companion, and the doctor fell, with no little weight, with me sprawling over him. But these Dyaks are lithe as cats, and as slippery as eels; he was on his feet before I was, and hastening to possess himself of the pounder, which had been jerked out of his hand. Again I was too quick for him, and, calling to my aid another of Tom Cox's boxing lessons, delivered at his head a couple of fair, straight-out hits, and floored him for the second time. But no sooner was he down than up again, screaming with fury, and making at me with all his limbs and teeth as a tiger might; and by this time the crowd of men from the village were half-way up the hill, every one of them yelling almost as loud as Anakraja, and clashing their krisses, and banging their little gongs, so that, on the whole, the reader may understand how thoroughly Tom Cox was stunned, since, through all this skirmishing and hubbub within and without, he lay as dumb as the pounder itself, and without a sign of life.

Ribut Bungat was at the head of the multitude that now surrounded our house, and, accompanied by half a dozen soldiers, he came in at the door while Anakraja and myself were still in the midst of our conflict; and no sooner did my antagonist perceive his master than he fell on his knees before him, and commenced howling louder than before, changing his theme, however.

"Here, O my chief, here are the arch-traitors! here are the crafty

ones who would have given the idol of his people to the fish of the
sea! Succour me, O my chief, for I am nearly spent in striving to
prevent this, the stronger ruffian, from escaping to the woods, out of
reach of your just vengeance."

At a sign from Ribut Bungat I was instantly seized by two of the
soldiers, and my arms pinioned behind with strings of twisted bark ;
but, indignant as I felt at this treatment, it was nothing to my vexa-
tion to observe with what looks of bitter hate and contempt the old
chief regarded me.

"And is it for this, O Orang Reu! that I have raised you from the
condition of a slave to be the companion of my right hand?   Can the
wretch whom my eyes now dwell on be he whose false tongue was for
ever preaching of mercy?   Miserable slave! yesterday I gave you a
necklace of pearls ; to-night a kris's edge shall make you one."

It was hard indeed to hear such reproaches from the old chief,
who, as he had truly said, had treated me as his own son ; but harder
still a hundred times was it to see the devilish Anakraja triumphing
—to see him fawning on the man whom he would have rejoiced to have
sent to a sudden grave, and favouring me with a grin full of satisfied
malice whenever he found opportunity. I was, however, pleased to
see that Ribut Bungat was in no humour to accept the affectionate
attention of Anakraja, and pushed him off with very little ceremony.

"May I speak, my chief?" I asked, being resolved to spoil the
ape's diabolical mouthing and grinning if it was possible.

"How may I deny you, after I have accepted your counsel to take
no man's life without first hearing his cause?" replied the old chief,
sneeringly; "truly Orang Reu you were wise to make such provision
for yourself."

"Though I meet my death where I now stand, O Ribut Bungat,"
said I, not heeding the taunt that accompanied his permission that I
might speak, "I can only declare, in simple truth, that never since I
have tasted of your generosity have I harboured one evil thought
against you. Since, however, I am to die, let me beg of you a little
grace—not so much that I fear death as that your chief enemy may
live to laugh."

I saw at once that Anakraja winced under this latter observation
and, half aloud, he whispered into the chief's ear—

"Be advised, O Ribut Bungat ; let not these dealers in magic live another instant. Say the word, and their guilty heads shall roll at your feet."

Now it happened that the soldiers having bound me to their satisfaction, turned to Tom Cox, and, finding that life still remained in him, commenced hustling him about, the better to secure his arms and legs. Their handling being none of the gentlest, Tom was roused from his insensibility, and recovered his wits in time to comprehend Anakraja's last observation.

"What does the villain say?" cried Tom, so suddenly that the fellows who stood sentry over him jumped again. "Does he talk of our guilt? Was it not he who hatched the infernal scheme, or set it ready for hatching? Was it not he who gave me the names of the head men who were in the plot, and who——"

Snatching a spear from a man beside him, Anakraja made such a lunge at Tom, that, had not his arm been struck up in time, there would have been a gash in my companion's throat that would have stopped his mouth to a certainty.

"Do you speak what is true?" asked Ribut Bungat, eagerly, and as though he more than half suspected that it was so. "Can you show me that you speak the truth?"

"Let your eyes convince you," replied Tom. "There is a pocket in the inside of my jacket; put your hand there, one of you fellows, and pull out a piece of paper you will find."

This order the man addressed obeyed, and, sure enough, there was the paper Tom alluded to, and on it were inscribed, in Anakraja's unmistakeable scrawling letters, the names of six of the leading men in the country, together with an intimation that they might be depended on, and would be found ready, "when the moment arrived, to take such measures as would ensure success for the scheme."

From that moment Anakraja had nothing further to say, but, silent, ghastly, and grim, held out his hands that he might be bound, according to Ribut Bungat's prompt command; and, while this was taking place, the old chief hurried away to the town to ensure the arrest of the other six conspirators. I may as well here state, however, that he was only successful in arresting three of them; the others, having no doubt of the fate in store for them, chose to end their lives according to their own devices, one of them swallowing poison, and the other two piercing their bowels with the sankoh, or native spear.

The administration of justice in Borneo—at least, in this part of it—is very different from what one finds in civilized countries. There are no prisons on the island—no places where a culprit could be confined for a single night without the strictest watching. Therefore such a punishment as imprisonment is unknown; instant trial with instant penalty is the order of the day, whether the said penalty be fine, maiming, or death—indeed, the executioner invariably sits at the end of the justice-hall, and the carrying out of the extreme sentence of the law is only delayed for just so long a time as the victim can be conveyed outside the building.

In accordance with this principle of speedy justice, we—that is to say, Tom, myself, and the villanous Anakraja—were marched straight from the hill to the familiar hall of audience, which now, however, wore a very different appearance from that it commonly presented. Even in the little time which had elapsed since the discovery of the plot, the white decorations of the hall had given place to a vivid red colour; the walls were daubed with it; the chief's seat was draped with red cloth; the very pedangs and dukus, or chopping-knives of the guards had their blades and their handles smeared with the sanguinary colour.

This was how we found the hall when we entered at the door, and all that I have described or shall have to describe was revealed (for it was now dark night) by the flickering, smoky torches the guards held in their hands. In his customary corner sat the headsman—a hideous giant, black as a coal, and with no other garment than a short petticoat of bark—toying with his tremendous chopping-knife, and jesting with two other fellows who from time to time directed his attention towards us, and grinned with devilish glee at the prospect of the tragedy shortly to take place.

I should like to have spoken a few words to Tom, by way of ascertaining his views as to the terrible mess we now found ourselves in, as well as to learn if he intended to offer any defence, and what; but there was no chance for anything of the kind. Three jailers stood between us; and once, when I uttered his name, one of the fellows brought the flat of his kris down on to my lips, and uttered "Dian!" (Be silent!) in such a threatening manner that I did not repeat the experiment. Anakraja was a witness to this, and, observing my disappointment, said scornfully—

"Patience, Orang Reu; there will be opportunity for your talk presently, when you mount with Tomcox to the fine place up there which you tell us of."

And he being a countryman, and quite a favourite with all who knew him, was allowed to talk on without check.

Presently, however, every one's talk was hushed, for, entering at the rear of the judgment-seat, Ribut Bungat made his appearance, clothed in a long red robe, and with a sort of skull cap, also of red, half covering his grey hair. Following him came the other six prisoners. Nor do I make any mistake when I say the other six, although, as I have before stated, three of them had died by the violence of their own hands. It would have been impossible to find a more vindictive man than Ribut Bungat when roused to a vengeful mood; and he was so roused now, and ordered that the lifeless carcases should be put on their trial as well as the living men, that, if found guilty, the body of each might be dishonoured and thrown as food to the crocodiles, instead of being given over to their female relations, that they might "wake" it (for this Irish custom prevails in Magindano), and roll it in fine mats, and kill a fowl over it, as a sacrifice to the spirit who guards the dead; and as the three dead men could not be made to stand, and there was no convenient way of propping them against the wall, they were ingeniously slung by the neck with a rope, and drawn up over the beams till their heads hung level with those of their guilty living partners, who were placed in a row with them.

Then our trial—if so it could be called—began. Ribut Bungat himself was chief witness as well as judge. In brief terms he explained to the assembly that on the afternoon of that day, while in council with Anakraja and some others, he had need to send written word (he had grown amazingly fond of writing, and would scarcely send a message next door without it) to one of his counsellors who was sick. Turning suddenly to Anakraja, he asked him for a piece of paper to write on, and the doctor, taken off his guard, thrust his hand into his pouch, and produced the only piece he had with him, which was Tom Cox's latest despatch concerning the progress of the conspiracy. When, however, I say that he produced this paper, it is not strictly correct. He only drew it partly from the pouch, and then, suddenly bethinking himself, thrust it back again with a stammering excuse that he had no paper, but would go home and fetch a piece. Observing

Ribut Bungat's rising suspicion, however, and knowing that there was no help but to produce the damning evidence, he affected an easy and unconcerned demeanour, and, again withdrawing Tom's note (which had no address), observed that here certainly was a scrap of paper, yet when he said he had none to give he was right, inasmuch as it did not belong to him—that he had picked it up just outside the village, where either Orang Reu or Tomcox must have dropped it, as it was in the handwriting of one or the other. His intention was to have returned it to the first of the white men he happened to meet. That was all he knew about it—he was ignorant of the contents of the note, or for whom it was intended. The chief might, of course, read it if he pleased.

Ribut Bungat did please, and, having read the note through, started up in a rage, and cried—

"Treachery! These vipers we have nourished are turning to sting us! Where is this Orang Reu and his villanous brother? Fetch them instantly, but without alarming them, lest they make off or rob themselves of that life which is no longer theirs, but ours."

"Orang Reu! Tomcox! treacherous!" cried Anakraja, with well-simulated indignation and amazement; "then let it be your servant's business to bring them here before you, and in so unsuspicious a manner that they shall never dream of the just punishment which awaits them."

With this he had started off before the chief could even say yea or nay, and, hurrying up the hill to our house, presented himself before us in the manner the reader has already been made acquainted with. This evidence, coupled with what transpired in the presence of the chief at the time of Anakraja's arrest, completed the case, and a pretty clear case it seemed against all of us. True, I was innocent; but when the three Dyaks had been asked what reply they had to make to the heinous charge preferred against them, and they simply pleaded "innocence," and when Anakraja was asked, and he, too, whined out, "My life is, as it ever was, in the hands of my chief, and innocent though I am, should Ribut Bungat decree that I have lived long enough, I shall die proclaiming his countless virtues, and how great, and good, and generous he is"—when I say that this arch-villain impudently asserted that he was not guilty (an assertion which, I am happy to record, Ribut Bungat received only with a gesture of impatience), what would it avail me to follow suit?　As it happened, however, it did not fall to my lot to answer next, but to Tom's, and—peace to poor Tom's soul!—he did a noble action, and one which wipes completely away from his character the stain of selfishness which had hitherto clouded it.

"Are you, too, innocent, Tomcox?" asked Ribut Bungat sneeringly.

"No, I am not," replied Tom.　"I am guilty of aiming at the lives of men who, in the eyes of the people of my country, are murderers. That white-livered calf (Anakraja) is the suggester and prime mover in the business, and I agreed to act under him.　The only innocent man standing bound before you is Orang Reu, as you call him.　He knew nothing of the conspiracy from first to last."

But conscientiousness carried to this extent was unknown among these people.　The chief shook his head, and one sage counsellor, addressing Ribut Bungat, earnestly warned him against trusting what Tom had said.

"Clear the land at once of these sowers of mischief," urged he; "we may as well have two of them among us as one, for no sooner will the bad spirit of the one whom we slay escape from its house than it will fly into the other, and, instead of two men, each with a devil's nature, there will remain to bring destruction on us one man with *two* devil natures, and what, then, shall we have gained by the death of one?"

This speech, ludicrous as it may appear, was evidently regarded as a marvel of wisdom by all who heard it, and there was a loud murmur of "Badas! badas!" (Good! good!) and as great an amount of head-wagging as though Solomon himself had spoken.

Ribut Bungat, however, neither cried "Badas!" nor shook his head.　As I have before intimated, the old chief and I had grown to be capital friends, and he was only too glad to have his inclination to think me innocent justified in so direct a manner.　Still, the question of duality of devil nature, as raised by the last speaker, seemed to have impressed him considerably, and, as the sequel proved, it was this very argument, raised for my destruction, that saved my life.　As I have before had occasion to remark, the Dyaks of this part of Borneo are extremely superstitious, and the chief was no exception to the rule; and, though his shrewdness was decidedly superior to that of his countrymen in general, that circumstance tended no more to his advantage than that it allowed him wider scope for his superstition. It was very well for his counsellors to say that if one of his adopted white men was slain his evil spirit would straightway take a lodging in the other white man, but what would be the result of killing both the white men? What security did he have that the two emancipated spirits of evil were so fastidious that they would not take up their abode in a couple of his wickedly-disposed subjects? Would it not be better to put one white man out of the world, and then to pack off the other white man to carry his double burden of devilry elsewhere? or, better still, so to manage that he should sink with the said objectionable double burden far out at sea?

I don't say that these were Ribut Bungat's cogitations as he sat regarding his prisoners perplexedly, and seemingly considering what his verdict should be. It would be uncharitable to say so, because he may have been actuated by a secret desire to give me a chance—certainly a very meagre one—of saving my life. Of this, however, the reader is as capable of judging as myself. Presently the chief raised his head to speak, and the crowd was hushed by the cries of "Dian! dian!" (Be silent!) uttered by the guard.

"This, my children," spoke Ribut Bungat, "is my decision. You have heard the evidence, and will agree with me that the prisoners are one and all equally guilty and worthy of death?"

"Bisi! bisi!" (Yes! yes!) was the loud response of the audience, while Tom Cox cast at me a pitying look, and shook his head deprecatingly.

"Then," again spoke Ribut Bungat, "all that remains is to settle the manner of their death. As you know, there is but one fate in Magindano for traitors—that they be beheaded, and their bodies thrown as food for crocodiles; and with all these criminals, except one, shall this law be carried out; and understand I make the exception in the case not of the least but of the most guilty. That one is Orang Ren. He, you know, has long been my close friend. How I have favoured him before all others in the land is no secret to you" (this observation called forth the cry of "Bisi! bisi!" most emphatically from all parts of the hall); "therefore it should have been his duty to have acquainted me with my peril. He did not, and therefore he is the greater traitor, and his death shall be the cruel one he, with the others, contrived for us. He shall be sent to sea in a sampan so leaky that, exert himself how he may, it shall not live many hours; and he will sink and drown in the depths of the waters, but where no man shall ever be able to tell. Thus will he and his evil spirit be wiped out from amongst us. As for the rest of the prisoners, the dead as well as the living, take them out instantly, and return to me with their heads."

And though it was dark night, so that you could not see to do anything without the assistance of the torches, the three inanimate bodies were hauled down and dragged along by the ropes about their necks, and the three Dyaks, and Anakraja, and, lastly, my poor friend Tom, whose acquaintance I had originally made in so singular a fashion, and who had, for so many years, been my constant friend and companion—my only companion, I may say—were carried off in procession, headed by the executioner. There was no opportunity for farewell or parting embrace; he could do no more than wave his manacled hands towards me and utter, " Good-bye, and God bless you, Reu!" when he was hurried out at the door, and that was the last, the very last, I ever saw of him. It was strange to reflect on the vicissitudes of human life as illustrated in poor Tom's case. Nobody at home would ever dream what had become of him. His mother at Stepney would have evinced no great surprise had he that very night knocked at her door. The blacksmith, his master, had, most likely, not yet forgotten him, but, on the contrary, ever kept a broad look-out for his runaway apprentice in any smithy he chanced to visit; while, during the greater part of the time, Tom had been among savages, eating, drinking, and dressing like them or nearly, and now he was about to die a savage's death, and his body thrown to outlandish monsters, concerning whose very existence the good folks of Stepney were more than doubtful. And were my prospects more cheerful than Tom's? Had not I been selected, on account of my superior atrocity, to die a death more cruel and lingering than that visited on Tom and the rest? Adrift at sea in a leaky boat! To see Death in the distance sauntering towards you leisurely, and to know of a surety that you will presently feel his cold arresting hand! Yes, surely the fate of Tom Cox *was* preferable!

In one respect at least, however, my sentence was less cruel than that of my companion. It was his hard lot to be hurried out of the world without opportunity for prayerful preparation, while in my case, as it fortunately happened, the terms of my sentence involved some necessary delay, for the sampan in which I was to float to my death was not to be simply a vessel leaky through long usage, but one regularly prepared for sinking after it had been out at sea a certain time. To my great satisfaction, therefore, when I had been in suspense for about a quarter of an hour, word came from Ribut Bungat that I was to be taken up to my house for the night, and there to be closely guarded till he himself came in the morning, and witnessed my departure in the leaky boat to be prepared meanwhile.

It must have been about midnight when, in custody of three well-armed Dyaks, I, for the last time, entered the wicket of the little garden where I had spent so many hours of content. The chief room was just in the condition in which we had left it, that is to say, in a pretty state of disorder from our scuffle with Anakraja. However, my custodians, who were all of a grade, and on capital terms with each other, seemed resolved to make their duty as easy as possible, and at once set about making themselves comfortable, merely fastening my legs as a precaution against my slipping out at the door. They lit the lamp and spread the mats, and, the night air blowing chilly atop of the hill, they made a fire; and, seeing them so inclined to luxuriate, I thought it not amiss to give them my good-will.

"If my brothers are hungry," said I, "they will find in the corner there a sucking-pig of this morning's cooking, and some baked rice and some sago-cake."

They needed no second invitation. The eatables mentioned, together with every other the cupboard contained, including a jar of pickled pumpkin—poor Tom and myself were getting along excellently in the cookery department, and had lately made good vinegar out of sugar and water—were quickly produced, and devoured with many expressions of admiration. They were even generous enough to offer me some of the meat, but, as the reader may imagine, I had no appetite for eating.

"If, however," said I, "you would do me a kindness, hand me a cupful of the old palm wine you will find in the keg yonder."

Now, palm wine was another article to which Tom and I had devoted considerable attention; we had tried all sorts of experiments with it, and at last had managed to bring it to such a state of perfection that, while in the mouth it was mild as milk, its potency was that almost of the best cognac. Their alacrity in serving me with wine was not less than that with which they helped themselves to meat, and when I had partaken of a cup, they, too, helped themselves to a brimmer, and so much was it to their palates that they ventured on another draught, and then laid down to smoke.

Exactly as I expected—nay, to admit the truth, as I had calculated—the old palm wine and the tobacco-smoke soon began to make their influence felt. The worst of it was, however, that their increasing drowsiness alarmed them. "What if they should all fall asleep, and I should escape?" they said to each other; so, by way of extra precaution, they shifted from the fireplace, and laid along the inside of the closed door, and then began to tell stories by way of keeping themselves awake. This pastime, however, was not vigorous enough to counteract the soporific effect of the old palm wine, and by the time the story-teller's voice had become a mere unintelligible hum, his audience—at least, his native audience—were in a condition to attest their appreciation of his eloquence by the heartiest snoring, and a very few minutes afterwards I was the only being awake in the house.

If my thought, however, had been to escape, I should now have found myself no better off than ever, for the bodies of the three sleepers formed an impassable barrier to egress through the doorway, and to have attempted to remove the obstacle would, doubtless, be to have courted a thrust from a spear, for they slept with their arms in their hands; but I had no desire to escape from the house, even if I had the chance. What good would it have brought me? There was the sea before me, and the vast, tangled, interminable forest behind me; but for any hope I could entertain of receiving a cordial reception from the natives residing at the further side of it, even if I had the good luck to reach it, for reasons with which the reader is already acquainted, I might as well have jumped into the ocean with the notion of arriving a live man on the other side of that.

If my object in making my jailers drunk was not that I might escape, what, then, was it? This: that I might possess myself of my great diamond, and some of the largest of my pearls, and my roll of bank-notes. They were altogether in a little unlocked box in our cupboard, but, unluckily, this same cupboard was at the end of the chamber farthest from me, and, as I have before stated, I was bound hand and foot. I managed, however, by dint of great exertion, to stand on my feet, but, at the very first attempt at putting one foot before the other to walk, I stumbled with no little noise; but the mighty old palm wine held the brains of my jailers in such strong fetters that they never heeded the noise, but snored away as contentedly as ever. Not caring, however, to risk another crash, I resorted to an expedient that should have occurred to me at first— that of rolling. I rolled over and over till I reached the cupboard-door, and then I got on to my knees and ransacked my jewel-box at my leisure.

My anxiety was where to stow the articles I was desirous of carrying off with me. For all I knew to the contrary, I might be stripped before I was allowed to enter on my voyage, and in such a case all the precautions by way of stowage I might choose to take would be of no avail. At last, however, it occurred to me that I might carry my diamond and four of my biggest pearls in my mouth. It was not probable that I should be called on to talk much during my stay at Magindano, and, even if I were, my choked utterance would doubtless be attributed to dismay and grief. As for my bank-notes, I laid them flat, and, dividing them, placed each half between my feet and the soles of my sandals; and, simple as the operation may read, it occupied me so long a time fumbling and pawing with my hands closely bound at the wrists, that by the time the job was completed, and I had rolled back to my original corner, daylight came streaming through the chinks, and the crowing of the cocks roused my custodians, who at first were in a great fright, but presently finding me, as they thought, calmly reposing, they bestirred themselves to clear away all evidence of the orgies of the preceding evening, and were presently in such trim array that it was impossible for any one to say that they had not fulfilled their trust like honest soldiers.

But, the reader may justly inquire, why all this artfulness and manœuvring? Of what use were diamonds, and pearls, and bank-notes to a man bound on a voyage to death? What now becomes of your hypocritical talk about poor Tom Cox's hard fate, in being hurried out of the world without an hour's grace in which to make his peace with his Maker, and of your own expression of thankfulness on the same account that you were to be spared till the morning? Would it not have been more becoming in you, as a dying man, to have devoted the few hours yet remaining to you to prayer? So it would, good reader; and so I give you my word of honour, I intended to employ my time when I expressed my thankfulness that opportunity was afforded me. But the more I came to reflect on the circumstances of the case—and you will be pleased to bear in mind that a man in such a condition as was mine thinks very rapidly—the less could I bring my mind to the conviction that I was really a dying man. True, there was nothing in Ribut Bungat's words from which hope might be drawn—no more, indeed, than from the leaky sampan to which he had condemned me; yet, if looks go for anything, and my despair had not made me incapable of correct judgment, the old chief had still remaining some friendliness for me. In his own heart he did *not* think me the most guilty of any of the conspirators; indeed, I think it will not be going too far to say that, since Anakraja's perfidy had been so clearly made out, Ribut Bungat had entertained almost perfect belief in my innocence. "Why, then," it may be asked, "why, then, did he not exercise the absolute power which belonged to him, and declare his belief?" For a mighty good reason: his was not the only life involved in the conspiracy; it was intended to send nearly a thousand men to their long account, and among this thousand were some of the most powerful under Ribut Bungat the land could show. Had I been a mere common slave, in whose welfare the chief could have no interest beyond my commercial value, he might with tolerable safety have interceded in my behalf; but, as the reader knows, and as every man, woman, and child in Magindano knew, I was Ribut Bungat's right-hand man, his confidant, and his secret adviser, and there might have been that between us which would have made it more important to him to exercise clemency than justice; at least, so the indignant host would have said, had he shown me any mercy; and, indeed, they could hardly have been blamed, for by what right could he forgive my murderous intent in its direction towards others, who were as free to prosecute and punish as he himself was? He dare not do it, especially as it was he himself who had denounced me. What he could do, however, if he believed in my innocence, was to aid me in secret, and by some underhand means endeavour to save my life. This thought it was that thoroughly possessed me, and prompted me to act as I did instead of how I should.

As soon as daylight appeared I began to grow anxious, but it was not till at least four hours afterwards that one of my guards, looking out, announced the approach of Ribut Bungat and his officers. The chief, however, was not walking, as was his custom, but was carried in a sort of sedan-chair, and, when he came close, it was easy enough to perceive that he was haggard and feverish, and far from well.

If I had had any remaining doubts as to his friendly disposition towards me, they would now have been quite dispelled. He evaded my eyes nervously; but when our glances met, there was that in his which spoke of pity and remorse as plainly as though his tongue had uttered them. This was comforting as far as it went, but what I sorely missed was any sign of assurance that I might *hope;* he looked sorrowful as a man who had come to see his friend die, and that was all! For a moment this plunged me to the depths of despair, but then came the cheering thought, that his sorrow might arise from the fact that he was about to lose me. Any how he *must* lose me; and though it might afford him some consolation to know that I was safe and sound somewhere else, I should be as dead to him as though I were at the bottom of the sea. His first act was one of mercy.

"What!" exclaimed he angrily, "are my guards such weak women that a prisoner is dangerous in the hands of three of them unless they bind him? Or did you tie him, that he might not escape while you slept? (My three jailers winced plainly at this random stroke.) Release him of his bonds."

This was at once done; and then Ribut Bungat, in the same petulant tone, inquired of me if I had eaten. My mouth being too full to allow of speech, I could only shake my head by way of answer, whereon he began to storm anew, declaring that my sentence was to drown and not to starve, and ordered some food and drink to be brought instantly; and much, indeed, should I have liked a hearty pull at the pitcher which was presented to me, but fearful that, if I attempted it, I might swallow my treasures, or even, perhaps, cause one to stick in my gullet and strangle me, I could only decline with a more mournful shake of the head than before, which caused Ribut Bungat to look more rueful than ever, and by way, I suppose of relieving his emotion, he smote one of my guards a tremendous whack over the shoulders with his staff for neglecting me. Then, turning once more to me, he observed meaningly—

"Orang Reu, though you are doomed to die, and cannot hope to live many hours, you do not seem to have made any preparation."

This remark not a little astonished me, as I thought to be sure he alluded to spiritual preparation; and though we had talked together more than once of death and what came after, he was always disposed to treat as a funny joke my opinions on the subject. Was it possible that he had taken our religious conversations really to heart, and was now distressed at seeing me so unprepared to die? If such a thought entered my mind it was not allowed long to remain there, for, observing my perplexed face, he continued—

"If you were at home in your own country, and were about to die, how would you be dressed?"

As well as my clogged utterance would permit, I told him that in my country a man was buried without his clothes, and simply wrapped in a winding-sheet; while, at the same time, I was growing more and more down-hearted to find that he continued to talk so seriously about my dying. My answer seemed to disappoint him.

"How is that?" said he. "Is your country so rich, and yet the people pay little respect to their dead? Have they no fear of giving offence to the spirits into whose custody the body will pass? With all the nations with which I am acquainted, it is the common custom to array the dead in their most costly clothes, and with their limbs adorned with their choicest ornaments. It is the law with us, and it is a good law. Therefore I command that you, who are as though you were dead, do adorn yourself with your golden rings, and ear-weights, and your necklaces, for, meeting your death at sea, the great spirit who controls the waters may ask you who sent you; and I, Ribut Bungat, who live by the sea, and thrive by grace of the great spirit who rules it, would be thought neither miserly nor ungrateful."

There was a murmur of applause when Ribut Bungat delivered himself of this speech. The majority of the hearers doubtless saw in it nothing but a tribute of respect to the sea, by which, as their chief had said, they one and all derived their sustenance. A few there were, I dare say, who in their wisdom penetrated the command, and found under it a manœuvre to be rid of me and all my devilish belongings at a sweep; though I firmly believe many a one would not have said nay to the offer of a pair of earrings or a few pearls from one of my costly necklaces, in spite of the taint of brimstone about them—

nay, it is not too much to say that, had all my goods been conferred on one individual, the rest would have been consumed with envy in consequence; still, as nobody was to be the loser, even of his temper, by the manner of their disposal, they were agreeable enough that me and my jewels should be packed to Satan together, and applauded the chief's decision as heartily as the others.

But Ribut Bungat's strange order bore a different complexion in my eyes. What other object could he have in insisting that I carried

The Old Chief does Davidger a last service

my riches away with me, than that I should be benefited by them? I knew the man too well to suppose that, from superstition, he would cast such valuables to the fishes. Evidently it was his desire that I should be saved; but how? I had no other friend on the island but himself, and *he* would not have the preparing the sampan for sinking; and I could not dare hope that those to whom the job was entrusted would bungle in a way that would serve me.

"Perhaps," thought I, "he thinks to save my life by casting about the doomed boat one of those ridiculous charms he has so much faith in." Never in my life did I so bitterly bewail the ignorance of the heathen.

This, however, was no time for explanation. There could be no harm in taking my goods with me; indeed, there was no opportunity to discuss the utility of the proceeding, for, under Ribut Bungat's direction, the fellows began ransacking the place, and laid all they found in a heap, from which, with his own hand, the old chief helped me to dress. The most massive and precious ear-drops I possessed he himself placed in my ears, and threw over my head all my necklaces, which were five in number, and all of more or less value. Besides these I drew on my golden wristlets and anklets, twenty-eight in all, and making together such a weight as made it a labour to lift either of my limbs; then, with my leopard-skin mantle on my shoulders, and my state headdress, composed of grey monkey-skin and ivory and gold, I signified that I was ready: and so we set out for that part of the beach that lay just under the brow of the hill.

On the shore were congregated a vast number of people, and at the water's edge was a sampan of the largest size, with its paddles, and two jars, one containing rice and the other water. Jars, paddles, and sampan were painted the glaring and ominous colour, and, amid the yells and execrations of a thousand voices, I was invited to enter the treacherous boat which was to drift me to death. As I stepped on board, Ribut Bungat was close by, and though, for the sake of appearance, he was forced to draw back from my proffered hand, he regarded me very kindly, and softly uttered the single word—a word which was as precious as all the wealth concealed within my mouth, and within my sandals, and draped about me from top to toe—

"North!"

CHAPTER IX.

TO a man in a little boat out at sea, and provided with neither rudder nor compass, it is no easy matter to steer in a given direction. Still, from the circumstance of the sun's setting exactly before the door of our house on the hill, it was easy to judge in which direction "north" lay, and, taking the paddles in hand, thitherward I pulled. When I had got some fifty yards from the shore, I halted for a moment to contemplate for the last time the country in which I had witnessed so many marvels, and received from the inhabitants treatment so various. Yet, on the whole, I had no fault to find with Magindano; and though, in leaving the place, I had been certainly bound for my own native land, much sadness might well have mingled with my sensations of delight; but as it was, now that I was leaving the domain of the friendly chief of the Sea Dyaks to seek a grave in the sea's bed, or, what seemed scarcely preferable, permission to live in any strange country, and among savage barbarians of any sort it might please the winds and the waters to cast me among—when, as I say, these reflections came crowding about me, my heart overflowed with bitter sorrow, and for half a pin I would straight have pulled back to the Magindano shore, and said to the angry mob there assembled, "Pray kill me; let me at least end my life among you with whom I have lived so harmlessly." But, even as I halted in my uncertain mood, the people seemed instinctively to know what my thoughts were, and, raising their arms, they made as if to drive me away, and caught up stones from the beach and hurled them towards me, and yelled and screamed so, that, despite my distance from them, their curses came distinctly to my ears. Knowing how little I deserved this treatment, however, it rather served me than otherwise. Had they seemed sorry for my departure, had they evinced signs of relenting in their hatred of me, then, undoubtedly, I should have rowed back to them, and, in all probability, met my death; but, finding myself hooted at, and cursed, and pelted, my tender thoughts rapidly faded, giving place to indignation and anger, and, flinging on my cap with much less deliberation and solemnity than had marked its removal a few moments before, I snapped my fingers at the savage crew, and uttering a shout of defiance, took careful bearings of the direction in which I should pull, caught up my paddles and laid to my work in real earnest.

So I pulled for two hours or more with no abatement of speed till the island was quite lost to view, and, though it was heavy work and the sweat ran down me in quick tricklets, I gave my shoulders to the work, and paddled with a will. Suddenly, however, a thought came into my mind which caused me at once to come to a dead stop. Had not I been a little too hasty? Might I not have overlooked the simple manner in which Ribat Bungat meant to help me? He had not joined the rabble on the beach in execrating me, but stood with his arms folded, and with the same sorrowful face he had worn since my persecution had began. What did he mean by the simple word "North"? That I was to paddle in that direction; but to what end? That I might find land thereabout, or that I might fall in with a prahu which he would send to my relief, which would carry me to some safe place of which he knew?

The longer I thought on this the more I was convinced of its feasibility, and wondered how it had hitherto escaped me; so I lay on my paddles, and kept a long and anxious look-out—so long that, by the time I grew weary of it, the sun was at high noon, and blazing down on me till I felt faint and sick. All this time I had worn all my finery, including my skin cloak; but now I removed them, and sat in my sandals and drawers, and with my cap, or rather helmet, for it resembled that article of European head gear more than any other, on my head. At the same time I took a drink out of my water jar, and so for a time assuaged my thirst and my impatience.

But now with the moments grew my suspicions that I was doing a very foolish thing. Ribut Bungat had *not* meant that he would send a vessel to my relief, and all this time I had idled away—all this time my patched boat was rotting under my feet! By this I might have reached the land the chief had hinted at; no doubt he had calculated the time it would take me to row the distance, and set it against the durability of the pitch with which the treacherous sampan was veneered! Now I should drown through my own folly! With the means of saving myself so kindly placed in my hands, I had let it slip through my fingers, and I was certainly doomed! And so over-powered was I by these bitter reflections that I covered my face with my hands, and cried aloud, and so wasted several more precious minutes.

At last, however, by a great effort I roused myself, and taking the bearings of the sun, began again to pull for dear life. Apparently there was as yet nothing amiss with the sampan, and, with the exception of the little water I shipped through paddling at so furious a rate, it was as dry and comfortable as when I set out. But my tremendous exertions began to tell on me; every muscle in my body was a-tremble, my mouth was parched, and I speedily found my back blistering under the scorching sun, and my head aching cruelly from the weight of my helmet, though, being aware of the danger of exposing the head under such circumstances, I was loth to remove it. At last the throbbing of my temples became so excruciating that I was obliged to remove the cumbersome thing, and, with foolish petulance, was for casting it into the sea; as good luck would have it, however, I altered my mind, and, instead, pitched it to the end of the boat. Then I took my skin cloak, and, ripping it in two with my knife, made it into a sort of hooded tippet, secured round my neck with a thong of the skin, which I cut from that part of the cloak I had no need for. Previous to putting it on I dipped it in the sea, and wrung it as dry as I could, and, though the damp fleshy side of the mantle was grateful and cool, there was enough of salt hanging about it to give my excoriated shoulders such a pickling that, had I not had much more important business to think of, would have caused me such pain as to make it unendurable.

As at this time of year the sun rises in Magindano about three o'clock, and as, to the best of my calculation, I stepped into my sampan about four hours afterwards, I had by this time been at sea

between five and six hours. As before mentioned, I had on board a
jar of water as well as one of cooked rice, but they were both small
jars, holding, I should conjecture, little more than about three English
pints. As to the rice, although it was decently dressed with oil and
spices, it at present had no attractions for me. But with the water it
was different; I had begun by taking a great swig at it, demolishing
a pint, I dare say. But no sooner did I take to the paddles and pull
for half an hour than I was as thirsty as ever, and felt inclined for
another pull at the jar, and, indeed, paused in my paddling for the
purpose of obtaining it; but when I raised the vessel to my mouth,
and had thus an opportunity of observing how low the precious liquid
within had already sunk—when I saw this, and looked about me and
saw nothing but blazing sky and salt sea, with no more promise of
land than though I had been in the middle of the Atlantic, it behoved
me to be prudent, and I took but a single steady gulp, and though,
through my having injudiciously allowed it to stand in the sun, it was
fully lukewarm, how delicious that gulp was! Had it been cool, it
would, no doubt, have been more delicious still, so I prepared for my
next treat by dipping the remainder of the skin cloak into the sea-
water, and wrapping it round my jar. I had resolved that I would
drink no more for an entire hour, by which time I knew from experience I could cover nine miles at least, and be brought probably
within sight of land; but, alas! my urgent thirst outstripped my
resolution by full half, my arms began to flag, and I had no energy
except to gaze on the reeking goat-skin that enveloped my treasure;
the nectar, doubtless by this time as cool as melon-juice, brilliant as
diamonds—more brilliant than my diamond, the great dull, yellow
one—the useless thing!—not worth a single splash of cold water, and
more harm than good to me, tucked with the pearls under the waistband of my drawers, and hurting me as I bent at my paddles; but
no, I must not yet drink more of my water. Suppose I ate some of
the moist rice?

The experiment might be worth trying, especially as I set so little
store on the contents of my second jar; so I plunged in my hand to
take a mouthful. But who can picture my disappointment, my rage,
my despair, when, at the depth of a finger in the jar, my fist encountered a substance that, from its hardness, was not boiled rice, and
which, when I withdrew my hand, proved to be a sort of black and

evil-smelling pitch! The sticky, filthy-looking stuff hung and clung to my knuckles, looking all the more odious contrasted with the white rice within my hand. Here, then, was wanton cruelty and treachery of the most refined nature, and that Ribut Bungat was well aware of it I could not but believe; for, now that I came to think of it, it was the chief's own man who had placed the jars, and Ribut Bungat himself had directed him. These reflections sent me into a very bitter mood, and in the midst of it I did a very wicked thing; I took up my water-jar, and in a deep draught drank to the eternal destruction of Ribut Bungat and all his false and hypocritical kith and kin. I think it likely that the toil and heat I had undergone may have touched my brain a little. I hope so; for when I think on that solitary boatman, with his Bedlam dress and his Bedlam rage, standing up in his boat with his jar aloft—when I reflect how close he was to death, and that he had no reason to hope otherwise—and when I hear him crying aloud for misery and ruin to fall on his fellows, I am ashamed of him. If there is any one who thinks I am too hard on the solitary boatman, I advise him to suspend his judgment a little while.

My great drink of water had much refreshed me, and, though I had become sullen and miserable (for what could I hope from steering north after my discovery of Ribut Bungat's treachery?), I still continued to paddle with a will, and, meanwhile, the afternoon grew. Now, singular as it may seem, since I had set out from the Magindano shore had I given scarcely a thought to what should have been my chief concern, the condition of my sampan—as I was led fully to understand it was to be an unseaworthy vessel in which I was to be sent adrift in—an artfully-prepared craft, which, at a moment when least expected, should fracture and send me at once, and without the least warning, plump down to the ocean's flooring. True, there was nothing, up to the present time, in the appearance of the sampan to recall the terrible terms of my sentence to my mind when it had once slipped therefrom. From stem to stern the boat was sound enough, and for many hours she had carried me over the smooth sea in the handsomest manner; but now, just as I was looking towards the sun, and thinking that at about that very moment it was creeping round the first row of palm-trees that skirted our little garden on the hill, and that by and by it would glow ruddily on the bench within the porch around which the little scarlet flowers trailed—the bench on

which Tom and I had sat many and many an evening, smoking our
outlandish pipes and drinking palm-wine—the bench in which our
names were cut, together with the names of our parents, and the
name of the street in London and the number in the street in which
we lived, and which made it all the more like "going home" when,
the labours of the day over, we went and sat on it—the bench on
which poor Tom and I had talked such various talks, about our prospects, about mothers, about turning good and becoming a little more like
missionaries than we were, about our boyish pranks and mischiefs, and
how our friends would stare when, some fine morning, we walked
down their street and knocked at their door, with our skins all
blackened by the sun and great gold earrings in our ears—the bench
on which, but a few hours since, poor Tom had sat while he let me
into his fatal secret. While I was so cogitating I was recalled to
my present condition by feeling water about my feet, and, looking
eagerly down, there, in the centre plank at the bottom of the sampan,
were two spots within a foot of each other, and as large as the palm
of the hand, sinking away from the surrounding wood, as it were,
while about the edges of the sinking spots the sea came gurgling and
rippling through. I put down my hand and felt at one of the leaky
places, and found it soft and yielding, and so feeble a barrier against
the pressure beneath, that it seemed a miracle that the water did not
instantly come spouting up, overwhelming me in an instant.

Now, indeed, the terrors of death appeared to me, and, clasping
my hands, I cried aloud to that very Being whom I so recently had
invoked for his wrath, to extend to me his mercy and forgiveness for
sins committed in a world I had so short a time to stay in. I seized
the cape and hood from my shoulders, and trod them over the
treacherous holes, and kept my feet pressed over them; but the sea
came steadily in notwithstanding, and my feet were invisible below
the ankles. Then I seized my helmet, which, it will be recollected, I
had thrown to the other end of the boat, and, sitting down, began
baling out the water might and main; and, to my great joy, in a few
seconds I was able to clear the sampan so as to be able once more to
see the leaky places.

Now was my time, if ever! How—with what—could I plug the
holes? I cast about me, and my eyes fell on the jar of pitch.
Reaching forward, I plunged in both my hands, and brought out as

much as I could hold of the black, slimy stuff, and pressed it closely over one of the leak-holes; and judge of my joy when I found that the stuff tightly adhered to the parts surrounding the vent, and that the sea no longer came through! To adopt the same course with the other hole was but the work of an instant, and—at least for the present—my boat was seaworthy again. Need I describe how anxiously I sat and watched the two tiny hillocks—the trusty shields that stood between me and death? Need I describe to the reader with what fear and trembling I poked at every other inch of the bottom of the sampan with the handle of one of my paddles, expecting at each poke that I should drive out a concealed plug, and that the enemy would assail me again? But—thank Providence and Ribut Bungat—there were no more leaky places, and those which were stanched held bravely.

After all, then, the good old chief had not deceived me. Instead of being a cruel device to inflict on me pain and disappointment, the pitch—I call it pitch for want of a better name; it was not pitch, however, but a mixture of resins and gums peculiar to Borneo—concealed beneath the rice was kindly provided by him, knowing how urgent would be my want of it. It was humiliating to reflect on the way in which I had anathematized the good-natured old fellow, who, barbarian as he was, had shown himself so much wiser than myself. Well, I only know that I blessed him many, many times more than I had cursed him, and I very heartily hope that he received full advantage of the balance.

There was one circumstance arising out of my temporary disbelief in Ribut Bungat's honesty, however, which it was impossible now to amend, however sorry I might be that in my foolishness I had allowed it to transpire. From the very moment of my suspecting my old friend, I had thought it no longer worth while to follow his hint about making for the north; indeed, after what appeared so manifest a revelation of his treachery, the north, of all quarters of the compass, seemed a direction proper to avoid. Consequently, I had, during the past four hours, paid no attention to the course in which I was proceeding, and, for all I know to the contrary, I might now be altogether on the wrong track. True, I could still glean a notion as to the way I should go by the direction of the sun; but when the sun went down—as it clearly would do within two hours—then what would become of me ?   However, no good could come of indulging in bitter regrets, so I righted my boat for north as well as I was able, and began once more to paddle as fast as my weary arms would allow me.

However, I might have spared myself my exertions, for I was destined never to reach the northern shore Ribut Bungat had recommended ; and this, not because my leak-patches did not hold good, or that my strength flagged, or that night overtook me, but because of a

Davidger Discovers the Dyak Prahu.

mishap that is likely to befall any one caught cruising in the China seas.

What happened to me came about in this wise.   It may have wanted about an hour of sunset, and, resolved on making the most of the remaining light, I was paddling my hardest, with my head down, as is the experienced paddler's method, when, out of the stillness which had lasted all day long, a sound of the blowing of a Dyak reed-pipe met my ear. In a moment I ceased to paddle, and, half rising in the sampan, looked longingly what I hoped was shoreward, thinking that my journey was so nigh at an end that I could hear sounds from the people among whom I must endeavour to find a home. But, look intently as I might, there was no sign of land in view; but when I turned my eager eyes in the contrary direction, I was no longer mystified as to the source of the piping, for scarcely a mile away was a prahu, and that I was perceived as soon as I descried the vessel was certain, for, while still irresolute whether to make off or run for her, the prahu lowered a sampan, and a man, springing into it, began paddling swiftly towards me.

The thought instantly possessed me—this was the prahu that Ribut Bungat had sent to my rescue! For a little time I was nearly beside myself with delight, and waved my paddles as a signal to the man in the sampan. He returned my signal, and at the same time raised a shout, but to my surprise not in any language with which I was acquainted. Was I mistaken? To my great grief I saw that I was. The ruddy light of the setting sun was glowing full upon the strange prahu, and, from the shape of her hull and the fashion of her masts, it was plain that she did not belong to the island of which Ribut Bungat was master. Then, again, as the sampan approached, the paddler turned to regard me, and I could see that he did not wear a scrap of clothing from head to foot, and that his hair was uproarious and hideously matted, which never was the case with the Magindano Dyaks, who, for savages, were rather scrupulous about such matters.

On discovering that I had mistaken the identity of the craft, my first impulse was to make off at my utmost speed, but before I had taken a dozen pulls the uselessness of such a proceeding occurred to me so forcibly that I came to a sudden halt; indeed, had I continued to flee from the ship's messenger in the sampan, his desire to come up with and overhaul me would only have been retarded by a few minutes, for he was a gigantic fellow, and managed his boat like one of long experience. Besides, I was worn out by the great exertions I had been making all the day long, while he, doubtless, was quite fresh. And, after all, what occasion was there for my fear?

What should I do? That I had met a vessel out at sea, instead of being allowed to make land, might occasion me disappointment, though why it should were hard to explain, as, without doubt, the one was just as promising as the other. If I had reached this northern island which Ribut Bungat had spoken of, I should certainly have found it an abode of pirates, and, let the worst come, the crew of the prahu in sight could be no worse. As for the fellow's unlikely appearance, there might not be much in that; his nakedness might be indicative of his total ignorance of civilization, but it did not follow that he was a greater villain for being without a petticoat.

Argue how I might, however. I could not reassure myself. The foreboding that it was an ill wind that had blown the strange ship into my neighbourhood had tight hold of me, and was not to be shaken off. There was, however, no time for deliberation. The savage in the sampan had already diminished the distance between myself and the prahu by more than half, and it would not do for me to remain any longer undecided as to the course I should pursue. How about my singular freight—how should I account for it? It might not be a very uncommon circumstance for these sea rovers to come upon a solitary man in a solitary boat; but then it would be a black man, and not a white one. Moreover, his cargo, if any, would be of a simple and ordinary character, whereas mine was about the most singular to be met with in any sampan on the face of the China seas. What explanation could I give of my business? Whither could a man be bound, or what was the nature of his business, whose cargo consisted of a jar of pitch, a bundle of golden anklets, some pearl necklaces, a head-dress fit for a prince, and, tucked beneath my waistband, jewels of sufficient value to buy a hundred slaves? How should I dispose of my riches?

Since, whether I liked it or no, they would rob me of everything I possessed, if it so pleased them, I thought it might be as well to give myself as dignified an appearance as possible; so, laying down the paddles, I put on my arm and ankle rings, and my pearl necklaces, and my helmet, reeking from being used as a bale, but still magnificent. My gay cloak was now such a matter of rags and flinders, that it would only have detracted from the splendour of my other ornaments if I had attempted to hang it on me; therefore I cast it over the side. My sandals had remained on all day, and it was only now that they were brought under my notice that I recollected the bank-notes they concealed, and that they must be pretty well saturated with sea-water. However, this was no time to attend to such trifles. There remained nothing for disposal but my three great pearls and my yellow diamond, and it seemed that they could not be safer stowed than they had been in the morning—that is, in my mouth. So, with my lips concealing wealth enough to buy an English estate, and with not so much as a shirt to cover my sunburnt back, with my naked shoulders laden with necklaces a queen might envy, and with a good quarter of a hundredweight of gold in rings on my legs and arms, I sat still to await the coming of the man in the sampan.

His surprise as he approached to find so strange a looking being as myself was unmistakable, and, indeed, it was no easy matter for me to preserve my composure when I came to closely inspect the Dyak. He was a man of a very different stamp from any I had seen at Magindano, even among the lowest field-labourers or slaves who worked in the woods or manned the war-prahus. As I suspected, he was literally naked, and so ill-savoured that I could smell him a good three boats-lengths away. His teeth were dyed a brilliant red, and his hair, shaggy as the mane of a bison, was matted and tangled, and hung about his fierce eyes. As he drew his sampan closely alongside mine, he continued to chatter at a tremendous rate, and from his tone it was easy to understand that he was asking a string of questions ; but though a word here and there betokened him a Dyak, all he said was high Dutch to me. Besides, even had we been able to under- stand each other, I had had no time for the concoction of a story likely enough to account for the peculiar circumstances under which I had been discovered ; and it would never do to tell this sea-savage, who, in turn, would carry the tale to his masters, that I was banished from Magindano for conspiring to destroy the fleet ; so I resolved to say nothing at all, but simply signed to the fellow that I desired to be taken aboard the prahu, and, without further parley, took up my paddles and made towards the great vessel, which was slowly bearing down towards us. My companion, however, kept close by my side, scarcely once taking his eyes off me ; and, long before our sampans reached the prahu, he began eagerly bawling to the people aboard concerning the prize he had picked up—how that I was a marvel and a wonder—a man neither white, black, nor brown, and whose like was never seen in the world—that I was dumb, and could not open my mouth—that I was covered with gold and jewels ; and all this in such

an eager voice and with such earnest gesticulations, that, had I been
a veritable water-king or an ordinary merman, greater fuss could not
have been made, nor a more anxious rush to the ship's side to see the
singular creature that was approaching. Even the slave rowers
became so daring in their inquisitiveness that they paused in their
labours, and, all of a row, turned their amazed faces and staring eyes
towards me. These latter, however, were speedily brought to a sense
of their indiscretion by a big giant of a fellow who presently stalked
among them, and struck and kicked them worse than I ever saw any
pack of dogs served. This fellow was evidently the commander of
the prahu, though there was nothing in his appearance to denote his
superiority, except that he was taller and blacker than those around
him, and wore enormous copper rings in his ears.

To tell the truth, I was not at all sorry to note all this surprise
and amazement at my appearance, as it seemed to denote that I should
be treated as a person of consequence. Already I knew what a superstitious race the Sea Dyaks were, and it came into my mind that if
these barbarians, even more ignorant than those whom I had lately
known—if they chose to think me ever so exalted a being—nay, even
though they should imagine that I had risen out of the sea or
descended from the clouds—I would not contradict them. I think I
must have been full of this conceit, for I prepared a little trick in
furtherance of it. When we arrived right close to the prahu, with my
heel I scraped away the pitch that covered the leak-holes in my
sampan; so that, as a pair of hands were lowered to help me aboard,
the frail bark in which I, the mysterious and unknown, was found,
sank with a rushing and foaming, and vanished instantly.

But I had reckoned without my host. Had these Dyaks been only a
little more ignorant than those of the island of Magindano, they might,
indeed, have been led by superstition to think me something more than
an ordinary man; but, unluckily for me, the villains were so utterly
and completely benighted that they were quite insensible to awe, and
so brutally matter-of-fact that had a flight of angels appeared they
would have seen in them nothing but a flock of a new sort of bird, and
concerned themselves no further than to inquire whether they were as
good eating as other winged creatures.

The hands that assisted me up the prahu's side were those of the
chief, and, with no other remark concerning the wonderful disappear-

ance of the sampan than a curse on me for my clumsiness in capsizing it, he lugged me aboard as unceremoniously as though I had been a sack of meal. Standing me before him on the deck, he examined the pearl necklaces, and felt the rings on my arms, and touched them with his tongue (the Dyak mode of testing gold) ; and, satisfying himself that they were really as valuable as they seemed, he laughed an ugly laugh which not at all improved his appearance, and followed this rudeness by another; viz., he snatched my inlaid helmet from my head, and perched it atop of his own tangled crop. This behaviour sent my spirits to their lowest ebb; and whereas a moment ago I had hopes of being taken for a demigod, I now saw that I should be lucky to escape being thrown into the sea ; that is, as soon as my finery was stripped from me.

" Well !" exclaimed the giant, whose conversation was somewhat more intelligible to me than that of the man in the sampan, after he had favoured me with a long stare, " who are you?   Whence do you come ?"

I might have astonished these savages, had they been capable of astonishment, by the marvellous exhibition of pearls and diamonds, instead of words, flowing from a man's mouth, but I plainly saw that neither words nor deeds would help me in my present strait, so I maintained my dumbness, and in reply to the chief's question only shook my head. However, thought I, since it is evidently your purpose presently to strip me, I may as well be generous at a cheap rate ; so I took off my largest necklace, and placed it in the chief's hands. At this he laughed contemptuously, and in a twinkling whipped off my other necklaces, and then taking my four limbs in succession in his great hands, as unscrupulously as though they had each been an eel for skinning, he stripped them of the gold rings, leaving me naked but for my drawers and sandals ; then turning to those about him said he—

" What think you—will he be worth his food ?"

" Since he has no voice to complain, I should say yes," replied one with a grin. And as though he had uttered a good joke, the rest laughed.

" He may be a stubborn brute who will not work," said another wiseacre, anxious in his leader's interest ; " see, he carries tally of the driver's whip on his back already."

"Why so he does!" said the chief, turning me about, and passing his hand roughly over my sun-blistered shoulders. "Here is a tongue which tells us plainly enough who and what he is. He is a slave. Yesterday, as on many a time before, he was beaten, and in the night he steals his master's gold and pearls, kills him, perhaps, and makes off in his sampan. It were too merciful a thing to drown so base a villain! Off with you! take your place among the other slaves, and work till you die."

This command he seconded by a kick, my excuse for not returning which must be that my manliness was utterly prostrated for the time by the cruel turn affairs had taken. I staggered to that end of the prahu where the paddlers were, and they, with many devilish jokes and grins at my expense, made way for me, and placed a paddle in my hands. Thus, within an hour—much less, indeed, for it was yet daylight—how had my condition changed! But a little while ago I was a free sea-rover, wealthy of hope and worldly goods, with such confidence in my good luck that to have presently found myself a prince or ruling chief would not at all have surprised me, and now I was a naked and forlorn galley-slave, whose doom it was "to work till I died!" "Better," thought I despairingly, "better to have died with Tom Cox, and have found a grave in the maw of a crocodile— better even to have let the leak in my sampan gone unstanched, and sank peaceably to the bed of the ocean, than live to become a thing so despicable as a slave to such human monsters as these;" but, at the same time, a little voice within me whispered that, if this really was the proper way to regard the matter, I was as well off, at all events, now as in the leaky boat, and that if by seeking the bottom of the sea my condition would be bettered, I had only to make one little jump and the trick was done. Not, I would have the reader distinctly to understand, that the little voice was a wicked one—so wicked, indeed, as to hint self-murder. On the contrary, it was the voice of my better self, and this was its method of showing me how contemptible and baseless were my arguments; and as I shut my ears to the jeers and malicious observations of my fellow-slaves, and gave the subject all my thoughts, I was not long in arriving at the conclusion that my rescue from the sampan, even by the band of cut-throats of the prahu, was, without doubt, a thing to be grateful for. Bad as were my prospects, when I came to think of it they were, at various times, quite as bad at Magindano, and that as " the sweet little cherub who sits up aloft " had protected me there, so I was here equally safe, and fairly in the way of any lucky breeze which might happen to blow.

These reflections tended to cheer me very considerably, and, fagged as I was with my day's exertion, I managed to keep stroke with the rest, so that the fellow who was set by the chief to watch my behaviour could find no excuse for exercising his stick on my shoulders, but even condescended to give me an approving nod. Over and over again I questioned myself whether it would be better to maintain my assumed dumbness, or to acknowledge that I had speech ; sometimes I thought that the latter course would be the more prudent, and that by giving up my three great pearls and my yellow diamond to the chief I might make a friend of him ; but, on the other hand, it was even more likely that he should regard me, or pretend to regard me, as a more daring and unscrupulous thief than he had before thought me, and he might be tempted, by way of concealing the source from which he obtained such valuables, to take my life on the spot. True, I might have spat the diamond and pearls into the sea, and so have avoided the last-mentioned danger; but, after all, there was certainly more danger of my coming to grief through talking than keeping silence, so I resolved, at least for the present, to keep my lips closed and my jewels safe behind them. In the course of the evening, however, perceiving that certain preparations for eating were being made, and thinking it not improbable that I might come in for a share, I took the opportunity to remove my jewels from my mouth one at a time, and slip them between the waistband of my drawers and the lining.

That the prahu was a pirate there could be no doubt: the brass gun at her bows, and the great array of small arms everywhere to be seen, were proof enough of this. This, however, was only evident to any one aboard of her. At a distance—and a very short distance too —she would have passed as a trader, as the brass gun was cunningly masked, and not a man bore even so much as a kris at his waist. In this respect the vessel differed from any I had yet seen in these parts, and these were not a few, for it was a common matter for other pirate commanders to touch at Magindano for the convenience of barter and the exchange of slaves, at which times there would be great feasting and festivity, and no one would suspect for a moment that it was a case of one great thief entertaining another. In all these instances the profession of the shipowners and commanders was not disguised; they were avowed sea-robbers, and honestly bade "Ware-hawk" to whomsoever they might meet; but the villains who manned the vessel on board which I found myself were rogues of quite a different stamp— petty, treacherous rascals, whose sole business was to attack by stealth and subterfuge, no game being too small for them, not even the humble Malay rice-boat, or the Dyak sampan, sparsely laden with beeswax and edible birds'-nests.

As the reader may easily imagine, I was very anxious to find out to what island the prahu belonged, how long it had been at sea, and when it was going home; but, to my great uneasiness, it seemed perfectly "at home" where it was, and, instead of making for any particular point, tacked about here and there to such parts as it was thought that prey would be found. And so day after day passed amid greater hardships than it was ever my lot to bear. Rice twice a day, with a few inches of sugar-cane, was all the victuals we had, and it was only when we made a haul of tamarinds or other fruit, or perhaps of a few goats, that any variety was made in our diet; all day long at the paddle, and all night—or as much of it as could be spared from my duties—stretched on a filthy plank, with as filthy a mat to cover me, with no such thing as a pint of water to use for personal cleanliness; so I passed seven long weeks on board this villanous craft, till I began to lose all heart and hope, and was fast arriving at the morbid con- clusion that it were better at once to throw over all my cherished notions of Christian decency, and take heartily to savagery. Nor was the temptation a slight one; for while I was the wretchedest being in the world, ever brooding and melancholy, my companions were jolly enough, and sang and laughed as though they had not a single care. At the end of the seven weeks, however, the weather began to look threatening, and, to my great delight, the prahu put about for home.

"Now," thought I, "I shall have a chance to escape out of the hands of these barbarians; at least I will try, though the attempt costs me my life."

And all that afternoon, though the sky lowered more and more and the waves began to rise, and, for fear we should not make port before one of those devastating hurricanes peculiar to these parts set in, the greatest consternation prevailed on board, I felt more cheerful than I had felt since the memorable evening when I escaped from the leaky sampan. But, alas! as their spirits rose mine fell; they neared land, and would presently see their friends and their wives and children, and all was joy and good-humour; but when I cast my eyes on the tiny island we were approaching, when I saw how bleak and dismal it looked, and that it was surrounded by the sea on every side, I began to fear that I might as well stay on board the prahu for all chances of escape there were for me.

Nor did my hopes revive when we touched the shore, and, with the rest, I disembarked and helped to unload the plunder. The village was but a few yards from the edge of the sea, and was composed of such a squalid collection of shanties as it was never before my misfortune to behold. When first I beheld Magindano it seemed unpromising enough, but compared with this it was a paradise. There the houses were tolerably clean, and on every side were to be seen wholesome-looking skins and mats, but here was nothing but filth and squalor; as for clothes, the inhabitants, both male and female, wore nothing but a wisp of dirty rag or a few shreds of bark about their loins, while the children ran about with their long hair matted about their heads and shoulders, and as naked as they were born. The huts were not built on a platform raised on piles, as at Magindano, but flat on the bare ground, and were composed of bark rudely stitched together, and plastered with mud from the shore. At Magindano, bullocks, and goats, and plump poultry were to be everywhere seen; but in this desolate place, with the exception of one or other of the animals mentioned, gaunt and wretched-looking, and picketed to a stump near the huts, no sign of a domestic creature was visible. The island, which was very flat, was, I should judge, not more than a mile in breadth any way, and bore not a solitary tree, and, indeed, as I afterwards discovered, no sort of vegetation except that loose, coarse sort of cabbage already spoken of as growing at Magindano.

Except from the children and one or two of the younger women, my presence attracted no observation, nor was there much reason why it should, since dirt and the sun had rendered my skin of as dark a hue as their own; and as to my features, they were doubtless accustomed to see brought home specimens of nearly every type of humanity to be found in Polynesia. In their eyes I was simply "one of the slaves," and as such, when the prahu was unladen, was told off one of a gang of ten, to which one of the hovels before mentioned was apportioned.

Now, I have before stated that I had placed my bank-notes in my sandals, and there they had remained during the whole time I was in the prahu, as never once in all the seven weeks had I taken my shoes off my feet. In the course of the evening in question, however, having partaken of a supper of rice and honey, I slipped off from my companions, that I might uninterruptedly consider my situation, and whether there was any help for it. I had got a hundred yards or so away from the hut, and, finding a convenient jut of rock, I sat down behind it. My first care was to see that my pearls and diamonds were secure in their hiding-place—the waistband of my trousers—and finding that they were, and that my drawers were extremely dirty, I thought I would give them a wash in the sea, and hang them to dry before the sun went down. Meantime, however, I must find a place for my jewels, for the four of them together made no inconsiderable bulk, and it was inconvenient to hold them in my mouth; besides, the edges of the diamond were very sharp, and my tongue and gums had already suffered considerably from abrasion by it.

Where should I conceal them? The hut in which I was lodged afforded no satisfactory place. I had no article of clothing except my drawers; therefore it seemed to me that the best course I could adopt would be to bury the jewels in the earth. The spot where I was seemed a likely one for the purpose, for evidently it was seldom or never frequented; so, taking the centre of the jut of rock as a starting-point, I took five steps forward, and, digging a little hole, dropped in a pearl, and, stamping the earth firmly down again, took ten steps and buried another, and then fifteen steps and deposited my third pearl, and finally seven steps more (for it occurred to me that, if it happened that any three of them should be found at equal distances apart, the discovery of the fourth would be certain), and there interred the most valuable item of my wealth, the great yellow diamond. This matter satisfactorily adjusted, it occurred to me that I might as well take off my sandals, and see if any of the notes remained sound enough to be worth further preservation; but, as I might have suspected, they had been so frequently wetted and so constantly trodden on, that they were reduced to a mere grimy mash, odious and useless.   So I sat down, with my sandals in my lap, and began cleaning out the insides of them.

Now this may seem a trivial matter with which to trouble the reader, and so, doubtless, in itself it is, and one about which I should have thought nothing, except for one little circumstance connected with it, and which—though at the time it appeared unimportant

Davidger is Watched as he Secretes his Jewels.

enough—was, as the sequel proved, weighty in the balance of my fortunes.   The little circumstance was this :—While I was busy turning out the black pulp from my sandals, a slight noise in my rear disturbed me, and, looking back suddenly, I was in time to detect a human face, wrinkled and hideous, leaning over the ledge of rock, and regarding me intently.   As soon, however, as the owner of the face found that he had been discovered, he came deliberately sliding over the rock, and, after regarding me curiously for about half a minute, limped off— for he was lame—with what seemed to be utter indifference, and busied himself among the small craft hauled up on to the beach. I felt very much alarmed by the old fellow's apparition, making sure that he must have seen me depositing my jewels in the ground; but at that very moment there was the sound of the beating of a gong, and, looking about me, I saw the slaves hurrying to their quarters for the night, and was obliged to hurry off too, leaving my washing for another day.

CHAPTER X.

OR many weeks after the events narrated in the last chapter,
my life was spent in a manner extremely wretched and
monotonous. The "rainy season" set in, and the weather
was so uncertain that the big prahu did not venture out to
sea, but lay on the beach under cover of a great reed-
thatched shed.

At first there was employment enough for us slaves in scraping and
caulking the prahu, and repairing her sails, which, as with those of the
prahus of Magindano, were made of skins of animals or grass matting.
When that job was accomplished, except for such domestic work as we
could find, we were idle, and lounged about from morning till night,
smoking when we could obtain tobacco, and now and then (for the
chief, although a great ruffian, possessed a sort of blunt good-nature)
indulging in a boose of palm-wine.

But, as the reader may easily imagine, I grew daily more and more
disgusted with my present mode of living, and lay awake of nights
hours after my fellow-lodgers were happily snoring, turning over in my
mind how it would be possible for me to escape. But, unless I had
possessed the power of flying, this seemed hopeless, at least for the
present, for there was no means even of attempting so daring a thing,
except by a sampan, and just now the waves were so unruly that so
shallow a vessel could not live a quarter of an hour among them; and
even had the sea been calm I should have been in but little better plight,
for the keeper of the prahus (the ugly lame man whom I had caught

peeping over the rock) was most particular, as the evening approached, to go down to the beach and make all secure, carrying the paddles up to the chief's house, and this not so **much because** there existed any suspicion that **any** slave would **endeavour** to make his escape, **as to** prevent the fellows **going out in the boats for their sport.**

Yet, from a slave's point of view, I **had less cause for grumbling** than **any man amongst them, as not one of them was so favoured.   Not by the chief, however,** nor any of the **people immediately about him ; for** although, **at first, and** when the story **of my singular introduction to the prahu** became generally known, I was **an object of some curiosity, at the end** of a week even this subsided, and the **chief would often pass me with** my helmet on his head and my gold rings **on his legs** without **deigning to cast a single** glance at me.   Only in **one instance** did **he** show me the slightest favour, and that was **when, for decency's sake,** I made myself a sort of cloak of **softened bark, and which everybody** about me persisted that **the chief would strip from** my shoulders the moment **he caught me wearing the ridiculous thing.** It turned out that he did not do so.   **He merely regarded me with comical surprise, and** bursting **into a loud fit of laughter, bade me stand still while he fetched** his wife, **whose covering was by no means super-abundant, and who** laughed as loudly as her husband; nevertheless, **that was the extent of their notice of my new cloak, and after that I was allowed to wear it** without molestation.

To return, however, to the point of digression.   **I have said that I was more** favoured and enjoyed more advantages than **other slaves,** and so I did, and at the hands of the ugly lame man, of all people in the **world. As I have already intimated,** his appearance was anything but prepossessing, and the occasion of **my** making his acquaintance was not such as to recommend him to my favourable consideration. True, if I might judge **from the circumstance of my pearls** and diamond remaining undisturbed (and there **could be no** question that I might), he had not watched where I had **hidden them, and so was** none the richer for his prying.

Strangely enough however, **(or so I** thought at the time) the instance above mentioned was not the only one, of my suffering **annoy- ance** from the ugly lame man's **curiosity.** From the very first day of **my** arrival at the detestable island, whether I was at work, at my meals, or even lying down **to sleep at night,** I could never be sure that the lame man was not watching me. The most singular part of the business was, that all his spying and watching was conducted with the greatest wariness, and as though he was patiently waiting for something that would certainly transpire, if he only watched long enough. Finding no comfort in the company of my fellow slaves, it was my custom to stroll away after work hours to some solitary place, and there sit and smoke my pipe and indulge in sober reflection. But I could never be sure that I was alone. Once I took my way to the beach, and sat in the shadow of a boat looking out on the foamy waters and wondering when, if ever, they would bear me away from the accursed crew among which I had fallen. It is a habit of mine when I indulge for any length of time in solitary cogitation to utter what I most earnestly think of aloud; it was fortunate for my assumption of dumbness that I was not now betrayed into this weakness, for after I had sat for full half an hour happening to look up there were the eyes of my persecutor just peering over the edge of the boat, I was certain of it, though when I started to my feet he was lying down in the sampan apparently fast asleep. Once again when by great good luck I had secured a little hut in which to sleep by myself, in the middle of the night I was awoke by a rustling noise, and there lay Katam (or "the crab" a name bestowed on him I suppose on account of his peculiar manner of walking), though how or when he came in was to me a complete mystery.

My first impression was that he was set on to watch me by the chief, and that simply that I might not attempt to run away; but by degrees I became convinced that this was not the case; he dogged me for his own ends, though what these ends could be was a sore puzzle. Was he simply an idiot? That could scarcely be, for he was keeper of the boats, and was entrusted with a considerable degree of authority over the slaves, which he exercised with much judgment and discrimination. He had authority over me among the rest, could order me to what work he pleased, and make my tasks light or heavy. It added to my perplexity, that he made them as light as possible, and in all his transactions with me behaved with what as closely approached politeness as a savage could be capable of. He acted in the strangest way at times. Once, when we were alone, he drew my attention to the crookedness of his leg, and then, pointing to the straight one, slapped them both, and looked earnestly at me, as though he expected I might be able to do something towards curing his lameness. Another time, when the rain was pouring down in torrents, so that some particular ship-work he had in hand could not be proceeded with, he came to me eagerly gesticulating, and waving his hands towards the clouds in a way that led me to conclude that what he meant was, would I be so obliging as to stop the rain. Believing that I was deaf and dumb, he never spoke on these occasions, and never so much as then was I so inclined to regret my shamming.

Nor was his kindness towards me confined to his making my work easy. On one excuse or another, he would always have me about him, either at his house or down on the beach among the shipping, and gave me tobacco, let me sit by his fire, and very often divided his comfortable dinner with me. He seemed uneasy when I was away from him, and took the greatest interest in anything I might be doing. To what I was indebted for his politeness and good-will I did not know, and was the more surprised at it, since to every one else he was surly and malicious, and often got a fellow a flogging he did not deserve.

This state of things continued for upwards of a month, and as nothing came of Katam's eccentricities, I began to grow used to them, and having no other way of accounting for them, began to settle to the idea that it was merely a case of one person " taking" to another, as the saying is; it would pass off presently, as such friendships frequently do, I thought, though I was in no hurry for the change, as I could not be else than a loser by it.

At last, however, and in the most unexpected manner, he furnished me with a key to the mystery. I had been assisting him in repairing a sampan all day, and the job at an end, he, as was not uncommon, asked me into his hut to share his supper. As a rule, these suppers of Katam's were not of a very magnificent character, chiefly consisting in a mess of rice and sugar, with sometimes the addition of a small piece of goat's flesh; not that Katam was too poor to keep a good table, but from the simple fact that food of a superior sort was not to be had on the island, and at hard times even the chief and his wives would frequently have no better dinner than their poorest slave.

On the occasion in question, however, Katam prepared a feast fit for a king. There was a fowl, some goat's flesh stewed with rice, fresh cocoa-nut (a luxury I had not tasted since I left Magindano), some bread-fruit, and a big measure of palm-wine. No other guest beside myself was invited, though there was enough for half a dozen at the very least; indeed, my host seemed particularly desirous, if I might judge by the cautious manner in which he from time to time looked out at the door, of concealing the fact, either that he had made a feast or had company.

My first thought was that perhaps Katam's religious creed was different to that of his neighbours, and that this was a festival of some one or something that he worshipped, and that, being a favourite, he had invited me to assist him in some mystic rite or ceremony belonging to the occasion; but I speedily found that, if the feast was in honour of any one, it was myself, for Katam waited on me as though he were my paid servant, and the expense of the dishes was defrayed out of my private purse. Amiable and polite as he invariably showed himself towards me, his behaviour now quite eclipsed any that had gone before. He helped me in the most obsequious manner, and could scarcely be prevailed on to sit down. He filled and refilled the cocoashell cup with wine, and this so many times, that had I not, according to my English nature, been rather tough in the matter of drinking, and, moreover, had a thorough seasoning as regards this particular sort of brew with my unlucky companion at the little house at the top of the hill, my chance of remaining sober would not have been very great. As it was, however—it was not much of wine, nothing like what Tom and I used to make—it had little more effect on me than so much ordinary English beer, and I was able to keep my wits about me, and held myself in readiness for the discussion of the business which I felt more and more convinced this grand display of hospitality was to lead up to.

After supper he produced a generous stock of tobacco and more wine, and after we had sat gravely smoking and drinking for some time, he assumed a look which convinced me that he was about to proceed to business. But what—after smirking, and grinning, and rubbing his hands awkwardly—he did was simply this :—He first pointed at his own naked feet, and then at the dilapidated sandals which still covered mine, and, as plain as dumb-show could, asked me the tremendous favour that I would give them to him. There was no mistaking what he meant, but he looked so very serious, and seemed to await my answer with so much anxiety that, instead of at once taking off the useless things and presenting them to him, I sat looking at him in astonishment, wondering what on earth he could want with them. I could make nothing of it, however, and shook my head to myself, as it were, in consequence.

But Katam immediately interpreted the **shake of** my head as an answer to his request, and was curiously affected thereby. The coaxing, fawning expression of his countenance instantly **gave place to** one of bitter rage, though **he turned his head suddenly that I might** not observe **it; and then, while his face was turned from me and** thinking, to be sure, that I could not hear him, he muttered—

"I knew it! I knew it! All along I suspected it, and now it is certain. But he shall not cheat me; I'll have them, though I take them from his dead feet."

As the reader may easily imagine, I was not a little surprised and alarmed to hear my **generous entertainer talking in this strain, and it** was a great wonder that I did not forget my pretended dumbness, and ask him what he meant; **but almost before I could have done so,** had I been inclined, Katam **turned to me again amiable and** coaxing as ever, and with five large sticks of tobacco in his hand; these he laid before me, again **pointing imploringly at my old sandals.**

I at once made up my mind that he should have **them. The paltry** things were not worth a single one of the **several sticks of tobacco he** offered for them—no, not a single pipeful even; they were, indeed, so completely worn out that scarcely a day passed that did not find me cobbling them in some way; it was only that very **morning that I** had pondered **whether it** would be worth **while to put them on** again. In his eyes, however, they bore a very different value. They were **worth acting the** hypocrite during a whole month for; they were worth no end of **dinners and** suppers—of this magnificent supper in particular, and **five sticks of** tobacco to boot; nay, according to his muttered threat, **they were worth** more than a man's life. I had no doubt in my own mind that he was altogether mistaken, and would speedily bewail **his bargain; but he had shown** himself in his **true** colours to me, and I was in no humour to treat him tenderly. Under these circumstances I made no **scruple,** since he had made **me so** liberal an offer, to part with my sandals, and, pulling them off, immediately gave them to him.

His conduct on receiving them was even more perplexing than had been his offer to purchase them. He did not attempt to fit them on—

he immediately began to tear them to tatters, tearing fiercer and with more impatience as he the more nearly demolished them, till at last, when they were quite reduced to flinders, he flung them from him, and stood stamping furiously and regarding me with the deepest malice. When, however, he found that his fuming had no effect on me, but that having filled my pipe from my newly-acquired stock of tobacco, I regarded him through the clouds of it with apparent calmness, he presently checked his passion and again sat down beside me, and affected to laugh in a shamefaced way at his own folly. Nevertheless, and even while he laughed, he muttered, thinking that I could not hear him. He bent his head and in a despairing whining voice said—

"Oh curse him! curse him! Shall I never find him out? Am I to come so near being rich and great, and be baulked after all? How shall I make him reveal to me the antu that makes him gold and precious jewels?"

It was fortunate that my tobacco was in full blast, and that at that instant I was able to emit a cloud that completely hid my astonished face from his view. It was all clear enough now. He, in common with the rest of the inhabitants, had heard the marvellous story of my discovery, and in his superstitious mind had found for the business a much less matter-of-fact explanation than had occurred to the chief of the pirate prahu. In his eyes it was nothing less than miraculous that I should be found possessed of such wealth, and he could arrive at no other conclusion than that my *antu*, or good genius, had provided me with it, and that I had more concealed about me. He had seen me, on the very first night of my landing, busy with my sandals, and no doubt, had ever since yearned to possess them.

Being so constantly on the alert to discover a means of escaping from my present wretched condition, it was not to be wondered at that the cherished topic now presented itself instantly to my mind. The lame boat-keeper was greedy for wealth; I was possessed of it; could not the lame boat-keeper serve me if I made him a rich present? Nothing, however, could be done while I persisted in remaining mute, so, resolving at once on active measures, I addressed my companion while the hazy curtain of smoke was still about me.

"I know thy mind, O Katam, and let me warn you to cast away from you all thoughts of harming me. If you killed me you yourself would instantly die. My antu watches over me and has ready cars to listen when danger is plotting against me, and ready though unseen weapons to strike in my defence."

At the first sound of my voice Katam bounded to his feet, and while I continued to address him, stood half out at the hut entrance, with his knees shaking and his countenance expressive of much astonishment and fear, and he held his fingers in his ears as though my voice had been loud as thunder; and, truly, to myself it sounded strangely gruff and harsh after my long silence. Evidently Katam was much more inclined to run off and spread the news that the dumb slave had found his speech than to stay and converse with me; but for him to adopt the former course was the very last thing I desired.

"Stay," said I, rising and putting my back to the door, "my antu is such as you never knew or heard of before, therefore for this one offence it will not harm you. Nay, if you desire anything that it is in its power to grant, I will, since you have been so very kind to me, intercede for you that it may be granted. Speak your thoughts, good Katam. They will not astonish me though they be clothed in the loudest words and not in whispers. Sit down and tell me how can my antu serve you."

But Katam could not so easily recover from his fright. All the while I was addressing him, he was busily employed with a shell of the mussel species, which he had taken from a niche in the wall, laying it on his eyes, on his lips, and on his breast, and each time that he completed the round, nibbling a little bit from the edge of the shell, and crunching it and swallowing it, which I suppose was a charm against the machinations of evil spirits, but never having seen it at Magindano, nor indeed in any other of the Polynesian islands it was my fate to become acquainted with, the reader must take the supposition at its worth. Anyhow his courage seemed much refreshed by the eye-rubbing and nibbling, and he presently adopted my suggestion and sat down with me by the fire.

"Tell me," said he in a low whisper, "is your antu so very powerful? Can it make dumb men speak—make those it favours rich in pearls and gold? Answer me, can it?"

"The Antu whom I and all my countrymen worship can do all you say, and a thousand other things even more wonderful," I answered evasively. "But tell me how can it serve you?"

"How!" replied Katam, in such a fever of excitement that the hand he laid on my shoulder fairly trembled. "It can do two things for me, for which my heart has been so long pining that it feels just withered up. It can carry me away from this accursed place; it can take me back to my own country, and give me such riches that I shall be everywhere welcome. Let it but do this for me, and ask of me any-thing—my right hand even—and I will freely give it you. You say your antu is all-powerful, and it needs only to look on the jewels and golden ornaments with which it had provided you, when you were taken captive, to be made sure that it is so. Ask it to grant me these two favours!"

And Katam looked truly imploring as he knelt before me, clasping his hands; but I shook my head.

"One wish at a time, good Katam," said I. "Shall I pray my antu first of all for riches for you, or that it may assist you to get away from this place?"

Katam was evidently much perplexed with the two stools between which I had placed him; he blinked his eyes and scratched his ugly head, and at last muttered—

: "Of what use would riches be to me here?"

"True, indeed," said I earnestly; "if riches could make one happy on this island, there would be few happier than myself."

On hearing me make this remark, a light seemed to dawn on Katam, and, regarding me suspiciously, said he—

"If you don't like the island, why don't you leave it?"

"If *you* don't like the island, why don't *you* leave it?" I retorted.

"Because," replied he, "I have no powerful antu at my com-mand; if I had! oh! if I had!"

And Katam looked at that part of the wall which was seaward with a longing gaze, and as though the partition of mud and reeds was no obstacle to his looking far away in the direction of that country he was so anxious to regain.

"It is there you are mistaken, Katam," said I. "My antu is indeed powerful, but it is not at *my* command, neither can I compel its good services. Otherwise, as you may depend, good Katam, my first hour on this wretched island would have been the last."

Katam was silent for a little while, but that he was busy revolving in his mind what I had said was evident from the twitching of his lips, and the restless twinkling of his eyes. At last he asked, looking at me keenly the while—

"How have you offended your antu, that he makes you live in such a place as this against your will?"

"But I have not offended my antu," said I; "that it is still friendly towards me you have already had proof. Did it not give me ears to hear your threats against my life, and fill my mouth with words to rebuke you?"

"True," replied Katam, "but it is your antu's wish that you should not quit this island."

"So far from that being the case," said I, "my antu would regard it as a great favour on the part of any one who would help me to make my escape from it."

"Humph!" grunted Katam in a satisfied manner; "and your antu, being so great and so rich, would reward any one who helped you, eh?"

"I have no doubt that he would," returned I, delighted to see that matters were so nicely sliding into the desired groove. "Indeed, I am sure that my antu would be so pleased with any one who helped me to escape from this place, that there is scarcely anything he might not venture to ask without danger of a refusal."

"Would he give such a one gold rings?" asked Katam.

"No, indeed," replied I, cunningly, "for he would consider such a reward too paltry."

"Would he give him ear-rings and a leopard-skin mantle?"

"In addition to more precious gifts, no doubt that he might," replied I.

"But there is only one thing that is more precious!" said Katam, whose eyes were now absolutely sparkling.

"Pearls and diamonds are more precious," replied I, "and those my antu would freely give to my friend—pearls and diamonds of great size."

Katam could not forbear a gasp of delight at the bare mention of the treasures his heart so coveted, but with true savage cunning he shook his head, and laughed as though he detected my purpose, which was to make sport of him.

"It is so easy to talk," said he, "but my hair is growing white, and I am wiser than a young man. Pearls and diamonds of great size do not fall with the rain. It is dew, not diamonds, one sees shining on the leaves."

"True," replied I, "but it is no easier for an antu to talk than to do. To talk, in fact, *is* to do. Tell me, Katam, if a man went out to-morrow night, which could he most easily find—a big sampan, sound, and such as would keep out the sea, with her paddles and enough of food and water aboard of her, on the beach, and ready to launch in an instant?—would it be easier, if one set out to-morrow night to make search, to find this, or big pearls and diamonds sprinkled over the earth, and ready to the hand of such as chose to pick them up?"

To the common sense reader it may appear mighty ridiculous that, having a matter of such tremendous importance to transact with an individual whose powers of comprehension were anything but brilliant, I should adopt figurative rather than downright and plain speech; but were he as well acquainted with the manners of barbarous nations as I am, he would know that they have a decided preference for the round-about, and will thus arrive at a stated point quicker than by the most direct and simple means; it is with them as with simple children at a dame's school, they might stare at a printed book till their eyes ached, and would then, on account of their ignorance of the art of reading, be as ignorant as before they began; but make up your text into pictures with figures and faces, and bright dabs of colour, and they will get the whole story by heart in a twinkling. So it was with Katam: not at all bewildered by the riddle, he sat regarding me with an expression of countenance in which avarice, and mistrust, and cunning were strangely blended. Presently he rose deliberately, and going to the door of the hut, looked to the right and to the left, and then, as though to make perfectly sure that the details of our little business should not be subject to eaves-dropping, he stepped out, and made a complete circuit of the hut, but in a sauntering, careless manner that was not likely to attract the curiosity of any one who might observe him. Finally, he returned to the hut, and pulling the mat securely over the entry, made it fast with four wooden skewers; though, if the same laws as regards privacy reigned here as at Magindano, this skewering was quite unnecessary, as, at the last-mentioned place, the mat, flimsy as was its material, as effectually secured the inmate of a house from intrusion as though it had been an oaken door strengthened by iron bolts and bars. Indeed, it is scarcely too much to say that the Bornean contrivance of woven grass is even more efficient than the

English door, for whereas the latter, in the eyes of a certain sort of folk, is only respected out of fear of the law and its consequences, the former is further secured by the toughest of all ties—those of superstition. When a Bornean, or at least a Dyak, hangs his mat completely over the entrance to his hut, it is distinctly understood that he is either out or is in no condition to receive visitors, and should any one be daring enough to lift the mat, though only for the mere purpose of peeping in, he offends not the occupier of the hut, but the household deity that there presides ; and it becomes a grave matter for settlement, and one in which the priest is the chief negotiator.

To return, however, to Katam. After he had secured the door in the manner described, I thought to be sure that he would at once proceed to the discussion of the business now so fairly launched ; but this is not the savage's plan. Katam, instead of following up the conversation at the point where it had been interrupted, began to load his pipe, which, with most provoking coolness, he lit, and proceeded to smoke to the last whiff before he uttered another word. I thought it time to jog his memory.

"Has Katam forgotten that my antu—the antu from whom he expects so much—awaits an answer ?"

Katam shook his head with a clever assumption of bewilderment.

"A question is a question," said he ; "but there are so many words to this one of yours, that I have forgotten many of them ; and should I speak in ignorance I might offend your antu, even more than if I said nothing."

"What are the words of my question which you have forgotten, Katam ?"

"If I knew I need not ask you to repeat them," replied he, with a twinkle in his cunning eye that plainly said, that if I hoped to trap him in so shallow a manner I was vastly mistaken.

So I again put the case to Katam, and in as precisely the same words as possible, strongly suspecting that the artful villain had not forgotten a single word, but meant to judge my sincerity by the accuracy of the repetition. I suppose I was successful, for at the conclusion he gave a nod and a grunt of satisfaction, and replied—

"The nights now are very dark ; certainly it would be much easier to find the diamonds and pearls if they were there. Diamonds hold

17

the light by which they may be seen; a sampan is a gloomy thing, and very hard to see even at a little distance in a dark night."

"There was never yet a night so dark," returned I, "but that my antu would make the gloomiest thing visible. Diamonds are more brilliant than moonshine, Katam."

"Great diamonds may be," replied the preposterous haggler. "The sky, full of little stars, does not give so much light as one big moon. If there were many big diamonds lying near the sampan might be seen."

So far it was evident that the lame boat-keeper understood me. To be sure, to hear him talk of the light of "big diamonds" as though they were common tallow dips was simply ridiculous, still, if I could only carry my point to a certain extent, he might be brought to his senses with the means at my disposal. Since the negotiation had proceeded so far, had it been an Englishman, or even a Scotchman, with whom I had to deal, I should have thought myself justified in dropping metaphor, and resorting to plain business speech; but my long experience at Magindano showed me that such a course is quite impracticable with a Bornean, so the next step had to be discussed in the same roundabout terms as the preceding one.

Said I, "It is as easy for my antu to spread the beach with big as with little diamonds, and no doubt that, since you desire it, the big moons instead of the little stars will be found, for my antu is very generous—generous to those who serve him as he is vengeful against those who mock him."

"How mock him?" asked Katam, with a somewhat less buoyant manner than had during the past few minutes distinguished him.

"Listen," said I, doing my best to look very serious and solemn, though I confess it was by no means easy to carry humbug to the extent I was now carrying it. "Suppose my antu—who, mind you, my Katam, is all this while, and although we cannot see him, in this hut with us, and listening to our conversation—suppose my antu, hearing your promise, and unwilling to believe that you would dare attempt to befool him, should spread the beach with such light as you speak of, and that afterwards he looked about in vain for the sampan?"

"Ah!" ejaculated Katam. It was quite evident that his superstitious mind was causing him no small anxiety, and that if the business in hand could have been accomplished without the intervention of spiritual agency, he would have liked it so much the better. Indeed, ever since I had assured him that my antu, although invisible, was with us in the hut, and listening to all we were talking about, he had become very fidgety, and glanced furtively about him in anything but a comfortable mood. "Well," said he, "suppose, although the lights were there, no sampan was to be seen? Just suppose it!"

"Then," replied I, "there would be nothing left but to let the lights die out where they lay."

"How die out?" inquired Katam in astonishment.

"In the way my antu might choose to direct," said I. "He who placed them there so mysteriously would be at no loss for a means of gathering them up again, when he discovered that they were spread in vain."

"But," said Katam, in a cunning whisper, "supposing they were gathered up before your antu came to look for the sampan, then it would all be dark, and he could not see; he could not hope to see; and if he is a just antu, he won't punish where he cannot judge."

But, in reply to this speech, which, full of artfulness as it was, overreached itself, inasmuch as it completely betrayed the speaker's disposition to cheat in the transaction if he found a fair opportunity, and consequently put me more on the alert to guard against him, I only laughed, and meaningly insinuated that I should be very sorry to be the man who gathered up the diamonds and pearls under such conditions.

"And why?" asked Katam.

"Because," replied I, "they would be jewels no longer, but only stones of evil; and whoever picked them up would surely die before the morning."

This view of the case seemed rather to damp the dishonest desires which, during the last few minutes, had found such favourable reception in Katam's unscrupulous mind. It was evident from his countenance that he was very much perplexed, and undoubtedly dread of my antu was the sole cause of his perplexity. If it was in the power of the invisible mystery to strew the beach with jewels, it would scarcely be wise to dare its anger. *If* it was in its power! Of course, up to the present time, Katam had only my bare word for the fact, so like a prudent general, he resolved to settle the "*if*" before the negotiation proceeded any further.

"It is very dark in the night under the shed where the sampans are," said he. "Even I, who am so used to the place, could not find my way there to bring out a sampan, unless I carried a light in my hand. A small light might do, but without a light I am sure that even I could not accomplish such a thing."

I seemed to reflect awhile, and then said—

"There is truth in what you say, Katam, and it seems to me that a soft light would be better than one that shone too fiercely. A big pearl would shed just the light required."

"Yes, yes," replied he eagerly, "that would do. Ah! how easy it is to talk!"

By this time it had grown quite dark, and being very eager to clinch the bargain with Katam, I rose to my feet when he made this last observation, saying carelessly—

"Let us go out and find this lamp with the soft light."

With his superstitious mind but half convinced, full of avarice and fear, the lame boat-keeper followed me out of the hut into the darkness, and as I made my way to my treasure-spot he hobbled in my rear. I need not say that I knew to the breadth of an inch where each pearl lay; and though, there being no moon, it was too dark to make out a man's figure at a distance of a dozen yards, I presently found myself standing immediately over the smallest of my jewels. I did not at once pick it up, however, but stood still with folded arms, and, while Katam looked tremblingly on, uttered some commonplace sentence in the English tongue with great deliberation and solemnity. Katam was the first to break the stillness which followed.

"Let me go back to my house," said he timidly; "you can bring me the lamp with the soft light for which you have called on your antu; your antu might be displeased to see me; I will go away."

And he was for sneaking off, when I stopped him.

"My antu is invisible," said I, laughing; "it has been, and it has gone again."

"And the lamp!" exclaimed Katam eagerly; "it did not bring the lamp! You have deceived me!"

But I had been quietly grubbing up with my toes the soil under which the pearl was buried, and now, stooping down, suddenly picked up "the lamp with the soft light," and placed it in his hand without a word. The effect was almost magical. He turned the pearl over

and over in his hands, he laid it on his tongue, he held it close to his
eyes, all the time muttering, and mumbling, and crowing with delight
as a child might ; then he suddenly turned and darted off at a speed
that I should have thought impossible, considering how much shorter
was one of his legs than the other, and made for his hut, with me
after him. He reached it first, however, by a long way, and when I
got in there he was lying flat on his belly by the fire, devouring his
beautiful prize with rapturous glances.

"Does the lamp with the soft light please you, Katam?" I asked.
"With such a lamp may a sampan be found on a dark night?"

"By the light of such a lamp, oh, my brother," replied Katam
enthusiastically, "a fleet of sampans might be found—a fleet of
sampans all laden to the brim with honey, and rice, and tamarinds ;
it is a star—nay, it is as lovely as a moon!"

And, laying the gleaming pearl on his clasped hands, the idola-
trous Katam, as he lay, rolled his forehead over it from side to side.
Suddenly, however, it seemed to enter his mind that he was doing an
unwise thing in making all this fuss about a single pearl, when they
were to be had in profusion at so cheap a rate, for he presently got up
from before the fire, and, affecting to handle the jewel indifferently,
observed—

"It is not the little lamp which makes me so glad, my brother ;
such things are common enough ; our chief has thousands of them"
(the lying rascal!). "I am glad that my brother has shown me that
he speaks what is true. To-morrow night the sampan shall be ready
to carry you away, and before you go we will take a basket and gather
it full of pearls and diamonds, with which you will ask your good
antu to strew the earth. We must take care, though, that we leave
none lying about," continued the greedy old fellow ; "we won't leave
one even so little as a rice-grain."

But this arrangement did not suit me at all. Despite his fair
speech, I knew Katam to be a treacherous villain, and even had it
been in my power to have provided him with a "basketful" of jewels,
it was more than doubtful if he would have kept his part of the
bargain respecting the sampan ; so I shook my head very gravely at
his suggestion, and told him plainly that my antu allowed nobody but
myself to see the pearls and diamonds he sprinkled on the earth, and
that, therefore, it would be useless for him to think of accompanying

me to gather them. That there was only one way to manage the affair, and this was it : he should get ready the sampan at the hour agreed, when I would steal out of the hut where I slept, and, picking up the jewels as I walked along, hide them all together in a certain spot, whence he might fetch them as soon as he had seen me fairly off.

Nor did I make the proposition without honourable intention ; I should have so left my other two big pearls for him, and those, with the one he had already in hand, would have made a very handsome reward, as, no doubt, he himself would have thought when he had got rid of his ridiculous notion of pearls by the basketful ; indeed, I should have made him the offer of the two jewels in a straightforward manner had I not foreseen that, in his present mood, the proposition would have been met by haggling and delay, which was the one thing I was anxious to avoid.

Katam, however, did not seem to see the force of my amendment to his proposal ; being a rogue himself, doubtless he had visions of me making off and leaving him in the lurch. Said he presently—

"Where would my brother go in his sampan ?"

It seemed absurd to run away from a place without having given even a thought as to where I was going, which was exactly my case ; however, I did not choose to satisfy Katam to this extent, so I replied vaguely—

"I am in the hands of my antu ; I shall guide my sampan as he directs, and, without doubt, shall find a friendly shore. Which is the nearest island from this, Katam ?"

"It is a long way to any island," replied he reflectively, "and the nearest, Battama, on the south side, is a place where none but a devil-antu would send a man."

"Is it a worse place than this, Katam ?"

"Does a man file his teeth sharp that he may eat rice ?" answered Katam enigmatically. "Is it the flesh of the bannana that drops crimson blood ? Are the heaps behind the huts of the Battama shells and husks, or are they bones of men ?"

I should like to have questioned Katam further on this subject, but it was no time for the discussion of any other matter but that which immediately concerned me. Not but that this might concern me, and that very closely, before I was many hours older. It was evident that these Battama of whom Katam spoke with such shuddering abhorrence were cannibals, and if there chanced to be other cannibal islands hereabouts, even though I escaped from the fire into the frying-pan, the advantage would not be prodigious, if it only led to my being properly grilled and eaten. That there were cannibal people in Polynesia I had frequently heard (would to Heaven, that at the present writing my knowledge was confined to mere hearsay) even before I left England, and I had read many accounts of their horrible massacres and feasts; but even then, and as a boy, it was easy enough to perceive that a good half of the horrors written down were impossible, and the remainder fairly open to doubt, so that in my own mind, I was by no means clear whether, except in the case of a shipwrecked and rafted crew, when tormented past human nature by gaunt starvation, the famished ones had drawn lots as to which should furnish a dinner for the remainder—(there was a lean, swarthy, Spanish-looking fellow, carpenter's mate on board the "Sultan" who, according to his own account, had been in some such dreadful pickle, and was able to give an account of the difference in flavour of black and white men)—I say I could not bring myself to believe, that except in such a strait man could be brought to eat his fellow. And even now, when Katam gave me so unmistakably to understand that there was a cannibal people so close at hand, I was loth to believe it. He was a stranger to Battama he said, and if the inhabitants made it a rule to devour all strangers who approached their shore, how did it happen that he had escaped? By the same rule if no one ever escaped, no one could for certain say whether they were cannibals or not. Still it would have been but fool-hardy to have chanced it and gone to Battama.

"You may rely then" said I, "that Battama is not the island that my antu would send me to. There are other islands, Katam, more distant perhaps than Battama but more to be desired?"

Katam was again thoughtful for several minutes, and at last said he, "I have no thought but for one island, and that is the most lovely of all. That surely must be the island to which your antu would send you. Listen, my brother. I too am tired to death of this wretched place, and had I possessed an antu such as yours, would long ago have fled. Your antu shall be my antu—we will go away together."

"But," said I, "where is this island of which you speak? How is it called? Are we sure of a kindly welcome?"

"Quite sure," replied Katam. "On the friendly shore of Magindano no matter how poor, or infirm, the stranger is always welcome."

The reader may easily guess that, as the wily old savage mentioned the name of the island with which I was so well acquainted, and on which my fortunes had been so various, I could not forbear a sudden start of astonishment, which did not escape the quick eye of Katam.

"I see," said he, "my brother has already heard of the lovely island, and no wonder, for its fame is wider than the sea, and the wind carries its sweetness to the earth's farthest corners. If my brother knows Magindano he knows that I speak the truth."

Although Katam said this with an affectation of perfect candour there was a twitching about his lips that told of another story. He was well aware that, if I knew Magindano, I knew that he had lied in at least one particular, in his description of that nest of sea robbers. He had said that the stranger was welcome on the Magindano shore, and so in truth he was—as heartily welcome as any other treasure of the value of a hundred dollars or so the sea might have cast up on to the beach; he was welcome to the extent of what he would fetch as a slave. And though it did not suggest itself to me at the time, when I reflect on what a base villain Katam proved himself to be, I think it not at all unlikely that his design was to lure me to Magindano, where, as a native of the place he would be secure from molestation; and then and there to dispose of me as his lawfully-acquired property. Only, that it would have been paying somewhat too dear for my whistle, it would have served him right, had I allowed him to convey me back to the people who had so falsely accused me, and driven me out to die a miserable death. I can picture to myself the consternation there would have been in the village when Katam led me into it. I can picture the fury of the people, and the sudden death which would have happened both to Katam and myself as soon as they had recovered their wits sufficiently to bethink them that they wore clubs and krisses! Otherwise I should have had not the least objection to return to Magindano. Many and many a time since I had left it, had I bitterly regretted that I had consumed so many hours, even at the height of my prosperity there, in wishing that I could devise some means of escape, and often when after an irksome day of slave labour, I have lain down to rest my weary bones in a place no bigger or cleaner than a hog-sty, have I yearned for the sweet little house on the hill, with its peaceful quiet and its rough and ready comforts, till my heart has ached.

But, under the circumstances, to return to Magindano was quite out of the question, and yet, after Katam had so fairly painted it I felt it not a little difficult to decline his offer, without explaining my true reasons. But Katam was himself so used to deliberate before he committed himself to an answer that I was able to avail myself of at least half a minute's reflection, without exciting his surprise.

"My brother is slow to answer," he at last hinted.

"Nevertheless my thoughts have been busy about your question," replied I. "I know nothing of Magindano, good Katam, but what you tell me; yet it is not the first time I have heard it spoken of, and while I was silent, I was trying to remember who had before named it to me. Now I recollect but too well. My antu has warned me, that I may not go there. It may be as fair as you say, but, were it ten times as beautiful, I dare not disobey my antu. But now I think of it, there is an island to the north of Magindano, to which my antu tells me it would be good for me to go. Do you know an island in such a direction, Katam?"

"I know more, as many as this," answered Katam, holding up his full number of fingers, "in the part you mention, but I don't know their names. Let it be so. I will make ready a two-man sampan to-morrow in the middle of the night, and we will go to this northern island together."

The proposition seemed simple enough; indeed, it should rather have pleased me than otherwise, for there was much more chance for what Katam called a "two-man" sampan in crossing to another island than for one of a smaller sort; but, endeavour to conceal it how he might, there was that about Katam's eyes which boded no good. I affected to fall in with the scheme readily enough, however, at the same time hinting that, since we were to journey together, I need not invoke my antu to send the pearls and diamonds until we landed; but at this Katam's visage fell, and, after much meaningless fencing, he bluntly refused to have anything to do with the business unless the jewels were carried away with us; therefore there was nothing left but to agree, though I did so with much misgiving.

I had made Katam a box to hold his tobacco—a common square little box with a shut-over lid, and before I left him he gave it to me as a handy thing to put the pearls and diamonds in.

As was arranged, I did not meet Katam through the whole of the following day, and at night retired to rest with my companions in the ordinary way. When I had lain about three hours, however, I crept stealthily out of the hut, and, making straight for the spot, disinterred my two pearls and the diamond, and, first half-filling Katam's box with pebbles, placed the jewels on the top, and, concealing the box under my bark cloak, hastened down to the beach.

To my delight, Katam was at least so far faithful; there was the "two-man" sampan, and in it were a jar of water and some provisions rolled in a mat. Katam himself was there, very anxious and frightened, and evidently only kept up by the prospect of the vast reward in store for him.

"Quick!" said he. "You have the diamonds and the pearls?"

I shook the box for his satisfaction.

"Yes, yes," said he; "but no man can know a diamond by its rattle; show me."

With pretended impatience that he should doubt me, I lifted the box lid sufficiently to admit my finger and thumb, and, taking out my big yellow diamond, held it on the palm of my hand, where it lay flashing luridly. Katam clasped his great hands and caught his breath at the glorious sight, and made a snatch at it; but I was too quick for him, and clapped it in the box again and shut the lid.

"There will be time enough for you to examine them when we are out of danger," said I, and tucked the box under my arm.

"Yes, yes," said Katam, "when we are out of danger. Quick! jump in! Let us get out of danger."

As I stepped aboard the sampan, I saw lying at the bottom, and only half-concealed by the mat, one of those formidable short clubs, made of stone, and with a bamboo handle, previously mentioned in this narrative. Catching it up, said I—

"How thoughtful of you, good Katam, to provide some weapons in case we are attacked!"

Katam uttered a passionate growl, which he turned off to an inoffensive grunt as he pushed off the sampan, and pretended not to have heard the remark I had made. Nevertheless, when I took my seat at the paddle, I let the stone club rest handily between my legs. Presently, however, I discovered that the savage's cunning had outdone mine own, for he had manœuvred so that I had the foremost seat, and my back was towards him. The box containing the jewels I placed at the bottom of the boat, and rested my feet on it.

On we sped farther and farther out to sea, and all in the pitchy darkness. Never in all my life had I felt my position so critical. That Katam meditated treachery I had no doubt, and it could be but of one sort—drowning me, and appropriating the contents of the little box, which, according to his calculations, was chokefull of pearls and precious stones. Truly the temptation was enormous, and I could not avoid the unpleasant reflection that, in so unscrupulously exaggerating the power of my antu, I had set a trap for my own snaring. My only chance seemed to be that Katam would repent his malicious resolution; my possession of the club I thought might tend to alter his previous views, for as unarmed men face to face I was much his superior—that is, if there is anything in height, and breadth, and youth—but the worst of it was, we were *not* face to face, and any moment he might fetch me a clout across my bare head with the paddle, which would at once put me at his mercy. So all I could do was to keep my ears well open for any suspicious movement behind me, and keep myself as cool and self-possessed as possible.

I tried to engage Katam in conversation, but he would not talk, cutting short my very first effort with the remark that a man's voice might be heard a long way on the water, and that I had better be silent. So we kept on till we were at least two miles from the shore, and I had begun to think that, after all, I had been over-suspicious, when, swift as a flash of lightning, came the long-expected assault from behind; not at my head, however, but at my lower extremities— such a tremendous lunge with Katam's lame leg, that I was lifted fairly out of the sampan into the sea. In the scramble, however, I instinctively grasped at what I supposed was the box; but it was not—it was the stone club; and with it fast grasped in my fist I sank deep down.

My lucky stars be thanked, however, I could swim like a duck, or, what is precisely the same thing, like a Dyak; and, despite the encumbrance of the club in my right hand, I rose speedily to the surface, with the intention of clambering into the sampan, and taking speedy vengeance on the villanous Katam; but, to my surprise, I could not see any signs either of the rascal or the sampan that had so lately contained us both. At last, however, casting my eyes about me, I spied the boat, bottom upwards, about twenty yards off, and moving away at a rate that at once told me how matters stood.

With nothing in sight but a capsized sampan drifting with the current, a person ignorant of the manners of these barbarians would have concluded that, after all, he must have been mistaken in supposing that the blow which sent him spinning overboard came from his fellow-paddler; it was more probable that some monstrous fish had floundered against the boat, overwhelming it, and bringing even worse evil on your unlucky companion than on yourself, for whereas you are hearty and alive, and with a boat within swimming distance, he, poor fellow, has gone to the bottom like a stone. But the real condition of affairs was very different. I was the " poor fellow" who was thought to have gone to the fishes, while my companion was little or nothing the worse for the sousing. It was not the current that carried the upturned sampan so swiftly along, but the strong arm of the villanous Katam. With one hand he was grasping the edge of the boat, while he swam with the other. No doubt that he thought it a very wonderful trick, and one that I could not possibly be up to; but happily he was mistaken. Ribut Bungat's fellows were extremely expert at all such water tricks, and being in the first instance a tolerably good swimmer, under such masters it would have been odd had I not become something of a sea conjuror myself.

Now, indeed, it was easy to see through Master Katam's manœuvring from beginning to end. How the sampan became overturned is more than I could account for, unless it had been caused by my awkward exit from it; but I had no doubt that Katam had secured the jewel-box, and that his intent was to wait awhile until there was no chance of my being alive, and then to right the sampan, and making his way home with all speed, to haul the boat ashore, put it in its proper place under the shed, and in a few minutes find himself in his hut with all his store of jewels, and no one the wiser. True, in the morning there would be a slave missing, but that would be no affair of his; had there been a sampan missing he might have got into trouble, but there were the contents of the boat-house safe and secure as they were left over night, and so it were useless to bother honest Katam about the matter.

As I have before had occasion to remark, when a man is in view of death he thinks very rapidly, and though it has taken a minute or more to write down my enlightenment as to Katam's rascally intentions, my mind had mastered them in almost as short a space of time as it took me to raise my head and give a look about me; with corresponding alacrity I made up my mind how I would act, and as a preliminary I stuck the club handle at my belt, and shot after the sampan faster than I ever swam before or since.

Katam is sent out of the world.

Purposely, too, I swam quietly; and, as he was not a neat swimmer, and puffed and blew considerably, besides making more splashing than a man whose legs were of a length, the noise he made quite covered mine; and I arrived at this side, as I may say, without him, who was on the other, suspecting it in the least. So we kept on for several hundred yards, and then he stopped (as did I), and listened carefully. Finding that no cry or any sort of sound broke the stillness, the rascal could not forbear giving vent to a diabolical chuckle, and proceeded to right the sampan. The side he was on, however, did not suit his purpose, so he came round to my side—that is, he was coming, but it was his fate never to get there. It was a wicked thing to do, but I humbly submit that the provocation was very great. He had deliberately planned my death—had armed himself with a club the more certainly to despatch me. Now this very weapon it was which was turned against him. I saw his ugly head just turning the corner, and swift as thought the mallet was raised and let fall.

The cry Katam uttered was not one of pain, but of unmitigated horror and consternation. The hand that pushed the sampan along had likewise upheld a paddle and the coveted box, and as he threw up his arms these articles were spun in the air, the box falling so close to me that it seemed sheer ingratitude not to secure it, even at the loss of the club, which, after the work it had lately done, I was by no means loth to part with. With little trouble I righted the sampan and secured the paddle, and then I sat for a very long and a very solemn time waiting for Katam, and expecting each moment to see the surface of the smooth dark water broken through by his woolly head; and not only did I expect, but most fervently hoped, that my enemy would presently make his appearance. Drowning men rose in the water three times before they finally sank, and Katam had not yet rose once. He was an expert diver, and I had better take care lest he presently made his existence known in an unexpected and sudden manner; even this I hoped, though at the same time I tried to make myself believe that I dreaded it. Anything was better than the dreadful thought that that blow on the head had caused his death. Truly it would seem that such was the terrible fact, as he had sunk like a dead man; but still, and although his complete disappearance favoured the supposition, it might not have been. No savage in the world, with the exception of the Australian Bushman, has a thicker skull than the Dyak; and though the blow that had fallen on Katam's head might have bewildered him, and perhaps delayed his reappearance, it might be that he would have risen but for some accident with which the blow of the mallet had nothing to do, and which might have happened to a swimmer under the most ordinary circumstances. These Bornean waters abound with sharks; it must have been one of these monsters that had hindered Katam from coming to the surface! So I tried to comfort myself, and to escape from the tormenting reflection that Katam's death lay at my door. A long time I waited, but, with the exception of the ripple of the waves against the sampan, the stillness was unbroken, and even when at last I paddled away, it was not without many an anxious pause and wide look out.

But whither was I going? A blind man in the midst of a wilderness could not have been more completely helpless than was I; indeed, such was my case, for what a dismal wilderness the sea is can only be known to those unlucky ones whose lot, like mine, it has been to be cast in a little boat flat on the face of it, as it were, and all environed by the black shadows of night; and surely it were no worse to be blind than to be possessed of sight where nothing may be seen. Mine was a strait in which there was but one course to pursue—to humbly place myself in the hands of Him who can make the ocean's bosom as comfortable and secure for a man's resting as the pillows of his bed at home; and this course I did pursue, paddling along steadily, and as often with my eyes shut as not.

So I kept on till the morning broke, and the cold wind of day-dawn swept over the wide waters. I felt it the more that, although I had continued paddling, it was only at a moderate rate, for these two-man sampans are awkward handling for a single rower. Besides this, I had not a rag to my back, except a pair of drawers made of Magindano grass-cloth, and which by this time, as the reader may safely guess, were considerably the worse for wear. When I set out to keep my midnight appointment with the wretched boat-keeper, I wore my bark cloak and a sort of cap of the same material, but they had somehow become detached from me when I had been so unceremoniously shoved overboard; and though they both had floated, I was too fully concerned for my life to give them a thought.

Nor was my nigh nakedness my only source of discomfort, I was both hungry and thirsty. With my momentous adventure before me, I had had no appetite for my usual supper; indeed, if I had felt inclined to eat, I should not have troubled about it, knowing that Katam would provide something good for the journey; and so he had if the presence of a wine jar and a copper cooking-pan might be taken as indicative of proof, but these had of course gone to the bottom when the sampan had capsized. So my entire worldly possessions were a pair of tattered drawers; true, there were the jewels, but since the boat-keeper's death I could not think of them without loathing, and would very willingly—although the yellow diamond alone ultimately brought to my purse nine hundred pounds—have given the lot for a good rough sea jacket and a sou'-wester, and a tot or so of rum and a few pounds of biscuit.

As the sun rose I was pleased to find that the course I was pursuing was north. Probably there was little or nothing in it, but when one is utterly helpless and dependent for succour and guidance on the mysterious and invisible finger of Providence, one is apt to catch readily at signs and tokens, and to take comfort out of the shallowest measures. Ribut Bungat had directed me "north" as the part where I might seek refuge, and it was a good omen—at least I thought so—that, after beating about in the dark for so long a time, the rising sun should find the bows of my sampan pointing towards the land of promise.

Comforted by this coincidence, I took fresh heart, and paddled with a will for full an hour, but when at the end of that time I looked around and found the broad ocean with no nigher boundary than the heavenly horizon, my spirits began to flag; and though the sun was by this time high enough to make its warmth felt, it brought no warmth to me. The sense of my nakedness, and hunger, and utter poverty returned to me with more than its former impressiveness, till, growing more and more despondent, I presently shipped my paddle, and, casting myself along the bottom of my frail boat, gave myself to tears and lamentations, and to cursing my hard fate.

And the more I cursed it, the more I felt inclined to, which was no more than might have been expected, since by so wicked an act I caused the ever watchful and pitying eye of Him " who holds the sea in the hollow of His hand " to turn away from me, and invited the devil, to whom cursing in any shape is more palatable than anything else. " It is indeed hard," I cried aloud, " that I should be singled out from among my fellow men to endure undeserved hardships such as these. It is unjust, it is cruel. Of what use is life to me? What are my prospects? To drift about the face of the ocean till I famish and die, or at best to be cast on some barbarous shore, to be made the slave of brutes in human shape, to live worse than any English hog, and to die even less regretted!"   And when I got to this stage of melancholy reflection I began to think how much better it would be if it were "all over," and then again on how easy a matter it would be to make it so, and raising my head I gazed over the edge of the boat into the smooth deep sea.   Surely the spirit of evil, whom my wicked utterances had evoked, was with me at that moment in the two-man sampan, for never in my life did I so strongly incline to that most awful of all crimes, self-murder.   It seemed so easy.   It was not like dying a violent death, (so whispered the devil's messenger) a single plunge into the calm deep and so an extinguishing of the life that plagued me so.   But at that very instant, and as though to unmask the specious arguments of the evil one, at least as regarded the quality of death I should be likely to taste if I threw myself into the sea, as I looked over the boat's side so intently into the fathomless depths, my eyes met those of a hideous scaly monster, lurking motionless a dozen yards below—a terrible looking fish with great round wide open eyes and a snout like that of a crocodile armed with teeth in double and triple rows.   As well as I could judge of its dimensions at so great a distance, it must have been at least three times the length of a man and with a body of the circumference of a barrel.

The sampan was very shallow, and as I leant over my face was within a few inches of the water: had the monster rose, he might have speared me to the brain with his spiky snout; and as I looked it *did* rise, causing me to start back with a jerk so sudden as completely re-called me to my sober senses, while at the same time, my very ears tingled with shame at the odious thoughts I had so recently encouraged. A pretty fellow I was to meditate suicide!   If I was not afraid of death what need was there for such horror at the sight of this fish, who would without doubt so promptly assist me on my way towards the dread domain of the grim reaper?   I should have been obliged to the snouted monster, and regarded his jagged teeth as pleasant instruments which were to effect my release.   But it was quite certain that I *was* afraid of death—afraid to meet him, even with the devil to back me, except on the very easiest terms.   Even though to *meet* death were everything, this would have been mean and pitiful enough; how then dare I engage in so rash a venture, the greatest danger attached to which remained

18

to be faced after death and I had made acquaintance? Death is only the guide and conductor, and in his simple self, is in no wise to be feared inasmuch as he keeps open gate for the vilest sinner as for the most perfect man; and beyond that gate, through which we all must pass, he has no jurisdiction. Knowing nothing of us, or our behaviour in life, he is of no sort of use as a witness at the Great Trial, and whether we be condemned or glorified, he is neither glad nor sorry. Nothing therefore is gained by the simple act of seeking death, but much—everything is lost, for what mercy can he expect, who, black with sin, thrusts himself insolently before the Judge, and demands to be dealt with.

I had covered my face with my hands in the first instance to shut out the sight of the sea monster who was waiting to devour me, nor did I as these grave thoughts possessed me, remove them, but very earnestly and humbly prayed, that the devil might not be allowed to tempt me, but that God would give me strength to continue in my endeavours to preserve my life, or if this was not to be, to die as became a man with a soul to save. And then, in a frame of mind more befitting one in my extremity than did the ungrateful and rebellious mood which preceded it, I again took to my paddle and laboured steadily.

But hour after hour passed, till the sun mounted high in the heavens, and I grew faint and sick under its fierce heat, so that I had no strength or heart for paddling, but lay in my boat turning this way and that to relieve my scorched skin, which, especially on my back and chest, smarted so that it was pain to move my arms; and it was not till I had endured this agony many hours that I bethought me of the simple expedient of jumping into the sea and enjoying the delightful luxury of a cool swim, keeping an arm on the edge of the sampan in the manner before described.

By this means I got over the hottest part of the day till the evening approached. I was terribly thirsty and hungry, the former to such a degree, that I was over and over again tempted to take a hearty drink of the salt water which encompassed me on every side. It was a sore trial to resist, especially while I was swimming, and the little waves came rippling against my lips. Once indeed I did venture to try the experiment of rinsing my mouth with the sea water, but the temptation was too much for my dry gullet, and before I was aware of it, as one may say, a good half of the mouthful found its way down my throat, and it was only by a great effort that I could bring myself to spit out the remainder of the poison, for clear and cold and beautiful as it looked and felt, it was nothing else than poison—as I had only to recall the sight of the agonies poor Tom Cox endured to convince myself.

And not only did the sea furnish great temptation to my thirst, but to my hunger likewise, for it happened about this time—six o'clock in the evening, as nigh as I could guess from the position of the sun—there came about my boat such a shoal of fish of a small size as I never in my life beheld. They were about the size of middling-sized salmon, and shaped the same, but in colour very different, being a buff, thickly speckled over with spots of a cherry colour, a sleek and clean-looking fish, and one that promised capital eating.

But what were they to me? Though they swam as thick as swarming bees not more than a yard below the surface, and did not seem at all frightened, how could I manage to capture one of them? I had neither hook, nor line, nor bait, nor net, and to attempt to catch fish without one or other of these was absurd, and there seemed no other way but to jump into the water and pursue them.

Yet it did seem a pity to go hungry with such abundance of food not only within sight, but within reach, if they would only remain still long enough to enable me to grasp them; but, tame as they were, they would not allow this, though once or twice my fingers had brushed against their slippery sides. Would it be possible to contrive some sort of net with my drawers and the paddle? Nothing, at all events, could be lost by trying; so divesting myself of my only articles of raiment, I so attached them to the paddle that they formed a sort of bag.

But they were not to be taken by so clumsy a machine; they would nose about it and butt their heads against it, and even nibble at it; but this was all, though I persevered so long that by the time I resolved to give it up as a fruitless job it was approaching towards sunset.

The sight of my neglected jewel-box lying all this time half-covered with water at the bottom of the prahu suggested another plan. I tore a strip from the waistband of my drawers, and selecting one of the largest pebbles from the number which the reader will recollect was placed in the box under the pearls, for the purpose of deluding Katam into the belief that the full amount of the promised reward had been provided, tied the pebble in a corner of my rag line. This I dropped among the fish, hoping that, according to the inquisitive disposition they had already evinced, they might be tempted to swallow the stone and as much of the line as was convenient, and that so hampered I might be able, by a neat upward jerk, to land one of them in my boat. But this scheme proved a more tantalizing failure than the one which had preceded it; the fish "bit" readily enough, but, instead of bolting the pebble, they cautiously mumbled it in their mouths, and, having dislodged it from the rag and discovered its nature, coolly spat it out, and gave the matter no further attention. However, they never grew tired of proceeding thus far, and afforded my ingenuity and patience a very lengthy trial. Over and over again I tried if anything could be done by "striking" as soon as they took the bait into their mouth, but only succeeded in breaking one "line" after another and losing my bait, till I had no more pebbles left in the box, and had reduced the depth of my drawers till they barely reached as high as my hips.

But though I had no more pebbles I had pearls, and I resolved to make just one more trial with a new line and one of these, and should doubtless have succeeded, even with so costly a bait, no better than before, but for a simple accident. Lying, as I have before observed, nearly covered with water, the wood of which the box was made had swelled to that degree, that it was only with considerable difficulty that the lid could be removed; and it so happened that, when I had taken out my last pebble, I had shut up the box as being of no further us efor the present, and thrown it back again into the puddle. Now that I once more took it up it was harder to open than ever, and in my endeavours to accomplish the job, the box, being wet and slippery, flew out of my hands, and tumbled overboard.

This, however, did not alarm me much; I knew that it would float, and therefore I was in no great hurry to turn about for the purpose of recovering it, but when I did so I was agreeably astonished; at least a dozen fishy snouts were poking away at it, with their heads half out of the water. So splendid an opportunity was not to be lost. Softly putting back my hand, I grasped my paddle, and, swift as thought, dealt a swinging blow at the cluster of heads. For an instant box and fish disappeared, as if by magic; but, to my unspeakable delight, there re-appeared at the surface, first the box, and then in rapid succession three fine fish floating and as dead as door-nails, and in a twinkling they were safely lodged in the boat. The weight of each fish was, I should guess, about six pounds. My only knife was the blade of my paddle, but with it I made very good shift to slit and gut one of my prizes, and then I sat down to supper. Under ordinary circumstances raw fish is not the most tempting dish a man could desire, but I can truly say that never before or since did I partake of so luscious a meal. It at once cured my hunger and quenched my thirst, and it was not till there remained nothing but his gills and fins that I stayed either jaws or hand.

By this time it was growing quite dark, and it seemed certain that I was doomed to spend at least one more night on the comfortless sea; but I was inclined to regard my prospects with much more cheerfulness than hitherto. So long as the weather lasted fair I should be able to keep my sampan, and, armed with those queer but very efficient fishing implements, the box and the paddle, I was not likely to starve for want of a dish of fish: and though, in all probability, it was a diet a man would quickly sicken on, I had no doubt that he might well keep life in him for at least three or four days, and in that time it was likely that I might find relief in one shape or another.

After the sun had quite gone I did not work very severely at the paddle, only exerting myself with sufficient energy to keep my blood from being chilled by the cold breeze, which now began to sweep the face of the ocean; but, though I did not tax my strength at paddling, I kept it up unceasingly, and, I have no doubt, covered a great space in the course of a few hours. Just before the night fell, and anxious to know whether I was to pass another long night out at sea, I stood up in the sampan and strained my vision for a sight of land, as only a man in my condition was likely to do. There was, however, no land in sight, nor any token that I was likely at present to approach it.

But all of a sudden, and after the night had set some four hours or so, I heard a strange sort of whistling noise, very faint, but unmistakable in the deathy stillness by which I was surrounded. It could not have been the wind, for that which was blowing was of a mild and even nature, and not likely to complain at so small an obstruction as my tiny boat presented. I sat still and listened, and, as the sound was not repeated, I settled in my mind that the sound I had heard must have proceeded from a fish, for, though I had never heard of a whistling denizen of the deep, I knew that in the China seas there were fish as different from those found in other seas, as the inhabitants of their shores differed from the people of civilized countries. So I took to the paddle again, and stuck to it, without interruption, for several minutes.

At the end of that time, however, I again heard the whistling noise, and this time so much more distinctly that it appeared certain that I was closer to it than before. This time, too, the sound did not seem nearly so outlandish as before, and even while I was considering, that since it was not a fish, what else could it possibly be, the sound made itself heard once more, and I at once recognized it as the voice of a *bird.* Nor, unless I was much mistaken, did it belong to any of the sea-going tribe, but to a sort of jay who hunted for moths in the night, and seldom or ever left the cover of the forest.

If this was so deliverance was indeed close at hand, but as already mentioned, at this season of the year the moon did not show, and it was impossible to see more than a dozen boat-lengths ahead. Had it been otherwise as I looked I might have easily have distinguished what I sought, for I could not have dipped my paddle a hundred times (they were vigorous dips, mind) when I was suddenly stopped short by the sampan grounding.

Whatever was the character of the inhabitants of the land to which Providence had thus directed me, it was certain that the shore itself was of a sort but seldom to be met along the Bornean coast, for whereas in nine cases out of ten the landing is rocky and precipitous, that on which I now was, was as smooth as the shore of an inland river, the waves causing but the gentlest ripple against the shingle of the beach. Tired as I was of the sampan, and much as I yearned to set my foot on land, I thought it would not be prudent to go ashore at present; it must very shortly be morning, when I could better see my way; for after all it might turn out that the people of the place were less placable, and harder to approach, than the place itself; indeed, for all I knew to the contrary, this might be that very Battama concerning which Katam had thrown out such horrible hints. Anyhow it would be better to lay off the shore till daylight, and this I did, though, as the reader may readily imagine, not without a considerable degree of impatience.

At last the morning dawned, and gradually I was enabled to distinguish that the island was a thickly wooded one, and that the forest growth extended to within twenty yards of the margin of the sea. From what I could make out it was not a large place, scarcely larger, indeed, than the villanous place I had lately left. As the daylight increased I pulled round about it, but though I searched very closely I could see no signs of shipping—not even so much as the smallest prahu—which somewhat astonished me, as, according to my present Dyak experience, the islanders were without exception seafaring. Another thing that struck me as singular, was that that unfailing sign of the human inhabitant, the rising fire-smoke, was nowhere to be seen. True it was yet very early, and as to the prahus it was not impossible that they might all be away on business.

If so, I was in none the worse case, for however bloody-minded the people might be, even though the island should be the terrible Battama, and the inhabitants hungry for man-flesh, they would not dare take my life in the absence of their chief, and so I might have a chance of making my case known in time. Anyhow nothing could be gained by delay in making an advance to the town, and without further thought on the subject I pulled in, and after having taken the precaution to secure my jewel-box, I hauled my sampan high and dry, and marched ashore, taking with me the sampan paddle as a weapon of defence, since I had no better. At least this was my idea at starting, but when I was fairly in the forest I found, as was the case at Magindano, that nothing was easier than to lose your way, and being very unwilling on account of my sampan that this should be, I was fain to devote my paddle to the more peaceful purpose of a finger-post—threading several great leaves on to it and binding it with the stalk of a creeper to a conspicuous branch which pointed exactly in the direction where the sampan lay.

When I had penetrated a quarter of a mile or so into this new country, I found that the wood grew more dense, so that, although the sun was by this time well risen, the shadows of the great trees on every side made a twilight like evening. Truly it was a lovely place. All about me, among the branches, birds of dazzling plumage, just awakened from their nests, busied themselves with their young, and made the air alive with their melody, while clustering about the great trunks in vast bushes were flowers the like of which I had never seen before, and which, only that the researches of modern botanists have confirmed their existence, the reader might very reasonably suspect were never seen at all.

Imagine a bush, symmetrical in shape, and with leaves of the most
vivid green, all hung about with wondrous lidded cups of such lovely
shape that the like never left a goldsmith's hands, and of the colours
of the rainbow—scarlet, pearly white, ethereal blue, delicate lilac, and
gorgeous purple—and all blending to make a spectacle most dazzlingly
splendid.   Nor were they *little* cups, or rather vases, or flagons—
indeed, I know not how to call them; they were of large size, large
enough to have held twelve bottles of wine, I should say (it would

Davidger Advances Further into the Wood.

have been a sin to have filled such glorious vessels with a meaner liquid)
and, as I said before, furnished each with a lid, hinged at the back
and standing more than half open, of the daintiest apple-green, and
reflecting the soft ruddiness of the cup's interior.   It might have been
the rarest Burgundy the lid reflected; but, peeping in, I found it
nothing but water sparkling like crystal, and that it was the cup's rich
lining which gave tone to the reflection.

I was weary from my hard night's work, and very thirsty. I sat down by one of these lovely chalices—for they grew very low—and, taking it in my hands, quaffed the cool nectar till I was satisfied. This, and the flesh of a ripe cocoa-nut picked fresh from the tree, made me a breakfast not to be despised, and, much refreshed, I once more set off happy enough.

Happy! houseless, homeless, without a companion in the world, ignorant even of the bare name of the country my fate had brought me to, with a bellyful of raw fish, without a shoe to my foot, or a shirt to my back, I say I was happy! And so I was, and so, by contrast with my condition such as it was a short twelve hours since, I had reason to be. Happiness is purely a matter of comparison. It is the most wonderful of all human attributes, for while it is of but one quality it is set to as many various notes as the wind can play on a reed, otherwise but one quality and condition of mankind could attain it, and the consequence would be that, in a very little time, none others but those of the super quality would be left to enjoy it. Even though it were set on but a moderately high pinnacle, with nothing but unalleviated misery to struggle through, who would have the courage to persevere till they attained it? There is happiness for the beggar who begs a penny and receives a sixpence—for the villain who doomed to be hanged is all unexpectedly rescued from the gibbet, and condemned to work in chains as long as he may live; for the prince who has a crown set on his head,—and each sort of happiness is the same according to the only method of measuring it, though it would be difficult to persuade the individuals in question of this, to the extent that the prince should give his crown for the beggar's sixpence, or that either should accept the convict's chains the murderer accepts with such glee. And so here was I naked, on a shore whose inhabitants might, for all I knew to the contrary, be cut-throats to a man—nay, cannibals even—stepping along with as light a heart as though nothing but pleasure was before me.

In a place so thickly wooded and covered with bushes and twining and creeping plants, it was impossible to make anything like rapid progress: still I should think I had not been travelling longer than a couple of hours at the outside, and that in as straight a line as under the circumstances was possible, when, to my great surprise, I emerged from the forest and found myself once more at the margin of the sea.

I say to my great surprise, but this was not on account of the little space of time it had taken me to cross the island, for, as before stated, I had seen from my sampan, and before I had landed, that it was but a little place; my astonishment was caused by the fact that I had not as yet discovered the smallest trace of a human inhabitant;—not a house, nor a hut, nor a felled tree even. True, I had as yet traversed but a portion of the island, but that portion was the centre, and it was very unlikely that any number of people would have been content to reside on the skirts of a country, and never find occasion to visit the interior— especially as, as a whole, it was scarcely bigger than an English country town—and there leave unmistakable evidence of their existence.

Having all along been so very doubtful of the character of the savages I expected each moment to fall in with, my first sensations on finding reason to believe that the island contained human inhabitants of no sort, and that I was quite alone, were those of satisfaction. Here it seemed was a beautiful place, abounding with wild fruit of every kind produced in these regions, and with birds grateful alike to the eye, and the ear, and the palate, and with millions of flowers more magnificent than anything that could be found in the conservatory of an English nobleman—all my own! My own to do exactly as I liked with! Never before in my life had I felt so exultant: I could not forbear clapping my hands and laughing aloud. "No more slavery!" I shouted "free! free and alone!"

But my presumption received a speedy rebuke. My delight was as brief as that of him who finds a rosy Dead Sea apple, and biting it, his mouth is filled instantly with bitter dust. "Alone! alone!" I shouted, and "alone!" was echoed back in that silent place, at first loud, but again fainter and fainter, as the voice of a man dying in his loneliness. Was I indeed alone? When startled to seriousness I thought on this and looked around me,—the extent of the riches, the thousands of trees, the flocks of birds, the vast size and numbers of the flowers even appalled me, and made me feel miserably little, and as though I had altogether blundered in my exultation. It seemed to me that the giant trees and the awful solitude I had intruded on ought rather to have lifted their voices and observing my smallness and helplessness, cried, "Alone! See him—he is alone!" in sheer derision.

Considerably sobered by this reflection, I set about a further ex- ploration of the little island, hoping in my mind that I might pre- sently have my new alarms set at rest by finding indications of the existence of some other human being beside myself. Nor could I comfort myself with the argument that, let the business terminate ever so unsatisfactorily, I could not well be a loser through my landing; there was my sampan on the shore, and I might either stay where I was or go away again, as I thought best. The difficulty, in the event of my finding that I really had chanced on an uninhabited island, would be to decide which *was* best. Had I "chanced" on the island? Was it "chance" that had directed my feet through all the perilous passes it had been my lot to traverse since the unlucky day when I stowed away in the hold of the "Margaret"? Was it chance I was indebted to for my life when threatened in that horrible darkness by death's three most active agents—thirst, hunger, and terror? Was it chance which launched me with the rest on that little raft, when we had escaped the bloody malice of Captain Jubal? Was it chance that rescued us from that frail partition between life and the ocean's icy depths—that selected me and but one other besides from the slaughterous attack made on the "Sultan" by the Magindano pirates—that placed in my hands means wherewith to raise myself from a condition of misery to one of affluence and power—that put it into the heart of grim old Ribut Bangat to take measures to save my life? How could I think on these, and many more signal instances in which the finger of Providence had undoubtedly been my guide, without feeling assured that the same Almighty hand had helped me this time, and that it was better for me to be on the solitary land than on the solitary deep? Nay, the veriest heathen must have seen that it was better, for on the island my food was certain, and I was no longer at the mercy of the capricious elements.

So I continued to think as I trudged along, yet not without a strong yearning that I might still discover something that would alter the aspect of affairs, which at best were melancholy. But though I kept my eyes and ears well open, and not unfrequently climbed up a tree the better to look about me, not a trace either of a human habitation or a human being could I see, nor indeed the smallest evidence to show any other than that I was the first two-legged creature whose feet had pressed the rank and monstrously tall grass. It was while taking a survey from a tree-top that I discovered that I had made my way back to my original starting point, for there was the sign-post I had erected pointing out the way where my sampan lay;

so that, having crossed and recrossed the little island, I could now come to no other conclusion than that I was indeed for the present quite cut off from human companionship.

My heavy labour during the preceding night, combined with my long exertion since I had landed—from the position of the sun I must have been wandering about the island not less than five or six hours—now began to tell on me, and I felt quite tired and done over. Nor were convenient resting-places wanting; on every side were gently-sloping hillocks thickly strewn with cool green grass, and scented with the perfume of flowers. Here, with the broad green boughs above me, and securely sheltering me from the fierce rays of the sun, which was now high over head, I might have lain and been sung to sleep by the sweet voices of the dazzling songsters that everywhere abounded; but at present I had not so much confidence in my new home as to avail myself of such seductions. That I was in no peril from carnivorous animals, such as haunt the forests of Africa, I well knew, but I did not feel as well assured on account of snakes or even of monkeys, for, although those I had at present seen disporting in the trees about me were but insignificant as to size, I was well aware, thanks to my experience at the happy little house on the Magindano hill, of their aptitude for tricks, and that it was very possible for very little monkeys to make themselves extremely disagreeable. Nor were these the only considerations which led me to seek my sampan as a place of rest. Rude and savage as the boat was, built as it had been by barbarous hands and hailing from a barbarous shore, still it was the work of *man*, and there was something of homeliness about it. "Very little, I should say!" the not over-reflective reader may opine, but let him defer his judgment until he is similarly circumstanced.

Between the place where I had erected my paddle as a sign-post and the place where the sampan lay might have been a distance of a hundred yards, or perhaps rather more, and, unshipping the waymark and carrying it over my shoulder, I made my way leisurely towards the shore. For the first fifty yards out of the hundred I had to traverse the wood and scrub was as thick as ever, but after I had passed this distance its density became less, so that I could see the way a bit before me. Presently I came in sight of my sampan; and not of my sampan alone, but likewise of something else which set my knees quaking. It was not a fair view I got of the boat from the

place where I was so suddenly brought to a standstill. Although not
so thickly packed together as they were further inland, the space
before me was plentifully sprinkled with trees, and they were, moreover, as is invariable in these Polynesian islands, laced and netted
together in such a way by climbing plants, that to look through was
like looking at a distance through fine lattice-work. There were men
in my sampan! two of them, black as ink and giants in stature. The
reader may recollect that when, by means of my novel bait, I captured
three fish, I ate but one, and preserved the other two; the savages
who had discovered my stranded sampan had found my fishy treasure,
and held each of them one in his hands, smelling and examining it,
apparently with the greatest curiosity.

I cannot find words which will express the tumult of conflicting
sensations that at once possessed me at the extraordinary and unexpected sight. After all it was nothing wonderful that I had overlooked the abodes, if abodes they had, of these savage inhabitants;
but, from what I could at present make of them, they were more
hideous than any savages I had yet fallen amongst, and I knew not
whether to be sorry or pleased that I had met them. What should I
do? If I made myself known, and they were barbarous as they
looked, I should have no chance against them, armed as I was with
only a sampan paddle; and if I did *not* make myself known, they
might take it into their heads to push off with my precious boat, and
leave me quite at the mercy of any others of their ugly sort I might
at any moment meet.

This last reflection decided me. My fatigue was at once forgotten,
and, screwing my courage to its best, I handled my paddle conveniently, and put a stout foot foremost, at the same time singing a
scrap of a nautical song, as though I were the jolliest fellow alive, and
cared for nobody.

Meanwhile, however, I kept as sharp an eye on my two savages as
the intervening foliage would permit, and, though their backs were
towards me, it was easy to see that my singing had reached their ears,
for they dropped the fish, and regarded each other inquiringly; and when
I paused for a moment to listen, I could hear them conversing together
in a loud tone, but in a language of which I had not the remotest
knowledge. I advanced several steps before I began to sing again,
and then when I did, my voice being brought so much more closely

to them, occasioned them all the more astonishment, and I had scarcely got through the first line,

" With a can of good flip, and of rhino a store,"

than, with a great shriek, they leapt from the sampan to the shore, and, facing about, disclosed the unmistakable visages of orang-outangs.

My first sensation was one of relief, and I could scarce forbear laughing aloud at the ludicrous mistake I had fallen into; but it presently occurred to me that there might not be much to laugh at after all. It was true that the creatures who had occasioned my fright turned out to be nothing but apes, but apes of such a sort as these were I never before had seen. There were some largish ones in the Magindano forest, and some ugly ones; but for either one or other of these qualities, they were no more a match for the beauties before me than I was a match for Samson. At this time they were not more than thirty yards distant, and, crouching behind a tree, I had an opportunity of observing the forest monsters without their being able to return the compliment, though their anxiety to do so was sufficiently evinced by the eagerness with which they gazed, chattering all the while, in every direction. In height they may have been about three inches shorter than I was, or about five feet five inches, but in breadth of chest I could venture on no sort of personal comparison; while, as for their limbs, I have no hesitation in pronouncing that the wrists of their fore-arms were as great in circumference as my leg at the ankle part, and their other joints in proportion.

But their bodies and their limbs, huge and hideous as they were, were quite forgotten when you gazed on their faces. They were absolutely appalling. I had seen pictures of his Satanic majesty, in which the virtuous artist had racked his imagination for a combination of features which should make up a whole horrible as would become the king of sin; but beside the faces of the creatures before me, the face in the picture-book—only that it possessed the advantage of being coloured a most inhuman green—was almost angelic. The glaring, restless eyes shone in their cavernous sockets through a tangle of what, I suppose, must be called eyebrow, and which hung down in a ragged fringe to the depth of nearly an inch, while above there was the retreating ridgy skull, surmounted by a crop crest of rusty-brown bristles. The hair on the face was likewise of this colour,

with the exception of the cheeks, which were bare and bald, and
glistening black. Their lips also were bare and jet black, and, parted
as they were in terror, revealed such a double row of fangs as made
tender flesh creep to contemplate. Should I go out to them, or should
I hide? How stood my chances? I had already roused their
curiosity, and if they sought the object of it I could scarce hope to
find a place of hiding secure from such cunning gentlemen as these.
Were there more than this single pair? If not, then my chances were
not so bad; if, as was much more likely, there were two hundred or
more, then my prospects were even better still; for, while they had
lurked so closely that I, in my exploration of the island, had been
unable to spy a single one of them, my appearance had so dismayed
them that they had not ventured to molest me. Either that, or
they had observed me—I could scarcely suppose that they were
all asleep—without any sort of concern. All things considered,
therefore, it seemed that I could pursue no better course than to
put as bold a face as possible on the business; so, grasping my
paddle—which was made of very hard wood, and with its double
blade formed a by no means insignificant weapon of defence—I
emerged from my hiding-place, and resuming my song at the part
where it had been so unexpectedly interrupted, I made my way to the
spot where they still stood, evidently quaking with surprise and
terror.

I had fully expected, from the fright which my singing occasioned
them, that when they beheld me they would be completely scared, and
at once take to their heels; but in this I was grievously mistaken.
To judge from their behaviour, they had concluded that the extraordinary noise proceeded from a much more formidable-looking
animal than I was; and when I approached them in full view, the
one that, from his extra breadth, I should say was the male, made at
me with most furious gestures, mouthing and stamping as though it
were his intention to exterminate me on the spot. I was glad to find
that my courage did not quail before the threatened danger—as it
might have done without much surprising me—and, finding that he
still came on, I stood still, and set my back against a great tree that
skirted the forest, at the same time grasping my paddle as I judged
best.

Seeing that I assumed this position, my monkey antagonist came to a stand too, though scarce a dozen feet in front of me, and seemed at a loss what to do next, which, as the reader will readily understand, was a very great relief to me, seeing that I had made sure that his purpose was to come on at once, and do his best to tear me in pieces. To be sure I had never yet met a man ape with such a sanguinary disposition, and had been assured by the inhabitants of Magindano, in the forest at which place, as I have had occasion before to observe, they abound, that these animals were harmless towards man, so long as they were not molested, and that even when they were driven to defend themselves their bark was much worse than their bite. But, for all I knew to the contrary, this might be a very different sort of man ape from that haunting the Magindano forest, and, to say the least, it was much bigger and fiercer looking; and of this latter quality in the specimen before me I presently had ample opportunity of judging, for, without moving a step closer to me, he began mouthing anew, and capering and clashing his jaws in a way frightful to behold. Evidently his intention was not to fight, but to frighten me.

As to his mate, she seemed to regard me as a creature too contemptible to be worthy her attention, for, after the merest inspection of my person, she returned to the sampan, and busied herself in another investigation of the two dead fish.

It seemed quite clear that my best course would be to regain my boat, and pushing out to sea, where, from their nature, it would be impossible for my monkey friends to follow, there consider what, under the circumstances, had best be done. As for the old he, I waited passively for what must have been as long as five minutes, hoping that he would presently grow tired, and remove from my path; but this he seemed not at all disposed to do. He seemed to have a knowledge of how extremely frightful he was making himself, and to be of opinion that if he persevered it was impossible that I could hold out much longer. At last, growing weary of such an unsatisfactory state of things, I resolved to make a push for the sampan at all risks.

The man ape made no attempt to oppose my progress. As I took a step forward he took one backward, gesticulating and barking harder than ever, and repeatedly looking over his shoulder towards his mate, who, having smelt and smelt at the fish till she was quite convinced they were not to her liking, had flung them into the sea, and was now mischievously employed in endeavouring to pick out the stitches which held the parts of my sampan together, a style of behaviour which made me none the less anxious to repossess myself of my property; and to this end I altered my deliberate walk to a run, an example which was immediately followed by the old man ape, who turned and ran too, and in three or four bounds was beside his mate.

This movement rather disconcerted me, for the sampan was at a considerable distance from the water's edge, and would be difficult to launch even were my efforts unimpeded, and to what extent their brutish obstinacy might lead them to interfere with me I could not tell. Had it been a single sampan I might have shouldered it without much trouble, but being a "two-man," with its inner side strengthened with coarse, heavy planking, it was much more than I could lift.

But I need not have troubled myself on the question of launching. If the fish had not suited his wife, the sampan suited the villanous old forest giant, and, while I was yet a few paces off, he caught it up in his tremendous arms, and swung it over his head, and, facing about, made for the wood, blundering up against and fairly capsizing me in his progress, his wife bringing up the rear, and, as I struggled to regain my legs, she fetched me a vicious clawing pat along my cheek, which, I believe, would have stunned me only for the smart and the blood-letting.

As I scrambled to my feet I felt, and I daresay looked, a match for the greatest monster the forest could produce. My hurts were not inconsiderable, but my rage and indignation far exceeded them, and crying out against them like a madman, I flourished my paddle, and went in pursuit, not so much of my sampan as the brute that had stolen it ; but, as I might have known, it was impossible for him to penetrate, with the cumbrous thing on his head, very far among the thickly-clustering trees. At a distance of about forty yards from the place where they had entered the forest, there I found my unlucky boat tightly wedged in the thickness of a thorny bush, while, as for my persecutors, they were no where to be seen. Nor was this the beginning and end of the disaster : the boat, being mainly composed of bark, at best of times would not bear much handling of a rough nature, but during several hours it had lain high and dry and baking in the sun, which had tended to make it more brittle than ever, and, though it still preserved its shape, no sooner did I begin my endeavour to extract it than its shattered condition became apparent. It was splintered from stem to stern, and, when I had **dragged it out** and stuck it up, and looked from the shady side of it, I found that it let in daylight in fifty places at the least, so that one might **as well** hope to float in a sieve as in such a wretched thing.

And how was I to mend it? Had I been a regularly apprenticed English boat-builder, with a full kit of tools at my disposal, I should have been sorely puzzled how to repair a vessel of such barbarous build as was this one; but taking the case as it stood, a shattered bark boat in the hands of one utterly ignorant of the principles of boat-building in the first place, and without a hatchet, a hammer—a pocket clasp-knife even—it would be hard to imagine anything more hopeless. Especially as, under any circumstances, my chief reliance was on **my boat.** Even though I had found the island a pleasant place to live on, the sampan was of use to me in endless ways. If there was **no flesh** food on the island, I could possibly, by adopting such expedients as that which accident had revealed to me, and which had been crowned with such signal success, provide myself with fish in any quantity. Even as a means of healthful exercise my sampan was invaluable, and on it, for all I could at present see to the contrary, depended my sole chance of escape. "How can my situation be **rendered worse?" I had bitterly asked myself** yesterday morning, when, with a sound boat under me and a pair of strong arms to grasp a paddle, I was free to take what course I pleased. How? Now I had found out how. It was worse—a hundred times worse—to be cast helpless **on** an island in the middle of the ocean, helpless and forlorn, and nearly naked, with no better companions than monsters, but just enough like men in shape to keep continually alive the bitter sense of my banishment from the society of my fellow-creatures.

In this melancholy mood I passed an hour or more sitting in the shade of my **boat** so strangely wrecked, till at last I grew somewhat calmer, and in a condition to consider what had best **be done.** Now it **was** afternoon—soon it would be night, and if I found the place horrible now that the sun was shining, how should I endure it when **the darkness fell,** and the nocturnal beasts, and birds, and reptiles began to stir? If I had a light—a fire—it would not be so bad, but how was I to procure a fire? Truely I had witnessed how, under tremendous difficulties a fire might be made, but even on the raft after we had escaped from the "Margaret," there was no lack of means such as was now the case with me, for among the company there were knives in plenty to strike sparks with, and some dry flax to catch the sparks; but I had neither one nor the other, nor any sort of substitute. Nor must the reader think that I had forgotten the world-renowned method of making fire prevailing among savages—that of rubbing two **bits** of dry wood together. I have no hesitation in declaring that this feat is not to be accomplished by anybody but a savage, and to recommend to a European in urgent need of a fire, to adopt the wood-rubbing process is only a shade less preposterous than to advise a person with toothache to fill his mouth with cold water and sit on the hob till it boils. The wood-felling slaves in the forest at Magindano, could accomplish the fire-making trick in question almost, or quite as soon as any one among us could **get** a light by means of a **tinder box**; but I **never could** accomplish it, neither could Tom Cox, though with the driest of wood and for no **other purpose than to beguile** our leisure, **we have** both tried it by the hour **together. Let** the reader comfortably seated by his fire-side try the experiment; **by the time** he himself is smoking through exertion he may succeed in making his two bits of wood smoke, but he has as good a **chance of blazing** himself as of setting his billets blazing;—unless **as I said before, he is a** savage **or the** close relation **of one.**

But I will tell him of a method by which he may "make fire" as often and as plentifully as he pleases, and though I have since heard of the same means **being** practised by the savages on the Guinea Coast, I was at the time when I sat puzzling in the shade of my crippled boat as ignorant of the way to **do it as I'll** be bound the reader is before I tell him. Let him obtain a piece of wood about as thick as his forefinger, as dry as possible, and tapered **off at one end like the** top of a sugar loaf; further let him take another piece of wood equally dry and of any shape, so that it will stand firmly on the **ground.** This block must have a hole scooped out at the top, about an inch deep, and of the same dimensions, or a very little larger than his stick. Let him sit on the ground, with the block conveniently between his legs, and insert the tapered end of the stick in the hole, surrounding which should be piled **some** finely picked cotton, or I daresay hay would do as well; let him then take **the other end of the** stick upright between the palms of his hands, and work his hands to and fro, in such a manner that the stick spins with great rapidity : when he has been at this for the space of a single minute, let him stoop his head and with his breath puff gently at the cotton, twirling the stick all the while, and unless he is more unlucky with all his civilized appliances than I was with such rough tools as the forest afforded, he will speedily have a blaze.

In my case, I was not so completely convinced that fire was not to be got out of two flat pieces of wood, but that I should have once more tried if I had had the chance, but even with the experienced savage, the pieces must be perfectly flat and where were such to be found? I broke two pieces of bark from the side of my useless sampan, and rubbed away at them till my arms ached in their sockets, and the pieces were ground to powder in the operation, but without raising as much as a smell of fire. Suddenly I bethought me of my jewel box with its flat top and bottom. The very thing! I clapped my hand to my waist-band where I had stuck it as I stepped from my sampan early in the morning, but now it was gone!

Which way was I to turn to look for it? There were not two such prime flat pieces of wood on the whole island as formed the top and bottom of that box, which suddenly assumed in my eyes a value superior to anything on earth ; as for the great yellow diamond and the pearls it contained, that their loss was involved with that of the box, caused me not even a pang of regret—I would have given the whole number for as many matches.

Where could I have dropped the box ? I had never once given it a thought since I had stowed it in a knot of the rag that girdled my waist, and I had traversed the whole breadth of the island knee deep in grass—had climbed trees, waded streams. It seemed quite useless under the circumstances to seek its recovery. Suddenly, however, my encounter with the man ape flashed to my memory, and how unceremoniously I had been thrown down. In an instant I was running like mad to the place where the scrimmage had happened, and, to my great joy, there was my jewel-box trampled into and half hidden by the shingle.

Securing my diamond and pearls in a corner of my ragged drawers, I hastened back to where the stranded sampan was, and speedily wrenching the box asunder commenced rubbing away with its flat parts as though my life depended on it. But no fire came, and the sun by this time was dipping into the sea.

But why had I failed in doing that which was easily accomplished by those who had little more sense than the man-apes about me? The reason was plain, I could not move my hands with sufficient speed, and without it perseverance went for nothing. One minute's rapid friction was worth more than an hour's merely brisk rubbing; and as I sat full of perplexity about the matter, I unconsciously twiddled a splinter of my box in a crevice of the broken boat. The splinter hitching in the crevice, called my attention to what I was doing, and all at once there came to my mind the easy way in which the trick might be done.

To find a small round stick was but the work of an instant, as well as a thick branch broken off by the wind, and long lain drying in the sun. Fetching a sharp stone from the beach, I scraped a hole in the bigger piece of wood, and setting it before me on the ground I proceeded exactly in the manner described already, with this difference, that at first I neglected to pack some inflammable material round the hole, and therefore had the mortification more than once to see flame playing about the end of my twirling stick which however died out as soon as I attempted to remove it. Finding this, I tore up a bit of rag very finely and placed it properly, and then just as the evening twilight was so far advanced that the nearest tree and bush had lost their identity, being merged in the thickening gloom, a little blaze leapt up with a suddenness that made me utter an exclamation of surprise.

Nor was mine the only cry that the sudden flame called forth. From every side of me—behind, before, and in the trees above, there issued a sound as curious as it was unexpected, "Heugh! Heugh!" accompanied by a rustling of boughs, and looking about me, I beheld at least a score of great glaring eyes, eagerly watching me, and blinking and winking in wonder.

For an instant I was filled with such fright, that it was a wonder I did not allow the blazing scrap of rag to die out for want of encouragement. Nothing but the glaring eyes were visible, but without doubt, every pair had an owner, and of what devilish sort he was I did not know; and as the unearthly "Heugh! Heugh!" continued, and the birds who had but recently retired to rest, awoke at the unusual noise, and set to chattering, and screaming, and flapping wings, it was like nothing else than being in a place enchanted. I was so bewildered that it was almost mechanically that I piled the sticks already prepared atop of my little fire which at once communicated with the big dry bough on which it was built, so that, almost instantly, I had a fire crackling and leaping and throwing about it a light sufficient for me to make out the owners of the eyes, as well as the eyes themselves.

As the reader doubtless has already guessed, they were the eyes of man-apes. So intent was I on my job, that I had neither seen nor heard them, as, when the shadows of night fell, they had gathered about me, which was the more remarkable, because of their vast numbers. My bonfire showed the woods on every side to be alive with them; but to my great satisfaction as I heaped more wood on my fire and increased the blaze, they slunk further and further away, so that their forms were but dimly visible among the more distant boughs and bushes.

Being thus fortified I set about making myself comfortable for the night. I collected a great heap of such rotten branches as were thickly strewn about the ground, and setting up the old sampan in a convenient position against a bush, cleared the space in front of it, and then gathering several armsful of grass made as comfortable a couch as any man could desire; and having thus prepared my bed, and being much easier in my mind, I began to think about supper, and no wonder, since as the reader will recollect, I had not eaten a morsel since the early morning. I felt a desire for something more substantial than fruit or berries, and thought longingly of those two prime fish which the mischievous she-monkey had thrown back into the sea. One of those prime fellows with the cherry-coloured speckles, nicely split and grilled would have been exactly the thing.

However, it was no time to be fastidious; fruit was better than nothing, so, taking a lighted brand from the fire, I went about among the bushes, and in a very few minutes collected enough of such simple fruits as I knew the nature of, as completely to fill the great "pitcher" flower I had plucked as a basket. But when I returned to my fireside, and was just about to sit down to begin my repast, what was my surprise to find that, in my absence, my supper had been otherwise provided, for there, plump on the glowing embers, was a bird bigger than a pigeon, and with his plumage completely singed from his body, in a fair way to become a delicate roast. Was there ever such a wonderful island! Ripe cocoas and rosy fruit for the gathering, and the very birds so obliging as to come down off the trees, and roast themselves for one's supper! What next would happen? Would a mermaid presently make her appearance, laden with an assortment of fish for my selection? Would it happen, if I only lay down and contented myself to let the island magicians have their way without interruption, that a couple of the fellows whom I had mistaken for man-apes presently made their appearance in black swallow-tail coats and white neckerchiefs, and lay a damask cloth, and the plate and the knives and forks? Suddenly, however, an end was put to my absurd speculations, and, in the most matter-of-fact way imaginable; all at once I was aware of a fluttering above my head, and falling through the column of thick smoke that rose high in the air, came a second bird, similar in size to the first, and lay on the fire frizzing. It was all plain enough now. Knowing nothing of the suffocating properties of smoke, the silly birds had ventured into it, and paid for their temerity with their lives. However, the substantial fact—the roast birds—remained, and they were none the less enjoyable because it had been proved that neither magic nor conjuration had placed them at my disposal. So, reclining on my bed of grass, I took a cleft stick, and devoted myself to the pleasant task of cookery; nor were materials wanting, for every few seconds a bird would come staggering down through the smoke, till it became quite a nuisance dropping my toasting-fork to wring their necks, for I could not bear to think that they might burn alive. Fourteen "head of game" so fell, which, hungry as I was, was many more than I could possibly eat. Nevertheless, I did not waste them. It might be that, after a little while, they would learn how dangerous it was to approach the smoke column, and then I might have to long in vain for that which was at present showered about me in such profusion; so I just added another one to the two which were already grilling, and taking the remaining thirteen, slung them in a row to a convenient branch.

My birds being done, I ate them with great relish, tapping half a dozen fine cocoa-nuts for my drink, with half a cocoa shell for a drinking cup. It wanted only a pipe of mild tobacco to have perfected my repast; yet, while I thought so, I could not at the same time help thinking that it was not a little preposterous in me to crave for a luxury, when, but a short hour since, I should have been grateful for wherewithal to assuage my bare necessity.

After supper I grew so drowsy, that it was with difficulty that I could keep my eyes open, which was no great wonder; I had had no sleep now for more than thirty hours—nay, I might say more than fifty, for, as the reader will readily believe, I had been in no condition for repose since the evening when Katam had first broached the conversation that had led to such a disastrous end for himself, and such perilous results for me. I should much have preferred keeping awake through this my first night on an island that had already yielded so many wonders, but since I found it was impossible, and that presently I should drop off to sleep without more ado, I saw that the best course was to make myself as secure and comfortable as possible.

The Birds cook themselves for Davidger's supper.

My comfort, as far as a soft couch was concerned, was amply secured, and that by a no more tedious process than involved the gathering of a few armsful of grass and moss. My security was my fire in the first place, and my paddle in the next; so I arranged the former that it might burn a long time, but not over fast, and then lowering the old boat a bit, so that it hung well over my couch, I pushed up my grass pillow, and not forgetting humbly to thank God for the great degree of mercy He had shown towards me, grasped my paddle in my right hand, and closed my eyes.

How long I slept I of course cannot say, since it was not yet daylight when I awoke, neither was it moonlight, but a light of so terrible a sort as makes my blood tingle to think on even at this distance of time. As it seemed to me, I had scarcely shut my eyes when I began to dream. I dreamt I was once more on board the " Margaret," and Captain Jubal was alive and commanding her. I dreamt it was just such another stormy night as that on which that unlucky tyrant met his death, and that the ship's ropes were rattling and chafing, and the sails were shrieking against the wind, which was tearing them away from the masts. As on that memorable night, I again heard the terrible voice of Captain Jubal but a hundred times more terrible than ever. When last I had heard him, his voice was nothing but a graff, roaring voice in one key, like the growl of a mastiff, but now it was made up of twenty different keys. It was deep as distant thunder, and as high and shrill as the shriek of a parrot, with all the intervening notes besides ; and when his men heard his orders, instead of replying, as was their wont, " Aye, aye, sir," they shrieked, and cried, and yelled too, until my poor dizzy head, as I lay on my bed of sackcloth in a corner—for there I thought I was— was like to split with the infernal din. Again the man came down, and fetched his axe, and told me to be damned when I civilly asked him what the matter was; again something came tumbling down the gangway, which told me the nature of our peril ; but this time it was not a body of water, but a body of *fire !*

In as great a fright as though it had been so I leapt up, striking my head violently against the shelving sampan as I did so, and then such a sight met my eyes as I shall never forget—the forest was in flames ! Fairly before my eyes was the prodigious bonfire, extending from the ground to the tallest tree-top—aye, and above that, till the restless forky tongues seemed to lick against the reddening sky. Stripped of their hanging branches, the tall palms became pillars of fire, and the bushes were like a red-hot cloud rolling over the surface of the ground. Nor were the sounds less appalling or hideous than the spectacle. How such sounds could be produced I leave to those more learned than myself; but had any one been standing out of sight of the fire, and yet within earshot, I am sure that they would have said that it was the thunder of artillery they heard, while the popping, rattling noise that accompanied it was, for all the world, like the report of small arms. I know nothing about battle-fields, but, as the reader is aware, I know what a fight at sea means, and am not strange to the demoniac noise which accompanies mortal strife and butchery by means of gunpowder, and clubs, and sharp-edged weapons; but what I had heard on board the " Sultan," compared with the horrible din that now assailed my ears, was a school-yard riot set against Trafalgar. Nor did the likeness of the scene before me to a bloody conflict cease at the banging and cracking—there were the *voices*. The voices of birds and little burrowing beasts and snakes, and, more terrible because more human-like than all, the voices of the monkeys and man-apes, driven from their familiar quarters, they and their little ones, by the merciless fire.

For a little while it seemed that I was surrounded by the flames, and I could do no more than crouch down under the old boat, and screen my eyes from the dreadful glare with my hands; but, as my scattered senses gradually resumed their uses, I could see that the fire was blowing *away* from me, and that, unless the wind chopped round, as at any moment it might, I was in no danger of being burnt. Still I could not muster courage enough to leave my shelter, and make for the beach, which, of course, was the safest place, until presently there came a furious peppering against the overhanging boat, which I took to be a shower of red-hot embers, and which I knew would ignite the dry bark like touchwood. This made me turn out quickly enough, but, to my great joy, what I had taken for falling embers was in reality heavy rain, and I could see that one of those short, but tremendous storms, which frequently occur during the hottest part of the year in these regions, was at hand.

This was the secret of the catastrophe. These rain-storms invariably begin with strong gusty winds eddying every way and whisking off and on high any light substance that may come within their scope. Such a gust had caught my fire and carried it among the bushes. Instantly following these uncertain gusts, however, there must have set in a strong wind from the south which drove the fire in one direction, and, by the will of Providence, that direction was contrary to that where I lay.

As I expected, the rain rapidly increased in violence, till presently it fell in a perfect deluge. But the fire had gained such strong hold on the timber that it was not to be easily quenched, and though by this time I had retreated as far as possible from the frightful scene, and standing close to the shore of the sea must have been a good hundred yards and more from the nearest burning tree, the hissing and seething occasioned by the fall of the water on the glowing mass, was extremely loud and indeed quite covered every other sound.

The tremendous rain continued unceasingly till the morning broke, by which time there was a visible abatement in the strength of the fire, but the smoke was prodigious, so that it was only by looking seaward that you knew that it was morning; all round about the island and reaching up to the clouds it was dark and dismal as a November night. Nor was it merely for the comfort of morning that I looked out to sea. So great a light as had burnt on the island all through the night, must have attracted the attention of the inhabitants of any other island, if such existed, within a distance of fifty miles, and their curiosity might induce them to come and see what the matter was. Of course it was by no means certain that whoever came would treat me in a friendly manner. It might even happen that the island I stood on was the private property of the chief of the next adjoining inhabited place, and if he sent to make inquiries, and found me, the miserable cause of such wholesale destruction among his ruined timber, it would probably go hard with me.

But such considerations did not deter me from most heartily wishing that I might presently spy a vessel of some sort bearing towards me. Even had I known that succour could only come from some such horrible tribe as that Katam had hinted at I don't think I should have preferred that they stayed away: nor I think would the reader, had he been in my plight—a burning wood to the right of him, the wide sea to the left of him, and he so nearly naked that a few flinders about his legs was all the difference, wandering up and down on the oozy beach with the rain pelting down saturating his hair, and sopping his shivering skin.

Earnestly though I looked, however, no such thing as a boat made its appearance. But though I got no comfort on this hand I did on the other, for the rain still continuing, towards the afternoon not only were the flames no longer visible, but the smoke grew so thin and light that it was evident that the conflagration was extinguished or nearly ; so I thought I might venture in among the trees and see what damage was done.

I found my " house" just as I left it as well as the bed from which I had so hastily risen, and, thanks to the shelter of the overhanging boat it was almost as dry as before the rain commenced, which, insignificant as it may seem, gave me at the time considerable satisfaction, inasmuch as it afforded me what I should have searched in vain through the forest for, a dry and comfortable seat. There, too, were the thirteen birds hanging to the bough of the tree just behind the sampan, and had they been cooked, I could have eaten two or three with a deal of pleasure; and I might have cooked them now, for within sight were many huge chunks of wood which, though at first sight they seemed black and dead, only wanted stirring about to light up again, but when I thought on the many affrighted and agonized voices I had heard coming out of that great roaring furnace, I sickened against cookery and for the present was content to consume a few of the plums which yet remained from last night's repast in my pitcher flower.

I remained squatting under the sampan till the evening, when the rain altogether ceased, and there was no longer to be seen the least sign of fire, or smoke even. It required no cunning to follow the course the fire had taken, for there, fairly before me, was a broad black road, wider than the width of Piccadilly, and longer than my eyes could reach. In place of hip-high green grass, flower-gemmed and lovely, were soddened pasty ashes, oozing and squelching loathsomely when trod on ; and all that betokened where had stood the forest monarchs emerald clad, and with their mighty arms stretching far and wide, were a few ghastly spars charred white and black, and looking all so still, awfully contrasted with the trees that the fire had spared, and which, now that the rays of the setting sun shone among them with a mellow light, waved their boughs as serenely as though nothing had happened. To be sure trees cannot feel, neither is there life, in a human sense, in grass or flowers—but when I contemplated the ruin which had been wrought through me, who was so complete a waif, and as utterly at the mercy of the elements as the grass or the leaves, I could not but feel a deal of sorrow.

Nor was this the only circumstance that tended to afflict me. Wandering through the soddened ashes and among the dead sticks,

from time to time I caught sight of my inquisitive friends the man-apes;
but they were curious no longer. They had been anxious to find out
who and what I was, and what was my business—at least so may be
fairly inferred from the marvellous interest they took in all my proceedings on the previous day—and now they knew all about it.
Torture and devastation was my business, and I had come amongst
them for its most merciless exercise; I had come armed with a weapon
more terrible than either fangs or talons, and my purpose was only at
present in part accomplished; I had come to burn the forest about
their ears; I was a monstrous creature, and one that it behoved man-
apes to shun!

If they did not think all this, their behaviour was just as though
they did. Did I, in my soft treading over the yielding ashes, come on
one of the great unwieldy animals unawares, he would turn, and
seeing me, utter a frightful cry, and make off with such prodigious
bounds, that I had need to have been a spirit of air, as well as of fire,
to have pursued and overtaken him. Never did man have so prime
an opportunity of studying monkeys' tails in all their variety; even
the smallest of the fry would not sit and grin at me till they had
mounted to the topmost branches, while the great she-apes, willing to
flee from my baneful presence, but hampered by more babies than
they could run with, put themselves into brave attitudes to fight me if
I came nigher. As the reader needs no telling, I was by no means
anxious for the company of such hideous creatures; but it certainly
did seem to make my situation all the more forlorn and lonely, now
that even the apes shunned me.

I found that the fire track extended in almost a straight line, at
the width before mentioned, and for the length of about three-quarters
of a mile, where there happened to be a widish stream across, which
the fire had not leapt; and, having thus achieved the object of my
exploration, and as the night was coming on, I retraced my steps
towards "home," for so, in my extreme poverty, I began to regard
the spot where the crazy old boat overhung the grass heap.

But, before I reached it, it was my great good luck to make a
discovery, which I am still disposed to regard as one of the most important that, under the circumstances, could have happened. I was
nearly home—indeed the boat was in sight—when traversing, as I
may say, the edge of the fire track just where the ashes were thin,

and the green vegetation began to show itself, a very familiar odour assailed my nose; it was just as though somebody lying in the grass close at hand was smoking a pipe of tobacco. Had I been in an inhabited country, I could have sworn that such was the case; but by this time I well knew that no being capable of smoking a pipe was to be found on the island, so my astonishment and perplexity may be imagined.

Although I stood still in wonder, I was so impressed with the idea that tobacco-smoke could only issue from the lips of a smoker, and knowing that a smoker was impossible, that I did not trouble to search about me, and I was bringing my mind to the conclusion that it was the charred remains of one of the surrounding trees that gave out the fragrant scent; but presently casting my eyes a little to the left, there I saw a little bush, scorched to the colour of an autumn leaf, with tiny sparks, twinkling like glowworms, travelling about it. It was from this little bush that the smell arose, and, going close up and bending over it, I had no longer any doubt that it was a plant of wild tobacco, which had been withered by the action of the fire that still smouldered in it.

The plant was more than half consumed, still there were eight or nine leaves remaining entire, or nearly so, and these I gathered with great care, and, rolling up a biggish piece, put it in my mouth by way of a quid; but, to my great disappointment, its flavour was so rank and bitter that I had no sooner got it in my mouth than I was glad to spit it out again. Athough not good for chewing, however, judging from its aroma, it was excellent smoking; but to one in my condition that was small consolation, but rather an aggravation. For the first time in my life I fully appreciated Robinson Crusoe's delight at finding the tobacco-pipe in the pocket of the dead sailor. No such luck could possibly fall to *my* share; not that I had much to complain of on that score, and as I instantly bethought myself as the expression of discontent escaped me.

Still my longing for a pipe of tobacco had been set so keenly on edge by the smack of its flavour I had obtained while standing over the smouldering bush, that I was very loath to abandon all thoughts of the luxury, if luxury it could be called. My fondness for the Indian weed dated from my friendship with poor Tom Cox—who himself, as he informed me, had smoked ever since he had a pocket to hold a pipe—and I had grown so used to it that any time I would sooner have gone without my dinner. It was among the chief of my deprivations since I had been cast away, and it was very tantalizing to come so close to what one so yearned for, and then to be denied it.

I tried to make a cigar by rolling a leaf the short way, but, though it looked promising enough, it leaked in every direction, and I could only keep it alight long enough to whet my appetite, and then out it would go. How I wished for a pipe! Was there no possibility of making one? What out of? What one wanted was a bowl and a stem. Where should I look for either? As for stems, had I wanted a million there they were—every stem of stalky grass furnished one. But the bowl!

Well, there was the bowl—a hundred of them, or at least the material out of which they could be constructed, for just at hand was a bush, or rather a low-growing scrubby tree, bearing nuts of the cob sort, only rougher and about half as large again, oval and nearly flat at the top, and peaked at bottom. All that was wanted was to grind off the peak, so as to make a hole large enough to admit one of the hollow reedy stalks, and to grind off the flat top, and scoop out the kernel. Plucking three or four, I marched home in much better spirits than I set out, and, having built a moderate fire, I went to the beach, and fetched a flat stone and a handful of sand, and, squatting down by the firelight—for it was now quite dark—set about the task of tobacco-pipe making, and, in the space of what I suppose must have been a couple of hours, contrived a pipe which answered capitally, only that every twenty whiffs or so the stem required renewing, as, as soon as the part that was inserted in the bowl grew hot, it either shrivelled and fell out, or split with the heat. But, as I said before, there was no lack of pipe stems, and I soon succeeded in smoking myself into a sufficiently philosophic mood to regard the act of a hungry man, who allowed a row of raw birds to spoil for want of cooking as mighty ridiculous; and so I prepared a roast while I still continued my pipe, which humble instrument, by the by, was rewarded out of the supper it had promoted, for the birds were of a long-legged sort, and out of one of their hollow leg bones a most excellent and durable stem was furnished.

Until very late that night I lay revolving in my mind what had best be done. It was evident that for the present, I must content myself to remain on the island, nor did I see any reason why, with a little in-genuity, I could not make out very well. My most urgent wants were food and shelter. Of the first I was secure, and as to the second, although I had no sort of tools I had no doubt that some sort of a shanty might be constructed; indeed, before I went to sleep, I had settled as to the design of my house, and of what materials it should be constructed. Among other trifles, Tom and I had practised by way of beguiling the time, which in the wet season sometimes hung rather heavily, was that of weaving mats out of grass after the native fashion, and though of course, after all our practice, our workmanship would have no sort of comparison with theirs, it was quite as durable, and ornamen-tation was the very last thing I cared about. What I purposed doing, was to drive some stakes into the ground at a convenient height, and so that my inverted sampan would rest on them and form a roof; that is, it was the bare shell of the boat I would put to this purpose; as I think I have already mentioned, the inside was lined with rough planking secured with wooden pegs; this I could take out, and by some means fix it to the outer edges of my roof and so widen it; having made my mats, I could hang them all round, and make quite a snug little shanty. And with my mind fully occupied by such thoughts as these, I fell asleep, and did not wake till the sun was high and the birds were sing-ing on the boughs.

All that day and the next, and for five more after that, I was engaged in mat-making, and though my progress was very slow, and, having nothing in the shape of a knife to trim my tags, not exactly satisfactory, it was good, clumsy solid work, and by constant application the week's work made a good show. It was not a little matting that I wanted, for my roof was a good twelve feet, long, which required twenty-four feet of " curtain " without the end pieces. I should have been content to have perched my roof no more than four feet from the ground, but having the good luck to find five stout and tolerably straight spars—young saplings they were, which had been charred short off at their roots—of about seven feet in height, and wanting but one more, and having as before stated (and as would be related scores of times to come if I made it my business to mention my miss of it every time it happened), no knife wherewith to reduce the length, I was bound to regulate the depth of my mats accordingly. To obtain my sixth prop was a tremendous job. It consisted of the lower limb of a tree, and my only implements were a sharp stone, and two or three shells of the mussel species. A handsaw would have accomplished the business in something less than a minute, but there was I astraddle on that tiresome bough from breakfast time (for I may tell the reader in this as in all other matters, I endeavoured to practice civilized habits, and took three meals a day, which I called breakfast, dinner, and supper) till late in the afternoon scraping and rasping, and grinding the skin off my knuckles. I believe I should have got through my job much quicker than I did, but, about dinner time, and when I had got more than a third through the bough (it was not more than four inches through) a bright idea occurred to me, and I could not help wondering how it was that I had been so foolish as not to think of it before. Why not *burn* the limb off? No sooner thought of than attempted ; but by the time I had nearly stifled myself with the smoke of the blazing torch I held to the partly severed branch I found that it was even slower work than pecking at it with a mussel shell; and the worst of it was, when I again took to the last-mentioned implement, I was disgusted to find that the wood was just charred enough to have become twice as hard as it was before, and as much time was consumed in going to and fro from the beach, to fetch fresh "saws" as at the actual work. So it came about that an entire day was spent.

My props being sunk two feet in the ground, left me five feet to cover with matting, and if the reader will multiply the length by the depth, he will find that I had little short of a hundred and forty feet of weaving to do before my curtains were accomplished. Five feet a day was as much as I could conveniently make, so that here went three weeks or more bating the Sundays, which I hope I need not tell the reader were observed by me as days of abstinence from labour. I wish I could say that these sabbaths were happy ones for me, but they were not. Having nothing to occupy me but my own melancholy reflections, and tiring of singing hymns aloud after the fifth or sixth repetition, I always had a bad night of Sundays, and was heartily glad to bustle about and begin my weaving on Monday mornings.

Although nearly a month elapsed before my curtains were ready for hanging, I did not wait all that time without deriving some benefit from my labour. After the third day's weaving, I had a quilt to my bed, and the hangings of my bedstead grew day by day. But, although this made me snugger of nights I began to get aches in my limbs, and was glad indeed when my "house" was finished, and my privacy was secured by four walls.

To be sure it was not much of a house after all. Even with the width of my roof eked out with the bits of board, it was barely five feet wide, though long enough to afford stowage for more goods than I was ever likely to accumulate. The purpose for which I chiefly wanted it, however, was as a bed chamber, and for this it answered admirably. In case of rain, I thatched the roof, and so made the entire edifice green, and at a distance it looked no more than a biggish hillock covered with verdure; after a while however the matting as well as the thatch dried to a straw colour, which certainly seemed to give to the whole an air of cosiness it had not possessed before.

And I may here mention that, during all this time I had never once been interrupted by the man-apes. Indeed unless I penetrated some distance into the forest, I did not so much as see one. The fire seemed to have completely frightened them, and though it may be objected that with such unreasonable brutes, such a thing could not possibly be, I have not the least doubt within my own mind, that having in the first instance seen me make fire, they were at least instinctively convinced that I was their most inveterate enemy, and that it would be best to avoid me. And I am the more inclined to this opinion by the cir- cumstance, that on the very first night when I was ensconced in my new house, missing me from my accustomed place, they came back to the deserted spot, and as I could plainly hear (for the site of my house, was a long distance from where I had at first pitched) cele- brated my departure from among them by a tremendous chattering and barking, the tone of which was anything but doleful. And a pretty consternation there was among them, when next morning I made my appearance, and a very lucky thing for me that I had not wandered far from my house when I was discovered.

It was lucky for this reason. Although, they were mightily astonished to find they were not rid of me, they did not manifest any- thing like that fear which my presence usually inspired among them. On the contrary, they drew together among the trees, and seemed to hold a consultation, and that it concerned me was easy to see by the frequent jerks of the head, and pointing to the spot where I was sauntering apparently at my ease, though not at all so, if the truth must be told, for never before had I observed the monstrous creatures to show such courage. It happened that I had brought my paddle with me, not because I had any idea that I might need it for self-defence, but for its utility as a spade, for by accident I had discovered that under the ashes were many bulbous roots, remaining from plants that had been consumed by the fire, and which were no bad substitute for the potato. Had it been made for the purpose, my paddle with its broad blade could scarcely have better served in digging these things up.

But now it appeared that the implement in question, might be required in a more hostile business than root digging, for after the man-apes had consulted some time, they sent off the shes with their little ones, which assuredly was a sign of war. Seeing this, and that the males on the retreat of their wives turned about and faced me I thought it might be as well to regain my hut, which flimsy as it was, would afford me some sort of protection; and to this end I turned my face in that direction, and began walking as sharply as was consistent with that indifference to the presence of my enemies, it was certainly my policy to assume.

But if I had entertained any doubts as to their hostile intentions hitherto, they would now have vanished, for I had not taken a dozen steps, when in a body they rushed towards me, beating their bellies with their great hairy hands, and uttering such hideous cries, as I dare say would have much alarmed me but for my experience on the first morning of my arrival, along with the villain who had carried off my boat.

Not that I may by any means lay claim to such an amount of courage or brag as to say that I was not at all alarmed. Had he been aware of his strength, or of my weakness, there was not a single one among that very ill-looking crew, who would not have mastered me, and here there were eight or nine. My great fear was they would arm themselves with the limbs of the trees, as I had heard was their wont; but they did nothing of the sort, which considered in connection with the great rage they exhibited, seems to me good evidence, that the tales of these creatures arming themselves for combat are the inventions of ingenious travellers.

On they came in a sort of semicircle still drumming on their bellies, and snapping their jaws together with a noise that made me shiver. My house was still a good eighty yards from where I was, the intervening space being sparsely studded with the naked and scorched trunks of the trees which had suffered in the conflagration. I made up my mind to reach my hut if possible, and the naked trees certainly favoured the idea.   More than all, they favoured it on account of their nakedness.   Had they been flourishing trees with branches thickly covered with foliage, they would have been worse than useless to me for purposes of shelter, as my nimble foes would have climbed into them and assailed me from above ; hanging from a great height by the toes of a single foot, and, making a dash at their victim's head or face, swing themselves up and out of danger before retaliation was possible.

Already had I gained one of these bare trees, and set my back against it, thinking that I would await their assault in that position ; but, on second thoughts, it appeared to me that, since it must come to fighting, it could not worse my position, and might possibly better it, if I had first shy; so, while they were yet within ten yards of my tree, and creeping cautiously up, I shouted my loudest, and, whirling my paddle round my head, made a sudden run at them.

At this unexpected attack they turned tail to run, but I was in time to catch the hindmost one, and dealt him such a swinging crack on the ear that down he dropped like a dead thing, and, though his companions at once turned when they heard the blow, and ran back towards him, I was enabled, in the confusion that ensued, to gain four trees towards my house, and there again stood to take breath, and prepare for another onslaught.

Nor had I long to wait.   The man-ape's head was much too thick to be cracked with so soft a weapon as mine was, and scarcely had I time to look about me when on came the pack again, headed by the one with the bleeding ear, who looked, if possible, more furious than the rest, and was evidently bent on mischief.   The others advanced, reared on their hind legs, but this one came on all fours, snarling like a cat, and giving me a fair view of his grinders.   Again I shouted and rushed at them, but with not so much success as before.   The crack the chief ape had received, while it had taught his fellows prudence, had goaded him to desperation, so that, while they were routed as soon as I shouted, neither shouting nor flourishing frightened him, and I speedily found that I must fight him face to face.

It would have been better for me if he had stood upright, and I suppose he thought so too, for instead he maintained his doggish attitude, and, when I had come very nearly up to him, he made a rush

at me with open jaws, and, had I not been startled to such an extra
degree of nimbleness as enabled me to leap right over him just in the
nick of time, I have no doubt that he would have taken a mouthful
out of my leg. As it was, having jumped over him, I instantly turned
about, and caught him a clip on the hind leg that made him squeal
again; and, seeing that he held it up, I thought it a chance to run for
my house. But no sooner did I attempt it than the entire pack, which
had during this second encounter stood aloof, were at my heels,
and pretty nearly at them too, at least my chief foe was, despite his
lame leg, so that I was obliged once more to set my back against a
tree. Hoppy still came on, and seemed determined to have me this
time, when, raising my paddle, I struck him with such force between
the eyes that the weapon was shivered to pieces, and the poor man-ape
gave a cry and a backward leap, and then staggered to the earth with
a skull cracked past mending.

Now, indeed, there was nothing left but to run for it, and run I
did; not so quickly, however, but that I was no sooner inside my mat
door than they were outside, and tearing at it to get in. Had they
succeeded it might have gone hard with me, for I was quite spent with
running, and trembled in every limb. However, by great good fortune,
I retained my presence of mind, and catching up a brand from the
fire—which I had lit to cook my breakfast, and had left to burn up
while I went and fetched my potatoes, as I called them,—I flung aside
my mat door, and struck left and right among them.

The effect was magical: in less time than it takes to tell, the man-
apes, uttering the most frightful cries, dispersed in every direction,
and in five seconds not a single one was to be seen. I don't know what
construction the reader will be disposed to set on this behaviour of
the apes, but to my mind it is clear enough. It was not me they had
been afraid of all along, but of my fire, and seeing me out without it
had thought it a prime opportunity to attack me. "Out without it,
Master Davidger!" says the reader; "do you mean to tell us that you
carried fire constantly about with you?" Aye, that did I, good
reader—in my pipe. As you may depend, as soon as my first stock of
tobacco began to dwindle, I could not be happy till I searched for
more, which I found, though not ready for smoking as the other was,
but green, and requiring to be dried. While I was at work my fire
was always burning near, and never on any occasion before this

morning had I walked abroad without having my tobacco at full blast. True, the apes could not see the fire in the pipe-bowl, but they could see the smoke plainly enough, and smell it too, I'll be bound, at a greater distance than one would think, and, as I firmly believe, it was because I was without my pipe that the man-apes ventured to assail me. As the reader may depend, never afterwards did I neglect such an easy weapon against my enemies; and whether or no I attach too much importance to my pipe I cannot say, I only know that never afterwards did I suffer the least inconvenience from my hideous neighbours. Nay, I turned the battle I had had to most excellent account, for, after some rest, I sallied out to the scene of the encounter, and, finding the body of my antagonist just as I had left it, I thought it no harm to divest it of its hide. It was, however, a much tougher job than I had bargained for, especially as I had no other tools to assist me than such sharp-edged shells as I could pick up on the shore; but, in the course of the day, I accomplished it, and, by careful drying and no end of rubbing, brought it to tolerable condition for the purpose for which I designed it, which was no other than to make me a pair of breeches; and, though the work in them was such as would have mightily tickled my father to behold, I much question if he could have done better without a knife or a pair of shears, and with a thorn for a needle. Out of the straggling bits that were trimmed off the sides I made me a pair of sandals—for I was unused to going barefoot, and the sharp shingle on the beach had on several occasions cut me rather severely; and even then I had a bit left for a cap. The reader will understand, however, that my man-ape skin breeches were not exactly *knee* breeches; they wanted full a foot of it, and, moreover, did not reach to my waist by several inches. Nevertheless, they were quite as comfortable as though I had been measured in Bond Street for them, and more durable, I'll warrant, for only that they were worn a trifle bald in places—for, for comfort sake I had contrived them with the hairy side outward—they were as sound and serviceable after a year's wear as when I first put them on. Besides my breeches, and cap, and sandals, I made me a grass-cloth jacket; but, except in wet weather, or when sitting within doors on cool evenings, I seldom wore it, for it was a cumbrous thing, and not at all fit to work in.

And now that the reader is aware how I was housed and dressed, I will tell him how I fared in the matter of food. Very few roast pigeons came to my share after that glut which fell so conveniently into my hands on the first night of my arrival on the island. Since they could not be procured without risking another tremendous conflagration equal to the first, I was content to forego the luxury. Now and then I managed to knock down one from off a bough with a stone, but this was rare, so much so, indeed, that, whenever it did happen, I invariably put by the dainty for my Sunday's dinner. I tried my hand at making a bow, and, after infinite trouble, succeeded pretty well, but, for want of a knife, my arrows were such miserable failures, that, had my game been as large as geese, I could not have hit them, unless they came very close and sat quite still.

Still I was not starved for want of animal food; a climb into a tree would always yield me a dish of eggs of some sort or another, and not unfrequently a few plump squales. Then there were the squirrels, which, when young, are not bad eating, and the wild hares, and, better than all, the wild pigs. Of these latter there were not a great stock, which, knowing how prolific an animal the pig is, rather surprised me, until I discovered that the man-apes had a deadly antipathy to piglings, and never failed to strangle them whenever they found an opportunity, which was just as often as the old pigs left them unprotected. It was by these means that I obtained a frequent dinner of baked sucking-pig, without the cost of so much as a thanky to the monsters who were my pork-butchers.

Then I had fish, and though, favoured by circumstances, I was enabled to improve vastly on the jewel-box and paddle system, to have seen me out fishing would have been an interesting spectacle for any civilized piscator who had been there to see. Having no boat, I tried my hand at angling from the shore, and, as I might have expected, took not so much as anything even of the size of a stickleback. This I tried within the first week of my residence on the island, and more as a pastime and relief from the monotony of mat-making than anything else; but when I saw how hopeless the case was, and that unless I could hit on some means of getting out to sea, I should be cut off from a most excellent article of diet, I began to think seriously of the matter, nor was I long in hitting on a scheme, and acting on it.

Among the ashes that strewed the great space the fire had cleared were many big boughs and branches, some as large as small trees, the bases of which the fire had attacked, and which had broken off by their own weight. Selecting half a dozen of such as I was able to drag, I hauled them down to the beach, and tied them together in a clumsy fashion with strings of bark, making something like a raft. My rod was a crooked stick, my line a length of twisted bird-gut, and my hook a thorn, which in these regions frequently grow fish-hook shape and of exceeding sharpness, as the wanderer in the woods often

Davidger building his Raft.

finds to his discomfort. For bait I took bits of bird-meat offal—the heads, legs, and so forth.

Launching my raft, I clambered on to it, but at first was so awkward that I was no sooner on than off again, soused over head and ears, while my tackle went to sea on its own accord; but, after two or three further trials, I contrived to climb on to my logs, and found that if I laid the cross way, and did not move much, they would bear me.

This was all I wanted. I was too good a swimmer to fear a ducking, and so long as my craft enabled me to get among the fishes and hook some, it might capsize the next moment, and welcome.

Letting the raft drift as it chose, I lay on my face quite still till I was about a hundred yards from shore, and then I cast in my bait, and scarce a minute had elapsed before a dozen fish, little and big, were at it, and, as I was annoyed to find, at my line too, which, as the reader already knows, was made of twisted bird gut, and, no doubt, smelt as savoury as the bait on the hook. Indeed, the gut line would have been bait enough, for, when I drew it in, they came up with it, and, never suspecting that so cunning an enemy lay sprawled along what I daresay seemed to them mere drift wood, I was enabled to thrust my arm between the logs, and gather them off like cherries on a stick. How many I might have taken in this way I don't know, for my line was a long one; but just when I had taken five, and was groping for the sixth, the villain gave it a nip which completely severed it, and put an end to my fishing for that trip. However, big and little, my five fishes must have weighed about a dozen pounds, which, together with the lesson I had acquired, was not unprofitable as an afternoon's work, so, sliding into the water, I took hold of my raft with one hand and swimming with the other, piloted my cargo into port. After this I fished with a strip of bark, which was tough and answered the purpose when I had discovered the right sort; some that I tried the fish would not approach at all, or if they did sheered off immediately. These sorts of bark I tasted, and found to be extremely bitter, and, being fresh from the tree, I dare say imparted their bitterness to the water immediately surrounding.

So I was sufficiently well set up for flesh and fish; of roots and fruits I had abundance. My stock of fuel was exhaustless, though I drew on it daily for a hundred years. My house was weatherproof, my bed was soft, and I had clothes enough. I was not entirely without company, for having one day discovered a litter of little pigs in a hollow of the bank of the little valley, through which flowed the only stream of fresh water on the island, I took one under each arm, and making a sty of stakes and boughs close to the rear of my hut, shut them in and fed them. It was not a wise thing to do, for the hatred of the man-apes towards their kind was enough to have brought on me a hostile visit from them, and I regard it as good proof that they dreaded me even more than they detested pigs, that my little grunters suffered no sort of molestation at the paws and jaws of their hairy foes. As it turned out, my two pigs were a boar and a sow, so that by and by I had little porkers of my own breeding. By this time the parent pigs had grown too big to be regarded as pets; indeed, they were anything but pleasant neighbours, especially when the wind blew from them to me; so I resolved to turn them loose. But this was not so easy as I had supposed; as for the boar, he scampered off eagerly enough, but her ladyship wouldn't budge. Whether it was affection for her squeakers, or for the constantly-filled trough, that governed her is more than I can say, but go she would not; all day long she was skulking about the sty, and so I left her when I went to bed. In the morning, however, I awoke to find that she had crept in under my mat wall, and was comfortably snoring in a corner.

It was not a little provoking, after having conquered the formidable man-apes, to be persecuted by a pig. Had any of the former gentry taken it into their heads to trouble me, I could only have found consolation in the venerable aphorism, " what can't be cured must be endured;" but it happily occurred to me, as I regarded her reclining sowship, that the old saw might be set the other way, and that in her case what couldn't be endured might be *cured*—I might make bacon of her!

I was always of an impetuous turn and no sooner did I get the notion of manufacturing bacon into my head, than I resolved at once to act on it. It certainly would be a great thing to have a rasher always at hand for one's breakfast, or to boil with a yam for dinner! Without further thought about the matter, I took up my biggest club, and she was a dead pig at a single blow.

My implements for bacon-curing were few. I had no *salt* in the first place, and, if I had given this a thought before I slew the sow, I think it likely that her life would have been spared; but now that I was in for it I did not like to give in, and resolved to make shift for salt by soaking the meat for a few hours in sea-water before I hung it up to smoke. My only knives were a sharp shell or two lashed to sticks, and, having lugged the carcase out into the open, I proceeded to bowel her, and then to scald and cut her up.

And here I am suddenly pulled up by the foreboding that, unless this part of my adventures is to occupy a hundred pages at the very least, I had best not dip into them too deeply. A little way back, I was speaking of *boiled* yam and bacon, and now again of *scalding* my pig. Of course I might eschew all explanation on these and such like points, and the careless reader would let them pass unchallenged; not so the diligent reader.

"Boiling! scalding! what do you mean?" says he. "It is true you have a fire, Master Davidger, but how did you come by your pot?"

"Did not I tell you, good reader, that, while on the island of Magindano, I learnt how to weave grass matting?"

"So you did; but, unless you wish to drive us to the conclusion that all you have previously written is the merest fiction, pray don't try and persuade us that you wove a grass *cooking pot!*"

My dear readers, I am bound to tell you that I did so, for it is perfectly true. "Was it a fireproof pot?" No, indeed; had I placed it on the fire it would have blazed up in a twinkling. It was a water-proof pot though, or very nearly—and I may tell you that had I been a skilful grass weaver instead of a bungler, I might have made the vessel as water-tight as a wooden pail—and the way I boiled my water was to fill my pot, and, getting several large stones, made them red hot, and dropped them into the water till it boiled. It is a common trick enough amongst savages. The Magidanoes did not practise it, because their trade with China merchants, to say nothing of their pillage from the ships of civilized countries, set them above such shifts; but the slaves on the island on which I had last resided followed the practice, and I have since ascertained that the American Indians adopt this method of boiling their meats in preference to any other.

And now, having explained the manner in which I scalded my pig, I have only to add concerning that animal, that she didn't make first-rate bacon. It was salt enough, but the meat seemed never to recover from its soddening in the sea, and altogether it was so like pork out of a forgotten barrel that I never repeated the experiment.

I find, on looking back, that it was in reference to the domesticated companions of my solitude that the bacon business came in for mention. Well, besides the pigs in my sty, I had song birds in any numbers. I used to take them while yet too young to leave the nest, and rear them within doors. I call them song birds, and so they were as compared with sparrows, and that sort of chattering, twittering creature; but the best singer of the lot was not fit " to hold a candle," as the saying is, to our lark or thrush. In plumage, however, they excelled anything my eyes ever beheld, and fluttering and chirping in and about my poor hovel, gave it an aspect of cheerfulness that was often a great comfort to me. I tried hard to teach the most likely-looking of my feathered friends to talk, but in that I failed completely.

On the whole, then, I had very much to be grateful for, and, looking back from this distance of time, I sometimes think that I was a foolish fellow that I did not resolve to end my days in peace and contentment. My bodily wants were amply provided for, my health was never better, and my soul's health, too, I should say for that matter; for receiving my daily bread so direct, as it were, from the hand of Nature, I did not dare show myself such an ill-conditioned heathen as to take it without returning sincere thanks; so, when I lay down at night, did I humbly solicit this protection, without which I might have been set on by man-apes, or consumed by fire or flood; and awaking hale and refreshed in the morning, my first act was to acknowledge God's goodness. All I wanted was the company of *one* other man; with one only I could have got along very well. With Tom Cox, for instance. With Tom, I think, before most men, for he, poor fellow, was of a very easy mind; and, while he got tobacco, and meat, and a good bundle of grass to lie and smoke his pipe on, would never have pined. It was not so with me. As soon as I began to make matters comfortable about me, when my house was thatched to my satisfaction, and furnished with a mat carpet, and a couple of mat cooking pots, and a stool, and a sort of table, and a few other useful articles; when I had half a dozen young porkers in my sty, and had learnt to catch fish, and to know the wholesome fruits and roots from the unwholesome; when, indeed, I had made myself as comfortable as, under the circumstances, was possible, then, instead of making up my mind to be happy, I at once began to be discontented, to feel lonely, and to fall to brooding on my miserable fate.

But, even while I felt so, I could not but be aware how ungrateful it was, and strove by hard work to banish my discontent; but I did not succeed. I had no tools to work with, and the result of my labours was *so* insignificant. It did not seem so when the articles I somehow managed to cobble together were required for my immediate use, but now it was very different. One day I would say, "I will make me another stool," and, going out, would spend the morning in selecting my materials, and the afternoon in scraping them into something like ship shape. But, after all, come night, what had I to look at as the result of a day's toil? Half a dozen ugly little stumps, not worth so much as a single halfpenny! "Now, here's a pretty way for a grown man to spend his time!" said I; "and, after all, what is it for? I have already got a stool, and another will only be in the way; it is labour in vain to finish my job." So I would have no more to do with stool-making, and spent the whole of next day smoking my pipe on the beach, or rocking lazily on the leafy bough of a tree, considering what job I should next be at.

At least, that was the pretence. What I really was thinking of all the time was, how I might get away from the island. It wsa impossible without a boat, and, as it seemed, equally impossible to build a boat without materials or tools. True there was timber enough—hundreds of stately trees, the trunks of which, properly hollowed and balanced, would make a boat capable of carrying twenty men. But how could I, with my few sharp shells and stones, hope to accomplish such a tremendous job? "If I were a beaver now instead of a man," thought I, "it might be done; I could eat through the trunk with my teeth." And this thought straightway led to others concerning beavers and their tree-felling, and the smallness of their teeth and their perseverance. I thought of the beavers and their doings all the way home, and as I sat within doors till bed-time, and for a long time after I was a-bed.

In the morning I was up and doing; I wanted a tree to make a canoe; I wanted a tree straight and clean, not more than seven feet round or thereabout, and as near as possible to the water's edge, else, after it was made, I should be unable to launch it, and it would be as useless as that which now served as a roof to my house. Hampered by requiring so many qualifications, my selection was not at all easy, and twice I made the entire circuit of the island, and notched at least fifty as worthy of consideration before I was able to decide. Finally, I chose a tree on the south side fit in every respect, only that it was much further from the water's edge than pleased me—forty yards, I should say, at the very least. However, I could do no better.

All next day and the one following I was busy getting my " tools " together, and making a rush basket of the regular carpenter shape to carry them in. As for my tools, I assure the reader that the refuse of an oyster-stall and the run of a flint-road would have yielded me implements for tree felling vastly superior to those I now possessed; for the shells to be found round about my island, although quite as sharp-edged as those of the oyster, were not nearly as large, and could not be used handily without they were fastened in a cleft stick; while, as regards the stones, although large enough, they were smooth and water-worn, and had to be broken up before they furnished a single sharp point. I should like to have met with some gutta-percha to use as tool handles, and endless other purposes, especially to have made me a vessel to drink out of, and another to wash in; but, though I searched very diligently, I could find no tree like those in the forest of Magindano, though, being but a poor judge, it is more than probable that it there existed.

My tree was nearly a mile from my house, and at first I had thoughts of shifting my lodging; but when, the first morning, I packed my basket with my tools, and did up in a great leaf a nice bit of cold roast pork and part of a yam for my dinner, and shouldered my basket and lit my pipe, it all seemed so nice, so like " going to work " in regular Christian fashion, that from that very moment I resolved not to shift my house, unless something more urgent than my job compelled me.

Up to the height of about sixteen feet my tree was without branches, and was perfectly straight from the ground upwards. I judged, for a width of say two feet three inches, twelve feet would be a good length. I commenced operations at four feet, and, by great diligence, cut to the depth of at least an inch all round the trunk by the evening. My tired arms, however, convinced me how hard I had been working, and, by the time I reached home and roused the embers of my fire, and cooked my supper and ate it, I was glad to get to bed.

The next day showed much less work done, and no wonder, for the labour of the previous day had worn out nearly all my tools, and I had to seek others before I could begin. Moreover, I found that, having got well through the bark, the wood was harder than I at first thought; and, though I worked all day at one side of my tree only, the cut was barely an inch deeper than when I began.

But I will not inflict on the reader an account of my daily progress at tree-felling; what he wants to see is the tree down, and the canoe made and launched. And in this I can sympathize with him, for, of all things in the world, that was what *I* wanted to see. It was a woeful long time before I did see it. It was exactly three weeks from the time I began my task, when, going " to work " as usual in the morning, I found that the stiffish wind that had blown during the night had broken off my tree at the cutting, and mighty glad I was to see it, for at least three inches remained to be sawn, and that meant four hard days' work. I made much shorter work of the other end, for I made a fire and burnt it off; and not only was the job executed in a twentieth of the time, but much more satisfactorily than though it had been sown off, for, with a little management of my fire and some bits of matting sopped in water, I was enabled to round it off handsomely.

But now came the toughest part of the job—indeed, now came the actual job, to which my three weeks' labour had been merely preliminary, the hollowing out of my log. My first intention was to chip it out with sharp stones and shells, and it was very lucky that my success in forming the bows of my craft had set this idea aside, otherwise I might have been chipping away to this very day if I had possessed sufficient patience, and still my boat would have been unfinished. The plan I adopted was to burn out the substance and leave the shell.

To effect this I made a mortar of earth, and pounded shells and water, and cemented the sides of my log, raising the cement on either side to the height of about a foot. This done, I built a fire over the top and between the " walls," and so managed it that in a few hours the whole surface was covered, to the depth of several inches, with glowing embers; and though the procuring of fuel and breaking it into convenient pieces, and fetching water in my mat pail to keep the mortar from cracking and falling to pieces with the heat was tedious, it was nothing like such hard work as hacking a green tree with a mussel-shell from morning till night.

The result of the first day's burning was satisfactory. True my log was little like a boat at present, but I plainly saw that I had only to exercise patience and discretion to achieve the object which, day by day, increased in importance in my mind. I was so anxious that the work should proceed with all speed, that, had it not been for the terrible lesson I had learned on the night of my arrival, I should have made up a good fire, and left it to do its work all through the night. But this I dare not risk, and, though I took care to use no more water than was sufficient to extinguish the fire, I did not quit the spot while a single spark was visible.

The next morning, the ashes being dry and still warm, I was not long in kindling a good fire, and kept it up till night; and so the next day and the next, till, come the sixth day, my fire lay in a deep trough, and required the nicest management lest it should burn through, and so spoil all my work. Three inches was my idea of what the thickness of my boat should be, and, having contrived some sort of a pair of compasses out of two bent sticks, I brought it to that substance uniformly, except at the bows, where the canoe was, I dare-say, nine inches through. Then I turned out the embers, and set to scraping the interior; and, in the course of another day, brought the charred surface to a state of perfect smoothness, and as black as ebony.

And now it was all ready for launching, and launched it certainly would have been that evening, late as it was, only that I found it impossible even to drag it a foot out of the forty yards that lay between it and the sea. Much obliged, indeed, should I have been to the man-apes if they had taken it into their head to have done me the same service, in a reverse way, as they had done when I first came, and carried my canoe down to the water's edge; indeed, I have suffi-cient confidence in the shrewdness of these monsters to believe that, if they had guessed my intention, they would have assisted at the launch with the most perfect willingness. As it was, however, there was nothing left but to put my own shoulder to the wheel, and this I did with an alacrity which was not a little absurd, considering that at present I had not even made me a paddle, or settled in my mind where I would go in my canoe when she was floated. But I could think of nothing but getting her into the water, and, though it was growing towards dusk, nothing would do but I must set to and break off from a tree a limb clean and round enough to cut into a couple of " rollers," and this I carried home, and worked half the night by firelight at shaping them, and making them ready to help my boat down to the beach in the morning.

By aid of my two rollers, it was easy enough to push the canoe down to the water, and, to my great delight, she floated very fairly. By dint of hard work I had, by evening, made a very good apology for a paddle; and, before I slept that night, I had taken a trip out to sea, much farther than I had ever dared to venture on my fishing raft.

I found that my canoe, although quite sea-worthy, was very heavy in the water, and that much greater speed would have been made with a couple of oars than with a paddle. But speed was not my object; all I wanted was to get out to sea a few miles this way and that, as my fancy directed, so as to give myself the opportunity of falling in with any prahu that might chance to be sailing that way.

And that was how I occupied myself, day after day, for over a fortnight, trying my luck east, west, north, and south, but all my journeys were fruitless; and as many times as I set out in the morning hopeful and eager, just so many did I return in the evening weary and melancholy, till the sight of the waving green trees, as I drew home to them, was hateful, and my little thatched house became as cheerless as a sepulchre. It *was* a sepulchre in my discontented eyes—a place in which I was as securely buried and hidden away from the world, as though coffined and lain in a twelve-foot clay grave.

By this time I had lived on my island, as well as I could make out—for, though I took great pains to bear in mind which day was Sunday, I grew presently rather bewildered as to the number of Sundays—about a year and seven months; and now I resolved that I would endure my bondage no longer. It was different before I possessed a boat, then I was a prisoner by compulsion; but, now that I had means to carry me to an inhabited country, it seemed very like folly, to say the least of it, to submit to my banishment a day longer than was necessary.

I resolved then to go, and, at all events, to have a long search— four or five days, if necessary—for another island. If I could not find one, I could return to my own. My preparations were soon made; all I needed was a stock of food and water.

But I had no sooner got thus far with my calculation than I found a rather formidable difficulty in the way. If I paddled out, say only a three days' journey—and with my slow-going craft I should be fortunate to make a hundred miles in that time—and was unsuccessful, and had to come home again, I should require water for six days.

How was I to carry it? A rush pot was very well when you lived within a stone's throw of a stream, but it was altogether a useless thing to take as provision on a sea voyage. Now more than ever did I long to discover that mysterious substance, on which I had built my fortune in Magindano—that gutta percha—and indeed spent a long afternoon in hunting for it, though, I had searched so many times before, I knew it was nearly hopeless.

It turned out quite so, and, flinging myself down by my fire, I gave way to an outbreak of bitter grief to think that a venture on which, perhaps, my life—certainly my happiness—depended, should be baulked for lack of so paltry a thing as a bottle or an old jar. I had nothing—nothing at all. I recollected how that Robinson Crusoe made himself jars out of clay, and baked them in the sun; but I also recollected what wretched things they were when finished, and I was not so clever as Crusoe by a very long way. Besides, I had no clay, so it was no use wasting further thought on that subject.

So I went on wishing that I had this and that that would hold water, till, with my usual good fortune, I hit on the very thing.

"Even a big bladder would do if I had such a thing," said I.

Well, I had bladders enough in all conscience, though, perhaps, not large ones. I had five young porkers in my sty, besides one or two sows that I had bred for breeding, and which, having no further use for, I had turned adrift; but, like the first mentioned—of which I had made bacon—they were not inclined to a wild life, and though they did not absolutely invade my house, hung about it pretty closely, and might be easily captured. Here were bladders enough, and, though it did seem shameful waste to destroy so much pig life on so small a pretence, I resolved that it should be done, and straightway fetching in the piglings one at a time, I knocked them on the head, as well as one of the sows, that was easily inveigled to the door by the offer of a lump of fish. Washing the six bladders quite clean, I blew them out and hung them close by the fire, so that by the following morning they were all ready to fill with water; and very capital receptacles they made—light, handy to carry, and extremely commodious. I should say that, in the six bladders, I managed to stow at least seven quarts of water.

These I conveyed into my boat, together with a large boiled fish, the half of a baked pig, three or four yams, and an armful of fruit.

Something else, too, I carried away, and which, though I have had no occasion to mention of late, were snugly put away—my pearls and my big yellow diamond. These I dug out of the corner where they were buried, and, having contrived a little pocket in my ape-skin breeches, I placed them within, and sewed up the pocket-hole with a bit of bird-gut thread. A mat I thought might be useful. I took also a good handful of tobacco and some touchwood, a bit of which I set a spark to, for if by chance my pipe went out, I should be in a pretty fix.

I did not remove my hut, nor anything that was within it, for, of course, I did not know but that I might be very glad to come back. Last of all, I set about extinguishing my fire, which I found to be a much sadder job than I should have supposed. It seemed cruel somehow—like killing a dog, or some such faithful companion, in whose life you had no further interest; and for that matter the fire had been my companion—my sole companion, through the whole time of my sojourn on the island. I was full of wretchedness and dismal despair till I had called it into life, and it had at once gladdened me. Through nineteen long months it had been my friend; it had kept me alive, and I had cherished its life night and day; never once had it died out since the memorable night when I sat rubbing two bits of wood together. Upon my word, as I stood with the mat bucket in my hands ready to douse it, and these thoughts ran through my mind, I felt almost inclined to "spare its life," as I may say, and leave it burning; but when I reflected on what a terrible thing my companion was when left to its own devices my sentimentality abated, so sousing the water over my hearth, I at once smote it black and dead, turned away, hastened down to the beach, and, stepping into my boat, paddled off.

But, after all, it was not my fate to leave the island which had afforded me so many simple pleasures, as well as anxieties and trouble, without a living companion. I have already mentioned that I had made friends of the birds in my neighbourhood, and housed many, and fed many more. There was one, however, who was an especial pet, not because he was very handsome or very clever as a singer, but because in his chirping he made a sound very like "patty." Now, my sister "Patty," or Martha, was my favourite sister, and in my loneliness I could not but be drawn towards the little creature who so

nearly uttered her name. I called the bird "Patty," and, by way of
honouring him—though I much doubt if he appreciated my kindness
—made him a grass-work cage, and hung him over my door, and fed
him with my own hand. It was when I had been on the island about
six months that I became acquainted with him, and so at the time of
my leaving I had had him over a year.

Just before I put my fire out I opened Patty's cage, and gave her

Davidger prepares to leave the island.

her liberty, thinking no more about her; but, judge of my surprise
when I was fairly at sea, to see Patty wheeling above my head!
"Patty! Patty!" I called, and down she came and perched on the
edge of the boat, and, though she rose several times seemingly with
half a mind to fly back to the island again, she came back, and finally
made herself comfortable, perching on one of my bundles which lay at
the end of the canoe.

It was then about noon, and I steadily paddled southward. Had my vessel been a sampan, I might have made a good thirty miles by sun-down; but, as it was, in my cumbrous machine, I could not have progressed more than twelve or fifteen miles in the time, for, with the last glimpses of daylight, I could not only make out my island, but even the trees that grew on the skirt of it. In a little while the stars began to shine, and, though but a poor hand at astronomy, during my residence in the island I had, as I smoked my pipe on the beach of evenings, made myself pretty well acquainted with the position of the chief stars, and, by observing them, was as well able to keep my course as under the sun's guidance.

Not that I paddled all night; nothing would have been gained by such a course. An hour or a day even made no difference to me. My intention was to allow myself four days for my search, and then, if I discovered no island, to turn back at once; after taking a spell of rest ashore to re-equip, and try my fortune for the same space of time in another direction. The sea was as smooth as a sheet of glass, as it invariably is at this season of the year, so I shipped my paddle, and lay in my boat, with my mat spread over me, and did nothing but smoke and watch the stars, and doze, till the morning wind began to blow.

So passed the next day and the next, by which time I began to grow rather alarmed about my provisions. The sun got at my meat and fish, so that I was glad to throw them overboard. This, however, was no great matter, for I had still four cocoas left and three largish yams; but it was my stock of water that troubled me. It was right and sweet enough through the first two days, but now it began to taste pretty much as the pork had smelt before I threw it away, and I plainly foresaw that by the morrow it would be impossible to drink it. There was only one remedy—to turn it all into the boat. It was not a nice way, nor one that I would have preferred had any other course been open to me; but, as it happened, it would have been impossible to have done better.

The bows of my boat being, as before mentioned, heavier than the other part, it rather dipped at that end, so that when I released the precious liquid from the evil-smelling pig-skins, it made a deepish pool at this end, and did not spread about. As I said before, the boat was quite water-tight, and the sea so smooth that there was little danger of my shipping salt-water. Then there was another advantage, which, although I had not at all counted on it, gratified me very much when I discovered it—the charred wood that lined the boat seemed to have an almost magical effect on the foul water, for, in the middle of the third night, when I dipped half a cocoa-nut shell full, I found that it was as sweet as when I had drawn it from the stream.

The worst of it was, that, on account of so large a surface of it, **being exposed to the heat,** it evaporated in an alarming way, so that **on the morning of** the fourth day, I plainly saw that, unless I made up my mind to endure a day or so of thirst, my excursion had better be **shortened; nor did it seem that to** shorten it would make me a loser, **for** not **a trace of** land, or any symptom of it, could I see, look which **way I might; so I resolved that** I would continue my course no longer **than the afternoon, and that then** I would have **a** bit of a swim and a **few** hours' rest under my mat, and start fresh for home in the cool of **the evening.**

And, without doubt, I should have done so, for, come the afternoon, land seemed as far off as **ever,** only that I was otherwise resolved by the curious beha**viour of my feathered** companion, Patty. Ever **since we had lost sight of my island, my** fellow-voyager had conducted **himself in the most decorous manner, taking his perch usually at the bows of my canoe, and contentedly chattering,** " Patty! patty !" **or hopping round the edge of the boat** by way of exercise. Not once, **however, had he taken wing of** his own accord, and, when once or twice I had taken and thrown him up, he would not fly a bit higher **than** he was thrown, but alighted immediately. Now, however—that **is to say, on the** afternoon of the fourth day from the time when I had set out—his behaviour was altogether changed. He grew restless, and began to flutter from one end of the boat to the other, and then to mount a little higher, and again a little higher, till his size, which was that of a blackbird, was reduced to that of a sparrow. Then he **came** down again, and was evidently more uneasy than ever, hopping hither and thither, **and crying, "Patty!** patty !" **at a** tremendous rate, and presently he once more took wing, and, after rising to a great height, shot away like an arrow.

I was just preparing for a bathe to cool my hot and tired limbs, **but** the intention was instantly forgotten. Clearly Patty had sighted land ! What other reason could there be for the bird's sudden flight ?

my eyes followed the bird till it became a mere speck, and presently vanished entirely; and then, my arms strengthened with newly-inspired hope, I bent to my clumsy paddle, and sent my canoe skimming through the water in the direction Patty had flown, faster than I should have thought possible.

Not so fast, however, but that the day closed, and the sun sank into the sea before my eyes were gratified with the sight for which it so yearned; indeed, when land did appear, it was growing so dark that I could not be sure, and it was not till the moon rose that I was convinced, and by this time I was not more than a mile from the shore.

Nor did I pause to consider what shore it might be that I was approaching. For all I knew it might be the very island from which I had escaped with Katam, or that terrible Batama of which Katam had told me; it might even have been Magindano; but, although these uncomfortable conjectures would force themselves into my mind, they did not cause me to slacken my paddling; my yearning for the company of my fellow-creatures was superior to every consideration, and I never halted till my canoe grounded, about twenty yards from the dry beach which sloped from the wood to the sea.

Leaping out, I waded shoreward, tugging my boat after me as far as I could, and then wrapping my mat round my shoulders, and taking my paddle in my hands, with my heart hardly thumping between hope and fear I made my way to land.

Although moonlight, it was only quarter moon, and I could not see about me very distinctly; indeed, all that I could see was trees, and grass, and tangle, just exactly like that on the island I had recently left, so that my spirits began to sink, lest, after all this trouble and commotion, I had only exchanged one uninhabited place for another. But presently my heart was lifted, and I could have cried with joy, for, kicking against something, I stooped to see what, and discovered a broken gourd, which had been used for carrying water, for in the broken piece there was a hole bored, and a piece of bark cord knotted through the hole. Insignificant as it was, it was the work of man's hands, and furnished fair evidence that the main object of my journey was likely to be achieved.

I should much have preferred continuing my exploration, till my eyes were gladdened by the sight of some more tangible proof, than the broken water gourd, that the island was inhabited; but about this time the moon was hid behind the clouds, and I thought it probable that, if I continued to advance at such an unseasonable hour, and in the darkness, I might, by some unlucky accident, bring about an introduction to the inhabitants, if any there were, not at all to my advantage, so I thought it prudent to make my way back to my canoe. By this time the tide had receded, leaving my craft dry; however, the shore was steep, and I had not much difficulty in setting her afloat, and, making myself comfortable in my mat cloak, and with a pipe of tobacco, I kept watch till the morning.

As soon as the sun rose I again went ashore, and cautiously made my way through the forest; but, though I now possessed the advantage of daylight, I could discover no fresh trace of a human inhabitant, and I began to entertain the dismal conviction that, although the island was at some time inhabited, it was now deserted. I had so walked for an hour at least—taking care, by breaking branches and by other devices, to provide a track by which to return—when all of a sudden my ears were regaled by a sound, the like of which had not met them through nineteen long months—the sound of human voices! My first impulse was to raise my own voice, and hasten towards the spot from whence the welcome sound was proceeding; but, on second thought, it appeared to me as well to exercise a little forbearance. It would, at all events, be no loss to me to see what sort of customers they were who were out thus early. Doubtless they were armed, as I might find to my cost if I too rashly made my presence known to them. As the reader may easily imagine, it was not a particularly lovely or inviting appearance; my skin was tanned to a foxy sort of yellow, and my hair and beard were of a great length. Indeed, the only way in which I could conveniently dispose of the former was by twisting it into a rope, and fastening it with a wooden pin in a coil at the back of my head, a-top of which was perched my ape-skin cap. My breeches, as the reader has already been told, were of the same material, while my legs and feet were bare, for the pair of sandals I had made were long since worn out, and since I had not been able to find suitable stuff to make another pair; nor did I miss them, for the soles of my feet had become as callous as leather. I had brought with me neither my mat cloak nor my paddle—nothing, indeed, except my breeches and the jewels in the pocket of them, and a pipe or so of tobacco; and so I climbed into a tree to overhaul the individuals approaching, and judge whether I might place myself in their hands.

By the number of voices the company was evidently very numerous, and, if I might judge by their laughter and cheerful talk, not bound on any very serious business. At last they came in sight, and I was able from my resting-place to count eleven men—nine, and two who seemed by their dress to be persons in authority. Each one bore in his hand a sumpitan, and they seemed to be engaged in the sport of shooting the small black monkeys which abounded in the trees, and

Davidger is discovered by Tran—ai's Hunting Party.

the skins of which, doubtless, were used, as in Magindano, in the manufacture of head-dresses.

From my first glimpse of them I had made up my mind to make myself known, for never before had I seen savages whose looks I liked so well, or who, from their decent manners and attire, promised such agreement with the habits of civilized folk. But I was presently spared even this trouble, for the quick eye of one of the huntsmen presently espied me; he pointed me out to the rest, and in a moment at least half a dozen sumpitans were directed at me, each one, as I knew, containing an arrow tipped with poison enough to strike me with death, though it only hit my little finger. So, as loud as I could I called, "Netu! netu!" (Wait! wait!) and waved my arms to let them see that I was a man, and not an orang-outang, as they, no doubt, at first suspected. But I doubt if even this would have saved me from an unlucky shaft—for my voice, from long disuse, had grown very harsh and unnatural—but for my constant companion; that one that I have so often mentioned, that I am afraid almost to have anything more to say about it, lest the reader should begin to suspect me of being a slave to it. By "it" I, of course, mean my pipe. But, before the good reader condemns me, let him consider of what inestimable service the little, ugly thing, with a nut-shell for a bowl and the bone of a bird's leg for a stem—the old original one I had made the day after the great fire—had done me! It had comforted me through my long loneliness; it had secured me from the attacks of the man-apes, and now, as I verily believe, it saved me from a poisoned arrow, for, almost entirely hidden among the thick foliage of the tree in which I had taken refuge, I certainly should have been taken for an orang-outang, but for the blue curling wreath that rose from my tobacco, and the savages' knowledge that man is the only animal that smokes.

It was evident, however, that my appearance caused them some dismay, for, though they numbered eleven, and could have had no dread of an attack from a single man, it possibly occurred to them that I might be the scout of a party lying in ambush; nor would they, until they had taken counsel among themselves, allow me to come down out of the tree to explain. As often, indeed, as I attempted to descend, I found myself covered by a sumpitan, and so thought it prudent to be quiet.

After a palaver of about ten minutes' duration, however, they retired to an open space some fifty yards from my tree, and then beckoned me to come to them. This I did with my hands open and held over my head, in token of peace and good-will; nevertheless, as soon as I came within their reach, they seized and bound me very securely, and then, as though satisfied with the "game" they had captured, trooped off at a smart pace, carrying me with them.

In the custody of two men, who walked one on each side of me, we brought up the rear of the small procession, and, finding that my custodians were inclined for conversation—though in so low a whisper that their masters, who were in front, might not hear—I very readily joined in, and gave them as much as I thought prudent of my most recent adventures, and how I came to their island. In return, they informed me that the island I was on was Maday, and that the two dignitaries in front were Orang Kalu, who ruled there, and his brother Orang Sapasis, who was only on a visit to the island, and who was a very great man indeed, being governor of Mompara, an extensive island about thirty miles distant, and renowned for its gold mines and its pearl fishery. I ventured to inquire what would be my probable fate, and was informed that that was a matter Orang Kalu and his brother would settle between them—that, being found on Maday, I was the property of the ruler of that place; but that, most likely, as Orang Sapasis was the owner of many slaves, and was always ready to pay a good price for them, I should be packed off to Mompara. So that it seemed certain that, though my life was tolerably sure on the one hand, on the other I was doomed to slavery; and I could not forbear sighing bitterly, and wondering if ever I should regain my beloved country, from which I had now been estranged so many weary years.

After a walk of an hour we came upon the village, as large as that of Magindano, and equally well built; indeed, in its shape and general appointments, it very much resembled it. After having been housed in one of the huts for a little time, and very plentifully fed, I was called to go before my new masters to be examined by them, and learn their pleasure.

CHAPTER XI.

AS I had anticipated this interview with the Orangs Kalu and Sapasis, I had, while in the hut, pondered whether I should make known to them my entire history, and appeal to their generosity to help me to make my way to England; but I could not help reflecting that there were many difficulties in the way. At that time, the Dyaks, as a nation, knew no distinction between Frenchmen, and Englishmen, and Portuguese; they were all classed under the hated catalogue of "white men," the daring invaders of their territory, the assailers of their prahus, the owners of the mighty ship of war which, by a single roar of its great cannon, could mow down fleets of sampans, and blow to atoms forts that it had been the labour of years to build. Under such circumstances, then, it was not advisable to appeal for mercy to my captors on the score that I was an Englishman. Truly, I might have demanded my liberty, and warned them of the terrible vengeance my countrymen would take if they discovered that I was detained against my will; but I had had experience enough of Dyak manners to know that, if they saw any difficulty in this direction, they would, without any scruple, by making me shorter by a head, effectually spoil all chances of my identity.

Again, if it had seemed politic to have declared my nationality, it would have been no easy matter to have convinced them of it, for certainly I was, at that time, the brownest " white man " the sun ever tanned; indeed, I had seen many natives—for, as among more delicate-skinned folk, there are fair and dark among the Dyaks—who were of even lighter complexion than myself. True, I wore a beard—a facial decoration seldom or never indulged in by a Sea Dyak. Since I had lost the services of poor Tom Cox, who used to perform for me the office of hair-cutter by means of a knife and a hammer and a little block of wood, my hair, as before stated, had grown to a preposterous length, and, for convenience sake, I was wont to bundle it up and secure it in a knot behind—very much, in fact, after the Sea Dyak fashion; so that in this again I might have been a Bornean. Of course there were differences which, to an educated eye, would distinguish me at once from a Dyak; my face was not of the Bornean type, my limbs were not of that spiderish cut so peculiar to Polynesian islanders, and, notwithstanding the hardships I had undergone, I might without disadvantage have measured shoulders and chest against the biggest man on the island.

When I was led into the chief house I found Orang Kalu and his brother reclining on their mats and smoking, while behind each was a slave with a palm-leaf fan to keep the flies from disturbing his repose. For full five minutes they did not condescend to notice me, but continued to smoke in silence. To a man in my position, who expected, at least, to create in the breasts of his captors enough of interest to make them inquisitive as to who he might be and whence he came, to be so treated was a little annoying, and put me on my mettle to observe as calm and indifferent a mien as possible. Orang Kalu was the first to break silence.

"How came you in that tree?" asked he.

"I climbed into it," replied I.

"Where do you come from?"

This was a poser, for by name I did not know the place from whence I had come. Even its geographical position I was not certain about, so I answered vaguely—

"From an island in the west."

"By whom is it governed?"

"It has no governor; it is an island without people. Now that I have left it, it is quite uninhabited."

At this Sapasis gave a short laugh, and winked at his brother as though to say, "Go on; humour the villain, and let us see how many more lies he will tell."

"And pray how far from this is this island?" asked Orang Kalu.

"Three days' journey in a sampan."

"But you must have swum," put in Sapasis, "or did you fly? Pray, where are your wings?"

"I neither flew nor swam," replied I, "I came in a canoe. It now lies on the beach in a line with the spot where I was found."

At this Kalu called a fellow, and gave him some whispered instructions, and then continued his interrogation.

"How did you reach this island you speak of?"

"In a sampan, which was wrecked as soon as I got there."

"Quite wrecked?" asked the sharp Sapasis.

"Utterly," I replied; "broken up completely."

"And yet you made your way here in it?"

"No; I built me another boat."

"What! without materials or tools?"

"With my bare hands, and with no other materials than a tree trunk," I replied, hoping that at last I had impressed them with the idea that I was not altogether a poor wretched slave, who might be bantered with impunity; but the effect of my last reply was vastly different from what I had anticipated. Orang Kalu rose to his feet.

"How, slave!" said he, "do you dare to mock us? Down on your face, base liar, and tell us the truth!"

He held a short bamboo wand in his hand, and, as he spoke, he waved it threateningly; but I had been without a master for so long a time, that my well-trained passions had run wild, and I felt foolishly resentful at such treatment.

"I am no liar!" said I; "I am an Englishman, and would scorn to say aught but the truth, though my life depended on it; and again I tell you that, without so much as a knife even, I made me a boat, in which to leave the island of which I had grown tired."

My answer seemed to provoke Kalu beyond endurance, and, raising his stick, he would have given me a severe stroke across the face with it, only that I caught it in its descent, and twitched it out of his hand. This was adding fuel to fire. Kalu raised his voice, and his guard entered.

"Let him die," said Orang Kalu, simply, and forthwith I was seized, and dragged out of the presence-chamber.

Now, indeed, I thought that it was all over with me. As at Magindano, one of the chief's attendants was the public executioner,

and this worthy it was who, as soon as we had got outside, bound my
hands with a thong, and, grasping my shoulder, marched me along.
The place of execution could not be far off, and there could be no
hope. Orang Kalu was the only being who could save my life, and,
if he had time to reflect on his hasty sentence, he might possibly do
so; but, as I well knew, in these Dyak countries " the word and the
blow " is the law, at least as regards the chief's sentence, and, before
Kalu's passion was cool, I should be cold—cold and dead.

Nor did Kalu save me, nor any other human power; yet saved I
was, and in a manner which, although it may, without proper explanation, seem like a barefaced attempt to impose on the reader's
credulity, was in reality very simple. It will be as well, then, for me
to pave the way for the reader's ready belief, before I state the circumstance that demands it. Throughout the whole of the Dyak
dominions, as among all other savage communities, superstitious
belief is unbounded. They are ruled in their most common-place
business, as well as the most important, by "omens." They seek
omens in the sea, in the earth, and in the air. They have voices of
warning in the whistling of the wind, in the chirping of beetles, in
the lowing of oxen, but more especially in the cry of birds. A Dyak
chief will turn a deaf ear to the cries for mercy uttered by the women
and children of a village he is pillaging, and kill and burn with no
other emotion than that of ferocious joy; but let a certain bird utter
its warning note, and straightway the bloody kris becomes harmless
as a reed, and the marauders flee like a flock of sheep, and hide themselves in the woods till the morrow.

There are several sorts of omen birds, possessing various degrees
of power; and, as it turned out, for more than a year I had entertained one of these terrible creatures in my home on the solitary
island; nay, I had not unfrequently teased it, and even had thoughts
of cutting its tongue, by way of making it talk. What terrible
things might have happened to me had I done so! My faithful
" Patty"—for this was the tremendous fellow—might have conjured
up a host of evil spirits more dreadful even than the man-apes, and
taken vengeance too horrible to think on!

But it is scarcely fair for me to make sport of a superstition to
which I am indebted for my life; for such undoubtedly was the case,
as I will explain to the reader in very few words. Our way to the

place of execution lay through a grove of trees, and barely had we entered it when I heard a most familiar sound—the voice of my little "Patty." The fellows who were conducting me, as well as the mob that followed behind, heard it too, and were impressed by it in a way which to me was unaccountable. They suddenly paused, and stood quite still, raising their hands as if in fright, and pointing at the tree from which the clear, thrilling "Patti! patti! patti!" proceeded. Even the executioner took his hand from my shoulder, and looked as scared as the rest. As for me, I was not a little affected to hear the voice of my little companion, and at once thoughts of my peaceful island home, and of dear native home, and of my sister, after whom I had named the poor bird, came rushing to my mind. I could account for the whole business in no other way than that the bird had recognized me; and, longing for one last sight of the creature who had recalled such a host of tender recollections, and at such a time too, I whistled, and called "Patty! Patty!" as was my custom when nearing home in the evening, after my day's labour at canoe-making, and, to my great satisfaction, now with the same result. Patty came to meet me, and seemed distressed that I did not as usual hold out my finger for him to perch on; but he hovered about my head, and kept crying "Patti! patti! patti!" incessantly.

But if the behaviour of the guard and executioner, as well as the mob, was unaccountable when they could hear the bird and not see him, now that "Patty" so plainly demonstrated that I was the special object of his solicitude, it was infinitely more so. The mob, uttering loud cries, turned and ran back towards the village, while the guards and the executioner fell flat on their faces, crying on their gods to save them from harm. Seeing how matters stood—for though, until I went on the uninhabited island, I had never seen a bird like Patty, I was well aware of the Dyak belief in omen birds, and undoubtedly in their eyes this was one—I thought it not amiss to make the most of my opportunity.

"Come," said I, "Orang KaIu is anxious for my death; is there none among you so daring as to disregard the bird, and obey your chief's commands?"

But though by this time Patty had grown tired of waiting for me to put out a finger for him to perch on, and had once more betaken himself to the cover of the boughs, it was a long time before

the executioner and his attendants mustered courage enough to raise
their heads; and even when they had done so, and encouraged by a
longish spell of silence on Patty's part, had got on their legs, they
seemed not at all disposed to adopt my suggestion, but stood in a
terrified group, whispering and pointing.

What course they would have adopted, had they much longer been
left to their own devices, is impossible for me to say; but, just as
things had arrived at the critical pitch above mentioned, a man came
hallooing and shouting from the direction of the house which the
brothers inhabited, at the same time waving a strip of white cloth in
his hand; from which sight I drew no little comfort, for, as I well
know and have already explained to the reader, white in these
countries is the emblem of peace and good will: and when I saw the
fellow waving his white rag, I was as well assured that my life was
spared, at least for the present, as though Sapasis and his brother
had shouted it from their house door. The emblem of reprieve had
come from the chief. The mob, which had fled back to the village,
had carried in the astonishing news, and this was the result.

The message brought by the chief's runner was, that I was to be
taken back immediately; so back we went, and were ushered—guards,
executioner, and all—into the terrible presence. Although Orang
Kalu's superstition had prevailed with him to consider his sentence
against me, his humour was not a whit improved; indeed, it seemed
to me that he was sorry he had allowed his weakness to betray him
thus far, and would very willingly have restored matters to the condition in which they were when Patty stepped in to mar them.

"How now!" exclaimed he, "has this insolent slave given you
all the itch for lying? Dare any one tell *me* that they heard the
voice of the spirit-bird?"

And Kalu looked so very fierce and threatening, that I much doubt
if any one present *would* have found courage to assert what it was he
had so distinctly heard. But, my lucky stars be thanked, the pipe of
my best of all friends was not to be put out by such unworthy
means; although I was quite unconscious of it, Patty had followed
me back to the village, and, now perched on the thatch, happened to
emit its terror-inspiring note just as Orang Kalu had uttered his
challenge. The effect was such that, had I been a disinterested spec-
tator, I am sure I should have laughed outright. As Kalu spoke,

daring any one present to repeat what the voice of the mob had informed him of, he stood erect, with flashing eyes and dilating nostrils, and with his right hand grasping the hilt of his kris—a very royal tiger; but no sooner had my cock sparrow, perched on the tiles, uttered its note, than the mighty fellow suddenly ducked his head, as though he had heard the roof splitting, and he raised his hands to his ears, and fell a trembling in a very pitiable manner. His brother Sapasis, who was by his side, was equally alarmed, though, being the cooler man, he did not show it.

"Let the hall be cleared," said he, "and leave the prisoner here."

When we were left alone, Sapasis conferred with his brother in a whisper, and then turning to me, observed—

"Prisoner, my brother is still inclined to mercy, and will spare your life if you will speak truth, and tell him how you came on this island."

But, before I could answer, the man that had been sent down to the beach to test the accuracy of my story about the canoe made his appearance. Eager as he was to tell his news, he was not quick enough to save himself from a severe blow of Kalu's staff, for the chief was full of baulked spite, and only too glad of an excuse to vent a little of it.

"Take that, you villain!" said Orang Kalu, "it may teach you to hurry when you are sent on a journey."

But, though the fellow was big enough to have swung Kalu round his head, and certainly old enough to be his father, he did not even flinch from the blow, but stood with his arms folded and his head, from which the blood was trickling, humbly bowed, and waiting permission. When I witnessed this rare instance of subordination, I could no longer wonder at Kalu's rage at the affront I had put on him.

However, the account the faithful messenger gave tallied with that which I had given. He would have been back long since, he said, but that the boat, of which he had been sent in quest, had floated off with the tide, and he had to swim out nearly a mile before he could reach it, and even then it was a long while ere he could reach the shore, for the sampan was such a clumsy thing—a mere log burnt hollow, and with a paddle such as he had never seen before.

Kalu seemed pleased that my account of myself should thus far receive confirmation, not on my account, as that it opened a way for him to allow me to escape, and that without very seriously compromising his dignity.

"Did you bring the thing ashore?" asked he.

"It is now high and dry on the beach, as your highness may see," replied the messenger.

"Then this rascal had better pack off in it, and go the way he came," said the charitable chief, alluding to me.

I knew not whether to be sorry or glad to hear him say this, but I was speedily relieved of the task of weighing the matter, for as soon as Sapasis heard his brother declare that I should go away as I came, he turned laughingly to him, and told him that, since he set so light a value on me, perhaps he would not object to giving me to him as a present. At this Kalu merely shrugged his shoulders, as though to intimate that he didn't care a straw what became of me, so that he was rid of me.

"Listen to me," cried Sapasis. "It is evident you are a liar, as all slaves are. Have you been used to field labour?"

"No."

"Can you weave?"

"No."

"Bah! he is both useless and a liar," said Orang Kalu. "You are welcome to him, Sapasis."

Sapasis merely yawned and nodded, and the fellows who had brought me in took me out again, and there was an end of the business; and I became the property of the chief of Mompara, who thought so little of his new acquisition that he did not think it worth a simple thank-ye!

Judging from Sapasis's behaviour, I had become the property of the best of the two brothers. Evidently he was an easy, good-natured fellow, on the best of terms with himself, and, so long as he wanted for nothing, ready with a patronizing word of pity for folks in distress. This, at least, was consolatory. Under such a master the meanest slave could not fail to have easy times, and, with this morsel of cold comfort for a pillow, I flung myself on the rushes with which the hut to which I was taken back was strewed, and fell into a sleep, from which I did not awake till I was roused, and informed that Orang

Sapasis was about setting out for the prahu which was to carry me home to Mompara. With more wretched indifference than I had ever before experienced, I followed my conductor to the spot where Sapasis's fellows were assembled; I fell into the procession, which made its way to the beach, and thence to the prahu which was moored there.

Early the next morning we reached Mompara, and certainly Kalu's people had not exaggerated when they called it a large and important place. A long time before we reached it, it was easy to see the long row of huts that were erected close down to the shore, while, further inland, taller buildings could be made out, with countless columns of smoke, significant of preparations for breakfast, and adding to the homely aspect of the place. There was one circumstance, however, which I could not account for, and which set not only my heart but my stomach—which was, I assure the reader, at times not at all fastidious—against Mompara and all its belongings. The wind blew off the shore, and bore towards us such an intolerable stench, as of fish in the last stage of decay, that I was fain to clap my hand over my nose and mouth, and keep it there. Nobody else, however, on board appeared to notice it, and even the luxurious Sapasis himself stood, with perfect serenity, on the deck, with his eyes, and consequently his nose, towards the island. The rising smoke having turned my thoughts breakfastward, I could not but associate the horrid smell with cookery. At Magindano rotten eggs were esteemed delicious, and pork considered to be improved by hanging a day or two in the sun. Here, then, was the same odious taste in another shape—stinking fish was the staple food of the Mompara islanders !

As may be easily guessed, these reflections tended not at all to raise me from my melancholy, and I was agreeably surprised to find that in this last surmise at least I was mistaken as to the habits of the people I was doomed to sojourn amongst. As we neared the shore, the cause of the stench manifested itself in the shape of many enormous heaps of oyster-shells, which, from their colour, evidently served for the graves, as they had served for the living abodes, of their inhabitants. I had forgotten all about what the Maday men had told me about Sapasis's pearl-fishing, but this was evidently the scene of the pearl-fishers' labours. "One thing is certain," then, said I to

myself sagaciously, " I shall never be a pearl-fisher ; or if I am forced
to the work it will not last long—the stench would kill me in a
week." I wonder what would have been my sensations had some
one whispered into my ear at that moment, " But you *will* become a
pearl-fisher, and, so far from the stench of the rotting oysters killing
you in a week, you will presently grow so used to it as not to notice
it as even unpleasant ; you will remain on this island as a pearl-getter
for ten years or more, and win renown thereby." Had any " little
bird " whispered such a preposterous thing I certainly should not
have believed it, but so it came about, and in a manner which I will
presently relate.

To return, however, to my first introduction to Mompara. As the
prahu neared land, the inhabitants came trooping out of the huts and
out of the town beyond—men, and women, and children. At a glance
it was easy to see that they were not all Dyaks, for there were men
with their faces carved and tattooed in a way never seen among
Borneans, and men with billets of wood stuck through their under-
lips and with rings through their noses, plainly bespeaking them
Malays ; and men with almond-shaped eyes and flat faces, and with
pigtails behind, who could be nothing but Chinese. But I looked in
vain among the mob of faces to find one that was English or Portuguese, or French even ; such a face was not to be seen. Still it was
comforting to find in all these people of different countries the same
amount of cheerfulness and clamorous delight to see their master
return. Moreover, there was an air of content visible on the majority
of countenances which could not have been falsely assumed ; and
though some of the mob were scarcely clothed at all, it seemed to be
from choice rather than necessity ; for there were others—evidently
workers like the naked ones—who were clothed more decently than
any people I had seen since I had left Magindano ; this was especially
observable among the Chinese, who all wore some sort of jacket and
trousers, and a cap on their heads. There could not have been a less
number of people on the beach than three or four hundred, exclusive
of the children, who counted as many again ; but this I afterwards
found did not constitute a tenth part of the inhabitants, who were employed, far from the shore, in the fields and in the gold mines ; indeed,
with few exceptions, the whole of the men in sight were engaged in
pearl-getting, and numbered about fifteen slaves to one free man.

So sickening was the stench on every side, that my stomach loathed the wholesome breakfast of rice and pork of which I might have partaken. Such an effect, indeed, did it have on me that I turned faint and giddy, and began to experience many sensations to which I had been a stranger since I was sea-sick in the hold of the ill-fated "Margaret." I made no complaint, but presently became so ill that an old Chinese woman, compassionating my condition, took me to her house, and made me up some sort of a bed, and, when I was somewhat better, prepared me a basin of broth, which, though it, like everything else to be met with on the island, was tainted with the odious fishy smell, was very comforting.

The gold mines, as I have before intimated, were situated at the farthest end of the island, and great was my anxiety to be taken there and set to work ; for, besides the advantage of getting away from the polluted air I was now breathing, the notion of " working in a gold mine " was not without its attraction to my mind, which, despite the many hard realities it had encountered, was still susceptible of romance. I think I must have entertained a vague notion that a mine of gold was pretty much like a mine of coal, only, instead of the walls, and the roof, and the floor being sooty black, all was dazzling and resplendent, and gorgeously hazed by the sparkling cloud of gold-dust raised by the picks of the workmen.

The only alternative, should I be disappointed in my desire to be sent to the gold mines, appeared to me that I should be set at field work. Judge, then, of my surprise and horror when, in the course of the afternoon, I was sent for to come down to the beach where the rotting oysters were, " that the driver might show me my work," the messenger said.

Rebellion I knew would avail me nothing, so, fortifying my nerves with a good quid of tobacco, I followed the messenger down to where the business of pearl-seeking was in full operation.

At a glance it was easy to understand the nature of the loathsome trade—that is, as regards the finding the pearl in the oyster. All round about the pestiferous heaps previously mentioned squatted men and women, with a sort of shallow tub before them. In each tub a man who attended at the heap from time to time pitched a shovelful of oysters, and to this the owner of the tub added a measure of water. The pearl-hunter's business then was to dabble amongst the dreadful tubful, to wrench the shells asunder and let their contents escape into the water, or rather into the slimy mud, for so it became after a single stir of the pearl-seekers' hands. The shells parted from the dead fish; the former were thrown aside, leaving nothing in the tub but the putrid mass lying at the bottom. This the man then literally took in hand, taking it up in convenient bits and passing it carefully over the flat of one hand with the fingers of the other, so that it would be impossible for a pearl no bigger than the smallest seed to escape him.

The driver was sprawled on a heap of empty shells, smoking a great roughly-made cigar of native tobacco, and evidently keeping a much sharper eye on the operatives under his control than they suspected. As he was a Malay, I could not readily follow his rapid nasal talk, but the substance of it was, alas! too easy to be misunderstood. I belonged to his gang, and must be there to-morrow morning with the rest. If I came to him in the evening he would provide me with a tub and a spoon, and then he would likewise instruct me as to the laws and regulations of the business. He had sent for me that afternoon, not to set me to work, but that I might have an opportunity of observing how it was done, and, by being enabled to go at it in the morning without bungling, save myself an aquaintance with the rattan he invariably carried with him.

Gladly would I, having received his instructions, have hurried away and refreshed my nearly-stifled senses by a breath of comparatively sweet air; but part of the driver's commands was that I should stand and watch the washers and learn the way, so there was no help for it. It was easy enough to learn, however, and, with my customary inclination to "take the bull by the horns," as the saying is, I had a great mind to screw up my courage to such a pitch as to enable me to try my hand at a tubful on the spot, and it was only a fear that I might faint over the stench and fall headforemost into the tub that deterred me from the attempt.

Fortunate indeed was it that I did not try my hand that afternoon at pearl-fishing, and for this reason. After awhile the signal was given for the men to strike work, and then each gang ranged itself before the driver, who inspected them one at a time most minutely. Any article of clothing they wore he took off and shook; he passed his hand over their head and ears, and with his forefinger searched round the insides of their mouths, and all for the purpose of ascertaining whether they had concealed any of the treasure their tub might, in the course of the day, have yielded. Now, although I have of late made no mention of them, my two great pearls and my diamond lay snug enough in the pocket of my ape-skin breeches, and, had I meddled with the tubs, more likely than not I, too, should have come under the driver's examination, with a result the reader may easily imagine.

The gang with which I found myself associated was composed of men of different countries, and, as is usual with communities of slaves, there was little of sympathy or good-fellowship amongst them. It seemed that one of the laws of the island was that, whenever a new slave was introduced into a gang, the whole number should at once assist in building the new-comer a hut; and no sooner had my gang partaken of their evening meal than they at once set about hut-building on my account. The helpers were many, and the materials neither numerous nor elaborate, consisting, indeed, only of a score of rough boards, a bundle of reeds, and a couple of bushels of mud; so that in less than an hour my habitation was finished, and my un-friendly fellow-labourers at once departed, and left me to sit in it alone.

Of furniture my house contained not a single scrap, and it was while casting about for something to sit on—for I never could bring myself to adopt the Eastern method of squatting on the ground—that I bethought me of the washing-tub which was promised me, and resolved to go at once to the driver's house and fetch it.

Besides the tub and spoon—the latter an iron scoop-like instrument to scrape round the washing-tub—the driver gave me an iron pot, a bag of rice, some salt, some sugar, and a couple of dried fish something like cod in appearance, but not so large. This, I was informed, was my allowance for a week, except a bit of pork or beef I should get on the Wednesday. He likewise instructed me as to the laws by which the pearl-washers were governed, and which, though they occupied a long time in delivery, may be summed up as follows:—
1. All the pearls in the sea belonged to the sultan, whose servant Sapasis was, and to whom Sapasis was responsible for an annual tribute of large pearls. 2. That it was death for a slave to conceal a pearl, however small its size. 3. That any slave who was fortunate

enough to find a pearl of extraordinary size and beauty should be free from work for a whole year, and be fed and lodged, and provided with tobacco and palm wine in plenty, at the expense of Orang Sapasis; but that if the pearl found should be of such great size as to cover the forefinger-nail, then the slave might demand his liberty, or his value in dollars.

As may be imagined, no part of the driver's harangue interested me so much as this last. How fortunate it was that I had been enabled to preserve my pearls! Why, the smallest of the two would cover, not only a man's finger-nail, but, if laid thereon, the entire top of his finger would be invisible! So elated was I at this sudden clearing away of the dark cloud that of late had enveloped me, that, with my iron pot and my rice and other eatables stowed in my tub, and the latter on my head, I marched back to my new house in so blithe a frame of mind as to indulge in whistling a brisk English tune; and I don't know which most astonished the lethargic inhabitants, a man bearing a load without creeping and groaning, or a man expressing a tune so curiously; for it strikes me as not a little singular in all my long experience among savages, that, although they have tunes which they sing and chant, and although they can whistle shrilly enough when hurt or alarmed, I never yet heard a savage attempt to apply his whistling abilities to music.

Naturally enough, my first impulse was to immediately put into force my very simple stratagem—so simple and apparent that it would be an insult to the reader's understanding to enter further into any explanation than to say that he is quite right in his surmise that it was merely to introduce one of my pearls into my washing-tub, and make believe I found it there in the regular manner. Upon reflection, however, it seemed that I had better not act too hurriedly over the business. Had the driver, like the governor of the island, been a Sea Dyak, it would not have made the least difference had I made my tremendous discovery within the very first hour of my being at work. It is a great chance if a Sea Dyak would have dreamt of any sort of trick; but the driver of our gang was not a Sea Dyak but a Malay, and of all people on the face of the earth there are none more suspicious, and treacherous, and cunning. And I don't say this because the individual, who is chiefly responsible for having set me roving, was a Malay. I owe her no grudge. On the contrary, I have a strong belief that she—the old lady whom Bill Jupp and myself encountered in the brickmaker's shed, of course I mean—was by many degrees the best specimen of her nation I ever met. But, after all, she could be scarcely called a Malay, having spent nearly the space of an ordinary life among civilized folks.

The more I thought about it, the less feasible seemed the plan of secreting and recovering one of my pearls the very next morning. It would certainly be better to wait for a week, a month, three months even, than spoil my excellent chance by over-eagerness. True, I should meanwhile have to endure the odious labour already described, but I had no doubt that the certain prospect of being presently released from it would make it endurable; indeed, strange as it may appear, even the few hours I had already passed at the nasty place had sufficiently familiarized me with its odours, that I could at least breathe without continually retching and shuddering. Before I went to bed, therefore, I stamped my treasure into the floor of my hut, and resolved to wake with a stout heart for the ordeal before me.

And truly I needed a stout heart, and a strong stomach, to bear up against the terrors of the work which the following day found me engaged in. But somehow I did bear up. I kept my mind's eye continually on the precious gem which was to redeem me from my tribulation, as the benighted traveller caught in a morass constantly regards the far-off twinkling light. Fifty times in the course of that woeful morning I was for kicking away the cause of my misery; but I managed to struggle through, and at the close of the day was able to give as good an account as the rest.

The next day I found my disgust decreasing, and the day following it was less still, and so on in proportion. It was nearly a week, however, before I could partake of my food with anything like regularity; and I saved quite a store of rice, which I can assure the reader was not wasted; for ere many more days had passed I could manipulate the contents of my washing-tub with as much indifference as though it were dough, and my appetite became so pressing for its arrears of food, that it took all my store of rice and fish to appease it. The disgust thus overcome, the rest was easy enough; for our food was wholesome and plentiful, and the labour required of us neither heavy nor urgent.

So passed more than two months, and I at last made up my mind to put into execution my long-cherished scheme, though not exactly according to the original notion. Undoubtedly the first simple plan was the best, the safest; but unluckily I got into my head the whim that since the other pearl was of no use to me, I might as well do a grand and unprecedented stroke of business, and find *two* immense jewels in a single tubfull of stuff. Up to the very last I am not sure that this second scheme pleased me, but at the very moment of my securing the bait which was to catch my long-flown freedom, the resolution to take both pearls predominated, and, putting them into my mouth, I set out to work as usual. Before I reached the beach I saw with full force the folly of the proceeding, but it was now altogether too late to recede.

There had been a dearth of ordinarily large pearls for a very long time; indeed, the last one which had turned up, a worker—a young Chinese, who did not belong to our gang—was detected in the act of swallowing, and only escaped the axe by dying of the tremendous doses of physic administered to him. There were rumours that Sapasis was dissatisfied, and accused his overlookers of insufficient attention; though to judge by the amount of rattan, and cursing and bullying, with which the drivers invariably treated their gangs, the accusation was without foundation. That Sapasis, however, was not satisfied, was evident by the frequency of his visits to the beach.

This, then, should be a good time for producing my wonders. For an hour or so I worked on steadily, and then, quick as thought, spat my pearls into the trough, and the die was cast. They were so large and so lovely, that the least stir of the mess revealed them; and presently, affecting to give an astonished cry I caught up one, and immediately uttering a still more astonished cry, seized the other and ran with them to the driver, who was standing alone some paces off.

" Take me to Orang Sapasis," said I. " I have found that which will change his sadness to joy."

And, opening my hand, I showed him the pearls. His first act was to snatch them from me with an ejaculation of amazement, and to retire behind a shell-heap that he might examine them, I following close enough at his heels, the reader may depend. When he had examined them, however, he seemed strangely agitated; and instead of, as I desired, hurrying off with me at once to Orang Sapasis, he loitered and lingered, and looked from the town to the beach, and from the beach to me, and seemed very undecided indeed. At last said he, in a cautious whisper—

" Do the fellows about you know of this ?"

" No," replied I, innocently enough ; " 'tis but a moment ago that I found them, and I came straight here."

" Good !" said the Malay, his little eyes twinkling with greed and cunning. " And do you know, Rusa" (or " The Deer," a name with which the driver had dubbed me)—" do you know, Rusa, the worth of these things ?"

" Riches and liberty !" replied I, shortly. " Take me to Orang Sapasis, and he will pay the price."

" Ha ! if such trash would buy riches and liberty, how rich we should all be, Rusa," replied Tangah, to whom a new idea seemed to have occurred. When you have been longer at the work, you will know pearls from dross. Get back to your tub, Rusa, and hope for better luck."

Worthless, however, as the cunning villain would have made my pearls appear, he took care to place them very carefully in his pouch.

Said I, controlling my rage as well as I could, " then it is only pearls that we fish for, for Orang Sapasis ?"

" Only pearls," replied Tangah ; " of what use is other rubbish to such a great lord ?"

" Then, as these two are not pearls, they belong neither to Sapasis nor to yourself, but to me. I must have them."

Tangah looked tremendously savage, and raised his rattan.

" If you dare," said I ; " bear in mind, Tangah, I am neither a Dyak nor a cowardly Chinese. Give me my pearls or I will cry my loudest, and demand to be taken to Sapasis. Let him settle the matter between us."

Tangah was cunning enough to see that I was in downright earnest. Had he dared he would have cut me down at once with his kris, and so shut my mouth effectually ; but slaves were too valuable to be destroyed at so cheap a rate. He was at liberty to beat me with his cane, but Sapasis was not a hard-hearted man, and any slave might demand a hearing of him. To drive matters to such extremes was the very last thing that Tangah desired, so, though fit to explode with the rage with which my last observation had filled him he affected to laugh, as though all he had previously said was a joke.

"Though you are neither Dyak nor Chinese you are wiser than either, my Rusa," said he; "now have I only just discovered it. Undoubtedly you have discovered a great prize; they are both pearls, marvels of beauty, and it was only that I feared that by confirming what you were near assuredly of, that so much joy coming so suddenly on you might hurt you. They are indeed lovely," continued

Davidger shows his Pearls to Tangah.

the cunning rascal, withdrawing them with a long drawn sigh from his pouch. "The like of them was never seen on Mompara before. One of them would purchase the liberty of twenty slaves, and all you will get will be the bare price of one." And then after a pause, and as though a sudden idea had possessed him, he said, "Listen, Rusa, the Orang Sapasis is rich, we are poor. You shall keep one of these pearls, and I the other. Quick! Hide this one [the smallest] in your belt, and get at once back to your work. We will talk the matter over in the evening."

So saying he turned away and busied himself at some distance, leaving me to go back and wallow in my wretched tub, with no better consolation than that the execution of my long-treasured scheme had left me poorer than before.

My first sensations were only of bitter disappointment and exasperation against the rascally Malay driver; but when in a few minutes I grew calmer, there dawned on me the reflection that disappointment might not be the least evil I might have to endure. From what I knew of Malay character generally, and of this man's in particular, he was far too cautious a fellow to allow a slave to share with him a secret, the betrayal of which would involve at least his utter ruin. This set me thinking more seriously; and it presently came into my mind that when a slave was found to have concealed a pearl in Orang Sapasis' absence, it was not customary to wait for the Orang's return, *but to deal with the culprit instantly.* It was so with the young Chinese, whose case I have already quoted. This recollection, coupled with the fact that Orang Sapasis set out the very next day for a longish voyage, at once resolved me how to act—as soon as work was over I would go up to the Orang's palace, and tell him all about it.

Even as I was thinking by a lucky chance the Orang himself, attended by a troop of his courtiers, came down to the beach to see how the work progressed, and to give his overseers final instructions as to their behaviour during his absence. Whether it was that I suddenly ceased work, or that I looked with particular earnestness towards the advancing party, I don't know; but happening to turn my eyes in the driver's direction, I saw that his sallow complexion was many shades paler than usual; and as I regarded him he laid one hand on his lips as a caution, and the other on the handle of his kris, by way of gentle intimation of what would be the penalty if I disobeyed him.

But my situation was desperate, and I resolved not to swerve from my resolution; and when the Orang and his party approached where I was sitting I started up, and to the Orang's surprise and alarm fell on my knees before him, and in as few words as possible narrated my story, at the same time producing my pearl in corroboration.

At first Sapasis looked incredulous, but as the story went on his brow lowered threateningly, and finally he looked round him for Tangah, the driver; and not seeing him called him aloud, and sent some of his people to look for him. And speedily the poor wretch was found behind a shell-heap, writhing and struggling on the ground in his last agonies—overmatched, beaten out of life by his own cunning. For no sooner had he seen me kneel at the Orang's feet than, having no doubt of my intention, he had for a moment hidden himself for the purpose of swallowing the evidence of his guilt; after which he probably would have come forward, and with much virtuous indignation denied my scandalous accusations. But Providence had otherwise willed. The jewel, hastily swallowed, had stuck fast in his gullet, stopping his breath and choking him.

The Orang was a shrewd man; and when his anger was excited, as cruel as he was shrewd. At a glance he saw how matters stood, which was not difficult; for the wretched driver was grasping at his throat, and making all sorts of horrid pantomime that there was the cause of his distress. Had help been promptly given undoubtedly Tangah might have been saved, but Sapasis would let no one touch him.

"Leave him alone," said he, with a cruel laugh, and at the same time turning away. "Poor Tangah is ill; he will be quiet presently, and then we will inquire what ails him."

And sure enough presently Tangah was quiet—quiet as death could make him. Somebody went after Sapasis, who had sauntered down to the edge of the sea, to tell him.

"Tangah is dead," said the messenger.

"Ah, well, I thought he would die," replied Sapasis, indifferently. "Look in his throat, and find the cause of his death; if you find it give it to the slave Rusa, that he may bring it to me."

So they looked in Tangah's throat, and of course found the jewel which had suffocated him; and bringing it to me bade me carry it to Orang Sapasis, and I did, delivering it to him as he was surrounded by his attendants.

"Now," said Sapasis, fondly regarding the instrument of the driver's death—gleaming pure, and lovely, and spotless as ever—now do I know, O Rusa, that you spoke truly. Rise, Rusa, slave no longer, and name thy double reward."

"Liberty, only liberty, my lord," replied I; "and with no further extension of your bounty than sufficient means to ——"

"Means to carry me to my own country," was what I would have said; but Sapasis, eager to display his gratitude and generosity, interrupted me.

"Liberty shall be yours," said he. "There is no part of my dominion to which thou mayst not go as freely as myself; and as to means, take thou the place of the villain Tangah, with his house and all he may have hoarded therein, with his wife, and his sons, and his daughters as thy slaves. "These are my commands," continued Sapasis, raising his voice and looking round on the crowd now assembled; "let all who hear take such part as they may be called on, to see them obeyed."

Although it was a sore disappointment to me that the Orang's notion of "liberty" should be circumscribed by the dimensions of his island, still surely I had no cause to grumble. At least I was free to go whenever a chance presented, and meanwhile my time could be passed easily and lucratively. Marching at once to Tangah's house I took possession, and immediately made inventory of the goods it contained, and which were not inconsiderable; for Tangah had been a driver several years, and what with his honest gains and his pilferings, had prepared a nest very well feathered indeed.

The nest was mine, and so was the brood; Tangah's daughters, two of them, and his three little sons. Tangah's widow was mine, too; and of this she wanted no telling, for she prostrated herself before me, and cried and implored me not to part her from her young ones. At this very moment came a message from Sapasis to say that since I might not have a use for all the slaves he had given me, he would gladly purchase such as I could spare; but to the utter surprise of all who heard me, I returned an answer to the Orang begging him to allow Tangah's family to retain their liberty, and that I could never be happy if I allowed myself to inflict injury on these innocent creatures. When this answer was carried to Sapasis he merely laughed, and said that I was a fool; but that he thought differently, was clearly shown by the constant kindness he ever afterwards manifested towards me.

And here I may say was an end to my Bornean adventures; for though, as already intimated, I remained among the pearl-fishers for the long space of eight years, one day was so exactly like another that almost any one might be taken as a sample of a thousand. Tangah's was a large house, so that there was room enough for the widow and the youngest children, which was a great accommodation to her and an advantage to me, as she proved a frugal and considerate housekeeper, and an excellent cook. My pay as driver was two dollars a day, which was sufficient to allow of not only good living, but of putting a something away to increase the store I inherited from Tangah.

I remained well in health during these eight years, and was every way happy except for the one circumstance that Orang Sapasis, who knew my urgent desire to leave his dominions, spared no pains to prevent me; and really he did this in so kind-hearted a manner, that I never could remonstrate very seriously with him. And so I should have remained a slave-driver at a pearl-fishery to the end either of the Orang's days or mine own, had it not happened that on a certain bright June morning, and just as the people were beginning their work, and I, having lit my first cigar, was strolling amongst them—had it not happened, I say, that all unexpectedly a ship hove in sight—a British ship, with the British colours flying!

Who shall tell the emotion which filled me as my eyes dwelt on the sudden ship with its white sails, and the white faces of her crew, which shone out against the dark shrouds? All that was English in me awoke as though my long seventeen years and over of experience among savage people had been but the dream of a single night. Home—mother—everything connected with the dear old country, came vividly before me, and, kneeling down on the shore, I most heartily thanked God that He had at last delivered me from my long bondage.

To my amazement, however, no one but myself seemed delighted at the approach of the ship; and when she came so near that her guns might be seen and counted, the consternation of the pearl-seekers increased, and they ran off to the palace of the Orang, and flocked there in a vast mob, begging that he would protect them. But the Orang was not at all dismayed, and, although a European ship had never before visited his island, he had had dealings through his agents with both Dutch and Peringuese, and therefore, like a hospitable prince, came down to the beach to welcome the strangers.

Great was the Orang's surprise to find that I had already boarded the first boat the "Pegasus" had sent off; indeed, I had not waited for it to touch the shore, but, as soon as I saw it lowered over the ship's side, had swam towards it. Rather indignant, too, was the Orang, and called out in a commanding tone that I should come away, and leave the business of greeting to him; but when for the first time I made known to him that, despite my tawny skin, I was of the same country as his visitors, his anger ceased, and when I expressed my intention of departing when the "Pegasus" did, he made no objection.

The business of the "Pegasus" was simply that of exploring and surveying; nevertheless, its stay at Mompara was protracted for full a fortnight—a weary fortnight for me, I do assure the reader. Not that I was idle meantime; I had various business to arrange, not the least important being the conversion of my worldly goods to the most portable shape. This, however, was effected, and, with three thousand dollars, my great diamond, and a pair of huge gold bracelets, heavy as fetters, which Orang Sapasis gave me as a parting gift, I joyfully sailed away.

Only that the voyage to England was very tedious I can tell nothing about it, my sole thoughts being engrossed with thoughts of home, and who had gone and who was left. My mother, I counted, must be by this time nearly sixty, and my father sixty-seven; so there was not so bad a chance that I might find them alive—at least one of them.

Within an hour of the ship touching at Portsmouth I was bowling along on the coach Londonward, and in good time was set down at the Saracen's Head, in Aldgate, which, if the reader is at all acquainted with that neighbourhood, he knows is but a short step from Goodman's Fields. I had a bag and a great trunk with me, but these I left at the coach-office, and set out to inquire for my relations.

My first journey was to the little house at home, of course. It was night, and the lamps were lit; and as I turned into *our* street—how narrow, and little, and untidy it looked!—my heart beat at a tremendous rate, as, starting with number one, I went on to number seven. A glance told me that the familiar board, "Davidger, Tailor, etc."—what the "etc." ever meant was a mystery to me—was not over the door. Still there was nothing in this; it might have been taken down—fell down—gone to be painted. Three, four, five, six steps more, and the dismal truth was revealed; there were lasts in the parlour-window, and a brass plate on the green street-door, inscribed, "Rogers, Shoemaker."

Mrs. Rogers came to the door. Did she know where Mrs. Davidger had removed to? Miss Davidger, she supposed I meant; "the old people are dead, you know—him five summers ago, and the old lady the spring before last." The Miss Davidger she alluded to was Miss Mary Ann, my youngest sister, who was a dressmaker, and supported her mother till she died. Where was she now? Ah! that was more than Mrs. Rogers could tell; there *was* a talk of her marrying a young grazier who lived out Hampshire way, and who met Mary Ann at a Whitechapel vestry-hall tea-meeting.

That was the extent of the information Mrs. Rogers could give me, so I thought I would run round to Cable Street, and see if my kind old aunt was in the land of the living; but, alas! the baby-linen shop was now a beer-shop, and there was singing, and smoking, and beer-drinking going on in the very chamber which used to be so sacred.

Now where should I go? It mattered little, for, finding myself so lonely, I verily believe, if the next turning had taken me to Mompara, I should have taken it. Stay; there was Bill Jupp!

I knew the way to the corndealer's well enough, and in a few moments stood before its well-known window, looking in. The name was still over the door, and the appearance of the shop had not at all altered, with this exception, that the person behind the counter was a buxom, bright-eyed little woman whom I had never seen before. Anyhow I would go in and ask after Bill; but, lo! as I entered at the door, Bill's head emerged from the hole leading to the cellar under the shop, and taking me, by my brown skin and the rings in my ears, for a distinguished foreigner, he hastened behind the counter, and politely asked my pleasure.

"A ha'p'orth of grey peas, Bill," said I.

If my appearance had altered, my voice had not, for by it he recognized me instantly, and in less than a minute we—that is, he, and his wife, and myself—were cosily sitting in the comfortable shop-parlour, exchanging histories. The reader knows mine, and the summary of his was, that his father had taken to farming, and left him the corn business.

Bill made room for me in his house, and there I am at present staying. My search after my relations has not been very successful. I can gain no tidings of sister Polly, but of Annie, the eldest, I hear that she has married Mr. Levy the clothier's son, and that the pair are now in thriving business in Liverpool. My next sister is dead. So is my Cable Street aunt. So is her brother Sampson, the stevedore. His niece Margaret I discovered alive, and charing at eighteenpence a day. Finding that her ambition soared no higher than a comfortable laundry business, with a mangle attached, it was instantly provided for her, and, I am happy to say, she is getting along very well. As for me, having written my Bornean adventures, I am reduced to sitting smoking at the window from morning till night, and wondering what I shall do next.

THE END.